William M. Baker

Blessed Saint Certainty

a story

William M. Baker

Blessed Saint Certainty
a story

ISBN/EAN: 9783337336042

Printed in Europe, USA, Canada, Australia, Japan

Cover: Foto ©Andreas Hilbeck / pixelio.de

More available books at **www.hansebooks.com**

BLESSED SAINT CERTAINTY:

A Story.

BY THE AUTHOR OF

"HIS MAJESTY, MYSELF," "COLONEL DUNWODDIE, MILLIONAIRE," &C.

QUI LEGIT REGIT

BOSTON:
ROBERTS BROTHERS.
1881.

UNIVERSITY PRESS:
JOHN WILSON AND SON, CAMBRIDGE.

TO

My Eldest Born,

MORE TO ME THAN A SON,

MY COMPANION ALSO, AND MY INTIMATE FRIEND,

THIS BOOK IS DEDICATED.

CONTENTS.

6 *CONTENTS.*

BLESSED SAINT CERTAINTY.

CHAPTER I.

GERALD URWOLDT.

ONE bright September afternoon, many years ago, the people of Ocklawahaw were aroused out of their habitual indolence by the arrival of the most distinguished visitor they had ever received. When I say that this was the finest horse they had so far seen, I must explain myself by saying that Ocklawahaw was the only trading-post of an Indian Reservation in the West. It was built along the crumbling edge of a bluff overhanging a great river, which toiled slowly past, so heavily weighted was it with red soil from the regions through which it flowed. The town consisted of many score of log cabins scattered about like dice, with a frame house upon the highest points here and there, — some of them painted red, with green shutters, — in which lived the leading men. There was a blacksmith-shop, a wagon-

most frequented

house, and a four-

served as a tav-

s the wonder of

the Reservation by reason of its size. Although built of frame-work and weather-boarded, it had never known the painter's brush. Two stories high, and broad in proportion, its size was glory enough. Of a dark brown, after years of sun and storm, the autumnal ripeness of the husk told of the richness of its contents, which were pork, meal, flour, ammunition, blankets, tobacco, tin-ware, domestics, calicoes, molasses, and whiskey. But a portion of the population were Indian, or even half-breeds. Negroes, at that time slaves, and white men through all varieties of traders, horse-jockeys, speculators in land, small farmers, loafers driven thither by stress of law elsewhere, gamblers, trappers, desperadoes generally, made up the inhabitants.

The town stood in what had been a dense forest. Barely enough of this had been cut down to allow of the erection of the houses; and the ways winding between the houses and dotted with stumps could hardly be styled streets, so thick were they still with enormous trees, which strove to comfort themselves for the absence of their slain by brooding so much the more closely, as with verdurous wings, over the homes now nestling beneath them. The forest surrounded the town, slowly giving way upon the northwestern side to prairies, which stretched hundreds of miles away to the mountains. It was in these open spaces nearest the settlement that the farms of cotton and corn were cultivated. In the boundless grass beyond these the cattle and horses belonging to Ocklawahaw were almost as much lost a.

the fish in the sea. Every spring the owners of the stock, mounted upon mustangs, scoured the plains, sweeping before them toward an appointed centre everything which wore horns or hoofs. There the living net was drawn closely about the wild and frantic creatures, until, the calves and colts duly branded, the struggling mass was let go again for another year into the freedom of nature. The process was repeated, at points of convergence twenty miles apart, over the immense expanse so long as colt or calf remained unbranded, and then the wild riders subsided for another twelve months into their normal laziness.

For hundreds of miles above and below the village the river rolled its floods of liquid mire through a dense forest of trees, elm and cotton-wood, pecan and live-oak, bearded from their topmost twigs to the earth with hanging masses of gray moss. The ground was covered with centuries of decaying leaves and rotting limbs, while the whole forest was woven as into one immeasurable cobweb by the grape-vines crossing from tree to tree like the threads of gigantic and antediluvian spiders. The village mourned more than one adventurous hunter who wandered into the gloomy woods never to return. To such perishing of cold and hunger, with eyes becoming dim in death, the vines must have seemed, instead, like living things, like prehistoric serpents winding themselves about the .ackened trunks, forcing their way through foliage nd moss to the tallest tops, leaping from bough to 'ough, knotted together in deadly wrestle in the spaces between. There was something horrible to any one in the way in which the anaconda-like vines seized upon and coiled themselves about each other until they sank into the flesh and crushed the bones each of the other in their deadly strife.

And yet through the slumber of the forest, too deep to be awakened by the winds, there flickered, like foolish dreams, the finer life of birds and squirrels, — a life flavored with wickedness in the innumerable snakes, with a relish even of merriment in scolding catbirds and shrill lizards, to say nothing of the conscious hypocrisy of raccoon and opossum slinking by, and of the chancellor-like gravity of owls enshrined as with spectacles and wig in the judicial seclusion of hollow trees. It was only upon the edge of the woods near the village that life emerged into self-consciousness in the children chattering together, laughing, fighting, swimming in the river, climbing the trees, swinging upon the vines, dashing about on colts whose manes and tails were tangled with cockle-burs.

Next in importance to the warehouse store was the log tavern, in front of which a mongrel crowd was assembled, as usual, on the afternoon of which I am speaking, — not a man of them without his rifle and revolver. When the horse already mentioned came in sight along the road leading from the east, the laziest there arose to his feet, the most drunken became interested. It was not that horses were scarce, — no man there so poor as not to own a score or so ; but these were of Spanish stock, scrubby mustangs merely. As the beautifully formed and spirited steed halted at the porch of the tavern, the crowd drew about it in almost speechless admiration. Here, at length, was a horse, — the horse of their dreams! The most imaginative among them had never lied, during a trade, in reference to his best animal to this extent. With the precision of a church choir the words broke in the same breath from every lip, " Morgan stock!" What with equal unanimity they thought, but did not say, was, " Worth a thousing dollars, by jingo!" But it was only the most desperate among them who said to themselves as they thronged about it, " If this animal is to be had, foul or fair, I'm bound to have it!" although the theology with which this resolve was sealed mentally was of another phrase than Amen.

When the crowd came to lift their eyes at last to the rider, they saw that he was an uncommonly good-looking young fellow of about twenty-four years of age, — a profusion of long and flaxen hair flowing about his neck from under the rim of his broad-brimmed felt hat. Whoever and whatever the stranger might himself prove to be, his steed had already established his rank in society; but his open face, broad shoulders, vigorous arms, unhesitating voice and manner, confirmed him in possession of the title of Captain, — Captain Urwoldt it proved to be, — which was bestowed upon him on the spot. Nor did he refuse to take a drink, when, having dismounted and tied his horse to a post, he stood upon the porch of the tavern. As the first step toward cheating him out of his steed, a man in the crowd asked him to do so, and he went for the purpose with the one who invited him into the house. But the supreme excellence of the horse was too great for the self-control of a villanous-looking rascal hanging about the steps of the porch.

"Doggon it, how grand we are!" he exclaimed, as the new-comer went in; and there was the ready laughter which awaited whatever attempt at a joke anybody might risk. On the instant the one aimed at turned, came out again, walked up to the envious gentleman, remarked, "Are you the chap who said it?" and slapped him full in the face. Having done which, the stranger stood ready, revolver in hand, for whatever might follow. For an impressive moment there was the silence and paralysis of utter astonishment, giving place to a laugh which arose at last into a general roar of amusement. Under any other circumstances the one struck would have replied with a shot; but, glancing with amazement at the comely and determined face of the stranger, the man yielded to the popular current, and joined in the laughter louder than any. As he did so, he grasped and shook with affection and respect the hand which smote him. In a few seconds thereafter the crowd were drinking at the bar upon invitation of the new-comer, every one assenting with many an oath to the universal affirmation that the owner of the horse was "some," and that "he will do!"

In the end it was discovered that the new arrival was a little better armed than most men, was shrewder at a horse-trade than the best, could drink as deeply, shuffle cards as deftly, as any. In a word, it was not a month before it was agreed by all that, unparalleled as the stranger's animal was, it was but in keeping with the qualities of the owner himself.

When Captain Urwoldt arrived in the village he had no definite intention of staying there. He was merely "prospecting" with view to any locality wherein he could do best for himself, and in any way, he cared little what. During the first week of his sojourn he learned that the headman of the Reservation was rich in lands, in cattle, in cash. He ascertained, on inquiry, that this headman was already an old man, and that he had but one child, a daughter, who would come, at his death, into possession of everything. Not knowing of any better opening in the regions beyond, Captain Urwoldt slowly made up his mind to remain. He had not as yet seen either the headman or his daughter, but his plans were extremely simple; he would ingratiate himself with the father and marry the daughter.

Concerning this adventurer I propose to say as little as I can. It may be added therefore, as briefly as may be, that he entered upon his schemes by selling his horse to the headman for half of what he would have demanded of any other person. Next, he secured a clerkship in the one store in Ocklawahaw, and toiled thereat soberly and steadily until he came into the complete control thereof. When business, as the time went by, was dull, he put up a sign to that effect, and took daguerreotypes, — the first artist of the kind in Ocklawahaw. He did not suffer it to interrupt his regular business of trading in pork and calico, rum, molasses, and ammunition, cattle and lands, and charged such prices for everything that it soon became evident to everybody in the Reservation that "the Captain was bound to be rich some time, you bet."

One day, leaving his business in competent hands, he disappeared from Ocklawahaw, but it was only to come back again, at the end of two or three months, from a hunting excursion upon the prairies and mountains beyond. A train of pack-horses accompanied him, laden with venison, buffalo skins, and the antlered heads of the bucks he had killed while away. But he was more than hunter and daguerreotypist, for during his absence he had made sketches on plain and mountain-side. Fitting up the loft over his store for the purpose, he stretched his canvas there, and, in the intervals of more lucrative business, devoted himself to painting. When he was ready for it, the curious public were admitted to behold the results at so much a head. Not an Indian or half-breed, not a white hunter or trapper coming in with pelts, not a mechanic supplied by the government or a speculator in horses or mines in all that region, but, sooner or later, visited the pictures, and spread the fame thereof far and wide. For years these works of art were the wonder of the whole country, and not merely because they were the first known to men in that region; for an amateur they were excellent, and it wɼ but proper that the Captain should become, as he d Major Urwoldt in consequence thereof. It somev

perplexed the simple-minded people when they saw
a man so gifted harder at work than any of them, in
his store and along the street, making money in every
manner possible. "The Major," they observed, "is a
genius," and they were right.

But, as has been intimated, it is not with him I
have to do in these pages; not more at least than is
essential to my story. There is mystery in the way
in which the rose and the lily, the peach and the
apple, draw from the same soil, growing side by side,
each its own peculiarity of juice or color, of fragrance,
form, and use. So with what is to follow. The Reservation was but the field, the people of whom I have
spoken but as the clods thereof, out of which sprang
the persons with whom we have our concern in what
comes after.

CHAPTER II.

BLACKBERRY EYES, AND WHAT FOLLOWED.

WHEN Gerald Urwoldt first came to the Indian Reservation he found it under the rule of a headman, or chief, whom the Indians spoke of in their language as Mogga-thirvan, or Thunder-tongue, but who was known by the whites as John Ross, by which name he himself preferred to be called. He was a very tall and spare man, over sixty, the only son of Scotch trader who, for prudential reasons, had married the daughter of the then chief of the nation; and in John Ross the Indian and Scotch peculiarities blended and mutually confirmed and ratified each other. Wary and silent, thrifty, economical, and unrelenting, Ross was possessed of absolute control of his savage people when the treaty was made with the government, in virtue of which they were settled upon their Reservation. How he managed it no one knew, but, as one result of the transfer of the tribe from barbarism to semi-civilization, their chief had made himself rich retaining all the more his influence over his people and the unbounded confidence of the government. He was, in fact, a natural-born diplomat, and might have made himself a Talleyrand and a Rothschild in one, had his been a European area instead.

When young Urwoldt rode into Ocklawahaw upon his fine horse, John Ross was a dry old man, wrinkled, exceedingly tough, and devoted to the management of his horses and cattle, and an almost unceasing use of a stone pipe, with an unsleeping vigilance toward all new-comers. It was rumored that in his earlier days he had been the most cruel of savages, sparing neither color, age, nor sex. However that may be, he was peaceful enough now, did not touch whiskey, and, except for his property and his pipe, cared only for the child of his age. This was a little girl when Urwoldt arrived, and she was known in the village as Mitchabuna, or Blackberry Eves. Her mother had been a half-blood Indian, who died when Mitchabuna was an infant; and the brown cheeked little thing would have died also, or, worse, would have relapsed as she grew up into the original barbarism of her kin, if it had not been for one thing.

Long before the girl was born, with the first settlement, in fact, of the Reservation, there had come to Ocklawahaw a young missionary who labored faithfully in the teeth of the native savagery of the people, and against the sort of civilization, worse still, with which the ion began its career as a ward of the government. After long and almost desperate efforts, the youthful apostle, Williams by name, disappeared from the village, apparently in utter defeat and disgust. But they knew little of the man who thought thus. He had only fallen back for a breathing space upon the New England Society which had sent him,

2

and in a few months he was back again, reinforced b
a wife out of a Female Institute there, more zealous
if possible, than himself. The well-mated pair wer
to work with zeal. Early of a Sunday morning th
husband would make his rounds among the tents an
cabins, persuading and urging the heathen inhabitan
to attend meeting at his cabin; and then, his wi
leading in the singing with a subduing force therei
unknown hitherto among the children of the 'orest, l
would preach to them in their own language. Du
ing the week the husband and wife taught school '
old and young, male and female, gently and unti
ingly herding them from the utmost skirts of tl
town into their own doors for the purpose, very mu
as partridges are driven into a net.

Almost from her birth little Mitchabuna had bee
brought into the school. Parson Williams was n
young when the black-eyed child first came under l
care, and, as the years of toil and privation passed b
he became an old and worn man. If Christianit
ever clothed itself in Kentucky jeans and yello
brogans, ever crowned itself with an old wool ha
and looked with pitying eyes upon the world throug
brass-rimmed spectacles, it was in this instance. Th
missionary had settled in Ocklawahaw to advanc
civilization, too; but, as the years elapsed, the civili
zation was, in a sense, forgotten by Parson Williams
and only the more durable Christianity remained
As he adjusted himself more and more to India
ways, the usages of a former life were laid aside, anc
then forgotten. Not even John Ross could speak th

Indian language as well as the old missionary, although his English became almost obsolete to him, became ungrammatical, somewhat coarse, and not free from phrases, when he did speak it, which astonished people not used to life on the Reservation. Very rarely indeed, and only by compulsion of his superiors eastward, did the old man show himself at their conferences. At such times he was as a John the Baptist among them, in his coarse garb, rough visage, queer isolation from even the best of them. When constrained to take part on Sundays and in prayer-meetings, it was as if a John indeed had suddenly arrived from Judæa and the days of Christ; and there was that in what he said in his laconic fashion which sent secret thrills of alarm for himself through polished pastor and distinguished divine, even while it filled their eyes with tears. But the old man was always in a hurry to get away again to his Indians who had come to revere him profoundly even when they hearkened to him least.

To Mitchabuna the missionary and his wife were more than parents, for they had but one child of their own, a girl, Persis by name, a few years older than the daughter of the headman.

"What ails you, Blackberry Eyes?" Parson Williams demanded of the girl one morning, when she was about twelve years old, for she had come to school with an unusual color in her brown cheeks, her eyes dancing with excitement.

"It is nothing," she answered in the same Indian tongue, and entered upon her studies with sober demeanor.

But it *was* something, none the less. Young Ur-woldt had ridden into Ocklawahaw upon his remark-able horse a few days before, and, for the first time, the two had passed each other under the live-oaks. It was an eventful occurrence. Mitchabuna regarded him as the handsomest man she had ever seen. Having already resolved to marry her, it made small difference to the adventurer how she looked; but he congratulated himself upon the fact that his predes-tined wife was both fairer of complexion and prettier than he had hoped.

"They say that this region is cursed with chills and fever," he said to himself that night. "But the ague has not touched *her*, that is clear. If she can stand it and look so well, I can. So here goes! I might as well try my luck here as anywhere else."

It was necessary that the fortune-seeker should be as wary as possible, and one of his many and diverse gifts was the possession of a cool caution which can work and wait. Keeping his own counsel, he seemed for the present not to know of her existence.

And yet, and from the first, the Indian girl had full assurance that the new-comer thought vastly more of her than either he or she allowed any other person to suspect. So far she had been more than contented with her moccasins and buckskin skirts and leggings, her beaded belt and cap, adorned with her own embroidery, and feathers dyed red by her own hand; now she affected calico instead, and a sun-bonnet. Heretofore she had hardly done more than to glance at herself in her little looking-glass of mornings before going to school; now she began gravely to study in it her complexion of pomegranate brown and crimson, her white teeth, her red lips. It was only when she felt sure that the handsome white was nowhere near, that she laughed as loudly as she pleased, shot with bow and rifle, climbed trees as she had always done, swam in the river, caught and rode at a gallop the uncurried, unshod mustangs, dispensing with saddle or blanket, her black hair flying upon the wind. Where it was possible for Captain, and then Major, Urwoldt to see her, no Eastern maiden could have obeyed the manifold admonitions of Parson Williams and his wife more faithfully than she. As she grew older she would flush with shame, almost rage, at the shade of copper in her cheeks, for fear that he might not like it. Poor child! It was little he cared, so that he saw in her the hue of her father's gold. He was a singular compound of miser and artist, of poet and money-maker, and took his own stealthy steps to carry out his deeply considered plans.

But old John Ross was as sharp-sighted in reference to his property, and in regard to his daughter the heiress thereof, as he had ever been when, in other days, deer or bears, a lurking foe or a possible bargain, was concerned, and one fine morning Mitchabuna vanished from the village.

Major Urwoldt was not long in learning why. From her earliest childhood Parson Williams and his wife had so carefully instructed the girl that, when she was over fifteen years of age, they agreed that she was prepared for something beyond their own teaching. For some time now they had been urging upon John Ross to give his daughter an education worthy her vigor of character and future possessions, that she might become a teacher and benefactress to her people. It so chanced that the missionary and his wife were going East, for the first time in years, and they could place Mitchabuna in the institution which had educated Mrs. Williams. And so Mitchabuna was sent away. It made no difference, so far as any one could see, to the energetic Major. He inaugurated only a more systematic making of money at the store. When summer came he went off on a hunt, returning with new pictures, loads of meat, stacks of skins. Indeed, he seemed to be the soberest and steadiest of men; apparently he cared not for anything beyond his merchandise and his pictures; but who could tell what so determined and exceptional a man might do some day?

The months, the years, rolled by. Major Urwoldt had imperceptibly become Colonel Urwoldt instead. He raised cattle these days, bought and sold horses, came into possession of large tracts of land. It was rumored that he had discovered valuable mines during one of his hunting and artistic excursions, and had preempted or bought the whole region somewhere among the mountains. With the consent of John Ross, and to the enthusiastic delight of Parson Williams, he had erected an academy of higher instruction in Ocklawahaw, himself subscribing liberally and draughting the plans. As a Christmas gift, he presented the good missionary with plans, specifications, and elevations, beautifully drawn, of a new church with parsonage attached, and assured him that the buildings should be erected in the next two years. He set up also a small weekly, the "Ocklawahaw Scout," editing and supplying it with poetry from his own hand, and copious prose.

During all these years he had managed to live on good terms with John Ross, now becoming a very old man. No mention of the absent heiress had been made by either. Colonel Urwoldt had grown to be by this time a large, heavily bearded man, handsomer than ever, peremptory of manner, and was reputed to be almost as rich as the headman himself. Managing matters with steady caution, he had made himself essential to old Ross, in his dealings with the government on the one hand, and his own people on the other.

Meanwhile Mitchabuna was receiving, at her institute in the East, the best education the times afforded. She was the one pupil there who possessed absolute health, and her intellect was inferior to none; nor was there any of the girls who had quite as intense a desire to improve. Her teachers flattered themselves that it was because she proposed to devote herself, upon her return, to the welfare of her people. They were mistaken. For some time before leaving Ocklawahaw there had been a singularly clear understanding between herself and Colonel Urwoldt. An active but clandestine correspondence was kept up ever since, and her marriage with him was the first event after her coming back, with the full consent of her father, who died soon after, leaving his son-in-law in full possession of his position and property.

The handsome adventurer was now General Urwoldt. There was no longer any need of a mask, and he revenged himself for the past by asserting himself. Portly, prosperous, positive, a marvel of energy and skill in money-making, he now added hard drinking to the list of his accomplishments. The Indians he openly despised, and dealt with accordingly, gambling and indulging in horse-racing as the humor seized him.

Meanwhile child after child was born to him, boys and girls, their skins fairer, and therefore their eyes blacker, apparently, than those of their mother. Parson Williams lost his wife, and was aided in his work by his daughter Persis, until she married a stockraiser, who broke his neck one day while riding a vicious mustang; and the young widow herself died in a year, leaving behind her a little girl, another Persis, as the sole companion of the old missionary.

Then came the small-pox, ravaging the Reservation with frightful fury; and it would have been hard to believe that Mitchabuna was as highly educated as almost any lady in the land, had you seen her during its desolations; with her dress hanging half off her shoulders, her black hair in disorder down her back, it seemed as if, in attendance upon her children, as they were smitten down one after another, she neither ate nor slept. She would fall asleep, at last, from sheer exhaustion in her chair as she sat by the bedside, or across the feet of a child dying upon it, to wake, as it were, a moment after, her hollow eyes drier, fiercer than before. Week after week she fought for her children with death, like a she-wolf for her whelps. But, now a boy, then a girl, they died, and it was all the old missionary could do to tear their bodies from her for burial. Not a child of those who died but breathed its last upon her bosom, and she held on to each in turn, her gaunt arms locked about the corpse, her lips drawn, when any one came near, so as to show her white teeth, her eyes tearless and glittering with silent ferocity.

The soul of white-headed Parson Williams was stirred within him. When only one child remained to her, little Ross, the old man locked the door upon all beside, and, like a prophet of old, denounced her for her stubborn rebellion. Then he knelt, and prayed for mother and child as never before. It may be that she was fain to yield from pure exhaustion. Suddenly she fell upon her knees beside her apparently dying child, and surrendered him, her last lamb consuming in the flames of fever, a sacrifice to God. Then she gave way to weeping, weeping the unshed tears of so many weeks, weeping as if she would never cease! It was like the rain of a tropical storm, for, when she arose at last, her sky was as clear as if it had never known a cloud; she was even bright and smiling.

To the astonishment of all, little Ross passed the crisis of his disease, and, first slowly, and then rap-idly, recovered. The pestilence departed, having slain its hundreds, and Mitchabuna was another woman. Many months before, she had given her husband as

serious a fright as he had ever experienced. From
the hour of their marriage he had been accustomed
to tease her, now about this and then about that,
generally about her Indian blood, in the wantonness
of his peculiar character. One day she was seated
so submissively before him at her sewing while he
did so, that he ventured upon the one step too far.
In an instant she stood erect, hot, her face pale, her
eyes so terrible to see, that, although she said nothing,
he recoiled in unfeigned alarm, nor did he attempt it
again. She had long ago come to see that he had
married her merely for what she brought him, that
he despised her race and herself. He had fled at the
approach of the pestilence, nor did he return until
long after the danger was over, and she had for him
a contempt beyond anything he could imagine. Of
his licentious life she had long known, and it would
have been eminently unsafe for any one of his many
mistresses to have come within her reach; but outwardly, at least, she was now the most patient and
submissive of wives. Now she had but one purpose in life, and that was to care for and train and
save, if she could, her last hope in the world, her son
Ross.

I write what follows concerning Ross Urwoldt and
those so closely associated with him because it is a
narrative, from my sincerest observation and experience, of the certainties upon which rests and rolls, in
whatever direction, the life of every one of us. I
am to speak of the evil that Ross derived from his
father and others; for there are certainties as inevita-

ble and as dreadful as the worst things in nature, —
deep valley, roaring torrent, rocky cliff, malarious
swamp. But there are blessed certainties, too, and
it is of these and because of these that I speak at all.
Infinitely more inflexible and adamantine than the
steel rails along which a train flies, these absolute
and unerring certainties span, thank God! every valley and river of our existence, pierce every mountain
range, bear us high and safe over every bog and
quicksand. Whatever befell my friend afterward, let
it be recorded here, that, as he existed at all, so he
continued to exist now, and as through death itself,
in virtue of this certainty, to begin with, — a mother's
love. It was small merit in him then; but oh, if you
and I could not merely recognize but rest upon our
every certainty until the last! could but so rest as
to let go and sleep in its arms, as he did when a
babe in the embrace of Mitchabuna!

CHAPTER III.

IN COLLEGE.

AS the years rolled by, General Urwoldt left his wife and child entirely to themselves, and plunged deeper into the mire of a money-making baser, if possible, than his dissolute courses. For as long as he could do so, Parson Williams assisted the mother in the education of her boy, obtaining after that a tutor named Amasa Clarke, from the East, to aid them therein. It was at the suggestion of the old missionary that Ross was first prepared, as he grew, for college, and then sent thither.

In due time he came on to Old Orange, the college which I had just entered, one of the youngest students there. We were Freshmen together, and it was impossible but that I should like Ross Urwoldt, and from the first. The face of the lad was only dark enough to give to his aspect a certain sternness and rigidity of purpose. You would not have detected the Indian in him at all, unless it was in his eyes. It was not that they were so large, so black, but that they had a steadiness of gaze, accompanying a peculiar motionlessness at times of his whole frame, as of one accustomed to watch, and for hours at a stretch, and with unwavering ken, the least movement of game or enemy far away across the prairie. Added to this, there was an erectness of bearing which was as much a part of his agility as the antlered head of a stag thrown back upon its shoulders is part of its flight and speed, — the result, no doubt, of a species of health so perfect as to differ in kind, not degree alone, from that of those of us who spend our lives in-doors. As I came, at college and afterward, to know him better every day, there was so much more to know and to like that I do not intend even to begin to describe Ross Urwoldt yet. Let me say merely this, that he had more of what I am constrained to style clear force than any other person I have met. There was a single-hearted straightforwardness in him, which he derived, I dare say, and almost from infancy, from sending his soul with arrow or rifle-ball, and to the very heart of squirrel or deer. Like the Greek heroes, he had enjoyed a training as under the centaurs, far away from cities, and there was more of the Achilles in him, heathenism and all, than I, at least, have found elsewhere.

"I wonder you did not injure your health by hard study," I said to him, when I came to know how thoroughly he had been fitted for college before he came.

"No," Ross replied. "My mother was too much on the alert for that also ᵕ ᵕ ᵕ des with me, goes hunting wit⁷ ⁷ ⁷ ⁷ ⁷ e so ever since I ᵕᵕ ⁷ ⁷ ⁷ ⁷ ⁷ .ιugs when I fired at them, ᵕ ᵕ — and his eyes grew proud as he ᵕ ᵕ —"is a better shot to-day than I am, with bow or rifle. I wish one of your starchy ladies could see her ride!" He laughed aloud as he said it, with pride and pleasure. "She has had lots of children but if you could see her," he added, "on Maggie, my mare, out on the prairie beyond the farms, and where the stock grazes, a west-wind blowing, and a long-eared rabbit scudding away before her for dear life If I was lying badly hurt on the other bank of the river, could *your* mother have plunged in," — Ross violated grammar to say it, — "and swum across, the river booming too, to save you, sir? Not at all!' And he looked at me defiantly. "But I did not intend to speak of her," he interrupted himself. "What a fellow you are, Guernsey, to make a man say things!"

I must have set him to thinking of his home That week he said to me when we chanced to meet on the campus, "What do you know of nature?' for I had called his attention to a gorgeous sunset which was consuming the clouds beyond West College. "You climb a mountain for an hour once in your life. In hot summers you stand for a few moments upon the sea-shore, look out upon water and sky, and say, 'Oh my! Is n't it lovely?' Guernsey,' he broke out, "poets are people who do more than stand apart and look and listen. A fellow must lose and forget himself in things; he must fly with the birds, blow with the winds! When you see buffalo or deer grazing upon the slope, ⁚ ⁚ must have in your mouth the flavor and sweetness of their mesquit grass. Many a time I have been simply another horse out on the prairie with the one I rode. If you want to know what luxury is, lie flat upon your back on the ground, hovering with the eagle that rests on its wings far overhead, moving with it in perfect poise, now a little to one side, then to the other — But what nonsense for a fellow to talk that way!" he interrupted himself, and let his hands fall to his side; "you won't understand!"

"Don't I?" I asked, for he seemed half ashamed of saying what he did. "Listen and I will tell you something about yourself you have not thought of. You told me once of seeing an oak struck by lightning. The lightning did not flash so suddenly then but that you had time to leap with it. What is more, and worse, when it struck the tree *you* struck and splintered it, and with all your heart, and then laughed to see how you had made the bark and fragments fly! Your only regret was that it was not Amasa Clarke."

I was almost sorry I had said it. Ross gazed steadily into my eyes with his own, which were so black and penetrating. "The fellows are right," he said after a while, "in what they told me about you."

"What do they say?" I asked, pretending to be alarmed, — "that I am impertinent?"

"Oh, no, not at all." Ross hastened to disclaim it. "But you know already, and I can't flatter a man to his face. You ought n't to go into men, Guernsey, as you do into mathematics and the languages. As to Amasa Clarke you are right. I did n't know that I had told you so; in fact, I know that I did not, but

I do dislike him. But you are wrong; if I was the lightning, I would n't strike a weed or a toad!" And I then saw how heartily Ross detested his teacher.

"Don't you remember telling me — never mind Clarke — about your bear-fight in the cañon," I said, — "how your dogs tore at him from behind when he tried to climb the pecan-tree, and how he would whirl about and knock their heads in with his paws? Now the trouble with you, Ross, is that your teeth were in Bruin's fur at one moment, and the next instant you were striking at the dogs, at your own dogs too, with Bruin's paws, and with equal zest. You throw yourself so heartily into things, man, that you give yourself no time to be just, no time to take the right side and to fight only with and for it."

"Do you think so? That is what they call Moral Philosophy, is n't it?" he asked with disdain. "Well, I have n't got that far yet, and I hope I never may. You are morbid, Guernsey. What do you and I care for such things?"

Coming from the Reservation, everything in college was new to Ross, and for a time he enjoyed Old Orange as keenly as he always liked or disliked anything. The fact that his father was headman of an Indian nation, and his own striking appearance made our class rather proud of him. Moreover, we were curious to see how such a man would turn out as a student. Just then the two literary societies were contending for supremacy as fiercely as Rome and Carthage during their day, and the one I concluded to join was badly disappointed when the other fellows contrived to secure Ross. The initiation of new members was, in those days, a serious matter. I remember how, as some of us Freshmen were convoyed that Friday night to our Hall, we heard the most unearthly uproar proceeding from the other. There were the clanking of chains, the blowing of horns, the jing-ling of bells, accompanied by crashes as of falling bodies, followed by direful groans. The novitiates of the rival society were passing painfully through their initiation, and we trembled for ourselves.

Of our own experiences soon after I refuse to speak; but there were rumors current, for a long time after, of events in the other Hall that night which had not been provided for in their programme. From what we could gather, the Freshman from Ocklawahaw declined to submit to what, it was vaguely rumored, he had regarded as personal indignities. It was said that he had kicked over the source of the blue flames, had torn off the shroud of a leading corpse, and had an out-and-out fight with the ghost of the man whom the society had been reluctantly compelled to murder for revealing its secrets. The members of their Hall were morose when questioned about it by any of us; but it was well known that the Sophomore who had been the ghost in question was excused for days after from attendance at recitation and chapel. In some way Ross Urwoldt's face had been badly scratched; but he was one of that kind of men of whom few of us cared to ask questions.

All that was forgotten as our class adjusted itself like a team to the harness and steady strain of what was, in the case of some of us, honest and severe study. We watched Ross closely, and soon saw that he was bending himself to his work with a will. So far as a Freshman could hope to be, he was a leader in all the sports of the campus, and was always more than ready for a walk, and the longer the better.

I do not know how it is now, but in those more leisurely days many a student went through the interval of his four years' course with, alas, as little genuine interest in or good from it as a Russian peasant through the crossings and genuflections of a church service. But it was plain that Ross was studying hard, because with some purpose more definite, although concealed, than was true of one student in a hundred. Through it all I could see that he was none the less restless and dissatisfied.

"It is because I am trying to get at the results of study," he explained to me one day when the term was nearing its end, "that I cannot stand the way we go to work."

"What do you mean ?" I asked ; for we had taken, as I have said, a sincere liking to each other.

"You are the first man I've mentioned it to," he said, bringing down his more rapid gait to mine, as I limped by his side, for I was then quite lame, holding on to his arm, "but what I mean is — everything ! It may suit you fellows who have lived all your lives in towns and cities, but you know," he continued, "that I am different. It is not the Refectory fare I object to, for I can digest anything. Nor is it having. to box myself up in a close room, for that I must do if I am to learn something more than how to ride, to swim, or to shoot. Perhaps the unnatural in-door life is telling upon my health, and I am becoming too impatient in consequence; but I cannot endure the slow and round-about stupidity of things."

"Hold up," I complained, panting. We were out on a Saturday afternoon walk to Jug-town, and Ross had brought me farther into the country from college than I had intended, and was rushing me along faster and faster as he talked. "Hold up, man, and listen to reason," I said. "You cannot go to college, and at the same time be out upon the prairie after deer. What you desire is to skim swiftly and like a swallow over the mere surface. If you are to be thorough, you must take time to go down into the depth of matters, man."

"I agree with you," he said; "but see here, Guernsey. When I am at home I spend half almost of every day, when it is warm enough, in the river. To vary the fun, I throw in a Mexican dollar and dive for it. But the water is muddy, the silver sinks into the slimy bottom, and I must dive down as direct as an arrow from a bow if I am to grab the money in my first handful of mud. It is different here. When we try to know anything, — language, mathematics, whatever it is, — we do not go straight for it; we plunge about this way and that, making the muddy water muddier than ever. And they insist upon it that I shall do the same. When I try to say a thing in the simplest way, they want me to put it into a lingo instead, like this: I must not say I know, but I apprehend; not I value, but I estimate, appreciate; not I live in, but I reside in, Old Orange," — and my friend illustrated his meaning at length. "And the religion is worst of all," he added.

"Religion!" But I knew, in making the exclamation, what he meant.

"If people would only say in sermons right out then and there, like old Parson Williams, what they have to say!" he exclaimed. "They wrap up even that in words, words! It is as if a man was dropping medicine out of a vial, drip, drip, drop, drop, either as if it was poison which might kill, or as if there was so very little of it the supply would give out. So of prayer-meeting. Fellows come into it at night, used up, and what a funeral they make of it! They fall, like medicine men, into the same old tones and phrases, like a cypress swamp full of frogs, and I can't stand it. I won't go any more."

I reasoned with him in vain. It was as if I were trying to have him abandon his free gait for my halting limp. There was that, then as ever, in Ross which I could not understand, and therefore did not know how to grapple with. As a general thing men and rifles are made so exceedingly alike, coming as it were from the same manufactory, that when you comprehend one man or rifle you comprehend all. The rawest recruit, in learning how to handle one weapon, knows how to use every other rifle in the army; and, knowing how to influence one man, you know how to approach every other. But, not to press the figure too far, this native of Ocklawahaw was an Indian bow instead, tough and strong, and I never did know — let me frankly confess it — how to handle him. Whether he was so tough or I was so weak I cannot say; one thing is sure, — I was never the Ulysses who could bend him to my way of thinking or acting.

We had much talk before we got through, but it did no good. "Professors and students," he said at last, "you all remind me of the crowd hanging about the old store in my town, — Indians, ragged negroes, lazy half-breeds, strangers on the lookout to cheat somebody; so you people seem to me to be loafing around, waiting for somebody else to do something."

He, at least, exerted himself. He stood high in his class, took more than one prize for languages and natural philosophy, was the crack orator, the most popular man in college. But alas for human calculation! As he drew near the close of his Junior year an event befell.

The largest of the college buildings at that date was an edifice of stone, four stories high, a brick-paved corridor running the length of each story, with dormitories opening into it upon either side. Ross had his rooms in this building, and on the highest floor. On going down the stone stairs one evening to supper he found that each of the great oaken doors was barricaded from within. There were no gymnasiums in those days, in which the wild fellows could work off their superfluous energy, and the intention of the insurgents was to keep out the tutors on their return from supper, and "have a little fun," as they explained to Ross, who was, on the whole, more of a born leader of men than any one else in college. He would not help them, and begged to be let out. This they would not grant. Not to interrupt their long and painfully planned arrangements, he attempted to go back to his rooms up-stairs; but this also they laughingly resisted.

"You must take command," they said; "you are the best man to do it." This he declined; but his blood began to warm as he saw what was going on. There were scores of fellows at work heaping ammunition of bags of sand at the windows over the outer doors, building fires upon the pavements of each story near by, laying in supplies of water, hot and cold, with which to repel assault. The ancestral savage in Ross arose within him as he was hustled about by the students, swarming hither and thither in their shirt-sleeves, their heads tied up in red silk handkerchiefs. His eyes kindled, his heart beat faster, even while he remonstrated with the rest and refused to take part.

As he did so, there arose a clamor, at the chief entrance, of students banging at the doors outside and wishing to enter. Then there was an awful silence within and without; the tutors had discovered the state of things, and hurried away in search of axes. Soon they were back in force, and their resounding blows proved how determined they were to force an entrance. But the besieged were prepared. Bugles sounded through the great building; drums and fifes sum-

moned to arms. Still Ross resisted the rising tide of
insurrection, fiercer within him than without. Nor
would he have yielded if a sudden panic had not
seized upon the garrison, and that he could not endure
to see.

I suppose something must be allowed for the wild
instincts of the lad, for he was little more. He had
chafed, too, for so long under restrictions to which
he had been utterly unaccustomed. In an instant he
had become commander-in-chief of the garrison. By
this time the assault had begun at every door, and
Ross, bereft for the time of his reason, although cool
enough in bearing, hastened here and there, directing,
encouraging, assisting. I am sure he must have
been, for the moment, as demented as Don Quixote;
for with his own scorched hands he hailed down
upon the head of the tutor plying his axe below,
ashes, coals, blazing brands.

Alas, before very long the besieged gave way at
other doors, and scattered to their rooms, where they
were discovered immediately afterward by the in-
vading force, in the act, every man of them, of dili-
gent study.

"It is not that I am expelled," Ross remarked to
me when all was over, and while he was packing his
trunk for Ocklawahaw. "That of course. What I
hate is that there was not one of the fellows who had
the manliness to stand up and tell the facts; and
that, although they had been planning the thing for
weeks! The Faculty have gathered from their silence
that I was the ringleader from the first. They will

not learn otherwise from me. But you cannot tell, Guernsey, how I hate it!"

We were alone together in his room. He at last locked and sat down upon his trunk. His eyes rested upon the floor between his feet, but they saw the brown face of his mother, saw the very beads about her neck. I am sure he had forgotten I was there, for, to my astonishment, the tears were rolling down his cheeks. I had already visited the Faculty on his behalf, not telling any one of it; but it had been in vain, and I could have wrung their necks as I saw the deadly mischief they were doing, and unjustly, to the one of their pupils who was worth more, or would be, than all the hundreds beside. What could I say now? He looked up and remembered that I was there. "O Guernsey," he said, "if you but knew!"

"Knew, old fellow?"

"Yes, about my—father. About my mother. How anxious she is, not so much for me, as for what she wanted me to be to our poor people. She was to have been a help to them, and — and married my father instead. That is why she had set her heart upon me, and what I might do." This, also, I had already urged upon the Faculty, for I had guessed as much before.

"They intend merely to rusticate you; in a month or two you will be recalled," I said.

"As if I would return!" he exclaimed with scorn.

I said all I could, but he had nothing to reply. It reminded me of the way in which his people were said to have yielded to pestilence from the first. That, also, was part of the utter nature in him, as in them, and it lit up his character to me as by a flash of light. As will be seen hereafter, and in affairs of vastly more importance, my friend was one to whom a thing may happen once, but never twice. Like thoroughly tempered steel, he could endure almost anything, but, in regard to any special matter, when he was done with it then, like steel snapped in two, he was broken clean off from it and forever.

He now shook himself, put back his hair from his forehead, bathed his face, and stood before me, cold and composed. "My chief feeling," he said, "is not contempt for those fellows, but that I should have yielded! There is not a man of them I despise as heartily as I do myself!"

A negro came in and took his trunk. Ross lingered a moment, drawing on his gloves; he seemed to class me with himself and all the rest, for, with scorn upon his face, he added, "Contemptible!" and walked out. I was the one in college with whom alone he had been at all intimate, yet he did not say good-by, or even look at me as he went.

I was but beginning to understand Ross Urwoldt. We have all observed how insects in passing each other will stop for an instant, examine each the other with quick movement of what children call their "feelers," and hurry on, satisfied each as to the morals too, I suppose, of the other. Now, my chief interest has always been in regard to my fellow insects; yet so little at last do I know of people in general that I have often said to myself, "Surely my antennæ are the shortest, the least sensitive, least accurate of any." But I came to know Ross Urwoldt. Owing to what befell him, I could not help but come to know him, not perfectly, but yet as one rarely does any man. He was worth knowing.

To keep things straight and clear, let me add here and now that I often wrote to my friend after this, wrote to him so often and in such a manner that he could not help replying to me from his home in the West fully and freely, especially as I was the only person to whom he did write. More than once he varied his expeditions into forest and prairie by coming to see me on my island off the Carolina coast. His visits were very brief; but it is from them and from his letters that I derived my perfect knowledge of what follows. But I know Ross best from knowing his influence afterward upon another person, and that a woman. You measure to a hair's breadth the climate of an empire by its varying effect upon the silvery thread in the fragile tube of a thermometer, and I came to my final knowledge of this friend of mine through his power upon Persis Paige. Of her I hasten to speak as soon as I can.

CHAPTER IV.

THE BIG MEETINGS.

DURING the absence of Ross at college things had not been prosperous in Ocklawahaw. Parson Williams was becoming so old and infirm as to have lost, comparatively, his restraining influence, and his assistant in teaching, Amasa Clarke, was too indolent a man to be of more than nominal help in the work. General Urwoldt had abandoned himself to debauchery. There was more gambling, horse-racing, stealing, murder, than the Reservation had ever witnessed, and an universal indolence and apathy had settled upon the people like a malarious fog. Then came a drought, parching the very grass of the prairies, until the cattle fed, in their desperation, upon the prickly pears, and perished by thousands, choked to death by the thorns and the thirst. The river became so low that it could be waded by the children, and the wells and springs gave out. In hastening, the next spring, to make up arrears, Nature sent such rains and freshets that the crops rotted along the banks of the overflowing river. After that the grasshoppers invaded the land in desolating myriads, until the hearts of the people seemed broken.

Then came a change. No one could say when it

began, or how, but there could be no doubt as to the fact. Ross described it to me afterward. "All at once," he said, "the huge church, so long empty, began to fill up on Sundays. Parson Williams would have given up and died in despair, had he been any other than the man he was. Now he was as much astonished as any, for the people began to flock in as they had never done. Then prayer-meetings were appointed. After that the people insisted upon sermons during the week, too. From over the whole Reservation, Indians, half-breeds, white settlers, came crowding in, each man as of his own impulse, bringing tents and provisions with them. Then the fact of the crowds became an event which drew others from farther around to see what it meant, until, at last, the church edifice was abandoned as too small. Parson Williams obtained missionaries from other stations to help him, and services were held two or three times a day, and far into the night, under an arbor in the edge of the woods.

"When I got back from college," Ross went on, "I was amazed. It seemed to me as if every man, woman, and child from a hundred miles around was there; and when the iron baskets, swinging from the rafters of the arbor and filled with pine knots, were kindled of nights, I assure you it was a sight to see, that densely crowded multitude.

"You have seen pictures," Ross continued, "of the Deluge, in which animals of all sorts — lions, apes, elephants, serpents, tigers, rabbits, doves, crocodiles, eagles, foxes, wolves — are crowded together in one compact and terrified mass, by the advancing flood, upon the pinnacle of a mountain. I was reminded of it when I saw that queer coming together of all varieties of people, as if under the compulsion of some dreadful and rising Deluge. They would crowd in, sit through long services, go off to one side to snatch a little food, to get a few hours of sleep, and hasten back again as if under a power which paralyzed them from even desiring to do anything else."

"Could it have been the eloquence of the speakers?" I asked.

Ross Urwoldt laughed. "It was not your idea of eloquence, Guernsey," he exclaimed. "Cicero would have been bewildered by it. Although, now I think of it, I am satisfied Demosthenes would have rather liked it, as every sermon began at least with a philippic more vigorous and unsparing than he had ever attempted at Athens."

"A philippic?"

"Yes; and each hearer was himself the Philip against whom the preachers thundered. Parson Williams had caught from the Indians a style of plain speaking which would electrify an audience outside the Reservation, and his brethren in the stand beside him were not slow in following his example when he had to cease for the moment by reason of exhaustion. He and they had long arrears of rebuke and denunciation to make up, for it had been but a sparse attendance they had enjoyed before. It is impossible for any man to tell another his sins more definitely than the hearers were told theirs then, and it was a black list, you may suppose. From being an aged and almost decrepit man, Parson Williams had become erect again, young, vigorous. He was not so much like one brought back again from his old age, as like a dead prophet raised again to life. For the moment he regarded himself as standing in the place of God, of an offended God. You know how little I believe in such things," Ross said, " but to listen to him it was as if he had really and truly passed out of his own hands into those of a higher power. Almost his entire sermon on each occasion was Scripture, and spoken with, I dare say, the very fury of the one who first gave it utterance. His eyes were, when in the hottest heat of his message, as coals of fire; his white hair flickering, as he spoke, like flames with the intensity thereof."

"In other words," I suggested, "the preacher was but the drought, the flood, the grasshoppers come to a climax, the wrath of Heaven taking to itself articulate speech."

" Yes," Ross added; "and Nature itself teaches us that nothing but tornado and tempest can break the rotting stagnation of things. Like men and women everywhere, the people needed a thunderstorm, and Parson Williams left them little to desire as to that."

" He could not have frightened them," I remarked, " if conscience had not anticipated and assented to all he could say. The axioms of mathematics are not the only certainties. When a man is forced to see it, penalty for wrong-doing is as axiomatically certain as that twice two is four."

"They were terribly frightened, that is a certainty. But," Ross continued, "if the Big Meetings, as they were called, began with Sinai, they ended with something else. The thunder and the lightning gave place to the story of Calvary and to — In your superior civilization," my friend interrupted himself, "your preachers rarely venture upon the terrors, and therefore they never come to such pathetic appeal, such irresistible persuasion, as can follow only upon that. You know," he went on, with the scene before him as he spoke, "that Indians are a silent people, and that all varieties of the whites who settle among them become so too. Except that now and then a woman would break out, unconsciously to herself, into the lament as for the dead, you could almost hear each of the yellow leaves of the arbor as it fell to the earth. It was very strange. To this day I cannot comprehend it," Ross went on, "but many were weeping to themselves — I had no intention of saying so much," he added, "and that is all. The phenomenon lasted for many weeks, and ended then only from exhaustion of speakers and hearers. While it continued there was no more drinking, gambling, fighting. Hundreds joined the church afterward. The schools were scoured, repainted, crowded with children, over the whole Reservation. People gave money like water to enlarge the church edifice, to repair the academy. Of course many of the converts fell away, but the meetings have left their mark upon the people to this day."

I never knew how far, at the time, Ross allowed

himself to be affected by the services of which he
spoke. His mother was disappointed at his expulsion
from college, and to please her he attended upon
them. But one morning during their continuance he
arose very early; after feeding and chaining up his
dogs from following him, he took a little parched
corn and jerked venison, and, leaving, for the first
time in his life, his rifle behind him, he went into
the woods. The only person he saw, as he passed
through the village, was Persis, Parson Williams's
granddaughter. She could not have been more than
twelve years old at the time, and had to do almost
the entire work of the house, they were so poor.
Occasional touches of the ague had left her as frail as
an autumn leaf. As Ross went by, Persis was coming
out of her door to cut cabbage for dinner in their little
garden near by. She was nothing more than a thin-
bodied, sallow-visaged, barefooted child in her calico
frock. You see scores of such country girls out West.
When you meet them going to school along the highway, or coming in from blackberrying, chattering
bands of them, with lips and hands stained from
their work, they look as much alike as a covey of
quails.

As Persis came out, Ross was striding by, his head
sunk upon his bosom in thoughts wholly new to him.
He saw her as one sees a familiar cat, and recognized
her with a nod. As he did so, she was in the act of
lifting the hand which held the knife to put out
of her eyes the brown hair blown into them by the
morning wind. A gleam of fun came into the face

of Ross ; he had not seen her before since his coming back from college, but up to his leaving Ocklawahaw he had known her from the time she, at least, could remember.

"Is that you, Persis," he said, "and lifting your knife at me ? You won't kill me, will you ? " He threw out his hand in feigned alarm, and laughed, and passed on. In ten steps he had forgotten her existence. But Persis did not forget as easily. If he had not seen her before, she had seen him, looking among the throngs at the meetings until she had found him.

"How he has grown !" she said to herself. " He must have learned more than grandpa in his college. I hope he won't go to drinking like his father. He looks more like his mother, though."

And then she continued on her way to the garden, lifting the old gate by quite an effort before she could get it open. She took breath after she had done so, and looked after Ross, who was disappearing among the live-oaks.

"He is not going off on a hunt, he has no rifle," she thought. "Why don't he take a horse ? " But with that she hurried on ; for Persis had more than enough to do, — breakfast to get; after prayers, the things to wash up, clothes to mend, dinner to put on, stockings to darn, a little ciphering to do if possible, her grandfather's shirts to iron after yesterday's wash, the tins to scour.

One morning before that, as Persis came home from the old spring with a bucket of water, it had occurred

4

to her when she stopped to rest, putting the bucket down for a moment, that she would see if she could not look steadily at the sun rising in the east. She did it as long as she could, but, for her pains, she had the image of the sun dancing before her eyes as she stumbled homeward, and for some time afterward. It was so now. She was an ignorant little country girl with plenty to do, but somehow she saw little beside Ross all that day and long after.

"I must make time to sew a little," she said to herself, "on my new calico. It's two months I have been trying to finish it. I must have it by next Sunday."

And so she did; but, alas, on Sunday Ross was not at meeting to see.

CHAPTER V.

A STRUGGLE.

THERE are some matters concerning which I have not cared to ask Ross Urwoldt too many questions, and what befell him during this expedition of his into the woods is one of them. I will explain why.

My own home is upon an island off the Carolina coast. On one side it is buttressed by jagged rocks, and, when the tide is in, there are secluded nooks among these, in which I love to bathe as a relief from hard work or severe pain. In some of these natural basins I feel entirely safe. My bathing is done in midwinter as in midsummer, and I do not linger a moment on the brown boulders overhanging such a pool, shivering in the wind, or scorching in the sun, but dash headforemost down and down to what I know is the sandy bottom, clean as a carpet and as smooth. But there are other stone-locked bits of clear salt water into which I would be a fool thus to dive. I know what they are from what I see when the tide is out, — basins broad and deep, but bristling with cruel rocks, upon which I would be gored through and through at the first plunge. And so there are friends with whom I can and do venture anything as the whim seizes me; but with this friend it is different. His depths are deeper than those of other men. Moreover, I have been with him enough, when the tide was out, to know of the jagged rocks which are there, whatever sea may be in. Not that Ross Urwoldt is not, as I have said, simple and straightforward; but, alas, he is so in the inmost and unalterable hardnesses of his soul also.

Persis Paige had always been afraid of Ross Urwoldt; he had been dark and stern, for one so young, ever since she could remember him. She had been toughened by hard work from childhood, had small time to think definitely of him the day she hastened to cut her cabbages and go in to her other work; but she had still been a little in fear of Ross even when she laughed with him. During the manifold tasks of the day, whenever she did recur to the scene of the morning, it was with a sense of sadness, too, which she could not understand.

Even his own mother feared, I know, for Ross, because she felt that she did not fully understand him; so much so, that when he had been gone for several days she could not rest, and followed him. How she tracked him, who can say? But she came upon him farther away in the depths of the forest than she had counted upon when she left the village. By some maternal, if not Indian, instinct she knew, at last, as she stole along through the tangle of drooping vines and hanging moss, and around the trunks of the great trees, that he was not far off. And then, creeping nearer and nearer with moccasined feet and stealthy movement, she crouched low among the dead leaves, and, parting a sumach growth between, she saw her son. At the sight she could with difficulty keep down the cry which rose to her lips, as of a dam after its wounded young; he had been away from her so long at college, almost from his birth it seemed to her, and was he not all she had? He had made a fire which was smouldering under a fallen log near by, and which gave out an acrid smell to the heavy air from what seemed to be a bank of ashes merely. On the other side of him a tree lay on the earth, prostrated by some strong wind, half of its roots projecting high above the pit made in the black earth by its overthrow, yet struggling still to live in every bough and twig; and the quick eyes of the mother marked the pouches of food stowed away therein as if unused. He had spread his Mexican blanket upon the dead leaves between the fire and the uptorn tree, and, lying at length thereon, he held a book in his hand, but was not reading; he seemed too tired to do so. With her keen glance Mitchabuna saw how pallid he was, how exhausted he seemed to be, as from a severe strife; and she understood it well.

Among all Indian nations — in every savage tribe on earth, in fact — it is the custom for the young men to go apart and spend a time in seclusion. It is an instinct; and the period answers to the putting on of the *toga virilis* of the Romans. From time immemorial, from years long before Columbus discovered America, such had been the custom in the nation of which Ross Urwoldt was one day to be the headman. In each generation it had been the pride of the young brave thus gone apart to spend as long a time as possible in the depths of forest or mountain alone, starving, often lacerating, himself until barely strength enough was left to crawl back to camp again. When the Spartans scourged their boys at the altars of their gods, it was by the same instinct. Not that Ross cared for the custom of his people as a custom; it was the blind instinct coming down to him along the current of his blood for a thousand years. Unconscious that it was a custom, he had felt that he could not enter upon manhood until after he had passed through a set period of utter seclusion. Especially since his expulsion from college, he felt as if he could not be at ease until he knew himself better than he did. How could any one rightly estimate, properly place him, while he himself was utterly afloat, tossed about, bewildered as to who and what he was?

"Parson Williams told me one day," he let slip to me afterward, "that a man cannot begin to live until he has gone off from everybody and found out two things. He must face what is called God, and find out for himself whether there is any Maker, and who He is. Not until he has done that can he say anything about God to anybody,—for how can he? he don't know Him. In the same way, if I am to assert myself to others I must first find out for myself who I am. To do this I must, according to old Father Williams, go off by myself, lay hold upon and halt myself, must look myself steadily in the eyes, and know what I am. What do you think of it?"

I am satisfied that Ross was alluding to this period in his experience. His mother understood all, as, crouched upon the earth, motionless, except for the beating of her heart, she watched him, and more keenly than when she had supposed him to be dying of the small-pox.

As she did so, her son seemed to arouse himself as from a stupor. He arose, walked hither and thither, stopped to listen, glanced with a wearied eye into his book, tossed it impatiently aside, put his hair from his eyes. After walking up and down more and more rapidly, he stopped, his face toward where his mother lay. As she gazed upon him she shuddered, for she had always felt, as in the case even of his father, a certain inferiority to him. For too many ages had woman in her ancestry been the slave of man for her to have rid herself wholly of that, and now she hardly recognized him. His head was thrown back; his eyes, larger, seemingly blacker than before from his long abstinence, were fastened, as if in expectation of something, upon the sky overhead. For some time he stood, eager, motionless, expectant, his hair fallen back from his forehead in dank masses. Then he slowly lifted both hands, the palms open, eager.

"If you are a person, say so!" he exclaimed. "You can see, can you not? You are not deaf, are you? Since you made my ears you can hear, can't you? I understand, and you — you have sense enough to comprehend, do you not? Say something. Do something. I want to know you. Here I am, waiting to know. Speak! Act!"

He held his hands aloft, his eyes straining as if he would force a way for himself into the unseen, his mouth slightly apart, while he breathed deeply, steadily, as if he were running instead of standing. "At least, if you are a person, you can love," he whispered, not so low but that the ear of his mother could hear. "If you love me, say so, and I will love you. My mother would. Are you less than a woman? It is now or never! Act! Speak! Here I am. Do something, something!"

To Mitchabuna, lying upon the ground, afraid almost to breathe, it seemed as if hours passed by. The great trees swayed their tops in the dull air far overhead; the river rolled on its muddy path near by with a kind of audible silence, as of time itself flowing on. The shadow of the recluse slowly shifted as he stood motionless. To his impassioned questions the only reply came in the derisive tu-who, tu-who of a distant owl. As the mother gazed upon her son her heart grew chill. It seemed to be impossible for anything not cut out of stone to stand in that appealing posture, the eyes fastened upon the heavens, the hands still held out, so long!

"He says I love him," the mother murmured to herself, "and yet I lie here as near him, yet as unseen by him, as God. Nor do I think best to answer to his cry and show myself. O my son, God is within you!" But she held her peace. It was as when we behold a person walking in his sleep and dare not stir lest we wake him. For her life Mitchabuna would not have had her son know she was there, and he continued to look upward, unconscious of the fleecy clouds which came between him and the abysmal blue. But at last his face grew paler as he did so, his eyes grew angry, his outreaching hands clenched themselves into fists, he shook them defiantly, blasphemed, and fell as if fainting to the earth.

It required strong effort, but his mother lay as motionless as before. Now she dared wait no longer to see what would follow. With wet cheeks she drew herself noiselessly backward until, pausing often to listen, she could safely get upon her feet again. Then she hastened back to the village, singing to herself, happier than she had been since the day she married the man whom she imagined to be a god.

Alas, poor soul! in this case she knew, if possible, even less of her son than she then did of his father.

"Did you ever hold a looking-glass before a dog, Guernsey?" Ross demanded of me one day long afterward.

"No; why do you ask?" I asked.

"Try it with an ox, say, when it is lying down and chewing its cud," Ross explained. "The thick-headed brute will chew on, looking steadily at its image in the glass, regarding it no more than if it were so much plank instead. The dog is a grade higher. It recognizes that what it sees in the glass is a dog, and barks at and would fight it, or recoils from it with terror as from self-recognition too dreadful to be imagined; but it gets, in doing so, to the utmost limit of its brains. It has, it can have, no idea that the dog it sees is itself. Guernsey, a dog is incapable of conceiving of itself," Ross added.

"I have thought the same thing about you," I answered gravely.

"You have!" Ross said it with more pleasure than surprise. "Well, you do have some little insight into people, Guernsey. In this case, at least, you are right. Once in my life" — and I knew that he was referring to the time just spoken of — "I set myself hard at work to project myself, as the Germans say, so as to stand apart from Ross Urwoldt and see what sort of a fellow he is, — to precipitate myself, a chemist would phrase it, and analyze the residuum, isn't that it? — but I could not do it. The harder I tried to grip myself, the more vigorously I slipped out of my own hands, like an eel. I could not grasp myself, and I gave up trying. Self-examination is what theologians call it; introspection is the scientific term. I know sickly sort of men who at certain set periods go in quest of themselves, like detectives. Such a man hunts for and chases himself down. Then, when he has got a firm hold upon his own throat, as it were, he lifts his prisoner from the earth, hurls him down, kicks and stamps upon him. That I never try to do. If I were to catch and take a good look at myself, I am satisfied I would kill my mite of a self! Do you understand me?"

"Certainly; but you exaggerate things."

"Do I? No, I don't. It is not that I look upon my inmost self as wicked, but as being so infernally small. In comparison with great nature it is so small

I cannot find it, can do very well without it, and I intend to. You know how the Italian gypsies spend half their time. Well, if I were to search my rags for that vermin-self of mine, the instant I secured it between finger and thumb I would crack it —"

"Do be silent, Ross!" I said. "How can you hate what you say you do not look for, have no idea of, do not believe in?"

"You are right, except for this, that it is the first time I have spoken in that way to any one, and it shall be the last. I once set apart a time to get at myself, but I did n't succeed, I was too microscopic, and I never intend to try again."

"I cannot understand men and women," was my reflection, made aloud. "There is Steven Trent. The one defect in his really royal character is his emotionalism. Well, you, Ross, are yourself, intensely yourself, and yet you have n't a particle of that about you. Who and what are you, any way? No one else so perplexes me."

"Listen, and I will tell you a little story. One day, when I was hunting in the woods near Ocklawahaw, I heard something crashing toward me from the way the wind was blowing, and slipped behind an oak. By some stupidity of mine my rifle was not loaded, nor did I have time to load it before a buck came along on a slow leap. As it passed, and in sheer deviltry, never thinking I could do it, I sprang for its antlers from behind, for I was all muscle and sinew and foolhardiness those days. To my own astonishment I got a grip upon the base of the antler with my right hand, and I held on until I could get another with my left. I was dragged along dreadfully until the buck stumbled and fell, when I contrived to get myself astride its neck, locking my feet together underneath. It was the grandest ride I ever took; an unbroken mustang I knew all about, but that was tame to this. If I was to hear any one else tell the story, I would believe it no more than you are believing me now; but it is a fact. I do not know how I contrived to keep my hold as we tore along through the undergrowth, almost dragged off by the vines a dozen times. But I tied my legs in a tighter knot about its throat, until I succeeded in forcing its nose down at last among the leaves and mud. Then I got my knife out with my left hand, for I have learned to use either, while I held on with my right, and struck through a white spot between the shoulders and to the heart. After I had done it I lay, my legs still about its neck and deluged with blood, for I don't know how long, and almost as dead as it was. I would not try to do it again, but was glad I was fool enough to attempt it then. This illustrates what I was saying."

"And quite clearly," I assented; "but Tennyson is before you. He has already told of the youth

'Who rode a horse that would have flown,
But that his heavy rider kept him down,'

except that, in your instance, it was a buck. You are right. It is thus that the body gets astride the soul, struggle as it will. But Heaven forbid—"

"That the rider should succeed at last in riding down his soul, in driving his knife into it?"

"You cannot do it!" I exclaimed. "Remember the saying of gallant Sir Walter,

> ' Stab at the soul who will,
> No stab the soul can kill.' "

"Very true — in poetry, but," Ross Urwoldt remarked coolly, "I am speaking of fact. It so happens that, in my case, the youth did more than master his Pegasus from flying away with him into the clouds. As I put my knife into the heart of the buck and made an end of his capers, so I did then and there with what metaphysicians style the inner self, the soul. You need not have such a horrified look, Guernsey. One day — no, it took a week or two — I had it out, as I have told you, with my inner self. I talk upon such things to no one else, and I will grant you that, for a time, my inner self, as you style it, proved to be rather a tough customer; but I ended the thing then, and once for all."

"Yes, it is in your blood," I said sadly. "You make so furious an onset to begin with, that when you do not conquer in the first rush you recoil in utter defeat. I had hoped you were a stronger man."

"Guernsey," my friend replied, "by reason of my birth and training I am not a creature, like yourself, of tradition, custom, convention. I am a perfectly natural, not an artificial, man. That there seems to be a struggle, as between an unborn Esau and Jacob, in every man, I acknowledge. It may be the conflict of the man with the foolish fancies he has heard from infancy. My own idea is that it is the uneven action of the right-hand lobe of the brain and the left; the one lobe gets to acting faster than the other, gets upon a contradictory train of thinking — who can explain it? For my part I am sick of introspection. I tried it there in the Ocklawahaw woods as faithfully as Thomas à Kempis could have done. Luther attempted it in his cell until they had to break down his door and drag him out half starved, unconscious, almost dead; but he could not have tried harder than I did. I am too healthy a fellow for anything of the sort. You want me to believe that I have in me a mammoth Kentucky cave, and that I must go crawling and groping about in the pitch darkness of it on my hands and knees, and I won't do it! I prefer to walk outside in broad day. You would have me eternally winding myself like a tapeworm through my own bowels, and I won't! Guernsey?"

He had grown very serious. He looked at me with his steady eyes, and spoke almost sadly: " If ever a fellow tried to get at the unseen, I did when I went back from college. Others may succeed, I cannot! For my life I can't get beyond what I see and hear, smell, taste, and feel. Nature is big enough, beautiful enough, for me. I can't get beyond it, and I don't want to. You may whirl about in the empty air with the tom-tits if you wish; I prefer to walk instead, and on solid ground. You can take the ghosts, and I will remain satisfied with men and women instead. Whenever I hear people wrangling about things unseen —"

"Gravitation, for instance," I suggested.

"About what is called spiritual things, it reminds me," he persisted, "of children — did you ever hold out your hands when a child, and whirl round and round until you were so dizzy you could n't walk straight when you stopped? If you are fond of such things, go ahead. I find too much to do, too much to satisfy me, without going into that, and I won't do it. You have told me once or twice that I was the finest animal you had seen inside or out of the Zoological Gardens. Very well, I am content. Good-by!"

But I could not let him off in that way. "Some men," I said, "bore for oil through iron rock; others strike down a thousand feet through the strata for gold. What I aim at in every study, as in my dealing with every man, is to get at the central fact of things, — the one, chief, absolute certainty; everything else is mere drapery, if not trash. Now, my fine fellow," I added, "when I grasp at things above me, the one, about the only, certainty I lay hold upon is the Person who made and rules me; when I grope within me, the solid certainty I get my grip upon, in the dust and darkness, is that soul within me which is my eternal self. First, the everlasting God; second only to him, my everlasting self, — these are the supreme certainties."

"To you, not to me," he replied.

My friend was as sensitive to an insult as any man.

He was quicker with a blow than most men. None the less, having him so completely against himself now, I risked whatever might come.

" Ross," I had him by the sleeve, meeting the almost savage and animal steadiness of his black eyes, — " Ross," I said, " there is an old author who declares of the man who says, even in his heart, there is no God, that such a man is a fool. If you say that you are sure there is neither Maker nor soul, if you say — listen to me — that you are satisfied to live without either, then are you an immeasurable — yes, liar; and no man knows that as well as you !"

CHAPTER VI.

PERSIS PAIGE.

IN the earlier days of his arrival in Ocklawahaw, and when he was seeking to establish himself therein, Gerald Urwoldt had done more than any one there toward building the church; but he had not considered it necessary to go beyond that and see to the putting up of a parsonage also, as he had promised to do. Why should he do so when Parson Williams, eager as a child in regard to the church, cared nothing for a house for himself? And so the old man continued to live in the double log cabin behind the sanctuary, in which he had made his home and his school too, until the academy was built, from his first coming. It had never been a good structure, even for a log cabin. A tall man could not do much more than get in at the doors, they were so low; but the missionary had formed such a habit of ducking his head on entering that he would have done so had the doorway been twenty feet high instead. There was no difficulty in his towering to his full height when inside, as the two rooms and a hall between, which composed the building, were open to the cypress shingles overhead. But the "chinking" of blocks of wood, daubed inside and out with mud to fill up the spaces between

5

the logs, had dried up and fallen out in many places. Like the doorways, the windows were out of plumb, and it was almost as hard work to lift a window as it was to persuade the heavy clapboard doors to open upon their oaken hinges; for the cabin rested upon eight two-foot posts, one at the corner of each "pen," and they were sadly rotten. The chimneys were built of logs to the level of those composing the rooms, and were completed up and beyond the clapboard gables with sticks, the whole daubed with plentiful mud; but the chimneys had parted company with the walls outside, and were reeling away to their fall. The floors were "puncheon," that is, of logs split in two, the level side upward; and it required some skill to walk over them, they rocked so beneath the tread, the wind coming up anywhere between. This last was an advantage in which the home of old Parson Williams surpassed many of the stateliest structures in the land, — it was thoroughly ventilated; the most fastidious Board of Health could have found no lack of that. A remarkable thing about the building was that what had not taken more than a week to erect should have lasted half a century, — the most remarkable thing, unless it was that an edifice so miserable should have sheltered hearts happier than are often housed in the palaces of kings. The cabin was a miracle somewhat like that of the barley loaves, not merely in this, that a thing so mean should have held out so well, but that, in this case also, the recipients were filled thereby and satisfied. The cabin itself could not have known this, or it would not have striven so to hide itself behind the church, weather-boarded and painted white by the missionary's own hands, which stood before and within twenty yards of it.

One night, some time after the close of the Big Meetings, old Mr. Williams sat with Persis in one of the two rooms of the cabin. The meetings, and the results thereof, had given him such an impulse that he was full of his new life. The fact is, the good old man had acquired such habit from long use, and of late such fresh impetus, in preaching and exhorting, that it was not easy for him to cease even when, as now, his audience was merely his granddaughter. He had been telling her how dismayed he was when he first came to Ocklawahaw as a young and unmarried missionary. Then followed the oft-repeated story of how he had gone back to the East, had selected a wife out of a Female Institute for the very purpose, and how she had come to Ocklawahaw to labor with him.

Persis was kneading dough at the table near by while her grandfather talked. It was a large batch of dough, for he lived chiefly upon bread ; her arms were not strong, and she panted from her exertion. Then the old man told her about the one child who was born to them, Persis, the mother of the girl, — of what a help she was to them until she married a young neighbor of theirs, a raiser of stock.

Persis was breaking off bits of dough, rolling them into biscuit, and putting them in a pan to rise overnight for the baking of the morning. "And they *would* get married !" she said.

"Yes," her grandfather sighed; "your father was a handsome young fellow, and, having done all I could against it, I was obliged at last to marry them. Your mother seemed to be very happy at first. They went on a ranch twenty miles out on the prairie, and you were born in this room, for your mother came in then. Every now and then after that, Persis — she was our first Persis, you know — would ride in from the ranch on a horse, you in her lap, and a basket of eggs for us hooked by the handle on the horn of her old saddle. It went on that way for three or four years. No," the old missionary said, " Jerome Paige did not drink, did not gamble, was kind to his wife, and loved his child. And he was as industrious as a man who rides around all the time, looking after his cattle, branding his calves, can be. But it was the most natural thing in the world, Persis, my child, when the neighbors came bringing the baby, — that was you, Persis, for you always seemed a baby until after that, — bringing you and your mother and your father in the wagon. Your father had been pitched over the head of a bucking mustang, or it was by his mustang stumbling in a hog wallow of the prairie, nobody ever knew which; but his neck was broken. It seemed as natural for him to end in that way as it is for a bubble to burst when it is touched. I won't speak evil of your father, Persis, for you look so much like him too ; but there was nothing in him, he had no purpose in life, because he never could come to have any idea about anything except his cows and calves and horses, — had no faith, as your grandmother said. Ah me ! you do look very much like him, dear."

His grandchild had put her bread in the pan ready for the morning, placing it on a stool in a corner of the gaping fireplace, with a clean towel over it. Then she got her books and sat down to study. She was quite grave; but that was partly because she was wearied with the work of a day which had begun at dawn, and which had not known a moment's rest since. Her grandfather had sunk into deep thought. With his hands asleep as it were upon the pages in which he himself found all his repose, he saw in the coals upon the hearthstone the persons of whom he had been speaking.

"Mother and I, we lived with you after that?" Persis asked, while she found the place in her grammar where she had left off. The old man returned to her slowly, toiling up to her from the days a dozen years before.

"Yes, my child," he said gravely, "and we were more than glad to have you. But your mother never got over it. Her life was broken."

"You mean her heart, grandpa."

"No; her heart was only part of it: it was her *life* which was broken in two," the other added with almost stern emphasis. "Up to the day she fell in love with that good-looking Jerome Paige," he went on, "she had a steady object in life. I never knew a brighter girl than your mother, Persis. She had learned to read before she was three years old. Whenever she was not helping about the house, she was reading or ciphering. She was only a child when she began to aid us first in the Sunday school and then in the day school. I almost feared she had a sinful ambition, she studied so hard. She saved all the money she could, and sent East for books and papers. Then she wrote letters to interest people abroad in the Reservation ; and they sent her books on books for herself as well as for the children. I never knew a girl improve as she did. ‘ If I had the money I would send her East and to school at your Institute,’ I told your grandmother one day. ‘ There would be no use in it,’ your grandma said, ‘ for she already knows, unless it is boarding-school manners, all they could teach her.’ Persis, your mother had learned to read Latin. She could translate a chapter in the Greek Testament far better than I could. She had come across my old books, you see. I used to read the languages, but had grown rusty out here. Persis, your mother,” the old man went on, “ was superior to my wife, but she was not as devoted a Christian. She lived in a different time, you know.”

“ A different time ? ”

“ Yes, my child, sixty years ago the people about us were savages of the wilderness ; their women something lower still. They were ignorant, the squaws especially, and more cruel than beasts. Now they are becoming civilized, and, I hope, Christian men and women ; and the next generation will be as much in advance of these as these are of their parents. Look at Ross Urwoldt: you cannot imagine that *his* ancestors were taught when boys to cut open an enemy’s bosom after a battle, to tear out the heart and bite off and eat the point of it to make them brave, yet that was so! So it is with everybody; we are superior to our ancestors, our children will be superior to us. When I was born there was not a railroad nor a Sunday school in the land;" and at some length he told of the progress made in discovery, invention, schools, charitable societies, donations to benevolent objects.

" Now, all advance," the shrewd old man added, " is by the rising of the man, the woman, to a pitch higher than that of the father, the mother. Your mother was superior to your grandmother, greatly superior in most things. And, Persis?"

" Yes, grandpa.".

" You must make yourself greatly in advance of your mother. If men are improving generation after generation, women, — and it is God's most wonderful providence of all,— women are advancing much more rapidly. Rich people are building magnificent colleges for them, colleges in comparison to which your grandmother's Institute was but a poor little school. God has some great work for them to do, perhaps greater than that ever given to men; everywhere people are coming to see that. They tell me that women are becoming artists, doctors, writers, heads of charitable institutions of all kinds. I don't understand it, my dear. On some accounts I do not like it, not at all. But it seems to be the will of God. The reason I tell you all this is that I have no one but you. I want you to get up early, to study hard, to have a purpose in life, and all for God."

Having said which, the old man wandered off into the oft-repeated story of the death of his wife and then of the mother of Persis.

"Since you were a little bit of girl," he added, "you have had to try and take the place of both of them. It seems hard, but that is the will of God. I mean that, in these days, double duty is given to women. You are a good girl, Persis, and have done all you could."

If he had not feared to spoil his granddaughter, he would have added aloud what he said only to himself, "Yes, and you may be as much superior to your mother as she was to hers; at least, so I think." All he did say was, "The times are changed. It is a broader world these days, and it needs men and especially women to match it. Do your best, my dear."

Her grandfather had often talked to her in the same way, and after he was gone to bed Persis sat thinking it all over, as often before. She was too young to be so dealt with. Her work was beyond her strength already. "If I could keep free from the chills and fever, I would grow faster," she said to herself. "Is it wicked to be so tired when night comes?" But it was late before she crept to bed.

None the less was she up earlier than usual the next morning. She milked the cow, cooked the simple breakfast, fed the pigs, gathered up the eggs in the tumble-down stable, did some washing of dishes and clothes, sewed a little. Her feet moved as swiftly as her hands; but it was not until her grandfather had eaten his dinner and gone out to visit a dying woman that, after a bit of churning and scrubbing, she could sit down. While she was drying her hands at last upon the coarse roller towel, her eyes were devouring her books on the shelf near by. Taking her little stool under the window, she put her hair away from her eyes, and bent over the well-thumbed volumes at what was at once the hardest and most delightful work of all. Her recitations were to her grandfather after supper was over, and he helped her as he and she found opportunity during the day. This afternoon she applied herself with renewed energy. She was too young for that also, but somehow, even while studying, the story of her father and mother ran parallel with the parsing. Her mother had done very wrong to marry the young stock-raiser. There was Ross Urwoldt. He never thought of her, of course, but if he ever should, she would never think of him, never! Then she scolded herself for such nonsense, and studied harder than before.

CHAPTER VII.

NEW INFLUENCES.

" I HAD a time of it when I got back to Ocklawahaw — with my mother, I mean," Ross Urwoldt
explained to me long afterward. " She was glad I
was back in time for the Big Meetings, but, after they
had passed by, she was sorry again. More sorry
every day. She had hoped I would take a full course
at Old Orange, and become a sort of missionary to
our people, — you would hardly suppose a mother
could be that much mistaken in her own son !" Ross
laughed as he said it, but I was not amused nor was
he. " She said nothing," Ross went on ; " but had I
been brought back in a box, a corpse, she would have
sorrowed so much less that in that case she would
have wept herself out over me and have been done
with it."

Ross rarely alluded, even with me, to his mother and
never to his father. I could easily see that poor
Mitchabuna had, in the expulsion from college of her
son, the sudden shock as of coming all at once to see
that Ross was, after all, to be his talented, worthless
father over again. But while I thought this, Ross
was saying : "There was but one thing for me to do.
I have told you of one of my expeditions into the

forest, but that was only one of many. Every week or two I took my rifle, a knapsack full of provisions, and broke for the woods. My dogs had gone crazy with delight on my return, but I fastened them up from following me. I had an old mare, Maggie by name, who had been a sort of mother to me from the time I was a boy. She came capering about me those bright November days, as lively as a girl, making believe she was as young as ever, whinnying and rubbing her old nose about my shoulder to induce me to take her, but I would n't, and pelted her back from coming after me. I was savage. Everything was black as night. The river was up, and it moved between the snow-covered banks like a big snake, purple from overfeeding, sluggish, slimy, winding on its way to do whatever mischief it could down South. Dante put the mouth, you remember, Guernsey, of his 'Inferno' in a dense forest. But he never saw a forest like ours at Ocklawahaw. The trees are woven together with great vines, the moss hanging so rank from the boughs that the wind cannot get at the malaria, nor the sun either. When I went on my expeditions I sank almost to my knees at every step in the dead leaves coated with snow. The worse it was the more I enjoyed it."

Now, if Ross had been in the habit of talking in that way to people in general, I should have known that he was a humbug. As I well knew, I was the one man living to whom he did thus talk. I doubt if he cared to think of such things when away from me. If he had made a custom of moralizing in that

style with me, even while I loved the man, I should
have despised him, as one does the sham heroes of all
grades who weep aloud in order to be wept over, precisely as clowns in a circus laugh in their queer coats
and daubed cheeks in order to be laughed at, pennies
of some sort to be paid at the door in both cases.
But Ross Urwoldt was not of that kind. He was
thoroughly sincere, with me at least, and I rated, as
well as loved, him higher than I do many a better
man.

"Your hell was in you, not in the dank forest.
Otherwise," I said, "you would not have gone there.
But you were going to tell me, you said an hour ago,
about Governor Beauchamp."

"Wait a moment. I had been lifted out of being
a half-Indian when I went to Old Orange. Rather,"
Ross said, "I had climbed up that high out of Ocklawahaw and savagery by my own effort. Up to the
moment I found myself surrounded that evening in
college by the fellows, wild for a little fun, all I
cared for on earth was to climb higher. You know
how it was. What with the bugle and drum, the
tutors hammering at the doors and the fellows about
you begging you to take the lead, weariness with years
of steady study and Nature itself boiling in my veins,
what could I do but go crazy? It was my fault, of
course. I had lifted myself that high with my own
hands, and with my own hands I dashed myself down.
It all lies in mere circumstance, Guernsey, circumstance contained in a minute, circum—"

"Circumstance to be grappled with," I interrupted

him, "in the instant, and mastered as you would a wild-cat leaping upon you. But go on, go on."

"A wild-cat? Do you know, Guernsey," Ross said, "I saw one in the forks of a pecan the first day I took to the woods. My rifle went to my shoulder as of itself, I had n't had a chance for a shot so lo..; but just as I was about putting a bullet between its eyes I lowered the rifle. 'Not a bit of it!' I said, 'we are too near of kin, old fellow; it would be murder. No; you go ahead, bite your best, fight, squall, scratch! What do I care?' Would you believe it, Guernsey, I blazed away after that at every blue-jay I saw, catbird, woodpecker. I had to kill deer for my food, of course; but whenever I saw a gray squirrel sitting out on the limb of a tall tree, its tail curved over its head, a nut between its paws, its bright eye glancing about, letting down a fore-paw now and then to listen — crack! my ball would strike the limb under it, and it would whirl high into the air and come down to the ground with a thud! I did not know I could be such a savage. If I had struggled up and out a little, I had taken myself by the shoulders, as with both hands, and dashed myself down deeper than I had been before."

"Well?" I said; for while I sympathized with him I showed the nature of my sympathy by the way I laughed at his stern face.

"That is all! I had plenty of powder and balls, and, although I was weeks about it off and on, there in the woods, I fired my wrath at myself away with my ammunition. But, Guernsey, there was not a bul-

let that was not aimed really at myself. What a savage loves best is to kill, *kill !* Only it was myself I —
Oh, that is all !" and I saw that he had regretted saying anything. I made no reply. What I never do is
to preach ; when a man's own conscience is in the
pulpit, I would be a fool to try to take its place.

"But what about Beauchamp ?" I asked.

"After I settled down at last from my expeditions
into the woods, I went," Ross told me, "to studying
again under Amasa Clarke. He had remained all this
time in Ocklawahaw teaching. They had made him
President at last of the academy. He was about
the same man, except that he weighed a good deal
more. The more there was of him the less I liked
him, even then. But I 'went to work — for I had
brought back the text-books of the whole college
course — like a savage, with a sort of ferocity in that
direction, too. I almost frightened Clarke, but I
grew at last to be as quiet and silent as need be.
How I studied ! It was partly from the necessity of
being occupied, partly from love of books, chiefly because I knew it would please my mother."

"But Governor Beauchamp ?" I asked. "You were
going to tell me how you came to know him."

"Was I ? Well, I had heard of the Governor,"
Ross said, "since I could remember. He was a poor
boy somewhere, who had managed to fight his way
upward, until he obtained an appointment to West
Point. From there he went as an army officer to take
charge of the Seminoles in Florida. After living
among them and drinking hard, it was said, for so

many years that he became himself almost a savage, he suddenly resigned and went into the practice of law and politics in the State next to our Reservation. There he engaged in a duel or two, a street-fight or so. Then he was elected to the Legislature, after that to Congress. One peculiarity of Beauchamp was that he was either very popular or the most thoroughly execrated of men. Defeated for Congress at the next election, he came back to the State, and married the daughter of a planter who died when Rachel, her only child, was a few years old. For a while he gave himself up to dissipation. Whether popular or the reverse, he was always pressed for money. It was little he cared, for his daughter grew up on the plantation under the care of her aunt, and General Beauchamp, as he was then styled, did as he pleased.

"It is too long a story to tell," Ross continued, "but in some way he was smitten by another gust of popularity, and sent back to Congress, to the lower House. So popular did he become that he was elected, after a tour of vigorous stump-speaking, to the Senate. Then came another period of unpopularity; no man was so heartily cursed throughout his State as he. It is wearisome to tell, but after this came a period of restoration to favor. It was like a cyclone, and he was made Governor of his State almost by acclamation. Heaven knows why, but in a few months thereafter he resigned, and disappeared from the knowledge of men.

"All my life," Ross added, "I had heard of him. The papers made such constant mention of him, for

and against, always with vehemence, that from a boy
I considered him the greatest of men.   The people of
Ocklawahaw were constantly coming and going, and
they sat about my father's warehouse on goods-boxes,
whittling cypress shingles, cracking pecans, chewing
tobacco, smoking by the hour.   They had much to
say about General Beauchamp, what he did and said
in Washington, his speeches, his fine horses, his virtues,
his rascalities.   With some he was a scoundrel, with
others he was a patriot and a statesman, but with all
he was a hero.   You have to live in such a section to
know how utterly one man can be the standard, can
fill the talk of its people.   Cotton, corn, horse, whiskey,
dollar, Governor Beauchamp, — the language seemed
to be made up of those words.   There was no man I
had heard so much about, was so anxious to see.

"All this," Ross continued, "was up to the time of
my return from college.   The Big Meetings were long
past, I hunted now only of fine afternoons, and had
gone to hard study.   It was very rarely that I went
into the village.   One hot afternoon I had to go to
my father's store for something, — to mail a letter to
you, I think it was, for the store was also the post-
office.   As I approached it, I heard a loud, slow,
steady voice as of some one rather reading aloud than
making a speech.   The building was crowded with
people, but the first thing which struck me as I went
in was to see a large man seated upon the counter
which ran across the great room at the other end.
In front of him, and sitting upon nail-kegs, tobacco-
boxes, salt-sacks, half-opened cases of brogans, whis-

key and flour barrels, about the store, were, as it seemed to me, half the jockeys, small farmers, half-breeds, cattle-raisers, gamblers, loafers, of Ocklawahaw. Some were whittling sticks, others were chewing tobacco and spitting between their outstretched legs, but all were listening, as if for life, to the man perched above them all, upon the counter. I knew that he must be some remarkable somebody, he was so very large and good-looking, and he was so entirely conscious of it."

But I will repeat what Ross went on to describe to me, in my own words.

"And so you see, my friends," the new-comer was saying as Ross went in, "Andrew Jackson was the same Old Hickory after he became President of the United States as before."

There was a deliberate drawl in the way in which, as Ross mimicked it for me, it was said which it is impossible to put upon paper. It was that of a very heavy and indolent man who enjoyed his own pre-eminence and knew how intently every word was hung upon by his admiring hearers. The slow dragging out of each syllable was an affectation which would have seemed absurd in a lesser man; now it was part of the pomp of a king.

"It happened," the stranger continued, "when Jackson was President. Donaldson was his secretary. When Donaldson told Jackson that she was waiting to see him in the East Room, he found the President, as usual, dressed out in the ragged old wrapper he brought with him from the Hermitage in Tennessee.

6

He was smoking his pipe. It was a cob pipe. A corn-cob pipe. With a six-inch reed stem. 'You go and tell the Countess,' Jackson said to Donaldson, — 'you go and tell her,' Old Hickory said, 'that I will be with her in a minute.' 'My Lord!' Donaldson replied, 'what are you thinking about, General? You won't see her with that old dressing-gown on, with your hair in that fix, with your cob pipe between your teeth!' Jackson's hair stood up all over his head, as you know, gentlemen. 'Donaldson,' Jackson replied — "

Here, as Ross related to me, the new-comer stopped speaking. He was carving something out of a cypress shingle, and he held it away from him to see how it looked. There was an unbroken silence. Taking his time to it, he resumed after a while his whittling and his story.

" 'Donaldson,' Jackson replied, 'you do as I tell you.' 'General,' Donaldson begged, 'the lady is a Countess. Moreover, she is writing a big book upon America. At least, leave your old slippers.' 'Donaldson,' Old Hickory said, 'I knew a man once who made a fortune by minding his own business.'"

Here the centre of the admiring group paused to take another look at his shingle, and then slowly resumed.

" If you will believe me, gentlemen, in half an hour after Jackson was in the East Room talking to that woman. He was dressed out in black broadcloth, his hair combed beautifully. She wrote in her book that President Jackson was the most polished gentle-man she met in America. In her knowledge of the nobles and kings of Europe she had never met a more refined and aristocratic person."

"You must imagine the speaker," Ross added as he told me of it. "Although he sat in a slouching way upon the counter while he talked, he was the most magnificent-looking man I ever saw. When he arose and shook himself from the litter he made in his whittling, I saw that he was of almost colossal height and breadth. That he was, or had been, in the army, I could see by his military bearing. His head was large and in keeping with his stature and yard-across breadth of shoulder; the brows retreating, but noble; the jaws as powerful as those of a bull; the face almost leonine amid its shaggy abundance of tawny hair and beard. I was amazed. To me he seemed in his copperas-colored suit to be an emperor in disguise.

"And so he stood leaning against the counter whittling, telling anecdote after anecdote, awakening now and then peals of laughter. At last, and in a momentary pause, my father introduced me. Of course all the world must know who the distinguished stranger was, and all that my father said was, 'General, this is my son Ross.' Had he been at once a king, a patriarch, and an affectionate grandmother, he could not have been more stately, more venerable in his manner, more loving. Removing his jack-knife from his right hand to that which held the shingle, he took in his own my hand, saying, 'You are a noble-looking youth, young sir. As I fervently hope, you are a virtuous.' He held my hand in his while he

said this. Then he laid his broad palm upon my
head. 'May God,' he said in fervent accents, —
'may God Almighty bless you, my son!' He said it
with such unction that, for a moment, there was
silence in the room; but then, to my astonishment,
beginning with a low titter, everybody gave way to
laughter, and peal followed upon peal, as if this was
the best joke of all. Wondering, I glanced around
the crowded store and then at the stranger. He had
resumed his whittling, and his broad face was benignant; but my study of his really noble countenance
was arrested by the angles of his eyes, the corners,
under his venerable beard, of his mouth. They
slanted in the lines of concealed — no, it could not
be — amusement! There was a certain indescribable
flickering, quivering, — no, the eyes were full in
mine, then furtive, then fastened with grave sincerity
upon the bit of wood which was taking under his
careful carving the shape of a heart.

"And this," Ross added, "was Governor, Senator,
possibly President Beauchamp! But that was merely
the beginning of my acquaintance with him."

CHAPTER VIII.

RACHEL BEAUCHAMP.

AND so, when Governor Beauchamp fled from the scene of his triumphs, it was in the Reservation that he found a shelter. The habits he had formed during his stay among the Seminoles in Florida had doubtless much to do with it.

"They say," I remarked to Ross, when we were speaking, long after, of the Governor, "that when a forest is burned there springs up in its place a wholly new and different species of vegetation, the seeds of which had been biding their time in the soil from creation. So of Governor Beauchamp. We cannot understand the smallest revolution in weeds or minerals ; how much less can we explain any man, and the queer changes which befall him ?"

"Man is himself," Ross replied, "one of the very least of the growths of the soil, the easiest understood of all. What is an insect like Beauchamp in comparison to magnificent nature ? We speak of the magnetic force by which the sun draws the planets toward itself, by which the globe compels its particles toward its centre ; did it ever occur to you, Guernsey, how nature drags to itself unceasingly the hearts, also, of all of us ? The dullest and driest Professor of

Philology will drop his dictionary, and be drawn, whenever he can find excuse for yielding, to the seashore or the mountain side, — it is the magnetic attraction upon him of mountain and sea. A man may have made himself as much of a money-making machine as if he were the contrivance for that purpose in a mint, yet, all of a sudden, he will have broken away and gone, — Europe has seized upon and drawn him across the water, precisely as a magnet does an iron filing. Did you ever observe how utterly men and women, as well as children, give themselves up in a picnic to the attraction of lake or forest? Our life is wholly artificial, against nature. Some take opium to escape; others, whiskey. Some fly to religion to get away from our unnatural life. We gamble, read fiction, plunge into poetry, go to the theatre, the race-course, — it is but a desperate effort to break jail, to get out of the wretched conventionalism of men and women, and back again to great nature.

"It is that," Ross continued, "which explains Governor Beauchamp. He was a large man, and nature drew him to itself with a powerful grasp. It was the surge of the sea he craved, the blowing of the wind, the flash and peal of the storm, something larger, more genuine, than the miserable trifles about him as Governor. He was as glad to get away from his popularity as from his unpopularity, — more so, for people pressed about and stifled him more in the first instance than in the last. He fled to us, and for years he was the biggest, most utterly abandoned, and happiest loafer in Ocklawahaw."

"How did he pass his time?" I asked.

"He spent it," Ross said, "as the Orientals do, as the Syrian Jobs and Isaacs did, in gravely and deliberately doing nothing. He found a luxury in being far away from Congress and the squabbling capital of his State. Like a mariner who had escaped from wreck and stormy seas, he simply sat high and dry on the beach, beyond the utmost reach of the waves, and in the sunshine, resting, doing nothing whatever. He found a luxury in eating as much as possible, sleeping as often and as long as he could, smoking the best tobacco in reach, talking when he felt like it, saying nothing when he preferred to be silent, — the existence of a king.

"If the truth must be told," he added, "the Governor was a sadly demoralized Executive, in more senses than one. He became very fat, I may say enormously fat, — too fat to hunt, to ride, even to fish in the river, as he did when he first arrived. As a rule he did not wake until late in the day. I am compelled to add that he got drunk. He said it was the only way he could escape chills and fever. By three o'clock in the afternoon he would be garrulously drunk, with a crowd about him; by four he ceased to talk by reason of the state of solemn and dignified intoxication to which he had attained, and his retinue withdrew. At such times he sat generally on a stone beneath a sycamore, in a condition of majestic and haughty isolation from every one, refusing to pay his usual attention to anything or to anybody. Leaving out of account his soiled clothing,

disregarding as far as I could the broad-brimmed felt
hat which rested at strange angles upon his noble
head, Governor Beauchamp was even then, and merely
to look at, the most commanding of men. When in
that stage, his great hands grasping the heavy stick
of *bois d'arc* wood which he always carried, as it stood
between his knees, poising himself with unspeakable
dignity, his eyes wide open and gazing before him in
solemn abstraction from all around, you could imagine
him a monarch awaiting an embassy ; at the very
least, it was easy to fancy him still in his seat in the
Senate, gravely considering the line of statesmanship
to be followed in some national emergency then pressing upon him.

"When he sat in silent state upon his stone under
the sycamore, you would not at first," Ross went on,
"have imagined that he had touched liquor. Taking
into account the rude scenery about him and his own
habiliments, it was easy to imagine him some mighty
Montezuma of old hidden in the wilds, waiting until
the justice of Heaven should destroy his foes and restore him to his throne. Alas ! within half an hour
he would slowly relax, slacken in every muscle, yield
as to an inexorable and mysterious doom, and, sliding
down from the stone upon which he sat, would lie
along the earth in majestic ruins, dead drunk."

"They say," I remarked, "that his Indian name
was 'Big-Drunk.'"

"Yes, 'Doora-Chup,' 'Big-Drunk;' that was the
name by which he was known, at least," Ross added,
"until she came."

"She? Who was she?" I asked.

"Be patient, and I will tell you. In those days," he continued, "I gave my mornings to hard study. It pleased my mother. And I had an ambition, too, to show her that I was not dependent upon any college for my education. I must have studied very hard, for I could not apply myself in the afternoons. With my dogs at my heels, my rifle in my hand, I would saunter about as the fancy took me. The sycamore of which I have spoken was upon the outskirts of the village, where the prairie began, — the coolest spot, according to tradition, anywhere about, by reason of a breeze which blew there, or ought to blow, from the expanse beyond. When any one sat upon the stone beneath the old sycamore, he could not help leaning against its gnarled trunk, which, worn smooth and shiny thereby, always reminded me of the knees of Parson Williams's Sunday suit. How often have I sat upon that stone whole afternoons! There I would remain for hours, with the Governor lying at my feet, too heavy for less than four men to bear away, and not a man in the village who cared enough for him to make the attempt.

"How well I remember those hot days in August! On one side of me rolled the river like an infernal Styx, slimy, silent, not a fish leaping out of it, not a bird skimming its surface, too muddy, too hot for anybody unless it was a boy to bathe in. When I turned my eyes toward the open prairie, there was not a living thing to be seen upon it, and the air between where

I sat and the distant hills flickered with heat, needing but a few more degrees thereof to become flame. Back of me were the woods, dark but not cool, full of rotting trees; and every now and then I could hear a distant crash which told of some falling bough or giant live-oak, upon which the slowly gnawing doom had done its work at last. Everybody in and about the village seemed to be dead or asleep. I knew that Amasa Clarke was lying flat on his back on the platform in the exhibition-room of the academy, as the coolest spot there, sleeping, with his foolish mouth open, fat and flaccid like a stranded fish.

"And there I would sit looking at Governor Beauchamp stretched out on the dead leaves, his great face full in the sun, the flies swarming about him as if he were so much manure. It was a lesson to me, Guernsey," Ross went on. "I said to myself, 'Here is a man who has made a desperate struggle of it from childhood. How hard and long he worked when a lad, when a school-teacher! This mass of bloated corruption took a complete course at West Point. He mastered there the toughest sort of mathematics, was taught the languages, was drilled for years by a stern discipline, learned how to dance, to fence, to ride, to fight. Here he lies and rots, and yet he fought bravely in the everglades of Florida, has bought and sold with the shrewdest, has made speeches, has figured in Congress, has filled the papers with his name. This man, with his hanging cheeks, puffy eyes, draggled beard, Roman head in the mire, — *this* man was esteemed the most perfect gentleman, the wisest statesman, the most finished orator, nothing in the world beyond the reach of his ambition, and yet — there he lies.'

"I have read of the ruined cities of Asia, have seen in imagination the fallen columns of glorious temples, the prostrate images of the Ptolemies and Nebuchadnezzars, but Governor Beauchamp lying at my feet those hot afternoons was as instructive a teaching as I could wish to have in regard to things, because, you will observe, I got thus at the facts. That is what I like to get at, the *facts!*" Ross added, not savagely, but with a sincerity which was, to me, exceedingly sad.

"I remember one night," he continued, "when I sat with his Excellency snoring upon the earth at my feet until darkness fell. There was no moon, but all the stars were out, and as I stood at last, my head bared to the night breeze beside the fallen monarch of men, I looked up at the immeasurable blue above me, and contrasted the poor worm at my feet, so debased during even his brief moment of existence, with the more than eighteen millions of suns known to astronomers, which have burned for millions of years about and around the speck of dust we call our globe. Guernsey, I got an impression then of the microscopic meanness of man and the grandeur of nature which I shall retain forever."

"From what you have told me I should think," I said, "that you might have learned something also from such a life as that of old Parson Williams, as your people call him." For I did not care to argue.

"Yes, he was," Ross consented, "a good man. He came to Ocklawahaw so long before only to do good. He had worked long and very hard, and he was very poor. His wife had worked even harder, if possible, and she was dead. I had to pass by his tumble-down old cabin on my way to the sycamore, and was pretty sure always to see him at work at something. He was about the only man in the village who did not take a long nap of summer afternoons, and when I strolled by I was very apt to see him hoeing at his cabbages or his beets, fixing a new handle to his axe, plastering fresh mud upon the chinking of his cabin, — an exceedingly plain old man, whose talk was as rough as his clothes. The only wickedness with which he could blame himself was that, as soon as he settled himself down to a book, he would fall asleep."

"And there was Persis, you told me," I began.

"Yes, Persis." It was really amazing the change which came into the manner of my friend as he repeated her name. His face lighted up, his tones were different. "As I told you," Ross continued, "she was the busiest morsel of a girl, those days, you ever saw. Her grandfather kept no help, of course, and the poor little thing had the household work to do. She was ambitious, more so than I was, to keep up in her studies too."

Ross had told me about her before. "I wonder," I now said aloud, but none the less to myself, "why you, why somebody — "

"Did not come to her help?" There was color in

his face as he anticipated my question, nor could I understand why his eyes, always so steadily in mine when we conversed, should fall to the earth.

"My mother had in those days," — and there was such unconscious gall in the accents of the speaker! — "no thought except for me. Nor did she have any means of her own. My father was not interested in her, — in Persis."

"Nor in any one else," I added, but this time wholly to myself, as I well knew he had always held every penny of his wife's possessions, too, in his own hand. Abandoned drunkard and unfaithful husband that he was, he did not relax, even at his drunkest, his iron hold upon his money. How his wife managed to obtain the means to prepare Ross for college, and to maintain him there afterward, was a mystery which perhaps some remains of Indian cunning in her veins could alone explain. It was small wonder that his son rarely or never mentioned his father to me. It struck me, as I came to know about General Urwoldt, how that, while his avarice strengthened with his years, his passion for poetry, music, painting, oratory, had passed into his son, giving to Ross a certain curve and color, a softness even and warmth, to what would have been otherwise the inflexible bronze of his strong nature. So far as the father was concerned, even the memory of having once possessed these gifts had rotted away. Except in business matters he never touched a pen. It had been a long time since he had opened a book. That he had once done excellent work with his brush was to him, when thought of at

all, a matter of contempt as for a folly of his youth.
For all taste was lost in love of liquor, all conception
of beauty in the grossest lewdness, all that remained
to the man of clear-headedness and strength was
where the making and keeping of money was concerned.   As it is, I would have disdained to give to
General Urwoldt a word here, or a thought, had it
not been for what there was in him of explanation
— excuse, dare I say? — of and for his son.

But I did not intend to speak of the father. "From
almost the first month after my return from college,"
Ross went on, "I did what I could for Persis, — in
her studies, I mean.   There was no merit in it.   She
was so eager to learn, so quick to apprehend, so
retentive of what she came to know, that I was glad
to do it.   Guernsey," he added, "women are brighter
than you or I, — at least, *she* was."

"Be good enough," I replied, "to tell me something
I do not know.   Have you done with Montezuma?"

"How well I recall one particularly hot afternoon!"
my friend continued, speaking as if to himself.   "I
was resting upon the stone beneath the sycamore, the
mighty son of Bacchus lying at my feet, when Persis
passed by, barefooted, on her way to the spring for
water.   She had seen the sight before."

Ross paused a moment.   Almost as if he had told
me so, I saw that he was thinking of his own father,
who was as hard a drinker as Beauchamp, except that
he locked himself up in his store, for fear of being
robbed, when he gave way to his potations.

"The girl was not as much shocked as you would

suppose," Ross went on, " she had seen so much of it; but she looked at the fallen man so pitifully as she passed that I stopped her when she came back, carrying in one hand the heavy blue bucket full of water, leaning away from it, her other arm extended to keep her balance, heartily ashamed of her bare feet.

"'Persis,' I said, "is n't it a pity?' She did not lift her eyes to me, she was looking at the drunkard. 'Yes,' was all she said. She picked up the vessel which she had rested for a moment on the earth in the other hand, and went on. I arose and strolled toward the river, and stood out of sight from the sycamore, looking vaguely at the water, and saying, like a fool, to myself, 'If this water, if all rivers which run, were tears flowing across the face of the world for the misery in it, they would not suffice, not if the brine of ocean were added thereto!' How sick I was of the awful problem! 'And how can there be a Christ,' I said as I turned away, 'when He stands by, if there is one, and sees this and ten thousand worse things every day and does nothing?'

"As I muttered it, I came where I could see the prostrate statesman. Persis, supposing I had gone away, had returned, and was sitting on the ground by his head. She had brought a book with her, and, holding it in her left hand, with a leafy branch she had broken from a chinquepin-bush near by in the other, was keeping away the flies from the bloated face. For some time I leaned upon my rifle, watching her. She was small, thin, sallow,—a little country girl, sunburned, and plain as plain could be.

Upon her head was a sun-bonnet of the same blue as
her calico dress, made, in fact, from the same piece.
It was tied under her chin by strings of the same,
and thrown back from her face, that she might study
the harder. Wholly forgetful of her bare and very
brown feet, she was conning her lesson over as she
sat, changing the brush for the book, and the book
for the brush, as her hands became tired, but studying and brushing away as steadily as a clock.

"'*Penna, Pennae, Pennae, Pennam, Penna, Penna,*'
came from her in the peculiar recitative of those who
are memorizing, and this over and over again. 'Pity,
pity,' she then added, and, laying down brush and
book, she wet a towel from a tin basin beside her,
which I had not observed before, washed off the per-
spiration and grime from the senatorial brows before
her, wiped the whole purple face, like the smallest
conceivable mother of the largest imaginable baby,
did it slowly, carefully, then, resuming grammar and
brush, she went on more rapidly, after a glance at the
setting sun, 'Plural, *Pennae, Pennarum, Pennis, Pen-
nas, Pennae, Pennis!*' over and over again. As I
came slowly up, she snatched in her naked feet under
her calico skirt in alarm, hesitated a moment, closed
her book, her forefinger in it to keep the place, but
kept the leafy switch in motion.

"'Studying Latin!' I exclaimed. 'Why Persis,
who put you up to that?'

"'Nobody,' she said, 'but I want to teach when I
grow old enough, and I must learn first, you know.'

"'Persis,' I said, 'listen to me. I am a man, and

you are only a little girl. You are very young, and I am years older than you. For you ever to study Latin is nonsense, but for you to study it now is wicked. You are too young. I am astonished at your grandfather.'

"'Grandpa knows nothing about it,' she said, smoothing her skirt down over her hidden feet. 'I took it up for myself.'

"'Well, don't do so any more, that's a good girl.' But, as I proceeded, I found I could not talk in as patronizing a way as I began. There was no assent to what I was saying in her eyes; they were opened a little wider, that was all. She was shy, but not afraid of me, not as docile as I had expected, and I paused to look at her afresh.

"No," Ross said, "there was no beauty in her face, none at all. She had worked too hard, was too practical. Besides, she was at the awkward age in a girl, even if she had time for those slopes and spirals of leisure which are the lines of beauty. I wished she could have laughed more readily, but there was nothing in particular to laugh at just then. The sadness of her eyes lifted to mine were sweetened with an utter sincerity which touched me. I sat down upon the stone again for the purpose of looking into them some more. We talked about her studies as we had done before. She took up the Latin Grammar again, but she did not cease keeping off the flies.

"'This man studied Latin,' I said at last, touching him with my foot; 'Greek too, I dare say. He learned all the mathematics; he learned everything, and look

7

at him!' Persis complied with my request, and turned her practical eyes upon the wrecked politician, but she had nothing to say. 'Persis,' I said, — for I was at just the age to do it, — 'this man represents a good deal. He stands for and illustrates multitudes of men,' for I could not help showing off a little before her. 'This individual is Darius after the battle of Issus, is Xerxes after his repulse from Greece, is Hannibal after he was driven out of Italy and had taken poison, is Julius Cæsar after Brutus stabbed him, is — this man represents all the Roman emperors, every soul of them, — that is, after they had reigned awhile.'

"'Does he?' Persis asked, her inquiring eyes fastened upon mine.

"'He is Napoleon at St. Helena. This poor fool,' I declaimed, 'is Babylon after its fall, Carthage, Nineveh, Baalbec, Palmyra, Rome, — a thousand empires we have never heard of which flourished and perished. He represents them all.'

"'Does he?' Persis listened seriously, plying her brush as she did so.

"'You think his is a peculiar case?' I went on. 'Not at all. As he lies here, so will everything in the end; the paths of glory lead but to the grave.'

"'Do they?' But Persis was not attending as she should, for it was time to go, and she got up, keeping her feet carefully out of sight under the edges of her gown. My talk was too large for her undeveloped mind; she merely said,

" ' I must go to get grandfather's supper, but I will wash off his face again before I go, and I can make up for it afterward by running.'

" I was so occupied with watching her do it that I did not notice another girl who had stolen shyly up while we were talking. The first I knew of her was a sobbing, then an outcry of grief as she fell upon her knees beside the drunken man on the side opposite Persis. It was a girl about the age of Persis, but she was as plump and full-faced as Persis was spare and sinewy. Her hair was flaxen, while that of Persis was brown; but her face, freckled as it was, had more play in it of white and red, and she lifted up eyes which seemed to be blue through their tears.

" Kneeling beside the prostrate man, she clasped her hands together, rocking herself forward and backward upon her knees in utter grief, weeping convulsively. Persis had stopped, and was staring at her across the drunkard with great eyes; but the surprise was drowned out, as in a moment, by her tears as she saw the distress of the other.

" We could not get a word from the strange girl for a long time, she seemed to be in such a passion of grief. But Persis was sitting at last flat on the earth by her, forgetful of her bare and exposed feet, and of supper to be got, weeping with her arms about the other, and trying to soothe her in a certain sober, old-fashioned way. I had an idea who it must be, although I did not know before that the Governor had a daughter, and I hastened away for assistance in removing him, not to his own cabin, for that was no place for the girl to see, but to Parson Williams's, for the night at least."

"And those two girls were more to you even then," I suggested, "than all the constellations of the universe! But I am not going to argue with you, man."

CHAPTER IX.

ONLY TWO GIRLS.

WHEN Governor Beauchamp sought seclusion in Ocklawahaw, it was because the Indian Reservation lay apart from all lines of travel, was least known, or, when known, the most despised, of all the regions of the West. After he came, however, a feeble current of immigration slowly set in toward the new lands beyond. To-day that first faint trickling of immigration is swollen to a torrent which has poured for years, and has opened a course for itself broad and deep, rolling three thousand miles farther northwestward. But the passing through the Reservation of the first pioneers was enough to uncover the secret of Governor Beauchamp's disappearance.

When he fled to the Reservation his daughter Rachel remained, as has been said, in charge of her aunt, upon the plantation of her father. As soon as she heard of his whereabouts she wrote to him. But it was in vain she sent letter after letter in her large school-girl hand; his eye was not to be pained by her misspelling, nor by the blotches of ink upon the page; it is doubtful, poor girl! if he opened one of her epistles. General Urwoldt was postmaster as well as store-keeper of Ocklawahaw, and it was in vain that he offered the Governor his accumulating letters.

"No newspapers, no letters for me, if you please," he would reply, waving aside the documents with an oratorical hand. "You will pardon me, General Urwoldt, but I did not come here to be annoyed with things of that nature. I will be glad, however, to take a drink with you, sir, if you have any whiskey you can conscientiously recommend."

And yet, through all this neglect, there was this much of her mother in Rachel that she loved her father still. As she grew older, there was also so much in her of her father, too, that she could not remain content to live quietly on with her aunt upon the plantation. She was not what is called a bright girl; in that, Persis was her superior. If she seemed almost as content to go and come from the school-house near by as the cows were content to come and go from pasture, she brooded, too, in her slow fashion, over her father's absence, and what she had better do, seeing that he answered neither her letters nor those written to him by the overseer of the plantation or by her aunt. Who can tell what passes beneath the bark, as it grows, of even a dogwood sapling? There are processes going on in the heart, if not the brain, of a blue-jay which are as inevitable as anything in the roll of the planets; and, as Rachel grew older, there were feelings which blindly determined her to do something for her father, she knew not what.

For every appetite growing within us there are parallel preparations of supply going on without us;

that, also, is among the celestial certainties of life. So in the case of Rachel. The day came, neither too soon nor too late, when the man who owned the plantation next to that on which she lived with her aunt sold out, and was soon to go West, and to a point beyond the Reservation, but by a road which led through Ocklawahaw. Rachel knew of this for months in advance of his leaving. Could she not take Seelye, her black nurse, and go with the movers? Very slowly her purpose was formed, and when the wagons started at last, Rachel had no more idea of staying behind than an oriole has when the new season calls it southward. And so she took her place with the wife and manifold children; and the caravan of canvas-covered vehicles rolled westward, the negroes, cows, dogs, following behind, — for all this was before the days of emancipation.

In due time the weary movers arrived at Ocklawahaw, and halted in front of the tavern. The emigrant planter stepped upon the porch, went to the cedar bucket upon its shelf in the shade, dipped into it the big yellow gourd hanging by its leather thong from a nail near by, and as he raised the water to his lips, he demanded of the owner of the house, seated in a hide-bottomed chair, his feet upon the rails of the porch, — a Mr. Jake Golson by name, — "Does Governor Beauchamp live in this town?"

"Governor Beauchamp?" Mr. Golson dropped his head to reflect. "Governor Beauchamp?" It was as if he had heard a name something like that in his childhood. "Oh, Governor Beauchamp? Well, yes." Since people seemed to have found it out, Governor Beauchamp *does* live in the town.

"This is his daughter," said the planter. For Rachel had landed upon the porch by this time with her nurse and her trunks, and stood by in trembling eagerness. As the tavern-keeper let his feet fall to the floor in astonishment, while he stared at her, there were abundant leave-takings between the girl and her friends. But there had been enmity between the Governor and this neighbor of his who had brought his daughter on, and, although he had not told Rachel of it, he did not care to meet the father. As soon as possible the wagons rolled on, and through the town to their next camping-place, and Rachel and her nurse were left standing upon the porch. But the tavern-keeper had suddenly forgotten whereabouts in the village the Governor lived; his forgetfulness was a credit to him, by reason of the condition in which the poor girl would have found her father's cabin. It was a wretched alternative, but what could he do? "The Gov'nor gin'ally spends his arternoons, miss," he said at last, "under a big sycamore in the fur end of the town." And Jake Golson walked with her in his shirt-sleeves, the nurse staying behind in care of the trunks, until he could point out the tree.

It was there she found her father, as has been described.

And surely she was as deliberately constructed — now I come to think of it — for her particular work, too, as a fish is to swim, or a bird, however young, is to fly. She was, as has been said, of about the same age as Persis Paige, but of a heavier cast, both of body and mind. Her forehead was not as high as that of Persis, but it was broader. She had not been overstrained by hard work, like Persis, nor did she possess either fondness or aptitude for books, while there was not in her the possibility even of ambition. She loved her father, was there, as by a maternal instinct, to do what she could for him; that was all.

Parson Williams became greatly interested in the matter, and in a little while the Governor was housed in one of the best of the frame buildings which chanced to be standing vacant in Ocklawahaw. It was the providence of the distant aunt, I suppose, who knew the father too well not to do it; but Rachel was sufficiently supplied from the plantation with money as she needed it, the house was painted and furnished, the fences repaired, the negro woman who had accompanied Rachel taking her place as housemaid and cook. "Old Seelye is my mammy," Rachel explained to Persis, "and I could n't have come here if Seelye had n't come with me. We can manage very nicely."

In the course of a month or so it was as if Rachel and her father had lived together in their new home for years. He was cleaner, somewhat better dressed, but his intemperance was nearly the same. His daughter, knowing his habits before she came, took them as part of the ordinance of nature, adjusting herself to them without a tear or a murmur. Her father had long been accustomed to do without money, and ran up accounts at General Urwoldt's store, not troubling

himself upon the subject of payment. But Rachel
paid for the eggs, chickens, butter, flour, venison,
and beef like a matron who had done so all her life,
while Seelye cooked, swept, scrubbed, washed, ironed,
as if she had never known any world but that of
Ocklawahaw. If Rachel had no thought except for
her father, Seelye, who despised the Governor yet
more, if possible, than she did Ocklawahaw, lived but
for her young "missis." What time Persis and Rachel could find from their household duties was spent
with each other.

"And this is my little friend Persis," Governor
Beauchamp would remark, when he came upon them
seated together, of a morning, under the sycamore-
tree. "Rachel, my child, I am glad you have found
such a friend." He was as sober as a man could be,
for it was not until after dinner that he began to
drink. In his hand he carried his big yellow cane.
His suit of jeans was beautifully clean, and neatly
brushed. Rachel had seen to that, as also to the
purity of his voluminous linen, the arrangement of
his abundant hair and beard. A more benignant and
carefully attired gentleman it was impossible to find.

"You seem to be a good girl, little Persis," he
would say after much grandfatherly talk, her little
hand, so brown and hard, still held in his own.
"They tell me, little lady, that you are the best and
most industrious person in Ocklawahaw. Bless you,
my child!" And he laid his apostolic hand upon her
head, which happened to be divested of its sun-bonnet.
"And you have your knitting, I see. A woollen

sock! For your grandfather, I suppose. And how is he, my child? Be sure and give him my regards. I have a profound respect for clergymen, and your venerated grandfather is one of the most worthy of them all. You go to school? Ah, yes. That is right, right, little lady; and what are you studying now? Grammar? Geography? Latin, too? Surely not Latin!—And you, my little dear, I hope that you are well this morning. No touch, I hope, of your fatigue now from travel?" This last to Rachel. For it was one of the peculiarities of the majestic speaker that he adopted to those nearest him the same tone and manner which he used to strangers just introduced. Except that he said "Yes, my dear; no, my dear," instead of "Yes, lady; no, lady," his manner had been the same to his wife when she was alive as it would have been to the wife of—let us say—a brother senator. It was so in the case of his daughter. He spoke to her, whether seated on his own porch, across the dinner-table, everywhere, exactly as he would have done had she been the child of, say, a general of the army, bringing her with him on a visit. It was part of the man, and Rachel took it as her mother had done before her.

"You do well, young ladies, to enjoy this cool and lovely morning. And how do you pass your time?" he would say to the two girls.

Except that he had nothing on earth to do, either then or, as it seemed, forever thereafter, it was as if he had descended the steps of the Federal Capitol the moment before on his leisurely way to call upon the

President. These young ladies were friends of his; he had met them at juvenile balls in Washington, to which he had been invited because of his well-known love for children. All this had taken place with Persis more than once before, but she could never fully understand. One day she saw him lying dead-drunk on the earth, and the next morning he was talking with her, as now, in the most benevolent way, by far the grandest human being she had ever beheld. There was conflict therein which bewildered her. How could a man lie in the dirt like a hog yesterday, and stand upon his feet a king to-day?—beneath the feet of everybody in the afternoon, above the level of everybody—oh, far greater than General Urwoldt, than any one ever seen before in Ocklawahaw—the very next morning! How could anybody be so very bad yesterday, so exceedingly good, benignant, venerable, to-day?—it was that which puzzled Persis most.

After talking with the two girls as long as Persis could find time to stay, when she broke away at last, taking her friend with her, the Governor lifted his hat from his head, smiled down upon her from his heights of benignity as of stature, and passed deliberately on, leaving Persis to study out her puzzle as best she could; and so from day to day.

Perhaps a day, a week, a month after, as the time drew languidly by, he would stop General Urwoldt, just lighting from his horse at the well-gnawed rack near the store. The two had parted only at noon the day before, but—what else was there to do?—the

Governor would demand, "Well, General, and how are you? You have been out at your ranch, I suppose? How are your colts thriving? If I was not such a poor man, I would raise horses myself. What are your prospects for the next race?"

Whereupon his friend would stand, one hand upon the pommel of his saddle, and talk to him for an hour, talking over again things already told a dozen times. Except that the Governor was a taller, stouter man every way, the two were not unlike. But General Urwoldt could no more talk as long and as well, than he could drink as much whiskey as the other. He had seen nothing whatever of the world in comparison with Governor Beauchamp, for a long time had read nothing, had not a tithe of the ability of the refugee statesman. It was in vain that the General, somewhat jealous of him, endeavored to reach the higher level of his distinguished friend by the frequency and violence of his oaths.

"I see that you indulge in profanity," the Governor would remark to him very often, as he did now beside the horse-rack; "most — I may say, all — of my friends do so, but I do not myself. Washington objected to it, as do the ladies also. Personally, I have no objection to it, none whatever; but I do not indulge in oaths myself. But you were remarking—"

The General was cursing him instead, but under his breath, as a humbug and an infernal old hypocrite. Now, as ever, the reputation of his guest weighed heavily upon the headman of the nation. "This is none other than Governor Beauchamp! It is a grand

thing to have such an old hero here! Confound
him," the General complained every day to himself,
" but I can't make him out even yet."

For that was the trouble where this distinguished
individual was concerned, — it was impossible to
reckon him up with any accuracy. He made great
speeches in Congress; but somehow he had never carried, while there, any measure of marked importance.
In the hours of his popularity he was the hero of
barbecues innumerable. He would take the stand at
nine o'clock, and speak on and on and on, interlarding
what he said with anecdotes, for hours, to a laughing,
hurrahing crowd. If the smell of the beef and pigs
roasting upon sticks laid across the long ditches filled
with fire had not drawn his audience away, he would,
on such occasions, have spoken apparently on and on
until dark. And yet nobody could make out the
next day what, at last, he had been talking about.
And however unanimously and savagely his constitu-
ency cursed him in the days of his intermittent
unpopularity, they were as unable to state definitely
what they hated him for, as they had before been
able to say why they had praised him so vehemently.
He was "a great man," — all agreed in that, — a
great scoundrel, great statesman, great rascal, great
patriot, — in any case he was *great!* Persis was not
the only one who was bewildered; he said such little
and yet such large things; did, at least attempted
to do, things so vast, and yet things so exceeding
small also!

Standing at the horse-rack, General Urwoldt resented

it, to-day as always, that he could not speak with the unbounded license which he allowed himself with every one else. He knew that his illustrious friend objected to no oath he could venture, yet, all the time, the portentous manner of the Governor, even more than his imposing size, half daunted the head-man of the nation. It was like blaspheming before an archbishop in full canonicals. In his impatience General Urwoldt broke all bounds, as he stood talking with him. To his oaths he added details of lewd adventure; but the Governor listened to that, also, but not as if he had been talking of the crops.

"I see that you are young, still young," he remonstrated at last, and shook his head; and, whittling all the time at a shingle he had picked up off the ground, there was that in the corners of his eyes, of his mouth, an austerity of manner, which discouraged the other from saying all he would; now it was like telling doubtful stories to the Pope.

"For myself," the statesman added as they parted, "I have for woman the profoundest respect. They nurse us in our helpless infancy, adorn our tables and our homes in the times of our prosperity, minister divinely to us in hours of pain and anguish. I yield to no man in my most humble devotion to them." And he lifted his broad-brimmed hat from his head with one hand, waving his homage toward the sex in general with the other, as he said it. Then, General Urwoldt being obliged to leave him, the statesman loitered along his aimless way, a Jupiter condescending to stoop from Olympus to the haunts of men, and all the more a god by reason of the clouds in which he continued to wrap himself.

But it is purely because of the influence of this man upon Ross Urwoldt at that period that I say what I do concerning Governor Beauchamp. It is with Ross, not him, I have to do.

CHAPTER X.

THE ROLL OF THE RIVER.

THE rolling by of the river was as if Time itself took visible shape in its lapse in Ocklawahaw, so slowly, steadily, did its turbid waters flow by under the bluff upon which the town was built. As things were to-day, so it seemed as if they always had been, always would be.

So monotonous did things become that Ross, who had been to see me once before since leaving college, now broke in upon me again on my little island on a rapid visit.

"I am reading as hard as I can," he told me before he left, "in a fashion as blind as that of a pawpaw plant which hopes to bear fruit some day. I am preparing for whatever is to come. It pleases my mother. And then, you see, it enables me to go back to nature every afternoon with new zest. After dinner I stray off, my dogs at my heels, into the forest, and, rifle in hand, I shoot at whatever I care to have in more complete possession. As often as not I lie on the ground examining some bit of moss or mushroom through a magnifying-glass, the fang of some snake I have killed, the feather of some humming-bird or woodpecker. I have given time to exploring with my glass the eyes

8

of an owl I wounded; I wanted to see in them wherein it differed from me. We would have made a funny picture, the owl staring steadily at me, as I held it from struggling between my knees, and I at it. At last it knew as much of me as I did of it, more perhaps. When the weather is cool and I feel in the mood, I mount my mare and take a twenty-mile gallop across the prairie. Maggie is as much to me as any woman not my mother could be. I say to her, as we ride, 'Maggie, I see a long-eared rabbit;' and she pricks her ears this way and that until she sees it, and then goes off after it without a touch of mine upon her flanks or mouth, and just as eagerly as I. As we gain upon it she lays her ears back, awaiting the crack of my revolver, and looks and waits. I know she laughs when, with the report, the rabbit gives a leap into the air and tumbles over. So when I see a stray buffalo off on one side, or a herd of does grazing. 'Now for it!' she shouts—"

"I did not know," I said, "that a horse could talk; but it does n't matter: go ahead."

"Her heart and mine are so entirely one," Ross explained, "that it is precisely as if she did talk. In fact, she does not need to say anything, for we have but one heart between us. Her legs are mine. When I think of her as of another it is merely that she is better than I, a woman who is stronger, has two feet more than I, who can go faster. In Ocklawahaw we do not," Ross interjected, "make as much difference between a squaw and a mare as you might suppose. I have never had so absolute a friend as

Maggie, not even in my mother." He said this last with an effort.

"Sometimes I light from Maggie at the foot of the mountains, that she may rest and graze a little while. I climb about among the rocks, clinking here and there with my geological hammer in search of specimens. I have broken many a shark's tooth out of the rocky ledges, have seen in rifts of old red sandstone the tracks left by gigantic birds. 'Yes, ye were here ages on ages before men,' I say, and am glad to say, for, with the single exception of yourself, Guernsey, I .prefer animals to men.

"I intended to have told you of the hours I lay upon the river-banks, fishing. Fish are stupid things. I have not often known even a negro to be more of a fool than a catfish, all mouth. Dogs are vastly ahead of both. I have sat for half a day, the nose of a dog on my knee, talking to it. It was not the response of its tail I cared for, but — you try it! Appeal to your dog, look steadily in his eyes, and you can see there his 'O master, I would talk if I could! But why say it? You know how I love you.' Guernsey," Ross added, "I believe in nature! It is the grandest thing I know. Men are as uncertain as the gnats which come and go about your nose on a hot day, or certain only in annoying you; but nature! it is as invariable in everything as it is in the rise and setting of its suns. There is unfathomable mystery in it, enough to satisfy what we call the religious sentiment; and you can rest in it with utter trust. You see it, hear, taste, smell, feel it, — *know* it! It amuses you,

— look at its owls and monkeys; and it astonishes you, — look at its cataracts, tempests, unfathomable oceans, unbounded atmosphere! Why should I delve into myself to find a something in me, and call it a soul? Why should I try, poor fool, to break through the blue skies and get at a Maker? I find in nature more than enough to satisfy my utmost — "

"Ross!" It was all I said, lifting my finger as I did so. But my friend must have felt, too, like a fibbing school-boy, for he added, —

"At least, this is true. I remember especially one summer afternoon when I had been lying deep in the forest under a live-oak. My dogs were chained up; Maggie was in her stable; I had studied hard all the morning, and I was thinking about Governor Beauchamp, and — " He paused, but he did not add "my drunken father," as he might have done. "I was thinking about poor, hard-worked, tough little Persis in her cabin; about square-faced, equable, stolid Rachel playing the mother for her distinguished dolt of a father, — oh, about a dozen things of the kind! The air was pure and motionless. I could see glimpses of the sky, could hear the low murmur of growing and decaying nature about me. As if soothed by a lullaby, I felt what an atom I was in the universe, what a merest animalcule of the myriad million I was; and, as I lay, I would so gladly, so peacefully, have lapsed out of existence if I could! A thousand things were softly dying beside me as I lay there, — blades of grass, insects, abortive acorns. It was but a question of a few years longer, and, with all the race, I would drop into dust anyhow. How sweet to cease from living! I was like a boy sliding down a declivity on his sled smoothly on and on, and if I could but slide down and down and out. — Ah, how sorry was I to wake after an hour's sleep and find — "

"I have read of you," I said gravely. "The poet Gray chanced to be watching you from behind a magnolia, — no, a beech-tree;" and I quoted, —

> "'There at the foot of yonder nodding beech,
> That wreathed its old, fantastic roots so high,
> His listless length at noontide would he stretch,
> And pore upon the brook that babbles by.'

You remember how, poor fellow, he drooped and died.

> 'One morn I missed him on the 'customed hill,'

and all the rest. It is very sad!" And I drew my handkerchief from my pocket.

"Guernsey!" Ross Urwoldt had been seated, a cigar in his mouth. Now he stood up, smoking still, his hands in his pockets, angry, but quite cool. "You are the soul of truth, if you are sentimental," he began.

"I? Sentimental?" I said. "Who was actually dying upon the grass of sentimentality?"

"As a truthful man, I ask you," Ross went on, "if I am a fellow of — of that sort?"

"No, you are *not!*" I was compelled seemingly to contradict myself. It was absurd to do otherwise; of all the men I knew, Ross was, then as ever, the healthiest. He was never sick in his life, —

after his recovery from the small-pox, at least; and that had left him unscarred, as if his was a constitution too tough for disease to mar. Even in his repose Ross remained sinewy and strong. He had not a particle of flurry or fuss about him, was never nervous or thrown out by things little or large, painful or pleasant. As I have said, he could remain absolutely still for a longer period than any man I know, because his rest, too, was as that of a bowstring drawn tense.

"I thought I might tell *you*," he now added. "Let me add only this, to be done with it. If there is a man free from toothache or rheumatism, headache or indigestion, everything of the sort, I am. You know that I have as keen a zest for enjoyment as you have, Guernsey, except that I prefer my seas and mountains, my sunsets and groups of cattle, in nature itself, and you affect a relish for them on a yard of canvas. I enjoy things as keenly as you do. Yes, and I take my full swing of satisfaction, where you halt, and throw up your lady-like hands and scream, 'Oh, it is wicked!' I do not care a snap for the hate or — love," but there he hesitated perceptibly, "of any one, you excepted. Well, let me say it and be done with it forever! I tell you, Guernsey, I have not known an hour when I would not rather die than live. I go to sleep when I first lie down, and that is more than you do, old fellow, and I sleep like a babe. Well, when I go sliding down, down, down into the depths, I almost invariably say, as I did that day in the woods, if I could but keep on and on and — *out!* It does n't pay to live. I am that much of an animal, if you please, — cat, eagle, pig, what you will!"

It was not because I was looking up at him in the way I did, that he colored a little as he ceased to speak. There was a Guernsey in the man himself ten times as contemptuous of such talk as I could be, and I knew it, and he knew I knew it.

"Do you go to church?" I asked him after a while.

"To please my mother, oh, yes," he said, "and it is very fine. You must have heard the tree-frogs, Guernsey. Don't you remember? As night begins to fall, you will hear from far away a single 'Tre-e-e-e-e,' as shrill as from a silver pipe. Then silence closes in upon it again, as darkness does on a taper which has flickered an instant and gone out. The rest of the frogs know better. 'That fellow is a fool, and has begun too soon,' they say to each other. In five minutes or so — and all nature is waiting to hear — another lizard — for of course they are not really frogs, — cannot endure the suspense, and tries to start things. 'Trll-l-l-l-l!' It comes sharper, shriller than ever; but it is dead failure again, the silence is deeper than before. So here, there, from this quarter from that, effort and failure, until at last the Mozart of the era has arrived. You start at his vigorous, vibrant 'Tree-e-e-l-l-e-e-l,' for now all the woods for miles around join in. Not a tree-frog of the myriad but is doing its best. It is as crisp to the ear, and as fresh, as the best celery to the taste, and for many an hour it is kept up. It is as if the air, as far as you can see upon every side, is full of fine hail, every glittering atom a shrill sound.) If the universal shrill ceases, lulls, for a moment, the old Mozart or some young Wagner aspiring to outdo him, begins again with intense enthusiasm, and all the world joins in. It is better than opera, now, is n't it?"

"And it is in that way you enjoy the singing at church?" I demanded.

"Yes; for I have got so, at last," Ross said, "that I hear only the sounds, — sounds wholly apart from the words, the sentiments. When Persis looks at me in meeting, and gives her head a little nod over the top of her melodeon, — for she plays it, — I wait for the beginning of the next verse, and strike in as heartily as any tree-frog of them all. When meeting is at night, we drown out the forest orchestra entirely, at least while we sing. In the interval between the verses the outsiders come in with a rush which threatens to drown us out. I enjoy the one, as I do the other, very much. But I care no more for the meaning of what is said or sung, than I do for what the frogs mean, than Persis does for the meaning of the Latin she studies."

For the best of reasons I had become deeply interested in Persis, as in Rachel too, for that matter; Ross had before this either written to me or told me upon his previous visit so much about them. But it was chiefly of Rachel that he talked to me now. She took care of her father, chaffered with the Indians at her gate for venison, went to the store with

Seelye at her heels, to buy supplies; he told me all about her, and I was strangely interested.

But a letter arrived for Ross from his father, and he left me as suddenly as he had come. As I afterward learned, General Urwoldt cared really as little for his son as he did for his deserted wife, and yet he could not fail to see that Ross had grown up into a son of whom even such a father could not but be proud. Moreover, that son must be one day his heir. That explained his letter. In a sudden fit of generosity or jealousy, — who can tell which it was ? — he now wrote for him, and "packed him off," as he himself phrased it, for a three months' trip to Europe. Ross made the most of it, travelling rapidly and seeing all he could.

On his return his father compelled him to take entire charge of the "Ocklawahaw Scout," for, by this time, alcohol had consumed in General Urwoldt the last lingering taste for literature, even of that kind, as it long ago had done for painting. Ross held himself as independent of his father as that father was of him, but he accepted the work of editing the little sheet. He took even a pride in it, writing much for it those days. But his father, driving hard bargains still, suffering no one to interfere in his management of the affairs of the natives, seemed to close in, so to speak, upon himself. Identifying his son with his quarter-Indian wife, he kept up, as well as he could, a species of contempt for both, saturating himself more thoroughly every day with whiskey and the lowest debauchery.

Rachel, meanwhile, would have studied little but for Parson Williams and Persis. She did so at the request of these; but her heart was in her housekeeping instead, and she grew more matronly, young as she was, every hour, feeding her hens in the backyard, having old Seelye stew whatever fruit came to hand into preserves, seeing about the washing and ironing.

Not that Persis did not have all that to do, and without any Seelye to help her, save when Rachel and Seelye came over unasked and aided her from pure love of Persis, and, still more, of the work itself. But with Persis the household work was a something to be got out of the way as soon as possible, that she might return to her books. Almost every afternoon, as Ross strolled by toward the forest, he would stop a moment to see if he could help her. For when the dinner had been eaten and the dishes were off her mind, Persis sat, when the weather allowed, in a certain shaded corner of the old porch which ran along in front of the cabin, with her books and slate heaped conveniently upon a "split-bottomed" chair beside her. So seated, she studied as hard as she could, when she was not helping her grandfather in the academy, until the time came to prepare for supper, or until some other household care as pressing drew her away.

One afternoon Ross reined in his horse as he rode by, and Persis looked up at him, but her eyes seemed to see only the page of her book as she looked in his, and her lips kept up, under a whisper, " $T\acute{v}\pi\tau\omega$, imperfect, ἔτυπτον, perfect, τέτυφα! Τύπτω, ἔτυπτον, τέτυφα!" for she appeared to be too much under the impulse to stop all at once. But all along she was aware that he was saying, —

"Why do you study so much, Persis?"

"Oh, Mr. Ross, I have told you so often! I am fitting myself to teach." She was more than two years older, and more determined now than when he had first come back from college. Deep down in her heart, hidden as fearfully from herself as from every other, she cherished a yet deeper purpose in studying which made her wish that he would go and live somewhere, anywhere, the farther off from her the better, while it was being accomplished by her. She was only an ignorant girl, but her purpose lay in her inmost heart, as the oak lies at the heart of the acorn, however blind and foolish the acorn is about it. In fact, the acorn cannot help itself; no more could poor little Persis.

"But you know enough already. What do you think the Ocklawahaw children care to learn about moral philosophy and trigonometry?" Ross replied. "And Greek, as I live!"

"I do not intend to stay here," she answered.

"Where are you going, Persis?"

"How do I know? But grandpa is very old; some day Mr. Clarke will take his place as missionary. You know he has been studying the Bible under grandpa, and is going to be made a preacher at the next conference."

"Yes, I know!" Ross said it sharply, for he disliked Amasa Clarke more every day, missing, it is to be feared, the whole meaning of the limp and colorless man, as he did that of the singing, only that Ross liked the mere sounds of the hymns, and he did not enjoy the outer man of Mr. Clarke in the least, — far from it; they were too unlike.

"No, I do not know where I will go," Persis said, with lowered eyes; "but I intend to teach. I must improve myself, and I shall know well enough where to go when the time comes."

"But Latin and Greek?" he said; and he laughed aloud. "It is absurd, and for a girl so young too! I thought your grandfather was more sensible than to allow such a thing."

Maggie backed from the fence as her rider said it, pawed, tried to go on; the conversation did not interest her. But she and Persis were of the same sex in this, that both had come of late to recognize a certain mastership in Ross Urwoldt, sitting erect in the saddle, dark, vigorous, the most efficient, at least, of the three. His steady eyes would have seemed so dark as to be cold, cruel, had they not been counteracted somewhat by the moulding of the chin, the fulness and curve of the lips. Before long the beard would hide a pleasure-loving softness therein which sweetened somewhat the face of the young man. He had no intention of producing that impression, but it was almost as if he had said, "Little girl, you are only a girl, and must obey your superiors, of whom I am chief. Be a good little girl, and keep to sewing and washing dishes."

At least, there was something in Persis which so

interpreted him to her, and did it as dumbly as the sun produces its effects in a spire of grass. By a stirring within her, in consequence, as vague and yet as inevitable as in the blade of grass which lifts itself toward the sun, Persis also arose. Holding her book in her hand, she stood up. "You have been to college and to Europe,". she said, "you are studying hard now; do you think I do not want to know something too ?"

Ross glanced at her with surprise; he had not noticed how tall she was coming to be. Who would have thought Parson Williams's granddaughter would put on such airs ?

"Good afternoon, Miss Persis Paige," he said, raising his hand to his felt hat. It was the first time he had done so, and, giving Maggie a cut with his switch, he was gone. Maggie did not care for the blow, rather enjoyed it, since it was Ross who held the switch. But, brown country girl as she was, Persis was the more hurt of the two. She turned away with anger, and she had no more to do with putting the glow on her cheeks than a rose has with the redness of its leaf. But when she took up her book again, it was to study harder than before, by such blind forces are all we molecules impelled.

"I have given up trying to learn Latin and Greek," she remarked none the less to her grandfather that night. "It was silly in me to try to learn such things yet. I am going back to arithmetic and geography, so that I can know them better to begin with,— know them better !"

"Are you, Persis? That is right, my child." The old man would have said that, whatever her remark had been, for he was very sleepy, and went to bed early these nights.

"But I will study them some day, yes, and everything else too," Persis comforted herself amid her tears, after she had blown out, that night, the tallow candle of her own making.

CHAPTER XI.

LESSONS IN LIFE.

IN virtue of his out-of-door life the health of Ross was more vigorous, if that were possible, every day; for he was growing to be a finer man, physically, than his father, the handsome adventurer who had won the hand and possessions of poor Mitchabuna. But the Indian fibre of his mother's blood was in him also, like a cordage which tightened what would otherwise have been in him also the slackness, moral, mental, physical, of his worthless father. By reason of his abundant and elastic health, when he went of mornings to his studies, he did so with edge and zest as keen as when at breakfast. He reviewed his college studies, edited his paper, hammered at the higher mathematics, bent himself to mastering French and German, so far as it could be done without a teacher, but found his chief enjoyment in natural science, obtaining for his reading the latest publications therein, the first sheaves of a literature which has threatened since then, like the coming of the thistle into Australia, to crowd out every other growth.

"I am too old-fashioned for such things, my son," his mother would say to him. Then, as so often, she fastened wistful eyes upon him, fearing the beginning in him of the contempt for her which her husband had entertained so long. General Urwoldt might have been kept in bounds by her, if she had not anticipated and encouraged his tyranny, under stress, poor woman! of generations of abject submission coming down to her in vein and bone. Ross was incapable of being to her either slave or tyrant. As to his feelings toward other women, that was another matter.

"If you want to talk about Cuvier or Comte," his mother ventured, "you should try to interest Persis in such things or — Rachel." But she laughed as she mentioned the name of the Governor's daughter.

"Persis!" Ross repeated the name with seeming disdain, and went out. And yet he could not remember when he was not more interested in her than in any other except his mother, and now from desperate need of some one to talk with, he undertook, as the months passed by, to open the mind of the girl to the wonders of scientific research. Persis listened, asked a question now and then, but reserved her own opinions. If she had not listened so well, Ross would have put her down beside Rachel Beauchamp, as too womanish to care to understand.

"Why do you not make more of a companion of Mr. Clarke?" his mother would ask. "That is the way with men," she complained when she saw the face her son made. "It is because he is not fond of hunting, or dogs, or horses. Mr. Clarke is of irreproachable character, he teaches faithfully in the academy, he is of an affectionate nature, he preaches good sermons."

Now, Mr. Clarke was so fair and fat, so conciliatory and harmless, that the Indian scholars of the academy had long since nicknamed him Pooga-Dooga, or Mush-and-Milk; and Ross had no reply to make now to his mother. Coming events must have sown in his mind their baneful seeds in advance, for the young man almost hated his unconscious tutor when he thought of him at all, which he rarely did.

"There is Governor Beauchamp," Ross said to himself, once while his mother was praising Mr. Clarke. "He knows everything. Why not learn from him all I can? It is a good idea. Yes, I will drop study for to-day," for it was over the breakfast-table he had been conversing with his mother, "and go and hear what the old — old enigma has to say."

Ross was very much the master of his own movements. His father rarely stayed an hour in his house. He occupied, instead, a room over his store, kept carefully locked always, and opening into his loft of dust-covered paintings. By fits and starts he would have his son assist him in the store, selling goods or in the keeping of his books. But the two saw little of each other. Even if the habits of General Urwoldt had not been such, he was jealous of any interference in his business affairs. For Ross to get an insight into these would be as if his wife did so; and, every day and more and more, he almost confounded the two into one.

"Yes," Ross communed with himself as he walked after breakfast toward Governor Beauchamp's house; "there is much to learn from the old — old —" It was hard to put into words what the Governor was. Scamp, man of the world, drunkard, decayed statesman, — who could say what he was? The refugee-politician did not himself know.

"He is a big and badly damaged encyclopædia. I'll turn a page or two of him before he goes out," Ross said.

He was just in time. The one he sought filled the entire doorway of his house, coming out as his visitor ascended the steps of the porch. His daughter had just given him a thorough brushing, and was handing him his yellow *sombrero* hat, which she had also brushed. It and his clothes needed it that morning. Rachel and Seelye had contrived, since they came, that he should get drunk of afternoons, if possible, in the seclusion of a back porch instead of beneath the sycamore. The afternoon before he had eluded them. Rachel and her black ally had to search far and wide before they found him at last down the river-bank, prostrate, bemired. There were stolid Indians and worse white men loafing about, but these were hopeless of stealing anything from pockets so often searched by them in vain. But Rachel had the money, she would pay them; and, a negro or two doing most of the work, they had him home at the end, — an object from which even Indian and negro recoiled.

His sodden clothes had been drying before the kitchen fire the rest of the night, and Seelye had given an hour's work to cleaning them, in the intervals of getting breakfast. He had wakened perfectly refreshed, had eaten a hearty breakfast, was ready for the doing nothing whatever of another day.

"Thank you, my child," he was saying to Rachel as Ross came near; "study if you find time, read the books I mentioned to you, improve your mind, my dear!" He laid his large left hand upon her hair while he gravely settled his flapping hat upon his stately head with the other. "Heaven guard you, my dear!"

Rachel had grown during these years as well as Persis, but she had broadened as she grew. Hers was a comely face, for it had a German simplicity and solidity, with fair complexion, red cheeks, flaxen hair, blue and sedate eyes. As to her father, he had always drank, always would; she accepted drunkenness in him as she did blackness in Seelye. As Ross came up the steps, she smiled upon him and nodded, bravely unconscious that hers was not the most virtuous parent alive, and went back into the house to see what there was for dinner.

Except in the dignified, not to say haughty, stage of inebriety which went before utter downfall, Governor Beauchamp was the most accessible of men, but under his own roof his affability became cordiality. Now his greeting was effusive, but it was gracious too. He was a great man in retirement, — George Washington at Mount Vernon. So thoroughly did the man think this of himself, that every gesture and tone was in accordance; so thoroughly did he think and feel so, that he compelled his visitor also into the delusion.

"I am delighted to see you, sir. Send us out chairs, my child. Sit down, sir, sit down. Glad to see you, sir!" And the statesman removed his hat, insisted upon taking that of Ross also, deposited them both upon the table in the hall, and came out again and seated himself in the capacious hide-bottomed rocking-chair which Rachel had drawn out.

"I thank you, my child," in round, detached, well-oiled, sonorous words which it is impossible to describe, so virtuous, benignant, they were made by the manner, also, in which they were given out like alms; then he turned to his visitor.

"And how is the lady, your mother? Your father and my .friend, General Urwoldt, he is well, is he not? It is delightful weather with which Providence has blessed us to-day."

But Ross was trying, as he sat, to get what a sailor would call his "bearings." He was constructed in that way; he must see clearly, must understand things. "If this was Falstaff, for instance, I would know how to act," he murmured to himself. "Falstaff?" and one glance at the statesman refuted the vile aspersion. "Falstaff? This is the Chief Justice of England, instead, who rebuked the fat knight upon London street." Ross Urwoldt was young and modest, but he was strong, too, and straightforward. Here were several men in one ample individual. What Ross said must be without special aim, like firing into buffalo in uncertain and changing mass.

"But then, all I have to do is to listen," he reassured himself; for his host was talking on, in his slow, affluent way, about the crops, about how much per bushel corn would be likely to bring, cotton also, sugar likewise. There was nothing for the visitor to do but to listen. He yielded himself as, when swimming, he might for his amusement have done to the flow of the river, turbid, full of cross-currents.

But what Governor Beauchamp said was worth listening to. He had seen all varieties of fortune, as of men. What he said was more than sensible. He seemed to know men from their depths upward; that is, he took hold of them by their most hidden peculiarity first, and as matter of course,— for the old politician speedily passed from crops to men. It was evident that the sugar, corn, cotton, like the sun, moon, and stars, were as nothing to him in comparison with these. He appeared to have known almost every leading man in America of the last two generations, — to have known him personally, perfectly. As he talked on and on, one name suggesting another, it struck Ross that his host was as impartial as if he were forever done with men, were dead.

It was impossible to get away. As the Governor talked, he produced a species of bone bodkin, and used it gravely and carefully in extracting the wax from his ears, examining the results as he talked and talked. Next, he drew out of his vest-pocket, leaning far back in his rocking-chair to enable him to do so, a wooden pair of combs, clasped one in the other. Holding one in his left hand, he combed away at his tawny beard, relieving that hand by using the other upon the other side, but talking, talking,

talking, in the most leisurely but unhesitating manner, as he did so; stopping now and then to disentangle, roll into a pellet, and cast away the hairs which the implement brought away, but never ceasing to talk.

Ross listened with interest. McDuffie, Jefferson, Adams, Clay, Van Buren, Jackson, Webster, Dallas, Cass, Silas Wright, Nicholas Biddle, Calhoun, Amos Kendall, Benton, George D. Prentice, Hayne, — the list seemed interminable. The Tariff, Nullification, Bullion, the United States Bank, Pre-emption, Internal Improvements, — the topics were many, but these were but the ligaments which held the men of whom he spoke into a sort of Siamese-twinship of uniform and absolute rascality. There was this to be said for one man, and that for the other; but, after all allowance had been made, the man was, at bottom, a knave. "Eloquent, sir, but a rascal." "Able, sir, but a thief." "A Talleyrand, sir, in diplomacy, and, like Talleyrand, wholly without principle." "And there was Jackson. He was a pure man, sir, Old Hickory was, and yet but a mere baby in the hands of his partisans; vindictive, too, as a devil, he never forgave an enemy." "Yes, sir, I knew the Senator of whom you inquire, knew him well; and although he was a statesman, he was unchaste, abominably so, sir."

It was a relief to his young friend when the Governor took occasion to add: "As you cannot but have observed, the men of whom I have spoken are weak or wicked, pitifully weak, very wicked. But it is not true of women, sir. No, sir! I honor the sex. They are angels, sir, — angels of beauty, angels of pity, angels of purity. Perish the tongue that speaks ill of woman! They have my poor, but unfeigned homage, sir." And the speaker lifted his broad palm, pressed it respectfully upon his ample forehead, and waved toward woman his profoundest regards.

"But for them, sir, our entire world is but a frost-bitten sweet-potato, worthless to the core. And, pure as they themselves are, they are powerless to restrain our worthless sex. I honor the clergy, but they, alas! are as helpless as woman. I have known the world long, sir, have known it well, have known it thoroughly. It is a bad world, sir, — thoroughly, hopelessly bad! You are yet a youth; when you are as old as I, you will have found it to be all I describe. I am not an angel, sir, far from that, yet have I fled from it. Never enter its broader scenes if you can. You have, I am informed, great abilities. They will prove to be but a curse to you, sir, if they impel you to forsake your peaceful and virtuous seclusion. Live in Ocklawahaw all the days your Maker may be pleased to allot you; die here, sir!"

The disenchanted statesman clasped together his wooden combs, drew out of his pocket a well-worn knife, and looked about in a helpless fashion. His visitor understood his need, and with a "Will you permit me, sir?" he descended the steps, searched until he found a half-shingle under the lee of the house. Coming back, he handed it to his host. It was not as clean as it might be, but Governor Beauchamp received it as he would have done an official document. "I thank you, sir! Accept my thanks for your thoughtful kindness." And he smoothed off the edges with his knife toward more elaborate whittling.

"You have had a varied experience, Governor," Ross said deferentially.

But his host continued to trim the wood for quite a time in silence. "Your remark is quite correct. I have had a long and, I may venture to assert, a diversified experience. Of men," he added, after a while. "Yes, you are correct in your remark, sir."

There was another pause. Ross could hear the jingle of spoons and dishes in the house, occasionally the subdued song of Seelye, of which the refrain was, —

> "De reapin' time will shore-ly come,
>   An' my good Lord will call me home,"

interrupted now and then by "Yes, Miss Rachel," followed by the inarticulate murmur of a household consultation between the two.

"Your assertion is but the truth, sir," the old politician resumed at last. His tones were lower than usual, he appeared to be in a more thoughtful mood, when, holding his shingle off from time to time to see if it was properly shaped, he told, as he whittled, the story of his life, from his earliest efforts as a farm-hand, then as a self-taught teacher, then as a cadet. From that he passed rapidly over his adventures in Florida, in political life, making no allusion to his flight from the Executive chair.

"It is too long a story to tell, my experiences of life," he summed up at the end, "but you can gather this, my dear young friend. I was ambitious, more so perhaps than you are now. I toiled night and day, endeavored to perform my duty to God and my country, endured every form of contumely. Nor have I been without my times of recompense. If men have hissed at and hounded me, they have also applauded. I have often felt as if I was about to be rewarded at last for all. And what is the result? To be impoverished; to be vilified; to be utterly misunderstood of even my apparent friends; to eat of the apples of Sodom which turn to ashes on the lips; to accomplish nothing worthy the effort. In vain, my young sir, does the infidelity of the day assault Holy Writ. All *is* vanity and vexation of spirit! It is a bad world, as I have remarked, — a miserably bad world! Save for woman, it is a botch and a failure. If I were its Creator," and the speaker ceased to whittle, looking at the other with a majestic sadness in his eyes, "I would," and he held out his great hand, examining the palm and then the hairy back of it, — "I would fling it from my hand," and he illustrated it by a gesture, "as I would a clot of abhorrent filth, — yes, sir, vilest filth!" his countenance expressing in every line his disgust.

"The best man in all my knowledge," he continued, after grave reflection, "was a Senator of the United States, with whom I was intimately associated, and for many years. He was a monarch among men, sir, broad and vigorous. I think he must have been, when of your age, very much what you now are; and he grew up to be, as I trust you will remain,

dark of aspect, because reticent and deep, steady and
strong. Of all public men in my acquaintance he
alone had no enemy, so modest was he and honorable,
so thoughtful of others and courteous. No Senator
had as little to say as he; but when he did speak, his
few, sensible words, always to the marrow of the
matter, generally decided the question. Sir, Daniel
Webster told me one day with his own lips, that he
regarded the Senator of whom I speak as one who
was wise, pure, true, to be thoroughly relied upon.
'He has the strongest native sense, original good
judgment,' Mr. Webster observed, 'of any man it
has been my privilege to know.' That Senator,"
Governor Beauchamp went on in lower tones, "was
rich, was secure in his seat for life, might aspire, if
he cared to do so, to anything higher in the gift of
the people. He never knew what it was to be ill,
to have a bodily pain. But he had worthless sons,
sir, — sons who drank. So long as his wife was left
him he could endure it. But she died, sir, — died.
The day after her funeral, he arose from sitting upon
the front porch of his house, as we are now seated
here, took down his double-barrel shot-gun, went
into the yard behind his house, and blew out his
brains! While living he had the weighty aspect of a
great statesman. He was like a statue of bronze
which is too large for its pedestal. This most miserable world was too poor, too mean, too wretchedly
small, for such a man! He could not find refuge, as
some have done, in drink; he found it — and who can
blame him? — in death."

It was plain that the speaker was narrating what was true. His eyes were moist, he was entirely sincere. His visitor arose to go. It was in vain, as the dinner-bell rang, that Rachel came out and urged him, with the smiling face of a housekeeper who has made special preparation, to dine with them. Her father added his urgency in vain. Ross had no appetite, and his ponderous host followed him down the front steps. As he opened the gate to let him out, "My dear Mr. Ross," he said, bareheaded, and retaining the hand of his visitor in his own, "I would not sadden your life, and you are capable of great things perhaps; but I am an old man, have seen the world through and through. It is a dirty dime lying in the gutter, not worth picking up! God bless you, my young friend, and remember that the only object worth living for is some virtuous woman! Heaven keep you, and good-by until we meet again. Stay," he added, when his visitor had closed the gate between them, laying his hand upon the shoulder of Ross. "I do not like men in general, but for you, my young friend, I feel a deep concern; there is that in you which warrants me in so doing. Listen. I speak of woman, sir. But I do not refer to all persons of that sex. I have known some of the most distinguished ladies of this and other lands — ladies of rank, wealth, beauty; ladies learned, gifted, brilliant; ladies who were leaders of fashion, artists, writers, queens of society. I have not learned to like men; the ablest are often the worst; and the ladies I speak of were unfeminine, — were, in my poor judgment, but abortive men at best, Voltaires in crinoline, Aaron Burrs in petticoats and curls. It is not of these, it is of *woman*, I would speak! Woman such as was the wife of Jackson, of Clay, of Walter Scott; woman living not for society, for herself, but for others, for her own sacred hearth; woman, sir, gentle, retiring, sensible, modest, loving, — woman as God made her! My wife, sir — " And Ross felt that the hand laid upon his shoulder was trembling. "It is of the mother of my daughter, — my most estimable wife, sir — " Ross let his eyes fall; adown the broad face of the Governor the tears were flowing freely. "She was the type of woman of whom I tried to speak. Of her, sir, I was unworthy — Had she lived — " And the old statesman turned away.

It flashed upon Ross, as he walked off, that he had heard something, he could not recall what, of the wife of the Governor. Yes, she had been an excellent woman. She had been, everything to her husband, who was said to have been devoted to her till her death. "One can see that in Rachel," Ross said.

Beside his mother, Ross really knew and cared for but two of the sex, — Rachel and Persis. "As to my mother," he now said to himself as he went, "I am afraid, almost afraid — " He did not put his fear into words, even to himself. Was it possible that, as she became older, she was losing her refinement of manner? Could an educated lady forget her education when left to live in a place like Ocklawahaw? Was it conceivable that, as the days passed, she could slowly slide back again into the degradation of her ancestry, and become, by unconscious degrees, merely a squaw again, a squalid squaw! This thing and that, little phrases she was coming to use, small negligences about her household and her dress, almost imperceptible indolences, coarsenesses, laughter at times without sufficient cause, and tears too, — the son put his remembrances from him with dismay. " It is because I inherit from her blood and from my father my base estimate of woman," he said, "that I imagine such things."

Ross Urwoldt was too healthy of body, as of mind, to suffer himself to be lastingly depressed. He did not care, however, to go home to dinner, and wandered, as often before, along the bank of the river, until, seated at last under a cotton-wood tree which overhung the water, he sank into thought. The muddy stream drew itself slowly along, more like a current of syrup, so thick and dark it was from late freshets, than anything else. A few yards to the left from where he sat, a well-worn path ended at the edge where the women, when any dead thing was found in the village spring, came for water. Just there, as at many places along the bank, the current turned upon itself, making an eddy which boiled up from below like a caldron. As Ross sat he heard, with a hunter's quickness, a light step along the path, and saw that it was Persis, bucket in hand. She had been sick for some days, and his heart smote him as he saw how thin and pale she seemed to be. Surely her dress was too poor and worn. She was studying too hard! She stooped over the river, and, holding the handle of

her heavy wooden vessel, plunged it in. Her haste
was such that she did it too deeply, was leaning over
too far. In an instant the swollen torrent had seized
upon the bucket, had dragged her in after it, headlong.

In the same breath Ross sprang to his feet, ran to
a point below where Persis had fallen, and leaped in,
astonished as he did so at the sullen fury of the
water. To him, in his clothes too, it was like a flow
of cold but liquid lead, and it was a perilous time before he could lay hold upon and bear out the poor
girl, at a jutting bank of mud a hundred feet below.

For a moment he was compelled to sit down, the
dripping and unconscious body in his arms, he was so
exhausted by his effort. Persis lay, her face white
and cold upon his shoulder, her hair in streaming
strings on either side. She was not beautiful. Her
pallid face was too intense, too pinched, yet, knowing
what her life had been, knowing the unselfish and
unconquerable spirit of the poor child, a sudden pity
seized upon her rescuer. He had seen, he now felt,
as she lay in his arms, how frail she was. Even in
her wet clothing she was so light that Ross wondered
at it. It was only her emaciated body he had saved.
"It was Persis," Ross murmured, "but it is Persis no
more. What a martyr Persis was, and Persis is
dead!"

More than once I remonstrated with Ross when
we were in college together. "You have less com-
passion in your make," I told him, "than anybody I
know. Do you know what it *means* to feel for those

weaker than yourself?" Perhaps it was because he had been so unused to such an emotion, but now a deep pity came upon him. It was the instant creation in him of a new faculty; his inmost heart was changed; the tears rushed to his eyes; he stooped down and kissed the poor lips by an impulse too native to be resisted; and then he arose and, forgetful of his clothes wet and clinging about him, he ran like a deer, the girl little more than a rifle's weight in his arms, nor stopped until he had laid her upon her bed beside her grandfather, who was pondering over his old Concordance at a little table. Parson Williams was the physician too of the town, and Ross said but a word to him, and ran more rapidly still to his own house to send his mother, and then to the home of Rachel.

"It struck me even then," Ross told me afterward, "that Rachel, I knew not why, could do more than anybody else for Persis. To this hour I am satisfied that it was Rachel who saved her."

CHAPTER XII.

IF the will of Persis had been upon the same scale with her body, she would have come out of her unconscious condition merely to die of exhaustion. Rachel, always wise where mathematics were not concerned, was particularly so in this, that, a few days after, somewhat sooner than other people would have done so, she told Persis the story of her rescue by Ross. It was not deliberate purpose in Rachel. There was nothing more in it than her intuition, wiser than all purpose; but it rallied to the help of Persis, more than anything else could have done, her staggering will, by kindling behind and beneath it those divine fires in and by which, in a woman, the will is shaped. Before Rachel spoke Persis was lying too weak to move, pallid as death, wilted into utter indifference to everything, feebly wishing, so far as she could frame a wish, that she had been left in the sweet rest and unconsciousness of her watery grave. Her eyes, half opened and colorless, hardly saw the face of her friend. Now, in the same breath of telling her the story of her escape, Rachel exclaimed, "What is it, Persis?"

Even Rachel was taken by surprise. She would not have been had she known what Persis had cherished in her deepest soul this many a day. Her eyes opened and almost sparkled; her color came; she laughed. "Kiss me, dear," she demanded of Rachel. Then she tried to sit up, saying, "I want something to eat. Get it, dear."

Rachel went to the pantry, wondering; but Persis was disappointed of her desire to be by herself if but a moment, for first her grandfather came back into the room, and then Mitchabuna. They were astonished at her appetite. It was a craving for the strength food brings, that Persis suddenly experienced. She had not been without will before. It was so much clearer now and stronger! Beneath it had lain before but a quivering spark, now the spark had shot up into a steady fire. For her life the girl could not have explained it to herself, was almost frightened at it. We have little to do with the processes within us; they are certain because they are divine.

As to Ross, he was astonished at himself that he should be so shy of seeing Persis, and that when there was nobody he wanted so much to see. What reason could there be for it? It was but once that Persis began to thank him. She did not try to do so again.

"I suppose it is because it is such a fine day," Ross explained to himself as he went out one morning, many weeks after Persis was able to get about, and it was of his almost extravagant spirits he was thinking. It was the fall of the year. The sky was cloudless and of a steel blue. There was an exhilaration in the air, as if it also had ripened with the maturing apples, as if it had, like wine, grown stronger with the passing of the seasons. Although he did not suffer his enjoyment to show itself, so to speak, even to himself, he never had felt quite so happy.

It may have been nature, but, if so, the happiness it awakened sank suddenly inward as he came upon Persis going toward the sycamore, book and slate in hand, for a quiet but more determined effort than before with her neglected algebra. A gentleness fell upon both as Ross walked beside her, pained to see how frail she still seemed to be, but saying, —

"Do you notice what a deep green the grass puts on, and the leaves, before they turn brown? See how it is brought out by the lighter green of the pine-needles overhead, the darker hue of the mesquit-bush sparkling with its red berries. Look, Persis, at the tender gray of the moss swinging from the trees, the bronze of the live-oak leaves, the iron blackness of its trunk and limbs level with the earth. Did you ever observe," Ross was surprised to hear himself say it, "how the colors of nature help each other out? You play and sing, and you ought to understand such things; it is like the varying chords, is it not, in music?"

Persis glanced keenly at him, and then let her eyes fall; if he was clearer of vision, as in every other sense, than before, so was she. But all she said was, —

"I did not know you were a poet, Mr. Ross."

She had become, young as she was, almost a woman, and he a man, all at once.

"A poet! never! I detest poetry," he replied. "I

love nature instead. It is a weakness to love it so much. That is for women to do."

"Here is the old sycamore. Good morning," said Persis; "I must study hard." And, strange to say, she was glad when he was gone. "No," she had replied to his offered help; "I want to do my problems by myself and for myself." For, almost as strong as her love for Ross, the purpose of Persis was becoming in her a passion. She knew how women were regarded in Ocklawahaw, what General Urwoldt thought of his wife. Was not this his son?

"I will be more than a squaw," Persis said, as she settled herself to her work. What Ross would come to be, she had never a doubt. Come to be? He already was; it was she who was not. As to his future, one might as well ask of the sun in the morning, "Do you propose to rise higher?" No; just now it was in herself she was most interested,—most interested, young as she was, for his sake. We know how blind must be the aspirations of a girl like Persis; yet all things were adjusting themselves in her toward one question in which her life was to be swallowed up, "He being what he is, and growing to what he will be, how can I make myself into something worthy of him?" She had always been ambitious; henceforth love added to ambition its deeper and more enduring flames.

The next day was Sunday, but Ross did not care to go to church. His mother said nothing, and went her way to the meeting-house. It was the only day on which she took any pains with her toilet, altogether too negligent of it at other times. Ross had become reluctantly accustomed to her wrapper loosely girded about her waist, to her black hair in disorder about her cheeks, and whom did she care to please except her son? Little did she know how much, and more of late than ever, her negligence was affecting, almost terrifying, him. But this was Sunday, and it was like civilization emerging from savagery when she came out of her room arrayed for church. With her black silk and lace neckerchief, her beautiful teeth, her hair cared for and a becoming covering for her head, her fine eyes and elastic carriage, she was a striking woman to look at, and Ross took more pride in her then than it had ever occurred to him to express.

Certainly Governor Beauchamp thought so as he met her that day on her way home from church.

"My dear lady!" he exclaimed, and removed his enormous hat, "I had not flattered myself that I would have so great a gratification! Pardon me if I detain you. You are looking remarkably well!"

Not Turenne or Marlborough could have presented a more chivalrous aspect than the magnificently formed cavalier, cane in hand, as he stood bareheaded in the sun, the wind playing with his hair and beard; not Leicester himself, nor Walter Raleigh, could have been more courtly had it been Elizabeth. Mrs. Urwoldt knew everything in regard to the Governor, yet she smiled and blushed as he continued to converse with her in the most deferential and respectful manner. The manner of the man was out of place, but not more so than was the man himself. His sincerity made even his extravagance of courtesy natural, and he was so grave too. He complimented her upon her son. Never had he known a more intelligent and promising young gentleman. She would be proud of him yet.

"He is devoted to you, lady. Extraordinary as he appears to be in point of talent and attainment, you can trust him, lady. Do I not know men? Yes, you can rest in him your hopes, he will not deceive or disappoint you. And how handsome Mr. Ross is! But with such a mother," with a respectful inclination and a wave of his hand, "it were impossible he should be otherwise!"

Rabelais tells a story of the wandering of his heroes around the world in search of that which, upon the whole, it is best for a man to do. After innumerable defeats at insufficient oracles, they are brought, at last, and as at the end of the world, to the sacred shrine from which, as all agree, the highest wisdom tabernacling in clay shall announce that which alone it is best for mortal to do if he would be happy. To the astonishment of the seekers, the supreme oracle proves to be a Bottle, and from its neck gurgles the sum of wisdom in the one word, "Drink!" To that point had the retired statesman arrived. To do him justice, he held, and sincerely, to his faith in woman; neither the bottle nor Ocklawahaw would have known him had his wife lived. He had not met Mrs. Urwoldt for a long time; he seemed unwilling, unable almost, to part from her.

"I congratulate you," he said once more, and with

all respect, "upon your appearance this delightful day."

Poor lady! She was but a woman. By reason of the lingering in her veins of ages of female subjection, she was, in some things, but a weak woman. So long was it since she had heard a compliment that she could not but be pleased with it. And this was the Governor who spoke! He might be a drunkard, but he was a gentleman. That he was a great man everybody knew. Her eyes sparkled; her color came.

"And if," the Governor added, — "and if (which may Heaven forbid!) my friend, General Urwoldt," and he laughed as he said it, "should be taken from us, you, madam, would have small difficulty in marrying again." But the gravity with which it was said did away with the coarseness of the compliment, and the courtly speaker, lifting his hat for a final wave before he replaced it upon his head, walked away greatly refreshed.

Not so much so, alas! but that he resorted to other sources the same afternoon. To Rachel nothing in nature had become more a matter of course, and she sat by his side, as he lay stretched out upon a pallet on the floor of the back porch, dressed in her Sunday clothing, matronly to look at, her hands lying powerless in her lap, and wondering if it would not be well to get in the winter's pork as soon as it should be cold enough.

Governor Beauchamp had spoken lightly to Mrs. Urwoldt, but King Saul also is at times numbered

among the prophets. Ross had passed what was to
him the most pleasant of mornings out upon the
prairie. He had lain upon the fragrant grass enjoying the luxury of existence. Maggie, his mare,
had spied him, and, after smelling out with her white
nose about his cheeks that he had no use for her just
then, had gone to grazing again near by. There was
a pleasure to her master in her enjoyment of the grass,
and of the ocean-like abundance of it to the far-
thest horizon. He had not disdained to watch a cloud
of .insects hovering in the air, objectless in their cir-
cling flight, and purely for the pleasure of being in the
air together. The wind rose and fell like the regular
breathing of the peaceful scene. A cloud floated far
overhead, a flock of crows flew cawing through the sky.
He cared nothing for the past, for the future, for anybody — except Persis? Why should he?

But the sun began to beat too hotly upon him.
He got upon his feet and loitered toward the cover
of the woods.

As he did so he heard the sound of wheels, and saw
that it was his father driving rapidly by in his buggy
along the road. To his surprise General Urwoldt
hailed him, reined in his horse, — a spirited bay, the
best he owned, — called him to his side, insisted upon
his getting in, and drove furiously on. A man had
stopped at the store that morning, journeying by on
foot. After he was gone, General Urwoldt missed a
Mexican blanket which had been lying upon the
counter, and was in pursuit of the thief. "I think I
know where to catch him, and I wanted some one to

hold my horse," he said, "when I do." Ross had never loved his father. How had it been possible for him to do so? This portly, purple-faced, boisterous man had never shown any special interest in him. He had lived at his store and among his squaws. His business matters, his horses, his quarrels with Indians, half-breeds, rough settlers from among the whites, had taken up his time. To him the studies of his son had always been the nonsense of a foolish mother and an idle boy. Secretly he was prouder of his son, thought more about him, than he had ever expressed; but Ross did not know it. Like his mother he had grown accustomed to doing without this bloated man who outswore, outdrank, outstormed, any man in three hundred miles around.

As the two rode together, Ross could not but smell the effluvia of the perspiring drunkard, who never washed his body these days. His wrath against the thief caused him to steam visibly as he cursed and swore, and told what he would do when he caught the offender. "For I gave the old scoundrel a plug of tobacco to be rid of him," he said with many oaths. "Let me catch him, that is all!"

In the course of a few miles the man grew more malignant as he grew outwardly cooler. At last, drawing near a fringe of timber which ran across the road, he checked his horse to a walk, grasping the heavy whip more firmly, peering out from side to side as the road descended to a stream. Sure enough, there was a white-headed foot traveller seated by the brink of the water, rolling up his trousers to wade across, the bright-colored Mexican blanket lying upon the ground beside him.

To Ross it seemed as if it were all over in a moment. His father placed the reins in his grasp, jumped out, whip in hand, with an oath, ran upon the man, knocked him down as he rose to his feet, and began beating him with savage fury, cursing him as he did so. The son drove nearer, got out, and, holding the bit of the struggling animal with one hand, he laid the other upon his father's shoulder.

"You will kill him!" he said.

Even as he did so, the whip fell from the hand of the infuriated man; he reeled to one side and fell heavily to the earth. For an instant Ross was sure that the thief, who had now struggled to his knees, had stabbed his father. But no; the wretch, his face streaming with blood from the blows, had not even a stick in the hands with which he had tried to ward off the whip. There was a moment of horror while Ross stooped over his father. The purpled face was turned upward, the eyes were starting from the sockets. As the son let go the head of the horse, the thief, rising staggeringly to his feet, wiped the blood from his eyes, took in the state of things, then dashed across the stream, leaving his hat and stolen blanket behind him. As he climbed painfully up the ascent on the other side of the water he turned his bloody face for a last look, and cursed his pursuer as only men of his kind can curse. Then he paused a moment, took another good look at the prostrate man; a grin of joy settled upon his countenance. "Damn you, did I say? You *are* damned, you old rascal!" he chuckled, and then hastened on lest the son should send a bullet after him.

It is the peculiarity of men like Ross Urwoldt to become cold and silent where other men grow flurried. Getting up from beside his father, he walked toward the horse, which was backing away from the fallen owner, its ears pricked up, snorting with distended nostrils. In vain he spoke to it. Almost upsetting the vehicle as it whirled around, it flew up the declivity, and when Ross reached the summit it was running away toward the village, the vehicle bounding into the air at every rut and stone.

There was nothing else to be done but to wait until help should come. He returned to his father, undid his vest, loosened his necktie, supported his head on his knee, while he bathed the death-struck face from the water which murmured by as peacefully as before.

It was but too evident that General Urwoldt had, in his wrath, broken some blood-vessel, for the blood was gushing from his mouth as he lay.

For two hours his son sat beside him powerless to do anything but wait. He had often shot a buck when it was dashing along in the beauty of its speed. He had seen the antlered thing spring, at his shot, as if in desperate effort to overleap the sudden leaden obstacle in its way, high into the air, to fall to the earth in a confused and sprawling heap, its grace gone from it with its life. In shooting a bull buffalo the animal, he remembered, always stumbled forward, struck its nose against the ground, and rolled over.

But this was the first time Ross had witnessed the death of one of his own kind, and there was to him a something more ignoble as it was more terrible than in the case of deer or buffalo. The years of debauchery, insolent self-assertion, cruel bargaining, raging passion, unreasoning vehemence in regard to miserable trifles, — there had been nothing of that in the beasts! A moment ago General Urwoldt was the rich headman of the nation, possessed of what was almost genius too, as painter and writer, in every way gifted beyond the average of men; and there he lay in a death more disgraceful than the dead-drunkenness of Governor Beauchamp, — a drunkenness out of the mire and shame of which this man would get up again no more. With the man as with buck and buffalo, this was the end of things forever! Ross looked steadfastly at his dead father, shuddered, and in turning away from him turned that much the more away from all men.

At last a number of people drove up from Ocklawahaw, Mitchabuna and Parson Williams with them; for the horse, with fragments of the buggy at its heels, had arrived at its stable coated with foam and dust, telling thus the tale of some disaster. The wife wept silently as they drove the wagon home, the dead man lying upon the Mexican blanket in the bottom. But Ross sat cold and still. Like the rocks among the cañons, which hold the track of bird and beast made in them ages before, his was a nature that, hardening every day, was to retain forever the impressions then made.

" Reward, sooner or later, — fitting reward, exact as to date, level as to measure, to the worst man as to the best, to General Urwoldt as to Parson Williams, — this also is," I said to myself when I heard of it, "one among the solid certainties we can count confidently upon."

CHAPTER XIII.

THE death of General Urwoldt changed everything at Ocklawahaw. There was not in
Europe a monarch more absolute than, in the limits
of the Reservation, its headman had been and for
so long, and his death was as that of a king in its
effects. It was the passing away of an era, since, in
this case also, the advance of the times made it impossible that his son and successor should be a sov-
ereign of the same sort. By universal consent, the
death of General Urwoldt was regarded as the greatest
good luck which for many years had befallen Ocklawahaw and its dependencies, since, as all agreed,
Ross was an unspeakable improvement upon his
father.

Governor Beauchamp was, of all the mourners on
the morning of the funeral, the most conspicuous,
not to say the most affected. Clad in his best broadcloth, draped still more deeply in the aspect of respectful grief, he occupied a front seat during the
services at church, added his voice to the singing of
the funeral hymns, was among the last who lingered
at the grave. After dinner he escaped from his

daughter by saying that he intended to visit Father Williams.

He found the old man returned to his week-day clothes, and engaged outside his cabin in mending a tub.

"Yes, reverend sir," he remarked to the pastor at the end of manifold moralizings upon the uncertainty of life, "as I have often observed to you before, I honor your sacred calling. No one can regret more than I do that I attend church so rarely. I hear your sermons, as also those of your coadjutor, Mr. Amasa Clarke, so highly spoken of that I the more regret it. But I am glad, even while absent, that the gospel is being proclaimed. May God bless your labors!"

There was more of the same talk, but the aged missionary did not cease his work to listen to it as attentively as he might. The distinguished reprobate was too large a problem for the preacher. If he was not edified, the Governor was, and he walked away in the end as if he had been listening to a sermon. It did not prevent him from becoming, if possible, and by sunset of the same day, more deeply intoxicated than ever.

From that time Ross had more than enough to do. It took some months of hard work over the accounts and among the assets of General Urwoldt, before he found out how matters stood. When he did he was astonished to see how much wealthier his father had been than he had thought. For the late headman loved money so much better than liquor, that he never allowed the drinking of the one to interfere with the making of the other. But it was a property almost as hard to reckon up and manage as were the multitudinous "brands" of cattle and the herds of horses in which it partly consisted, and which were at large over the prairies for two hundred miles around; the Indians and half-breeds who attended upon, and at regular seasons corralled and branded the stock, being the hardest to control of all.

Hiring clerks to take care of the store, and who had themselves to be closely watched, the new owner almost lived in the saddle, while he learned not merely the condition of his live-stock, but the quality of his large, carefully selected, and widely separated tracts of land, upland, river bottom, cedar brake, Pecan forest, mineral. Whenever, in exploring the live-oaks, he heard the rush of animals through the dense undergrowth, it gratified him, even in the act of bringing his rifle into readiness, to see that instead of deer it was a drove of hogs, the ear slits of which showed that they, with every pig following them fast, were his own. So, when halting upon a knoll of the prairie, he unslung his glass and swept the horizon carefully around, deer, buffalo, antelope, verdurous grass waving in the wind, and golden clouds dotting the distance, were impertinences now, since it was first for stock he was seeking, and then for the big U on the flank of cow or horse, which proved the stock to be his own. So of his land.

"A man can no more grow and develop than can a tree, unless," he said to me one day, "he is rooted in soil of his own."

General Urwoldt had held his possessions so exclusively in his own panther-like claws that the mere ownership was for a long time a new sensation to his son, who, really, had not thought much about it before.   Often, in riding across the prairie, he would rein Maggie in upon the top of some eminence, and, after examining the expanse for stock, would try to realize that the earth itself, and as far as he could see in every direction, was his own.   As he did so he sat more erect in his saddle, drew deeper breaths of the air and sunshine which there at least were his own likewise.   It was as if he felt the sap ascending from the soil along every vein, as if every pore of his body drew in a stronger life.

It was natural that this Antæus, too, should thrive by touching the earth, as he did; and he throve indeed.   I do not know if he ate on a larger scale, but he slept more profoundly, grew deeper of chest, broader across the shoulders, wore the graver aspect, as of a many-acred earl, as the months wore by, especially as there were possessions of his which were not so passive in his hand as lands.   There were all sorts of men in his employ, not one of whom did not wear revolver and butcher-knife in his hip pocket handy to his grasp, and whom he had not to pay only, but to guide, compel, control, sober or drunk, content or discontented, pleased or growling vengeance through their beards; and the condition of remaining master of these was, that Ross should, under all circumstances, remain master of himself.   It was excellent discipline.

"It was easy to confront such men," Ross explained to me afterward, "easy to knock them down if necessary, easy to anticipate them in shooting. The difficulty lay in so speaking, so acting, as to govern them without an oath, a blow, or a bullet. I had to have long patience and practice, — severe drill, in a word, with and over myself, before I came to it."

Many months were gone before Ross was aware. When one event befalls a dozen follow. While the new master was accustoming himself to the sceptre and throne, Governor Beauchamp was suddenly smitten, swept out of Ocklawahaw, and far along, by another of those gusts which were as much a matter of course to him as breezes, or, at best, trade-winds, are to barks of lesser tonnage.

"As I told you," Ross wrote me, "his entire life has been but a series of sudden changes. Either he is lying flat on his back in contented obscurity, or he is the Julius Cæsar of some great triumph; with him — and he is as quiescent through everything as a baby — any middle condition of things seems to be impossible. I used to see him loafing about Ocklawahaw, talking to whatever group happened to form around him, accepting with affability whatever homage was rendered to him in hand-shakings, offered tobacco, proffered drinks. I used to see him here and there about the place doing this day after day, week after week, month after month, until it was hard to imagine he had ever done anything else all his life. There was not a child in Ocklawahaw that was not as familiar with his colossal size, dilapidated yellow

11

hat, broad brows, copious hair and beard, courtly manner, drawling speech, everlasting whittling, as it was with the sycamore at the end of the town. Ten, fifty, a hundred times, it seems to me, have I seen him in his garrulous, then in his solemn and digni- fied, intoxication.

"One September day, more than a year after my father's death, he had been struck by drink away from the house, and lay, as of old, upon the grass under the sycamore. I had not noticed that Persis and Rachel were with him, or I would not have gone nearer. As I went up to see if I could do anything for him, I saw them seated on the stone with their books and their sewing, and pretended not to notice the Governor lying prostrate on the earth, a little apart, the broad-brimmed hat over his face.

"The girls were young ladies almost by this time. They had grown larger, but were the same: that is, Rachel was as mute and motherly as ever; Persis Paige, quiet enough, but, if possible, more energetic about her housework and her studies than before. They were talking together in a low tone when I came up; at least, Persis was speaking in her eager way, quiet as she was, telling what she had read, what she wanted to read. But there was silence when I sat down; they seemed almost shy of me. Although I did try to be a brother to them."

"Did you?" I sympathized with him smilingly, as I read his letter.

"Beside my mother, they are all the society I have," Ross wrote. "Busy as I am, I need some companionship. But I cannot understand them. That is, I can understand Rachel. She has that kind of broad, clear, open, old-fashioned face which I suppose Mary and Martha Washington had. When I talk with her it is like standing outside of an open window in summer time; almost as if you were to lean your arm upon the window-sill and look in and see everything in the room. It is different with Persis, very different! But it is of the Governor I was speaking. As I sat trying to get Persis to say something, the sleeping man moved his arm, his hat fell from off his face. His hair had grown whiter of late, and it was tangled, as he lay, with bits of moss and dead leaves. The face was exposed to the glare of the sun, and he made, with his immense and utterly relaxed length, the great palms lying open upon either side of him, a Silenus in the last stages of degradation, and many sizes larger than life. Rather, he was like a whale thrown high up upon the beach. I could almost detect in the air the effluvia of his speedy dissolution; and then I glanced at Rachel sitting there so young, yet so sedate.

"'You old sinner!' I said, almost aloud; 'it is time you were dead and buried!' And I strolled away to send somebody who could carry him home.

"And yet," Ross added, "in three days after that the Governor was gone! There was a political revolution in his State, as I learned soon after. His own party had long ago cast him off with horror to save their reputation as the party of law and respectability. In a dearth of leaders of their own, the opposite party saw a golden chance lying neglected in the former Executive. A delegation came in haste to Ocklawahaw. Governor Beauchamp received them on his front porch, as an exiled monarch might have received an embassy from his repentant subjects. He was, he said, wholly satisfied where he was, had no desire whatever to return to public life. For some time, however, he had known and bewailed the madness of the party with which he had heretofore acted. As a wholly impartial spectator, he was free to say that those who sought him represented the only hope of the State in its present serious emergency. He hoped they would carry the next elections, hoped so as a mere outsider. I need not add that he yielded at last to return with them."

"For the first time I am reading the papers with interest," Ross wrote next. "They are full of the Governor, abusing or praising him. He is making stump speeches over the State. There are columns upon columns detailing the processions which go forth to meet him, the barbecues with thousands in attendance. His speeches are given at length, filled from end to end with parentheses of laughter, applause, vociferous cheering. It is another Napoleon returned from Elba."

That was all Ross could then write. In a little while, as I saw in the papers for myself, Governor Beauchamp had carried the State for his new friends by overwhelming majorities. He was elected Governor by a larger vote than ever, and the papers rang with eulogies upon his eloquence, his statesmanship, his inflexible adherence to principle; upon the self-sacrificing sublimity of his return from dignified and opulent retirement to overthrow the base, ignorant, and corrupt minions who had fed themselves fat upon the vitals of the people!

"I had already learned many things from the Governor," Ross wrote me soon after, "from what he was as much as from what he said. Now I learn another lesson, and that is, that everything lies at last in opportunity, in mere circumstance."

"Circumstance? Yes," I wrote, reminding him of it again. "Circumstance once leaped upon you from a pecan-tree in the shape, I remember your telling me, of a wild-cat. Unless I mistake, you had quite a time of it that day with circumstance. Instead of yielding to circumstance you fought with and killed and afterward nailed up the striped skin of circumstance upon your stable door. Sometimes it comes in the horns and hoofs of the devil, and sometimes in the person of an angel. Persis is a circumstance, so is Rachel. Don't let us argue about it, man; everything lies in resisting or in yielding to what befalls us, and you know it."

"Oh, well," Ross replied, "have your way! But this, too, I gathered from the case of the Governor: first, how low a man may fall, — how very low, and from what heights; second, that although a man falls as from the stars, and into the gutter, the fall need not slay him. I had not imagined that there was such toughness in humanity, such elasticity, so much bounce; India-rubber is nothing to it!"

" My dear fellow," I wrote back, " some day you will learn that a man is so exceedingly tough as to endure when all nature beside, having served him, shall perish, every forest with its dead leaves, every ocean more utterly than the spray it casts into the air. Out of all we behold, man and his Maker are the only things which survive; and as to the power in a man of rebound, — yes, and from a depth deeper than even the Governor reached, and not only to the stars but beyond them — But we won't argue about it; tell me in your next what Rachel thinks of affairs."

CHAPTER XIV.

FINALITIES.

FOR very many years now had Parson Williams labored in the Reservation. From his earliest manhood, by day and by night, teaching, preaching, visiting from house to house, he had given his life in every faculty, during every hour, to his work. It was he who did what he could to counteract the evil influence of General Urwoldt, to settle the quarrels continually arising among the people, to urge them, and by the example too of his own unwearying hands, to industry. He it was who acted as umpire in every case of dispute, whether it had reference to an acre of land or to an unbranded colt or calf. Wherever was sickness there was the good old man also, to heal if possible, to prepare the dying for death, to bury the dead, to console the survivors. Against a thousand discouragements, as poor as the poorest, he had done his utmost, his very life prolonged by the steady intensity of his purpose, which had never for an instant a reference to himself.

As his granddaughter sat sewing beside him one afternoon, she was saddened to see how very, very infirm he was. His old Bible lay open upon his knees as he sat, the spectacles placed so as to mark the

verse upon which he had been meditating. But he
was thinking of Persis. She changed color as she
looked up, he was gazing so intently upon her. "I
am afraid to leave you," he said to her almost
sternly.

"Afraid, grandpa!"

"You are too ambitious, my child; you study too
hard. Women should not want to know too much,
Persis; that was the sin of Eve which ruined the
race."

Persis ceased sewing in astonishment. "And you
yourself have always urged me," she said, "to study
as hard as I could in order to teach others."

"Yes," he replied; "but that was when you were a
child. What I desired to do was to give direction
to your path. I ought not to have said as much as I
did. You are going along it too fast! I wish you
were a little more like Rachel. A girl should not
read too much. It is as if a weak stomach should
take too much food, my dear. A man can stand it,
but God has made women differently. You should
know only enough to love wisely, and to help — in a
woman's way, mind! — those you love. That is all.
I am afraid for you, Persis!"

She should have had more regard to the words of
the good old man, since they were almost the last he
spoke. For, one day, it became known through Ocklawahaw that Parson Williams was dead. He had done
all the good which had been done in the Reservation,
even if he had not made saints of the savages.

The whole Reservation came to his funeral, — the

women with outcries of sorrow; the worst men silent
with a deeper grief, consternation almost. "It is as
if we were burying God," one of them said. Amasa
Clarke officiated at the grave, taking thereafter, so far
as he might, the place of the dead apostle. "But
he is only Pooga-Dooga, Mush-and-Milk," was the
unanimous remark.

Long as Persis had looked forward to it, the blow
smote her heavily, or would have done so if she had
not been so busy with the additional care and work
it brought her that she did not find time, at first, even
to weep.

And then the old cabin in which the two had lived
so long had held itself up only, it was evident, until
the aged missionary was done with it; for it almost
tumbled down the day after the burying. Mitchabuna begged her to come to her house; but Ross lived
there, and she would not. Moreover, Rachel took the
poor girl into her motherly heart and home from the
first. Then came the reaction. For weeks Persis lay
ill under the care of Seelye and Rachel, who became,
as in a moment, the oldest as she always had been
the strongest. For a while Persis, weeping and worn
out, clung to her friend, as if she were a mere babe.

There had long been years of trouble impending
between the North and the South; and Ross Urwoldt
was called away, the day after the funeral, to attend a
political conference in regard to it in a distant city.
Almost alone in that he took strong ground there
against secession, he exerted himself to his utmost to
prevent it; hardest of all, he had to keep himself

cool under pathetic appeals, vehement accusations, from the overwhelming majority who opposed him. What tried him most was that the power had already passed into the hands of mere passion; he might as well have endeavored to stem a thunder-gust; and he returned homeward before the conference closed, more alarmed at what the South might suffer through its own folly than what the North might accomplish by force.

The last few days of his journey back were upon horseback. He had often ridden by himself, for hundreds of miles scarcely seeing a human being, and the habit had come to him, thus, of slow, steady, continuous reflection, for the conclusions of which he must rely upon himself alone. The war which threatened brought back his mind to that which had already exercised it so long,— Persis! Now that the country was being precipitated into a strife of which no man could see the end, what ought he to do in regard to her? He loved her with all his heart. Perhaps she would marry him? She was so young he regarded it as almost brutal to speak to her about it, even yet. What ought he to do?

And then he thought of his mother. He knew only too well the way in which women were regarded in Ocklawahaw. When they were young and pretty, they were petted very much as if they were kittens. Sometimes a young wife, if very pretty, and when first married, would put on her poor little airs, would scold and wheedle, would venture even to pout at and vex her husband. Alas! the first curse from his lips, the first blow from his hand, struck her back into what she knew all along was her place, — a place hardly higher than the dogs, by no means as exalted as that of a blooded horse. Having the father he did, it was impossible but that Ross should be at least uncertain in regard to women, doubtful of them, even vigilantly suspicious of them. He had loved his mother, had gloried in the fact that she was an educated woman. In his struggle against his hereditary estimate of the sex, she was the one woman upon whom he rested his faith. Persis he loved, but in his mother he had trusted from his birth. But now —

As he rode through deep forests, day after day, in solitary thought, he strove against any doubts in regard to her, with the double dismay that they involved Persis also. He reached his result at last. With it came a sudden gladness. He put spurs to his horse and rode on more rapidly till he reached Ocklawahaw.

When, the day of his arrival, he stood upon the porch of the house in which Persis lived with Rachel, his heart bounded as he saw Persis herself, seated, book in hand, in the corner where the vines grew thickest. The girl held her book from force of habit. She did not know what book it was. Her tears were all wept. What work was to be done she had finished. Her past was as hazy to her as her future. She was still weak from illness. The one thing she did was to go on thinking of Ross.

When she looked up and saw him standing before her, she could not control herself. There was that in his eyes which would have frightened her had it not gladdened her so much. She sprang to meet him. Rachel would not have lost herself for an instant, whoever and however much she might love. But Rachel was not Persis, and it was a Persis so weak from long suffering, so electric with intense feeling long suppressed! She had to say something. In the sheer foolishness of her joy, "O Ross," she exclaimed, "it will distress you so much!"

"What is it, Persis?" He overmastered her, she was so happy, so weak; he stood there so strong, loving her — she could see that — so much. The matter she alluded to had filled her talks with Rachel for many days. Except Ross, she had thought of nothing else. It was the childishness of a young, a very young girl, too happy to know what she said. She took for granted Ross must have heard her news before this. No; Rachel would not have said it. There was the utter surrender in it of a too impulsive child to the man she loved so well, the man who was there to take her to his heart.

More than frightened now at her folly in doing so, she told him all. He had not imagined such a thing! Not even Ross himself could have supposed that the event would have struck him so hard. There was a revulsion in him of feeling. He almost reeled before it. Persis was forgotten. There came into his face a change from which she recoiled with a cry. He stood motionless for a moment, his eyes darkening as they fastened themselves upon hers. Then he turned, and, without a word, was gone.

For what Persis had to tell him was that his mother was married to Amasa Clarke, —the indolent and apathetic man whom, for so many years, Ross had disliked and despised beyond all men! She had not dared to tell him of her intention, and had seized the opportunity of his absence to carry it out.

What took place between mother and son in regard to the marriage, who can say? No one cared to speak to Ross of it. People were almost afraid to enter the house of the mother after it was known that her son had broken with her. At their coming in, her eyes flashed upon them like those of some wild animal. She had her fits, too, of girlish laughter, of violent weeping. But it was long before Ross saw Persis again. He had made an idol of poor Mitchabune, and, with her, his faith in the sex was gone.

Then came on the war between the North and the South. Ross went to another political conference, and on his return he gave himself up, colder and sterner than ever, to raising a regiment of men for the war.

CHAPTER XV.

A DECISION.

IT was little that Ross, or any one else, had said to Persis or Rachel concerning the impending war. When he should go into the army it might be different, but so far his chief feeling was a sense of resentment against all politicians, — a sullen anger such as a drop of the ocean might have against the billow which was gathering it up to dash it upon the rocks. But he could no more resist it than he could the marriage of his mother; and he was glad when he called upon the girls the day before he left and found them not at home. It was better so.

The next day, as he rode out of town, he dismounted at their door, fastened his mare Maggie to the fence, and came in merely to say good-by. Having reached the certainty of things, he had lost his wearied look. Perhaps he was the more erect by reason of his new uniform, his captaincy, his sword and pistols. Moreover, if he was sterner when with men, he had now the aspect, rather, of gladness, as of one who feels fresh and strong for a great journey which lies before him. Persis was by herself upon the porch at the moment, for her friend had been seized with a quiet mania for knitting innumerable socks for the soldiers,

and had gone to the store to buy all the yarn which
was to be had. While Ross waited her return, he and
Persis said everything to each other but that which
lay nearest their hearts. When on the prairie, rifle
in hand, Ross could pick out of a herd of deer,
grazing in the distance, the one deer he wanted, could
pick it out because it was so much the best of all,
and yet he could not now see that Persis was as much
superior to poor Mitchabuna as is gold to copper, as
is Cordelia to Cleopatra. But his mother had been,
and ever since he could remember, the chiefest of
women to him, and with her the sex had perished.
Persis knew it. She could do nothing now; but it
deepened into a religion within her, — the purpose to
prove to him some day what she was.

" By the by," he said, as he rose at last to leave,
" my mother knows how much you wish to go on
with your education, and that Ocklawahaw is no place
for it. That is the chief thing I came to say. She
begs that you will consent to take a full course at the
Institute where she was educated. She has money,
and will gladly pay all your expenses. What can
you do here during this foolish and horrible war?
I know of people who are going North while they
can. You must go with them. And you must get
ready right away."

Persis arose. It was always more natural for her
to stand than to sit, to move about than to remain
still. She now stood, her clear eyes in those of her
visitor, her sunburned hand upon the top slat of the
high-backed, split-bottomed chair in which she had

been seated. While he spoke she stood straighter, took her hand from the chair, and put her hair back from her forehead with it. If her color freshened a little, it was merely because she saw Ross through and through. But she was practical enough.

"Thank you, Ross. I mean," she corrected herself, "I thank your mother. Yes, I want to be educated. I intend to be educated some day. And I intend to go East to do it since I cannot do it here. But I cannot go in that way, even if I could leave now. I'm going to educate myself," she said simply. There was no sentiment about it. She spoke as if it was of a pie she was about to bake, a dress for herself she was intending to make.

"But you have no relations, Persis," Ross persisted. "And you have no —"

"Money? No, not a cent. I don't know now how I will do it. But I will know some day. I'm going to learn everything girls learn or ought to know. But," and she looked at him, steadying herself to do it, "I'm going to do it for myself. That is the best part of it. You will see."

"But, Persis —" he began.

At this moment Rachel came up the steps, her big bundle of yarn in its blue paper wrappings in her arms. There was as much more, but that was to be sent after her, and she wanted to begin at the socks at once. Rachel was sick at heart to see Ross go, for was he not like a brother to her? The tears began to trickle down her face the moment she seated herself, she could hardly see to put the first stitches upon her needles. Ross went down the steps and to his mare tied at the post. "Maggie is eager to be going," he explained as he came back, "and I was afraid her halter might work loose." But he did not care to remain. Rachel might have complained of his parting with her, it was so evident he was thinking of something else as he bade her good-by. As he held the hand of Persis in parting, "You will do as I wish!" he almost commanded.

"Thank you, I cannot." It was said in a gentle voice; but her face, her manner, must have suggested something to him he had not thought of before, for during all the days which followed, whenever Persis thought of Ross, — and that she never ceased to do, — what she saw was his great black eyes fastened fixedly upon her in sudden, searching, perplexed, almost insolent inquiry. There was something about her he could not understand.

He mounted his mare, rode rapidly away; the sound of the hoofs was dying away in the distance when Persis lifted her head suddenly, listened, and arose in agitation, white and trembling.

"O Rachel!" she exclaimed, "he is coming back;" and while she said it he was dismounting again at the gate. It was cruel to subject her to another parting, but she strengthened herself to endure it.

When he came in he seemed not to see that she was there. "I forgot one thing," he said to Rachel.

"What is it?" she asked, with doubtful eyes.

"Only a gourd of water, if you please."

At the shadiest end of the porch was a shelf

12

scrubbed white, on that a cedar pail, the wood and brazen hoops doubly scoured until the red of the cedar and the glitter of the brass was as of a utensil sacred to the gods. Over this hung, trebly scrubbed, a long-handled gourd, pure yellow without, pure white within. With eyes full of doubt, Rachel dipped it into the cool water, lifting the white oak cover which, like a more solid flake of snow, hid the water from dust, to do so, and handed it to Ross, who remained standing. He drank and held the gourd in his hand.

"By the by," he said to Rachel, "you are determined, are you, to stay in Ocklawahaw?"

"What do you mean? Why," she asked in wonder, "must I tell you again? Of course I intend to stay. I told you that Persis and I will be happy together." What she did not tell Ross was that she had endeavored in vain to induce Persis to go East with her to some place in which their education could be completed, but Persis would not. She earned her bread, as it was, by helping Mr. Clarke in the academy; she had no money, she resented the idea of depending upon her friend. All this Ross knew very well.

"It is impossible for anybody to understand you!" He turned almost angrily upon Persis. "When you know that Ocklawahaw is no place during such times as these for girls like you two!"

"What do you mean?" Persis was surprised out of her grief.

"You are so fickle. I can remember when you were eager to go East, eager to be educated."

Persis could not comprehend him. Her astonishment held her silent. It was easy to check her tears. Her long and bitter weeping of nights, weeping so bitterly over the loss of everything now, had drained them dry. She looked full in the eyes of Ross at last. "I can study where I am," she said.

"But it perplexes me," he insisted, "that you should value land as you do in comparison with education."

"Land?" Her eyes grew larger as she asked it.

"Yes, land. Your grandfather's property is yours. Since you wish," Ross continued, "to go East, why not sell your river tract? It is heavily timbered; the soil is rich; it will be valuable some day when emigration is coming in. Sell it to me. I can pay cash for it, and I will hold it for speculation."

The colors as of a new life were flushing the face of Persis; her lips parted; her eyes sparkled. "I did not know grandpa owned any land. Why didn't he tell me about it? Are you sure?" She could hardly speak.

"That is the objection I had to Parson Williams," Ross said angrily. "He was so taken up with his preaching that he forgot everything else! I can pay you enough on it for you to go East and make a beginning, at least. After a while you will be prepared to teach there; the money will hold out with economy until then. At least I would suppose so." And he entered rapidly, but at length, into how many acres there were, what it was worth now, how much he might be able to sell it for hereafter. He did not say so, but the impression he produced in

Persis was that, in some way, very long ago her grandfather had come into ownership of the land by virtue of being one of the first settlers of Ocklawahaw. Ross had much to add as to the danger of their remaining in Ocklawahaw, as to the advantages of schools elsewhere; he seemed to have forgotten how important it was for him to be off. Persis was not listening to him, although she stood with drooping eyes; the surprise of her joy was gone. How could she go so far away when Ross might any day be brought back to Ocklawahaw, brought back perhaps to die?

"Curse Ocklawahaw!" he ejaculated irrelevantly, savagely. "For my part, I never intend to enter the place again!"

Persis lifted her gaze to his face in a wild conflict of feeling. Tears were in her eyes while she almost laughed. Then her eyes fell again.

When he first spoke, Rachel drew back a little and looked at him. His face, already dogged, became more so as he felt that her wise eyes were upon him, and he talked on. Long before he was done Rachel dropped her eyes; she understood sufficiently, and kept her secret forever after. Had Persis not been of so excitable a nature, she might have suspected, but at first she did not. The change in her plans was so sudden! She was lifted from her feet, bewildered. Was it possible that her one life-long wish could really be fulfilled? It was only of that she thought, except of this, that Ross was evidently so glad to get her land! He had long wanted it, he told her; he would

make money on it. Even then, sweetest of all to her
was it, that she had it in her power to let him have
what he wanted. It must be a matter of great importance, he had been in such dreadful haste to leave.
Rachel went into the kitchen to hurry Seelye about
the supper, for now Ross must ride all night to make
up for lost time. He left her, and went to drag the
chicken trough out through the gate. Then, without
taking the saddle off his mare, he brought from the
crib behind the house an armful of ears of corn, at
sight of which his mare began to whinny, pawing the
earth with her impatient hoofs. Persis stood in the
porch, her hand upon the railing, watching him as if
in a dream. She saw him throw the ears upon the
ground at his feet, saw every motion as he picked
them up one by one, stripped off the husk and threw
the corn into the trough. She heard the noise made
by the mare while it ate, was keenly aware of every
line of Ross's face as he stood at last beside the
animal, his right hand upon the pommel of the saddle,
his feet in the litter of yellow shucks, looking down
into the trough. He seemed struck for the time into
the bronze of a statue, so still he became. His face
was almost sharp, it was so worn and thoughtful in
comparison with what it used to be.

Then Persis was filled afresh with the vague horror
of a war which nobody could understand, — why it
was, what it was, how long it might last, how it might
end; war coming irresistibly on like the shadow of an
awful night. And Ross was so utterly cut off henceforth from everybody.

"But he is sufficient for anything," Persis thought, her eyes upon him, "sufficient in himself!" And with the glow of pride in him came the new resolve deeper than ever, "Thank God, I am going where I can make myself into something beyond what he thinks —"

After a while Ross went into the house, asked Rachel for pen and ink, not looking her in the eyes as he did so, and wrote out a long paper for the signature of Persis. The girl did not read a line of it, signing it with a hand which trembled.

"What a fool I am! Why should it?" she asked of herself, pretending afterward to read the document, but not making out a single word.

"Ross!" She said it suddenly, sharply, planting herself before him.

"Are you not deceiving me?" she asked, endeavoring to hold her eyes very firmly to his.

"Deceiving you!" He was astonished. "If I have not given you enough, say so," he remonstrated. "I buy on speculation, you know. As it is, I may lose money."

"No, no!" she said impatiently, "not that! Did my grandfather really and truly own the land? Why did n't I know of it before? Are you *sure* —" But Rachel was calling them in to supper. Their guest talked rapidly of everything else as they ate, and before Persis had emerged from her amazed condition he had shaken hands with them, had mounted his horse, and was gone, this time for good.

Persis watched him with such intentness that she

noticed he said something to Rachel, in the act of his
hurried parting with her. It was merely good-by,
Persis supposed. The words so smote upon Rachel,
low spoken as they were, that she looked up astounded.
And yet they were only, "For God's sake, Rachel,
take good care of her!" and he was galloping away.

At last, Persis was but a girl. With the next day
came the very desperation of getting ready to go before the war would make it impossible. Again and
again she stole to her room to count over and over
the little buckskin bag of gold Ross had left as the
first payment on her land. "I did not know I loved
money so!" she laughed, catching herself kissing
each coin as she took it up, and again as she laid it
in its own row. "And, O you darlings, how can I
bear to spend you!" Then she laughed and cried,
conscious mainly of who had paid her the gold.

Mitchabuna, now Mrs. Clarke, did what she could
to assist the young girls in their packing. She was
dressed like a bride of eighteen, and was laughing
and chattering accordingly. "I am glad to have
Seelye," she said. "Mr. Clarke likes good cooking."
And she blushed a little. "And, oh, how sorry I am
that you are going away!" But it was very evident
that it was of her new husband, so many years
younger than herself, she was thinking. Having
him, it was little she cared for any one beside; it
brought color into even the placid face of Rachel to
listen to her.

"Who would have thought it?" Rachel said to herself a dozen times a day, in the little while left her

before leaving Ocklawahaw, — said it, but not of the bride, for Persis seemed another person. She could not be got to bed before midnight, and Seelye found her up before her, when she arose at daybreak to get her "salt rising" ready for the baking. All day Persis was in and out of the house, up stairs and down, helping and hindering Rachel, now full of their plans, then silent for long spaces, and seeming to hear little that was said to her. She had moods of sudden affection for Rachel, hugging and kissing her, then she would steal away and lock herself into her own room for a cry, or slip on her sun-bonnet and hasten out on a remorseful visit to her grandfather's grave. After that her face would beam out more brightly than ever, and she would laugh and talk until even Seelye felt compelled to say, " Law me, Miss Persis, how you *do* carry on! You act like as if you was possessed. Look at Miss Rachel; she is goin' too, an' she is as still as a mouse. An' you is goin' out into de wide an' weeked world; you better be sayin' your praars, Miss Persis!"

CHAPTER XVI.

EXPLANATORY.

I DO not intend to go into any detail of what befell my friends or myself during the war between the North and the South. Like every man, South and North, I had a general idea, before it began, of the political questions involved; and, with almost every soul of us, North and South, I was unprepared when the smooth flowing of our national life so suddenly quickened toward the cataract. The wholly unexpected rush of things whirled my little bark, also, round and round, and made my heart as dizzy as my head, — like most people, the country over, in this also.

Although born of New England parents, and in the North, my home had been from infancy upon a little island off the coast of South Carolina; and whatever ripening of character I have known has been under a Southern sun. Old Orange was, at the time I was there, largely attended by young men from the South, although it was across the lines; and as any one, in making a wreath, would naturally and for very variety's sake weave together oak and olive, palm and pine, so I chose my friends from the one section or the other, according merely to their diversity of excellence. After leaving college I was in Europe for a while, and spent my time thereafter in North or South, as nature worked in me toward the same variety of enjoyment.

Up even to the first shot of the war I was almost as ignorant as a baby of the possibility of such a thing. ?I dare say I had studied the question as much as any man of my age, yet *I* had no intention of cursing, much less of killing anybody, as a step in the direction of settling it. And so it happened that, one day, before that first shot was fired, I was lying at length upon the sandy side of my island, dreamily solving, as well as I could, the political conundrum, when a low sullen sound came to me over the water from toward Charleston. Understanding on the instant what it meant, it fell upon me, that single sudden sound, like a great drop of blood, — the first of the rain that was to follow. Let me change the figure. When I was in college, our professor of chemistry held before the class, one morning, a goblet of what appeared to be muddy water. Holding up the glass with his left hand, he tapped upon the edge of it with the little finger of his right. It was but one slight tap, but in an instant the floating sediment had crystallized into a solid substance, leaving the water transparently clear; and there it was at the bottom of the goblet with angles mathematically accurate and sharp as steel. So it was with me, as with millions more on the one side and the other, that eventful morning. The moment before, my mind was merely a bewilderment of floating and conflicting opinions, and I had as little to do with what befell to me thereafter as the professor with his chemical results. Yet, as the distant cannon struck my ear, I rose to my feet, my soul crystallized into exceedingly accurate shape, and in the clearest of atmospheres.

The next day I turned everything over to th ׳ ׳ are of my overseer and came North, remaining the׳é, except as I was employed in the sanitary service occasionally, during the whole war. I did not fight, an infirmity of heart as of health preventing that; but I had acquired, before the strife began, some little reputation as a writer, and I did what in me lay, for what I thought the right, both upon the platform and with my pen. And I will only add that I did not know before that I had as much soul to put into anything as I had then. There was not the smallest merit in it. I simply yielded to what was my conscience in the matter, as a man does to gravitation.

Among the most intimate of my friends is Dr. Steven Trent. We were classmates in college; but it was his marriage to a Miss Revel Vandyke which brought us into the close relation in which we stood to each other ever after. Not that she was of kin to me, or that I had enjoyed any measure of acquaintance with her before her marriage. I venture even to doubt whether I could have come to like her as I did, if she had remained single, charming as she must always have been. The fact is, she was one of those women to whom marriage makes all the difference in the world. It may be that it was her union to precisely such a man as Dr. Trent; but, as a result, she bloomed out into what I must always consider as, one woman excepted, the flower of all the wives I have known. I like people in general; but Mrs. Trent had this in common with her husband, that she suited me exactly, minutely, mathematically; and there is only one person beside of whom I can say that. Unless I am grievously deceived, the Doctor and his wife like me "only a little less" — they have solemnly assured me — "than we like each other."

"As to Jean," Mrs. Trent has added in regard to their little daughter, "I am afraid she loves you more than she does her own parents, because you spoil her, as you do your namesake also;" for their little boy, when he came, was named after me.

It happened that, almost from the hour of the marriage of Dr. Trent and his wife, I was a visitor, off and on, in the city in the East in which they lived. Whatever literary successes I had were enjoyed by them more than by myself; for I found it impossible to estimate either my books or myself as highly as they did.

During my years in college I suffered terribly from a malady which caused me to receive, because I craved it so thirstily, a larger measure of sympathy, interest, affection, than is given to people in ruder health. After leaving college I slowly recovered from it by my trip to Europe; by living a simple life upon my island; most of all, I think, by hard and enthusiastic work. But it left a certain impression upon my character. People persist in making a

difference in my case. I enjoy without fully understanding it; but I am singularly favored somehow.
Perhaps it is because I have so sincere an interest
in them; but people do manifest an interest in me,
the more as we know each other better, which is very
delightful.

Dr. Trent was a medical man by diploma of nature,
too, and had achieved an extensive practice as a
physician. He would never have made himself rich
as such.

"Steven's interest in a patient," his wife was wont
to say, "exhausts itself in caring for and curing him.
As to being paid for doing so, *I* have to see to that."

The family were poor enough, as I chanced to know
only too well, when, not long before the war, an old
uncle of the Doctor died. Donald McGregor was his
name, and he was very rich. He bequeathed Mrs.
Trent a handsome amount; but the bulk of his fortune
he left to little Jean, appointing her father as almost
sole trustee.

"I can see now," Mrs. Trent told me, "why it was
better that Steven should care more for his practice
than for money. Now that it is not necessary he
should be paid anything, he has gone into it with
more interest than ever. He is so ardent, you know,
in regard to whatever he undertakes. Now he can
be independent, can take only the worst cases if he
chooses. But I tell him that he would never have
been made Professor in the Medical College if people
had not an idea that he was rich."

Mrs. Trent laughed as she said it. I liked to hear

her laugh. She was not a slight and delicately
framed woman, neither was she so large as to sug-
gest coarseness. Without an atom of mere sentiment, singularly sensible even in regard to the Doctor
and her children, she had a power of loving which
fascinated me with her as one is in the smooth
and silent flowing of a deep river. Her husband had
been driven almost beside himself during the days of
their poverty, for he was the most sensitive of men,
you could see that in the cut of his lips. It was his
keen sensitiveness to suffering which made him the
physician he was, it put him so completely in the
very place of his patient, it gave him such intuition
as to remedy. So terribly did he suffer when poor
and crushed with debt that he would have killed
himself or gone crazy if it had not been for his wife.
And it had been good practice for her, having to sus-
tain him then as she did. When they became rich,
and suddenly, with the long habit there came to her
a vast power, now, of helping whoever needed help,
and she yielded, governed by her native sense, to her
habit of loving, to her love of loving, to a degree
which made her the happiest woman I knew. Her
health, also, was such that one day I rehearsed it
over to be able to say to her, "Mrs. Trent, I know
a black woman of about your age down South who,
from sheer animal perfection, cannot cease at least
to smile from dawn to dark. You ought to hear her
laugh and sing! Now, disrobe Corilla — that is her
name — of her color and excess of flesh, purify her of
her ignorance and frivolity, make her happiness to

be free from the faintest taint in blood or spirit, and
you yourself are Corilla over again! Pardon me,
madam, but the sugar on the plantation is dark, I
know, and even dirty, and yet the article upon your
breakfast-table, as pure and white as drifted snow,
what is it but the same plantation sugar refined?
Yes, Mrs. Trent, you are Corilla refined. I heaven
you will have been put more thoroughly through the
same process."

I say, I went over this remark in my mind, intending to say it to my friend, but, on the whole, concluded not to do so. Some day we can be franker of
speech to each other than, now and here, we dare to
be. Allow me to record it, however, toward explain-
ing things.

The only reason I have spoken of myself at all is
to say that I was in the city in which Dr. Trent and
his wife lived when Persis and Rachel came thither
from Ocklawahaw. Ross Urwoldt had told me a
great deal about his home when he was with me in
college. Moreover, I was, as I have said, his only
correspondent afterward. My long and frequent letters may have stirred him up to it; but he wrote me
often from Ocklawahaw, and always informed me
concerning the two girls in his letters.

And so it was that I came to have quite a part in
Persis and Rachel before I saw them. The fact that
they had come from such a dismal region at such a
period, especially that they came for such a purpose,
made me almost eager to meet them.

"I think you will like them, Mr. Guernsey," Mrs.

Trent said to me before I called on them. "Dr. Trent does. I do not know when I have seen any persons in whom I have taken such an interest."

There is not a more sensible woman than Mrs. Trent, and we are sworn allies; but the scientific accuracy of the times prohibited me from accepting blindly what she said. She was so round and rosy a matron, because, as any one could see, her heart, warm and abundant, came readily to the surface in behalf of whoever had any claim upon her. The more helpless such persons were, so much the more promptly did she class them with her two children, Jean and Guernsey, and become as a mother to them right away, — as she was also to me, and that although she was, by some years, the younger of the two.

CHAPTER XVII.

NEW—COMERS.

THUS it was that I called so soon upon the young ladies. Now, to me the dreariest abode on earth is a city boarding-house. " Poor things ! I hope," I murmured to myself as I went to make my visit to them, "that there will be an exception in this case." But there was not. The building, when I reached it, was what is styled, with unconscious sarcasm, " a swelled front," that is, a brick five-story house, the face thereof toward the street protuberant, and with windows like eyes starting from their sockets as if straining itself in envious emulation of the structures upon the left hand and the right. There were few better streets in the city ; you could see that the house was conscious of that. As I feared, there was a highly scoured condition of pavement in front, of door-steps and bell-pull, which assured me that the building was not a home, but a public institution prepared for inspection. The colored man in a white apron who answered the ring was, as I expected, a public functionary ; and I was let in as one of the many restless atoms coming and going in and out as of a post-office or a custom-house. I was one more troublesome thing, not a person, and

13

I knew that my death in some upper room, had I boarded there, would be less, except for the additional bother it caused, than the breaking of the pier-glass of the front parlor into which I was ushered.

"There are the same marble-topped tables, the identical lambrequins to the windows," I complained, as I took a seat upon the extreme edge of a linen-covered chair. "Beatrice Cenci, of course, over the bronze clock on the mantel. If she would but turn her everlasting head a little farther around and twist it off! Yes, and yonder is the Whatnot, — the Synonym, it should be named, — with the same china images, gilded vases, books for show. No children are allowed in this institution, that is evident. Yonder, behind the half-opened folding-doors, is the drawing-room, smaller, darker, gloomier than this. Is this Sahara? or is it that, from living on my island, and in the open sun and air, I am become a Fiji savage?"

But at this point I checked all tendency to lounge upon my starched seat, for the inevitable lady of the house dropped in, with the same snowy puffs on either side of her face. She was a widow, I knew, — one of the best of women, I made no doubt; but how could I help knowing, too, that it was not to let in the lawless air that she lifted the sash an inch, nor was it to correct a tidy upon a corner chair that she gave it a twitch. Had I been a book agent she would have known it. Were I a gentlemanly sneak thief, she would have had the police in forthwith. If I had called as a lover I would have assured her, unquestioned, — she had such investigating eyes, — that my intentions were honorable. But nothing gratifies me more than to see, or fancy I see, how even hard and suspicious faces, of women also, soften a little as they glance at me. I like them, whoever they are, and I dare say they see it in me. Had the prim lady been forty years younger, she would have been perched upon my knee in two minutes, perhaps allowed me to kiss her before I left.

I was glad that the ladies I came to see were not in at the moment, but had left word that they soon would be. That I understood. "They are new-comers to the city," I reflected, "and cannot keep within doors. They are right." And then I went back in memory to the dull town in which they had lived so long, as Ross had described it to me, its ponderous live-oaks draped with gray moss, its dense river bottoms, its lounging population, its ignorant, contented stagnation. "It must be like heaven to them," I said, "these bright streets and busy people. They will be as new to me as everything here is to them. One likes to open a letter, to cut the leaves of a magazine just out, to untie a bundle —"

At this moment a young lady came into the parlor. I have a positive zest for people, not when they are before me in the mass, like the sea, but singly, like pure water in a glass to a thirsty man. Now I modulated myself to the proprieties of a first acquaintance, as I arose and took the hand, which, according to the custom of her own region, she held out to me.

"Dark hair," I rapidly enumerated to myself, "dis-

posed, Greek fashion, upon the small head. Bru-
nette in complexion, too. Fine eyes. Good features.
Intelligent face. Voice in keeping." And I continued to hold her hand.

"I am delighted, Miss Persis, to see you again," I
said; for she seemed a little afraid of me.

"Again?" she asked, her eyes kindling.

"Certainly," I said, and went on to tell her how
often Ross had written or told me, on his visits, about
her. "It is as if I knew you in Ocklawahaw, for
years now. Had I met you on the streets, I do not
see how I could have failed to recognize you!"

Her eyes fairly shone with pleasure. It would not
have been as flattering to me at the time had I known
that she was enjoying a surprise. Not in regard to
me! Ross had been enough interested in her, and
for so long now, as to write, to talk, about her. She
had not thought of that!

"He used to read us your letters, used to tell
us so much about you. Ross," she added gravely,
"thinks more of you than he does of anybody." And
she looked at me shyly, with a species of curiosity.
Dr. Trent and his wife must have exaggerated fearfully in what they too had said to her about me, her
way of regarding me was rather that which one be-
stows upon a landscape, a cathedral, whereas it is
impossible for a boy of ten to feel smaller than I do.

"I insist from the start," I said in the end, "that
our friendship shall begin from your earliest childhood. Let us take our time to it." And, entering at
once into the spirit of the thing, she laughingly con-

sented. In a little while, assuming our acquaintance
from that date, we gradually talked ourselves up
through the years between to that hour. It is
pleasant to see how rapidly a mutual liking can ripen
where there is sun enough. Besides, Ross Urwoldt
had told me so much, had written of late so many
details, that, apart from what the Trents said, I was
in sympathy with my new friend from the first.

"You have come here to study?" I remarked at
last.

"As hard as I can," she assented. "My life so far
has passed in the Reservation. I have had no opportunities. Now I intend to make up for lost time."

"You have learned everything already, Ross writes
me," I said. She opened her eyes, looked at me as
if to detect a jest.

"Even what little I have learned," she said, "has,
my teachers now tell me, to be unlearned. No; I am
at the beginning, with everything to do. There is so
very much to know. I had no idea how ignorant I
was until I came here. All the methods are different,
and I am learning in order to teach, — to teach here
if I can. I must study hard, very hard. Rachel and
I have not begun yet." By this time I was allowing
myself to look away from her to what she wore.
What a lady's dress is made out of, — the name for
it, I mean, — how should I know? But I fancied,
from something in the pleating of it here and there,
the sharpness of the edges of the rufflings and puck-
erings, that it was new. Coming so recently from
where she did, it was reasonable to suppose the dress

was made since she came to the city. Now, the love
of dress, of ornamentation, is a quality which God
puts into the nature of every woman. It is sometimes
carried, like everything else, to excess; but a faculty
and a fondness for such things is as inseparable from
her as is her sex. Somebody sings that

> " The world, which knows itself too sad,
> Is proud to have its women glad."

I, for one, like to see a woman indulge herself and
me in dressing as beautifully as she can. And to
me the freshness now of my friend's clothing had the
charm of the first leaves of spring. Surely the crocus
enjoys breaking out of the earth, the cold, the darkness, into the silent laughter of its golden petals;
and, knowing how much this new-comer took pleasure
in the newness of all she saw and heard and wore, I
enjoyed it too, — enjoyed it the more by reason, perhaps, of a longer, deeper practice and experience of
other people's satisfactions.

We conversed all the better for it, — I exhilarated,
through her, by the novelty of everything, until I
made, as I am too apt to do, a longer call than I intended. As I rose to go, begging pardon for having
stayed so long, Rachel Beauchamp came into the
room, and I sat down again, having — and I was
not sorry for it — my whole visit to make over
again.

Now, I have not said that Persis Paige was beautiful, not even that she was pretty. I do not think
I would have been specially struck with her appearance had I seen her in, say, the saloon of a steamer

upon which I happened to be travelling. Because I like people, women and children chiefly, in general, it may be easier for me to deepen like into love when I come to know any one in particular. Miss Rachel was not in the least like her friend, but what I have said of beauty was equally true of her. In this instance we were something more than fellow-passengers on a boat, and, as we talked, I did not have to study her fair face and pure eyes very closely to see that she too, like her friend, was well worth becoming better acquainted with. There was in her, too, the same dew of freshness. The change from Ocklawahaw to the famous city was very great, and if she was not as intellectual in her tastes as Persis, she too showed her pleasure in their new life. Many a time I have taken Trent's little Jean to a show, have given her a new book, purely to watch the sudden dawn as of a new morning in her eyes. Heaven knows there are sadder sunsets to be seen in the eyes of people than anywhere else, and thank God for the brighter sunrises than the east knows which can be seen in happy human eyes. So now.

"How can a peach refrain from its down, the flower at dawn from its evident gladness?" I thought, as I observed in Rachel, too, the same exhilaration under the novelty of things. But she did not have as much to say as her friend, was not as quick to anticipate. I could see the reply coming in the eyes of Persis, could see it before it parted her lips to be ready to speak when I ceased. Not so with Rachel. She listened with placid eyes, heard me entirely through.

Not until I was done did she begin to frame her answer. I could study the freshness of her toilet, too, while I listened, for she spoke slowly, putting a certain definite weight of good sense in what she said which was as pleasing to me as the more rapid utterance of her friend. When Rachel came into the room, Persis was talking almost eagerly with me, her spirits were so high, the topic of what she had to learn from this teacher and that was so interesting to her. With the entrance of her companion I saw that she quietly checked herself, silenced herself, at last. She did more than leave the conversation to Rachel instead; she listened with interested eyes to what her friend was saying, helped me to draw her out. It pleased me, the way the more brilliant girl of the two did this, better than anything she herself had said.

The war made me, as it did many a better and richer man, very poor. Coming North when it began, I was obliged to work very hard. My daily bread was earned as a writer, but I never touched my pen. after dinner. It was in the afternoon I made my visit. A first call should have been shorter, but I am ashamed to say I stayed until the tea-bell rang.

"Mrs. Trent could not come with me until to-morrow," I explained to the young ladies, as, hat in hand, I lingered in the doorway of the parlor; "but I could not wait, and came to-day. One ought not to postpone a pain, and why should I put off a pleasure? I am, although Northern born and a Union man, from

a questionable part of the country, and people are shy
of me; at least, I know very few of them. On that
account, except in the mornings, I have more time
than I can use. Whenever I can be of any service,
please be so kind as to command me. If you will let
me speak of myself, I would say that I feel old enough
to be your grandfather, Miss Persis, Miss Rachel, and
young enough to go into whatever you may wish me
to do, as if we had come here from Ocklawahaw together upon a picnic."

I think that we had at least begun, when I left, to
be good friends.

Within a week after my first call upon the
ladies I met Dr. Trent and his wife rambling ..
with their children in a gallery of art. I told them
of my visit, and of how much interest I was coming to take in our new friends. Mrs. Trent had an
hour's worth of talk with me about them then and
there.

"Steven's care for them will begin when they are
taken sick," she laughed. "To him well people are
the most stupid of mortals. I have warned them not
to get sick."

"There is not a healthier city than this," I suggested. "In comparison to Ocklawahaw, low, damp,
with its malarial river bottoms and dense forests, it
is as Paradise for pure air; the trouble is that there
is too much oxygen in its bracing atmosphere, it is
too stimulating. But the young ladies have lived
simple lives, have laid up reserves of strength notwithstanding some severe shakes of the ague."

"It is that," Mrs. Trent remarked, "which helped determine them to come East. Would you believe it? Persis thinks that her early sickness out West has done more than interrupt her studies. She has an idea that it has weakened her intellect almost. That is one reason which urges her to study; she has to make up for lost time, has to restore the tone of her mind. She is very ambitious."

"I saw her on the street yesterday," Dr. Trent observed. "It was where the crowd of cars, wagons, carriages, was thickest. She was waiting her opportunity on the curbstone, with her friend, and suddenly she left her and ventured across. It was a risk, but she managed it very well, looking up street and down as she went, darting hither and thither between the vehicles. When she reached the other side she beckoned to her friend in triumph. But Miss Rachel was more prudent; she waited deliberately until a policeman had halted the torrent of wheels, and then she walked across as slowly, her skirts in her hands, as if she were attending a reception. I went over to admonish Miss Persis," Dr. Trent added, "but she laughed at me. 'I do it for the exercise,' she said. 'I am training myself in athletics. I want to get strong and well for what I have to do.' She is a bright girl. I think we will be proud of her some · day. But she must not overdo it."

"Rachel told me," the Doctor's wife interposed, "that the severest exercise she took was to go into one of our largest and finest dry-goods palaces, and then tear herself away from the display, which must,"

Mrs. Trent added, "be something wonderful to one who has not seen anything of the kind before. Like every genuine woman," Mrs. Trent laughed, "she loves such things dearly! It will take a long time to become an athlete in that. Miss Persis is eager to learn. When she is not studying she is to go with me to every art-gallery, lecture, reading, concert, she can. It is part of her education."

"I hope I may have a chance," I said, "to help you. You know me of old, madam. One man finds his pleasure in the growth of a new variety of roses, in producing a more delicious strawberry, a larger apple, than Horticultural Fairs have ever beheld. Some men have a passion for pug-dogs, for rearing swift horses. As one is most like the Creator he regards men and women as the most interesting objects in the world. If these two country lasses had been lads instead, we would have been interested, under the circumstances, in them; but girls are so much more flexible, pliable, you know. There is a divine possibility in a young girl which one does not look for in a boy. You cannot help hoping for her what a music-master does for the girl in whom he sees a possible Jenny Lind, a Grisi, a Nilsson,—a something greater, perhaps, than men have ever known. That is the interest I shall come to take in our new friends; who knows what we may be able to make them?"

Mrs. Trent was interested, but she was looking, while I spoke, at a life-sized painting near by of a Judith.

"Look at her, Mr. Guernsey," she said. "See how the muscles stand out in the delicate arm with which she holds up the heavy head of Holofernes. It is terrible, her face, is n't it?"

"She looks," I said, "like an older Miss Persis."

Dr. Trent, standing by us, muttered something to himself as he glanced discontentedly at the aspect of the bronzed heroine.

"What is it, Trent?" I asked.

"Your Judith had better look out," he growled, "that she does not play the devil with her own head!"

"You are studying too hard, man," I exclaimed. "What can you mean? You are growing morbid."

"Am I? Well, perhaps I am," he said. But Jean and Guernsey, worse than indifferent to paintings, as children, curiously enough, always are, bore down upon us at this juncture. They were hungry and wanted to go home. Now that they suggested it, we all were, and went away together.

"Men like yourself, with large heads and comparatively small bodies," Mrs. Trent remarked, as she pressed upon me another slice of beef at her hospitable board soon after, "ought to see to it that the rest of the body, as Steven here says, keeps abreast of the brain. Electrical people cannot eat too much pudding," she further suggested at that stage of our repast.

"Meaning me? No, madam," I said. "I am the most stupid of men!" For I was trying in vain to puzzle out what in the mischief Trent meant by his remark about Judith. The more so as the Doctor is a man who, from long accuracy with drugs and surgical instruments, is very apt to mean something in what he says.

CHAPTER XVIII.

WAR.

ROSS URWOLDT went into the war in his way, and I went into it in mine. He raised company after company, contriving, when he had used up one, to have another ready for the slaughter. No captain on that side fought harder, endured more defeats, won more victories. After a while he found himself a colonel, was wounded in the battle of Pittsburg Landing, was captured, made his escape, fought again, was again taken prisoner and wounded so severely this time that he could not escape. It so chanced — but not at all. I do not like the word! Let us adopt the divine Hebraism and say, It came to pass that my work had taken me South just then with my medicine-chests, boxes of books, hampers of clothing, and such delicacies as convalescents require. One day, as I limped about among the wounded in an extemporized hospital, I saw my friend. We had not met more than once or twice since he left college, and Ross was one of the very few men whom to know once is to know forever. Drained of blood as he was, I recognized him at sight. The great battle had been fought just before; the surgeons had followed upon it with their passionless fury, so to speak, of steel, cold and swift, and the place was like a butcher's

shambles. Ross was lying upon a pile of army overcoats for which their late owners had now no longer
any use; many of these last stretched out here and
there, quite young, most of them, but passed into a
winter where neither youth nor health, thick clothing
nor the frenzy of fight, would avail to warm them any
more forever. In the act of recognizing Ross I knelt
beside him, confident that he was one of these. The
college stripling was grown into a vigorous manhood,
not large but sinewy, not robust but singularly compact of body. His hair was cut close, and it and his
mustache were of a deeper black because of the pallor .
of his gaunt face. I must have mentioned it before,
it was such a characteristic of the man, but he had
beyond any one the faculty of becoming at times
stone-still. I dare say he inherited it from generations of ancestors who had learned to become like
logs or rocks for stillness when lying in wait for game
or foe; but Ross became absolutely motionless at
those times when other men are most agitated. The
sudden peril, the instant exasperation, which shook
other men like an aspen leaf, or hurled them about in
a rage, petrified him instead; he became silent, intent,
ready to put forth his best strength in the moment
and manner only in which he could effect most thereby. It was so with him in lesser, things. He gave a
more fixed attention to a friend in ordinary conversation than was common; but when he was profoundly
interested he fastened his black eyes upon the person
speaking with a certain statue-like intentness which
held the other also as in a vise.

It was so now. He lay so still that I was sure he
must be dead. It was only exhaustion, however, for
he was terribly worn also from a forced march all
night before the battle. He had fought, too, with his
usual ferocity till, at the end of the stubbornly con-
tested conflict, he had fallen badly hurt. Whenever
he slept it was with the motionless repose of an image
of stone or iron thrown to the earth from its pedestal,
and it was natural it should be so now. In camp he
could be as hard, as cruel, as any. If there was good
to come of it to the cause for which he fought, he
could lie with eyes steadier than any other, could
have a coward drummed out of his regiment as coolly
as he could hang a weeping and shrieking spy. From
exchanged prisoners I had learned that, while other
Confederate officers expended their wrath upon their
own panic-stricken soldiers in oaths, Ross had
stemmed their retreat in silence, but with cold lead
and dripping sword, colder still. Had hate and rage,
the brute fury of battle and the intoxication of victory, or the deeper excitement of defeat, — had these
aroused in him passions baser yet? But had he
ever been other than himself? If he had so much in
him of the native savage, I was enough of one myself to like him all the more that he was a variety
upon the stereotyped fashion of men, that he was
thoroughly sincere and true to his wild and sturdy
self.

I did not disturb him at first. For a long time I
sat on the floor by his side, thanking Heaven that the
law by which the planets roll was not more accurate

than that which had seen to it that we two should come thus together once more. They used to tell me that my severe malady had overquickened my brain; perhaps it may have caused my heart to beat too full and too fast; but at last, and as there was no woman there to do it for me and to do it better, I could refrain no longer, and bent over and kissed him upon the bronze-like forehead.

What windows for the soul the eyes are! Ross awoke at the touch; awoke, and I could see him, in his eyes, coming to me, — coming to me through all the years since we had met last; coming to me through the smoke, since the war began, of the battles. Yes, I saw him coming toward me in his eyes; coming to me through, first, the haze and daze of weakness and weariness, through the momentary bewilderment as to where he was, through the fierceness of fight flaring up in him; coming at last to see that I was Guernsey, — that I was the one man he had cared most for. What followed between us concerns no one but ourselves. This only I will say, that what came after, and before he could help himself, was a revelation to him far more of himself than of me.

I obtained permission, as soon as I could, to take him, by slow stages, away with me, to the nearest city in the South, but within the Federal lines. Securing comfortable rooms at a hotel therein, I gave up everything else and nursed him until he recovered. We could not be always playing chess, nor could I always think of something new to tell him concerning Rachel and Persis. He would not allow me to mention him

14

in my letters to Dr. Trent, lest they should know of
his wounds ; nor did he ask me in regard to the young
ladies, not, at least, after his first inquiries. I was
surprised at it. I did not know he had become so
cold and hard. I was disappointed in Ross, was
indignant. Afterward I came to know him better.
The fact was, that he had come to care for nothing in
the world but Persis ; but he was by no means certain
concerning her. His experiences were compelling
him toward an utter distrust of everybody, as of
everything. Persis was little more than a mere
country girl when he saw her last ; he dared not trust
himself to what she might come to be. He knew
that she must grow into a woman of marked character,
but of what character? There was nothing for him
in the future but Persis ; meanwhile he must wait.
If he was not killed in battle, he would some day
see for himself who and what she was. So deeply
did he feel, that he was, at this date, afraid to ask
me about her.

"I believe you would rather not hear about them,"
I said one afternoon when he turned almost impatiently away, as he lay, at the mention of Persis.

"You took your course," he replied irrelevantly,
"under stress of conscience ; with me it was conscience plus circumstance."

Had I understood then, I would have known that
Persis Paige was to him as to the beggar is the last
coin left sewed up in his rags, and who dares not
examine the coin, not knowing whether it be gold or
copper, good or counterfeit ; but I fell into his mood.

"There was no merit in it," I said. "When the war began, a something in me stronger than myself came upon me, lifted me, powerless to desire even to resist, off my island, and took me North. As a tree is torn up, so this something tore me up and out of my soil, roots and all. Why talk about it?"

"That is it," Ross exclaimed. "You will indulge your imagination as to this, that, and the other, — as to phantasmal somethings apart from yourself. You believe in a silent tornado which tore you up, — a tornado not yourself, yet peculiar to yourself! Now, I do not believe in anything apart from myself." He was lying upon a lounge which I had drawn into a bay-window looking southward over the suburbs of the city, and then over the gardens, orchards, fields, and so toward the distant hills. We were very quiet, for the war had rolled far down toward the southeast, and the city in which we were lay like a bunch of sea-weed, no longer torn and tossed by the ebbing tide. Ross had regained his vigor of mind; but a shattered leg was very slowly recovering, and he had use for his faculty of holding himself still. Now, I am so constituted that I cannot have motion enough, and it was a pleasure to me to have to move about for my friend also.

"That is where we differ," he persisted. "You are mastered by ghosts, I am not. When the war began there was an outside pressure upon me to do as I did. It surrounded me on every side, pressed upon me like the atmosphere. What did, or do, I care? In this world one thing is about as bad as another.

I did the easiest thing to do, I yielded to the pressure. If I had cared to fight it, I could have done so, — the fiercer for the pressure. But I don't care. Why should I? You have your baggage of principles, theories, — you thought so and so, didn't believe in slavery, did believe in one great republic, and so on, and so on. I am as naked of such things as a Comanche. I am simple, unencumbered, move straight forward. I found myself in the war. Very good. There I was. I raised men for it, marched, lay down at night, and slept. When morning came, there was breakfast to cook and eat. I ate with appetite, drank, marched, camped, encouraged the men. When a good joke came up, I laughed at it; when a bridge was to be built, a railroad to be torn up, I did that. When a fight was on hand, I fought. Do you understand? Why should I stop to argue? I stick to nature; what else do we know? The more I am like a mere part of nature, like a river, a bird, a buffalo, a cinnamon bear, the easier everything is. Why should I bother myself? Whatever lies nearest, that I do. Whatever is to be done, at that I go, with all the force I have, until I break or am broken, till I wear out, till I die and there is an end of me! You *will* make me talk. Nobody else can do it; and I have nothing to do until I get well. As of this war, so is it of everything else in this infernal world. The one thing I am glad of is that there is no other! Cæsar told the Senate, you remember, that to believe a man lived after death was all nonsense: the thing to do was to take this bit of life as it is, enjoy your-

self, lay on with all your might, if that is the thing
in hand, then die and be as dead — although he did
not say *that* — as Julius Cæsar! Cicero was one of
your philosophers; but, you remember, he sprang to
his feet when Cæsar sat down, and said that Cæsar
was right."

He had spoken more to himself than to me, with
his face to the wall as he lay. I made no reply. A
rooster crowed, a clock struck. After a while a brass
band went by in full blast. They were playing "Hail
Columbia," with the breath of battle in their horns;
the drummers were whacking at rebels rather than
sheepskins; there was a sudden uproar of cheers, then
the bells began to ring. It was plain that rumors of
a victory somewhere had arrived; yet I am sure that
Ross cared little more for it than he did for the buzz-
ing of flies on the upper panes of the window at which
he was lying. But it proved to me how dissatisfied
he was with his own conclusions; for, after a long
silence, he contrived to roll himself over, and looked
at me as I sat.

"Why, Guernsey, will you indulge yourself," he
demanded, "in lies?" He had seized upon me, lying
motionless as he did so, with his strong black eyes
as with the hands of a powerful, but drowning man.
They were such famishing eyes, too, that the tears
would have come to my own but that I thought it
best to look down at him and laugh instead, as at a
friend who must be humored, seeing that he is sick
and not himself.

"Mine are the only certainties," I said, "and you

know it. You are passing, now as every day, through the gymnasium which fits you for your eternal existence after this little bug-like life is ended. There is no endurance apart from that, no happiness. It is the only thing which assures you that you are not altogether a bug. Listen, old fellow!"

I think there was something in my face which held him to me as I said it, and I talked away at a great rate. A man knows when he is dealing in facts! It was wine I was pouring out to the weak, and the aroma was in it, not in me. However small a window may be, however dusty its half-washed panes, it knows when the sun is shining through it. For the moment I thought I could see its light lying upon the cold face of my friend, but I was careful to say too little rather than too much.

"It is little I know of the One who rules the world," I said, "but among my surest certainties in regard to him is this, that he is mathematically accurate in his dealings, unswervingly precise in regard to nations as to planets, unlimitedly just to the race as to the individual. From the beginning so far he has always compelled things from the lower to the higher, and I have, can have, no shadow of a doubt as to the result of this war!" But it was not in good taste for me to be as exultant as I was.

"The certainty to which I have come," Ross groaned, "is that men are invariably knaves or fools."

"But the King is strong enough," I said, "to control even fools and knaves to his own ends!" And there the topic dropped from between us.

It was easy to see that the fierceness of his fight had not been with the Federals only ; but why should we talk about men, whether in gray or in blue, at all ?

" Of all living creatures," I said to him at the end, " I suppose the cuttle-fish is the most horrible. And yet every red fang of its diabolical jaws, every lens of its goggle eyes, every peculiarity of its swarming and snake-like arms, is constructed with a wisdom as wonderful as that which gives the colors of the rainbow to the harmless dolphin. I do not know what it was made for, but I do know that it is as essential to whatever the purposes of its creation are, as Shakespeare is to his."

" So of this war ? " asked Ross.

" So of this abominable war," I assented. " There have been worse ones in history, but, like every other, this, also, is essential to the final results. Every man will receive his own results in himself; but, thank God, my faith is not based upon the whirlwind of miserable men, but in the Person who makes and knows, loves and manages, them all. Down with the prince of doubt and of darkness ! *Ave Optimus Augustus, Imperator !* "

" I care little for your theories," Ross replied. " I confess that I wish I could be as serene and happy as you are. It lifts and rests me merely to look at you."

Let me say here that Ross Urwoldt was afterward one of the best known of public men. As such he mingled among men of all sorts. So far as he could accustom himself to do so, he associated with them on equal terms, — laughing, talking, suggesting and receiving suggestions, saying vigorous things and having to endure energetic replies, outwardly the most affable — so far as he could compel himself to be — and practical of men. When he got inside my door, it was as when a man pulls off a mud-bespattered overcoat, kicks off dirty boots, and takes his ease in dressing-gown and slippers. What he tried at such times to hide from me was merely what he tried to hide from himself. But, bless me! what good did it do? He may have known me better than I knew myself. I certainly knew Ross as I hardly think even Persis, not to speak of Rachel, ever came to know him. I knew him at his best, but it was because I knew him at his worst that I loved and took most interest in him.

That was the way in which, one afternoon during his long confinement, he came to talk to me about his mother. He would not have done it had he not been enfeebled by having me with him; that undermined him, I think, more than his wounds.

"You have no idea, Guernsey," he said at last, "what a woman my mother once was. The first memory I have of anything is of her. She nursed me through the small-pox when I was a baby, and my first recollection is of looking down at her one day, when I was getting well, as she held me with her strong arms high in the air above her head. All the other children had died; I was the last that was left her. She was almost worn to death herself, but she had saved me as from the very grave, and I have an idea now that she was holding me up, giving me to God, or something of the kind. Yes," he added in softer tones, "I remember it perfectly. I can look down now, as I hang suspended in her lifted hands, and see her head thrown back, her hollow cheeks, her black and eager eyes! She had everything then and after that to bow her to the earth, to break her spirit, and she would neglect her dress, her appearance. But once or twice, when I was not much more than a child, I have seen her angry. How erect she became, how her eyes flashed! When I brought home on my mare, before me, the first deer I had shot, how well I remember her! I had ridden up to the door, and, before I could get off, my mother ran out of the house like a girl, her long hair down her back, her cheeks as red as a rose, her eyes so full of love and pride — Guernsey," Ross added, "I can see, as I tell you of it, the very whiteness of her teeth as she laughed, — she had beautiful teeth! I do not know how she managed it, but she fairly lifted me out of my saddle, held me up, kissed me, and then she put me down all at once, turned pale, shrunk from me as if she had thought of something, was suddenly afraid. I understood afterward what that meant!

"It makes a fool of me to be with you," he added almost impatiently. "What I intended to tell you is this. We did not say as much to each other as is common to mother and son elsewhere, it isn't our nature to talk much; in fact, the more we feel the less we talk. I used to think my mother was the best woman in the world, fit to be a queen. I wish now I had told her so! What I am coming at is that I hated to have her marry anybody. But, of all men living, I despised Amasa Clarke most. That she should marry him was the hardest blow I ever had. About a year after the war began I was sent back to Ocklawahaw to beat up recruits. I had to see her. Guernsey," he said, "I used to worship my mother, but I never want to see her again!" Had I known it, he had ceased, as he spoke, to think of his mother; he was thinking of Persis instead, but of Persis Paige dragged down with the rest of her sex into what he regarded as the downfall of his own foolish delusion of what a woman might be.

After that he went on to tell me of some of the uncleanness and of the atrocities common to both armies. He did not seem to care in regard to it himself, and I am sure he enjoyed shocking me, as he assuredly did. But what would I have? It was the downright devil in Ross which made me try to hold on to him the harder. And I wanted to save Ross Urwoldt; I had a strong purpose to save him if I could, because, of all the men I knew, he seemed to me to be the man best worth saving.

As is the case with everything, whether it be a tree, a lion, or a man, which possesses a natural and therefore perfect health, my friend recovered almost as rapidly from his wounds as Homer describes of the stricken Mars.

Upon the afternoon before we parted we were seated together for the last time in the bay-window of which I have spoken. Ross, now entirely restored, except that he was somewhat paler and thinner than was, I suppose, usual with him, had been looking out upon the landscape for a long time, smoking his cigar in silence. His father was, as has been said, in his younger days at least, a poet and a painter, and he asserted himself now, so I fancy, in his son, taking advantage of the mood of Ross as another father had of the midnight leisure of Hamlet. In a word, this Confederate colonel from Ocklawahaw yielded for the instant to the sentimental, which generally he despised.

"It has been a great contrast," he said,—"the life I have led of late to what went before; after such experiences of swamp and struggle, of the worst sort of moral mud and all kinds of murder and brutality, to be here, and with you, Guernsey. But the other is the rule; this is the brief exception. I have got up here out of this horrible war but for a moment; to-morrow I plunge into it again, and deeper than ever, for who can say how long?"

Very rarely did he speak thus, even to me. I said nothing in order that he might say more.

"Not that it is all bad in camp," he corrected himself. "In our army, as in yours, some of the hardest cases show, when the time comes, a courage, headlong yet cool, which Murat would have envied. Better still, I have seen in many of our worst fellows a patience, endurance, self-sacrificing devotion, equal to what one reads of Christian martyrs. Guernsey," he added, "I have often wondered, even in the heat of battle, at the joyous disdain of themselves with which my men dashed into certain death. A man tosses away his life then as coolly as if it were a squeezed lemon, does it rejoicingly. It proves what a little thing life is. It is all a man has," and he tossed the end of his smoked-out cigar through the open window, " but it is such a miserably small thing at last."

It was because he was so free from all humbug that I respected even his self-contempt. " Is it not queer," he went on, " that a man cannot get used to the low and rascally course of things? The discontent at it, the loathing of it, — is not that the oddest thing of all? A snake, an alligator, might as reasonably object to the stagnant pool in which, like its ancestors, it has always lived, always will live. But there is another thing which astonishes me yet more. Fancy an eel or an alligator passing its time in imagining itself to have a soul, a Creator, and all that, making its dirty pool ten times dirtier, its vermin estate a hundred times more offensive to it, by such contrast and contradiction! Why will you imagine such diabolical nonsense? "

It was said angrily, for what he put into words was but a small part of what he thought. Very little did I argue with him; it was with himself the fury of the argument lay.

" You talk about a God and a hereafter! What do you get out of it all? Nothing but what you have first put in, and you know it!"

" What I see, hear, taste, feel, smell, that is all I believe in! Certainly!" I mimicked my friend's tone as well as his frequent assertion. "Ross," I added, "do you suppose even an eagle ever saw a flower or a star? Does an elephant admire a landscape lying in full view before it? What do you suppose a lion cares for a sunrise, a sunset? except to slake its thirst, what does it care for the cataract which thunders to its very paws? We see things which these cannot, because we are more than these. Now—"

"I am speaking of spiritual things, things you do *not* see! Don't let's discuss it, Guernsey. I'm glad I go to-morrow. For myself," and he stood up erect and vigorous, "I deliberately prefer to be merely what I am,—an animal, one of the finest animals living, if you say so, but an animal only. I want no more. I wouldn't be any more if I could. I am satisfied to live, to die such, as fifty generations of my fathers have done before me."

A new idea smote me as I considered the face and bearing of my friend. A man can extinguish his intellect by drinking alcohol enough. Nero is not the only man who has rid himself of his heart. There are dozens of people a day who, with rope or razor, free themselves of their bodies as easily as one does of a nail-paring. We are free agents, frightfully free. Who knows but a man can rid himself of his soul also? It was a foolish notion, but, as I looked Ross full in the face, he was so sincere in what he said, that I had no more to say to him upon the subject than if he was, as I have already said, a leopard or a lion. But, being a man and not a brute, I know myself to be the master where the finest animal on earth is concerned, and how could I help the silent exultation of face which goes with such a certainty? Ross was conscious of this in me, and resented it. Yet why should I say anything? His quarrel was not with me, it was with himself.

He had already arranged his exchange, and the next day he was gone, to plunge, as I was soon to learn, into the thick of the fight again. From the first, I had not said a word to prevent, it was so evident that he had rather go South and fight than stay with me and argue.

CHAPTER XIX.

GROWTH.

IT was impossible for me not to like Persis and
Rachel more as the days wore on. I was such a
stranger to the city that I was glad enough to add
these girls to the home I had made for myself in
the society of Dr. Trent and his household. Of
course I was selfish in the matter. The admiration
one has for a landscape is but an expansion of the
pleasure he has in the trees and grass of his own
yard, and I am quite sure that I admire a wheat-
field more for the solid satisfaction which I get out of
a loaf of bread. Especially was this a reason for the
growing interest I took in Persis. She had, from
her first coming, an eagerness to know all she could
about the city and region in which she found herself,
and who could tell her more about it than I? Her
eagerness awoke within me again that which I too
had felt on my first coming there, and I enjoyed
everything over again, renewed and redoubled, in
going about with Rachel and herself. Although but
a dozen years older than they, I was as a father who
lives his childish pleasures over once more in the
companionship of his children.

While I had a very wide acquaintance with men

and women in audiences when I lectured, in hospitals
where I served; while I was not without a sense of
the friendship between a wide circle of readers and
myself, — my personal relations were with so very
few, that I could not help studying these two when I
was with them as closely as it was unconsciously. To
me they were new types of their sex, also, and wholly
unlike each other. In her more silent way Rachel
was glad of her new world, but she allowed Persis
to say almost everything for both. The only thing
which seemed to elate her was the enthusiasm of
Persis. More than once, when Persis was prevented
by her studies from going with us to see pictures, or
to concert and theatre, Rachel sat by my side, happy
but quiet; yet, when Persis was there too, the very
happiness of her friend gave a new glow to her cheek,
a brighter light to her placid eyes; she had more to
say, smiled more, was so much the prettier in her
simple toilet, because Persis, the more demonstrative
of the two, was with us.

Not that Rachel did not have decided likes and
dislikes of her own. Where books and authors, for
instance, were concerned, she did not always agree
with Persis and myself.

"The thing I have looked forward to," Persis told
me soon after coming, "next, that is, to my studies,
is to knowing the men and women who wrote the
books I like best. I have read some books," and she
mentioned them, "over so often that I almost know
them by heart. You have taken us to see the monu-
ments, parks, public libraries; please, Mr. Guernsey,

can't you arrange it so that we can make the ac-·
quaintance of —" And she mentioned hesitatingly
the names of several authors of note who lived in
or near the city. "We would rather see them than
anything else, would n't we, Rachel?"

I cannot conceive why it is, but sincerely as I
admire distinguished people, I have an aversion to
attendance upon them. From the day almost of her
coming Persis alluded to her wish; it so chanced that
I was the only person at that period who could gratify
her, and, sorely against the grain, I arranged at last
to do so, Mrs. Trent abetting me.

One day, within the first few months of their
arrival, I called in a carriage at the house of the
young ladies, by appointment, to take them to see a
celebrated authoress. Rachel declined to go. At the
moment she had something in hand — a music-lesson,
I think it was, — which interested her more, but her
friend was delighted at the opportunity.

"I would rather see her than Victoria," she said as
we went; and I noticed that, so far as her wardrobe
allowed, she was arrayed as if she was going to Court.
For which reason I could not understand why Persis
was so silent when, after what seemed to me a very
pleasant visit, we rode back. No lady could have
been more affable than the one upon whom we had
called, but my companion seemed almost ashamed of
herself for taking me there.

It was cruel in me to do it; but, when science
demands, even vivisection is a virtue. "Lady teachers," I reflected aloud, "cannot, I am told, endure to

have a lady principal over them. How strange! Ladies prefer to do their shopping with masculine clerks behind the counter. It is very singular!"

"Women can write," Persis fired up, "as well as men. Some day they will do almost everything as well as men, perhaps better!" She made it as an assertion, but her troubled eyes fluttered about mine, making it an interrogation rather.

"I sincerely hope so! Men," I replied, "have made a horrible bungle of it for sixty centuries. Who knows but that woman is to take the world out of men's miserable hands and complete things?" But my companion watched me so closely to see if I was not laughing, that I could not keep from doing so.

"Men always joke when a woman is concerned!"

She said it in such a manner that I could not help replying, with the accents, and, as far as I could, the eyes of a grandfather, "What do *you* care, my dear Miss Persis, for such things?" For she was so young, had been shut out so completely from the world! Moreover, she was giving, of late, promise of becoming so pretty, perhaps beautiful. "It amazes me," I continued to meditate aloud, "how swiftly an idea becomes universal. Here is this question of what women may yet be and do. The time was when chivalry had no more existence than telegrams or steamships. Queens of beauty, knightly devotion to woman, — do you know, Miss Persis, that the entire sex was elevated with the Virgin Mary? There is more in it than there was in the worship of the

Virgin, or woman would not hold her throne while' the worship of the Virgin is perishing from Christendom. The position of man has always been a something clearly defined; but of woman? Somehow, as for ages past, so now, she is still upon the stairway of unceasing ascent. Don't you see it, Miss Persis? If you and your sex are not to slip off the steps and back into something lower, you must go on climbing, you must come to be something more than you are! I believe with all my soul in the new chivalry toward woman; my trouble is that I do not wholly understand anything about it except this: heretofore woman has been lifted by the hands of men, hereafter she is to lift herself. I accept it in advance. O queen, live forever!"

My companion had forgotten her authoress. It was very flattering to me that her eyes — a slight suspicion still about her lips — were drinking in what I said, and growing brighter as they did so.

"People *do* have a new idea, then, of what we can do? I hoped so," she said, "but I was not certain." ·

"Certainly!" I assumed the prophet in addition to the grandfather. "There is a new conception coming in of what your sex can be and do, *must* and will do and be, which is swelling so much like an ocean tide along the entire coast, that I can no more measure than I can understand it. Whatever you or I or anybody may think or say, Miss Persis, it is rolling in all the same. But that *you* should know of, or care for it — "

"Because I was in Ocklawahaw?" she demanded

modestly enough; but she was not afraid of me, venerable as I was. "We had books, we read, we —"

"Does Miss Rachel care for such things?"

It was an impolite interruption. If the face of my companion fell, it was but for the moment. "Rachel," she said a little defiantly, "is the sweetest, most sensible girl alive, but she cares more for — other things." And I could see that her friend had very likely laughed at Persis about it. And then, by some odd association of ideas, Persis added, "That is because Rachel had such a father." And she went on to tell me, knowing that Ross must have already informed me of it, the whole story of the drunken statesman, and how he had been for so long like a big baby in the hands of his daughter.

I had observed long before that if I wanted to make Rachel talk, I had but to mention Persis; and now, with the devotion of Rachel as a topic, I had never known Persis to converse so eloquently.

I cannot give date or circumstance to my association with these girls. My life was a very irregular and uncertain one during the war. I almost lived on the railroad, coming and going thousands of miles, North or South, East or West. It was a hard, and often, if I had yielded to it, a most trying and unpleasant life. One is hurled about, at such periods, almost as if he were a dice. Mine was a mission of mercy, and I went rapidly in this direction and that, having almost as little to do with the sending of myself as if I were a carrier-pigeon. On which account I was very glad when I could rest for a while in the house of

Dr. Trent, and in the companionship of the young ladies.

It was not often that we spoke of the war then raging. Living as they had done for so long in the Reservation, neither Persis nor Rachel had grown up with deep convictions as to North or South. Parson Williams was no politician. I doubt if Ross had ever spoken to them on the subject. Rachel was deeply anxious in regard to her father; but to that she had been accustomed since she could remember. Knowing him to be opposed to secession, although in the South, it was not unnatural that she should share his views. But to be calm, to await the inevitable, to endure without unnecessary worry, — this had become her nature.

As to Persis, it was different. For quite a while after her arrival she could be as enthusiastic as any one for the old flag, where it was spoken of in general; but people learned not to stir up either Rachel or herself by too much mention of the iniquity of the South. That Persis was intensely anxious for news from Ross, I knew very well. It was an additional motive with her to hard study, that she could thus divert her mind from his perpetual danger; but no one was more eager to know the latest news from the war than herself.

Dr. Trent and his wife, beginning with mere interest in them, grew into esteeming and loving them exceedingly, doing all they could to make them happy. Persis did not care to talk about Ross, even with Rachel. By one of the marvellous intuitions of her sex, she seemed, in her strongest moods at least, to count confidently upon his coming out of the war unscathed, and he remained, as he had been for so long, the chief impulse with her in all she did.

This I pass over lightly, for the reason that it was impossible for me to know, during the war, much about it. Until afterward, my chiefest interest was in them as in young girls in a strange land, thrown largely upon themselves, making the best they could of their opportunities.

I recall distinctly how each looked the day I first saw them, but not, stage by stage, the process in them afterward of change, as I was thrown sometimes with one, then with the other, during my intermittent visits to the city in which they lived. What helped to interest, and aided me toward understanding them, was their growing divergence of character as the years rolled by. One day, for instance, I arranged to take them with me to see an author, whom, of all her favorites, Persis had long been most desirous to see. As before, Rachel excused herself. Wearied out as the author was with many years of homage, I was more interested in his evident interest in Persis than in anything else in his house or himself. Had he been an emperor, she could not have enjoyed it as much; and the almost tremor of her enthusiasm was so pleasant to him that, when we came to leave, the old monarch, holding her hands in his, gave her a kiss upon the brow which flushed her face with pleasurable pride.

"I could not have imagined it," I told her, as we

rode back to the city, "of the great authoress whom you remember we called upon."

"That *she* should kiss me? Certainly not!" It was said so indignantly that I laughed aloud.

"But why not? She was old, old enough to be your grandmother," I insisted; but Persis only drew herself back still more, as if from the distinguished lady in question, and deigned no reply. "It puzzles me, too," I went on, "that Miss Rachel did not care to go."

"Not if you knew her as well as I do," Persis said. "She is different. You forget what a father she has. It makes her very shy of men, especially of men who have a great reputation. She cared for her father apart from all that, against all that. Rachel loved her father, — loved him, Mr. Guernsey, a great deal more," Persis said almost angrily, "than *I* could love any man."

I laughed outright, she was so much in earnest, as always, and it was merely to turn the conversation that she added, "That is the reason, Mr. Guernsey, why Rachel is so shy of *you*."

"Of me? What do you mean? I cannot," I said, "see any connection — "

"She does not care for authors as girls naturally do. And then," Persis continued with archness, "her father was a distinguished man. *He* was a genius, too, Mr. Guernsey, but," my companion said with mocking lips, "men of genius do not stand as they should with Rachel. From her experience of her father, of the father of Ross too, I believe she has almost a horror of them." She laughed merrily, seeing how much I was teased at being considered to belong to the illustrious class specified.

"It is the absurd exaggeration of Mrs. Trent in talking of me to Miss Rachel," I protested. "Unfortunately Mrs. Trent measures me, as she does everybody, by her liking. And so Miss Rachel imagines," I added with an uncomfortable laugh, "that, when I am out of her sight, I am lying drunk somewhere." But my companion would give me no further light upon the subject.

In fact, she went on spoiling me instead; she seemed to like to talk with me. Whenever we met, at her house or elsewhere, I had but to mention a book for her to ask eagerly about it, if she had not read it. It was a pleasure to talk to her in regard to it or anything, she listened with such zest, anticipating what I was about to say, quickened into suggestions, assenting, dissenting, praising, at times almost scolding. To converse with her about an author or a book was to interest me in writer or volume much more than I ever thought I could be. So of what she had read, of what she intended to study, she was so full of attention, so rapid in reply and remark, her color came and went, her fine eyes never wavered from the topic.

As the time rolled on, her growth was as by an unceasing succession of summers of enthusiasms. Her eyes were larger, darker, more full of soul and purpose, she had richer color, her tones were fuller and sweeter, her hair seemed to be darker and more abundant, as her cheeks became more rounded, her form developing into that of the complete woman.

I knew, when I began, how difficult it would be to tell all this! The worst of it was that she gave me, when we met, an impression that I knew so much, and that she was so glad to learn. For my life I could not help feeling as if she was a fine painting which was growing — what a fool I was to think it! — under my hand. Not that I ever said so to myself.

And then she did so sincerely believe in me! Not so much in me for myself, but for what she rated me as having done. No, not as having done! Heaven knows that my ideal of what I hoped to do was immeasurably beyond all I had so far accomplished, and, in her eagerness, she did not see me as I was, but as I would be some day, — a day, alas! which so far has never dawned.

As the war slowly drew its bleeding length along, the girls derived, I feel sure of it, a goodly part of their education from it. They had a complete course of study always in hand. Every day, every hour, seemed to be systematically given to lessons of one kind or another. Teachers came to them, and they went to teachers. They were members of classes, they belonged to conservatories of music, they took courses of lectures. And yet the war was the great instructor. There were periods of municipal depression, of hilarious exultation, as the banner fell or rose upon the distant fields. Orations were frequent, lectures from returned philanthropists; societies arose to devise means; sanitary fairs were held. It was impossible to hear so much military music, to see the flag so often, to read the daily papers, to live in such ever-varying enthusiasm, to take part in so much vigorous conversation at table, in parlors and everywhere, and not be developed by the contest as by a perpetual and powerful impulse. For the period, at least, the bullets slew idleness in the city as surely as it did soldiers at the front. Frivolity perished at the cannon's breath, as surely as did slavery. To Rachel and Persis, as to all of their age, the war was a Spartan education which would leave its pupils, nobler, more unselfish, stronger, and better every way than they could otherwise have been.

For there was, as we were to learn afterward, more of Spartan broth in the fare of Rachel and Persis than even Mrs. Trent imagined at the time. Even if Persis had been careless as to money matters, Rachel possessed both an experience and temperament which insured a wise economy. Notwithstanding their utmost thrift they found it hard to keep out of debt. Ross Urwoldt, as we were to learn afterward, had elected himself their guardian and treasurer. It must have been the hardest work of his warfare to keep his charges supplied, thrown hither and thither as he was, with sufficient money. I do not know what fictions he resorted to as to proceeds due Rachel from her property, as to instalments on her land which he was owing to Persis. What I do know is that he kept himself stripped to the last penny of even his depreciated Confederate money that the girls might not suffer. I used to wonder at times as to why Rachel seemed so sober, why Persis had, even in our most animated interviews, an absent manner. Poor things! Being often in so tight a place myself, I might have guessed, from the intuition of sheer sympathy and fellow-feeling, why it was. But they ... kept the story of their needs as closely to themselves as I kept my own. With all her feminine wit, under the impulse even of her heart, Mrs. Trent no more found out their secret than she did mine. Not until afterward.

And thus the war drew to its close; and, upon the whole, I am inclined to think that, more than the mere war, more than their books and lectures, it was the privation Persis and Rachel endured, on occasions at least, which had most to do with their education at that date.

Even now I do not understand Ross well enough to know why he should write, as he did, to me, and not to them. Military discipline may have had much to do with it, but his remittances to them always passed through the hands of Dr. Trent or myself. To us he said, in enclosing it, all he could say; to them he merely sent his regards. But, as I write, I recall that where he was most intent, there, as I have described, he was most silent. In regard to nothing in the world was he as intent, these dark days through, as in regard to Persis. Yes; that, I feel sure, accounts for his course. He was as a scout who leans forward, silent, motionless, because he is looking, is listening, for his life.

CHAPTER XX.

A VISITOR.

ONE noon, some months after the war was over, I lounged in the doorway of a bookstore in the city, catching a glimpse of every person who passed me, going up or down. There were portly men among them and comely women; but I was struck to the heart as I saw how many of the women were invalids. Dr. Trent had suggested the fact, and now each pallid face of these confirmed his almost savage remarks. Why should the cheeks of the woman of thirty, who has just passed, be so very thin? Here again comes a pigeon-chested girl! This is a buxom lass, but evidently Irish. A girl with the beauty of health and refinement in her aspect passed by, but not often. Here is a colored woman, overdressed, and stout enough in all conscience! Alas, with the next woman who went by, began a new series of the sallow, the fragile, the languid. "If these, when dressed for the streets, are so sickly of appearance," I thought, "what must they seem when in the undress and negligence of home? And what is the cause? hard work? poverty? care? consumption? neglect? Do they lace too tightly? eat too little? Can it be possible that they exist upon pies or doughnuts? Through what have these women passed that so many of their faces are as worn as that of Liberty upon the current coin?"

I was looking up street as I thus reflected, when I saw coming toward me a man whose aspect arrested my eyes by its unlikeness to the generality of the men. People glanced at him a second time in going by, so foreign did he seem. Except for the unkempt look of his clothes, the slouch of his felt hat, and that he was taller, darker of visage, with blacker eyes, hair, and mustache, there was nothing to distinguish him beyond a military bearing so military as to be that of a soldier among enemies. His foreignness appeared to be deeper than that of land or language; it was not disdain so much as it was an unconsciousness of the crowd among which he moved. He looked, as he came, neither to the right nor to the left, but straight before him over the heads of the people, and with a steadiness of gaze which I never saw in any other.

Now I knew a little of what had befallen Ross Urwoldt since I last saw him. From what I had noticed in the papers, from what Persis and Rachel told me, I was aware that he was one of the best known of the Confederate officers in his region, popular for the ferocity with which he had fought through the war. Since the war he had removed from Ocklawahaw to the State of which Governor Beauchamp had been so often the Washington or the Arnold. There he had been dragged, as by his ardent and restless temperament too, out of planting, into the practice of law, and out of that into politics.

He would not have seen me in passing if I had not stepped out of the doorway, taken his arm, and limped — for I am still a little lame — along beside him, as if he had come that way on purpose. He returned my salutation, but I was hurt to see how cold in manner he remained even after he saw who it was.

"I live," I said to him, when we came to the next corner, "at the hotel near here. For many a day I have wanted your strong arm to help me along. You were a long time coming. I am glad to see you." And I adopted a tone as indifferent as his own while we talked of what had befallen us since we parted. But he hesitated when he had seen me to the hotel, had helped me up-stairs and to the door of my room.

"I am here for merely a short time, on business," he said, giving me his hand for good-by.

I suppose, confound it! that I *am* too much of a woman. Otherwise I cannot understand what he saw in my face, for I said nothing. He came in, pitched his hat upon the sofa, sat down as if he was tired. Then he straightened himself up again, consented to a cigar, and seemed to be thinking. It was not agreeable to see that I was little more to him, I fear, than a poodle. If I had not known the man better than he knew himself, I would have dropped him from memory and heart. Looking at him as he sat, I weighed him to an ounce, as if in scales. He was clothed from head to foot in prejudice, ignorance, utter mistake about almost everything; but his clothes were not the man, they could be changed, would wear out of themselves. Upon the whole, I knew no man intrinsically more valuable, I could not afford to lose him. More than that, he could not afford to lose himself.

By slow degrees he told me of how he was situated in many things, and it was disagreeable enough. Then I offset what he said by certain matters wherein I too was sorely tried. "At last it is," I said to him, " only temporary circumstance. Ten years hence to-day's circumstance will have perished; just now it is scaffolding about us, — scaffolding essential, Heaven knows why, to our upbuilding. You, Ross, are more than the war, more than the region in which you live, more than the miserable politics in which you are mixed up." He had informed me enough concerning his present position for me to say that much. He looked at me, stroking his mustache with a hand which, I now observed, was slashed across the back with a scar.

"You are Guernsey still," he said. "Has n't the war beaten your metaphysics out of you yet? Theorizing still! I never could do it, never will. For my life I cannot help seeing things as they are. My eyes are too strong to wear glasses. Why can you not be sensible, practical?"

"That is a fact," said I; "let's go down to dinner." There is no better cooking in Christendom than at that hotel, and I am sure Ross enjoyed his dinner; men of his health and unceasing exercise always do. We took our time to it, and by the end of dessert we were back again to and with each other as we were when he lay wounded under my care during the war. When he lounged, at last, in my easy-chair up-stairs, cigar in hand, we had got back pretty much to what we were when together in college.

"You know my opinion of men in general, North, South, East, West," he said to me in course of conversation. "I wish I could delude myself about them as you do. Not until my imagination has mastery of my reason, is that possible. Not that you are a sentimentalist, Guernsey; we all know —" And he must needs go into the exaggerations in which Steven Trent, too, was apt to deal, as to my powers.

"Thank you," I interrupted him, "but I am too practical a man to puff myself up or to be puffed up. Measured by the money I have made, I am next to nobody. Estimated by any influence I have exerted, my severest critic, alas, cannot rate me lower than I do myself. But let us speak of other things."

"The trouble with you, Guernsey," Ross persisted, "is that you will not confine yourself to iron facts. It may be from excess of force in you, but you will not keep to the solid soil. So long as you walk the earth I can keep company with you, but you are sure to leave your legs and take to your wings, and then we part. No, Guernsey, I can't fool myself about things as you do. I hate to undeceive you. It is like corrupting a child."

"Never mind me; go on," I said.

He did so at length. I verily believe it was the first time he had talked unreservedly to any one since we parted. He told me everything that had hap-

pened to him in the chaos which came upon his
region with the collapse of the Confederacy. My
purpose does not lie in that direction in these pages.
It is with Ross. Urwoldt, and those associated with
him, that I have exclusively to do. It would be
worse than useless to detail what he told me. He
had more to say, and it was newer to me, than if he
were just ashore from a long sojourn across the Atlantic. Never mind the items; the upshot of all was
his deepening disgust with his kind.

"As you know," he summed up, "I could not live
in Ocklawahaw. Especially since Persis and Rachel
left, what business had I there? When the people
where I now live urged me into politics, I told. them
they would be sorry for it. Guernsey," Ross added,
"you can have no idea how, from the start, I talked.
to my people. If I had not fought as I did, they
would have hung me." And, with that, he went over
again the miserable catalogue of folly and blunder
against which he had striven, and striven in vain.
"That is one reason I am here," he wound up. "I
have come like a doctor outside of a sick room to get
a breath of fresh air. They are a noble people, but
it is too close down there!" And he drew in a deep
breath as he sat. "Not that it is not worse up here,"
he hastened to say; "but, then, with these people I
have nothing to do."

"Yes," I assented. "We are not as lazy as your
people are, but we are too sharp, too greedy for gain.
You have the freedmen, and here we have the dregs
of Europe. With you political murders prevail; here

are the murders of unborn children, brutal massacres
for gold; lust, revenge, rum, have their victims.   The
community fails with you to punish crime; here
criminals escape by the use of money or politics, even
when convicted.   When I was a little boy I remember," I added, "standing on tiptoe at the kitchen
table to see our old fat cook make cake.   She would
roll out the yellow dough, and then cut it into shapes
for the oven with tin cake-cutters, round, square,
heart-shaped, star-shaped.   Ross," I urged, "into whatever shape we happen to be cut we are all from the
same dough.   But I must say that I think, on the
whole, we up here have the advantage of you."

"In situation.   Yes," Ross assented; "the highway
from Europe to Asia lies across the continent and
past your doorsteps.   If we are off the track to the
southward, so is Canada to the northward.   There is
no merit in situation."

"Of course not.   But it is not merely that, as you
say, the Broadway of the planet runs through our
part of the country; it is because the ventilation is
better!   Whatever topic comes up here is so thoroughly discussed, is so severely thrashed and sifted,
that we get, at last, down to the clean grain of whatever is good in it.   A man ought to climb to where
he can take a wide look all around.   Pull your feet
out of the mud, old fellow, and try to get up toward
the way God looks at things."

"I don't believe in God," he growled.

"Very well," I said.   "Take the separate sections
of the globe as you do the manifold squares of the

multiplication table; bless you, the same arithmetical working runs through the whole." But I saw in his eyes how, as I said it, he was lying in wait for me.

"That is what I believe," he exclaimed. "That is what Buckle and Comte say, what every sensible man is coming to see. It is all — nations, religions, civilizations — merely a vast machine. Suns, planets, winds, waters, men, lower animals, vegetables, minerals, — all grind together, but parts of the same complexity of wheels, and wheels within wheels. We originate, we live our brief moment, we perish alike. The greatest, the only certain, thing I know of is the sublime order of nature; the meanest of all things is man. Not that I do not recognize the intellect by which he comprehends nature; it is the miserable meannesses which invariably accompany this of which I speak."

"Of course. And," I said, "what then?"

"If a man is ambitious, let him enjoy himself that way. Most likely he prefers," Ross added, "to eat and drink and die. Every man to his taste." My companion suddenly checked himself. "What is the use of talking?" he said. "I am tired of talk; only do not try to fool me at least with fancies of vice and virtue, God or devil or soul. I live upon what I see and know. I am a — Positivist is the word, isn't it?"

"You know nothing about men; what," I asked, "can you know about God? Don't be such a bigot. Don't disgust me with *you*, Ross!"

He looked up at me as I stood over him where he

sat. In his silent way he was very angry. I saw that. What a fool I was to discuss such topics, any topics! My friend was so chafed by long years of disappointment that little was left of him beyond the original savage; so to speak, he was worn down to that. His ancestors learned, ages before his day, to grow cool also as they grew hot, cool that they might strike, when they did strike, to the heart; and Ross, I long ago had observed, grew slower and darker as he became more angry. He arose to go, arose very deliberately. If he did go, we would be done with each other forever.

"Ross," I said, and, reaching up, I grasped his shoulder, looking with as bright a face as I could into his sullen eyes, — "Ross," I repeated, "don't go. I want to tell you about the young ladies."

"Young ladies? Ah, it is Persis and Rachel, you mean." And it gave me a new knowledge of him, the coldness with which it was said.

Ross was the most aboriginal man I ever knew. His education neither altered nor obscured that. There are crystals which must be dug up, broken in two, and the surface ground smooth, before the native angles and colors can be seen. So with Ross; education and trouble had ground him until the nature of the man, hard and brilliant as crystal, was revealed, not changed.

Yes, I got a deeper glimpse into the man in the coldness he showed as to the two girls he had known so long. It was to me as to the Arctic sailor is the lifting of the fog which reveals new regions of boundless ice. But such a sailor knows nothing of the boiling geysers which may be at the heart of those realms of winter, and what I did not know then was, that it was the very intensity of his interest in regard to Persis which held him silent. Really that was his sole business there, to see her. During the whole war, through his growing disgust with everything else, his love for her was the one hope of his life; so much so that, brave in everything beside, he was a coward in this. He was positively afraid to see her, to ask after her. Who could say what changes the long absence might not have wrought in her? Most probably she had, like his mother, gone the way of her sex, and fallen into some womanish whim which had ruined her for him. She must have studied herself by this time· into who knows what affectations, new-fangled notions, bookish eccentricities! He had not seen her since she was a girl, an Ocklawahaw girl, and now she was a woman, a city lady, an educated lady, while he had lived in camp, among savage men. Moreover, how could she fail, by this time, to have fallen in love with some college professor, some long-haired monkey of a music-teacher, — who could say?

I did not know then what he thought, but I went on to tell him how faithfully the young ladies had toiled, how greatly they were improved. He stood before me as I did so, yielding to me from head to foot the same motionless attention which fastened upon mine his steadfast eyes. Not one word had he to make in reply, but he could not hide from me how pleased he was. The next day, and afterward, it was of Rachel he spoke, never of Persis. The same afternoon I went with Ross to show him where they lived, asking him, as I did so, " Do you happen to know a Major McAllister ? "

"Yes," he said; "I know at least of a man so named. He was an official under Governor Beauchamp when Secession began. When the convention of his State deposed the Governor, McAllister disappeared. It was known that he went over to the Federals."

"It is the same man. He held," I said, "some appointment in the army which enabled him to grant or refuse permits to wagon cotton through the lines. It was a post of great trust, and was given him for the sake of his friend the Governor. Let me tell you a noble thing of him. One day, during the war, a well-known adventurer came into his office, to secure a permit. There were grave reasons for hesitation in his case, and Major McAllister told him he would consider the matter and let him know next day. The other man bowed, looked at him in a meaning way, laid a brown paper parcel on his desk, and was about leaving, when the Major beckoned to him to halt. The room was full of army people. The Major opened the parcel before them all, found it to be, as he had conjectured, a roll of greenbacks. Springing to his feet, he hurled it with an oath at the head of the one who tried so shamelessly to bribe him, and ordered him never to show his face there again. The bills flew all over the office, — many thousand dollars, I was told. The man gathered them up, and was not seen again. It made quite a sensation at the time, the army correspondents were full of it. I am glad to know the Major."

" Is he here ?" Ross asked indifferently.

" That is the reason I spoke of it. He is a medium-sized man," I said, "middle-aged, somewhat bald, with side whiskers, and the appearance in general of a well-to-do banker. It is because he boards at the same house with Persis and Rachel that I tell you of it. Mrs. Trent hints to me that he is showing devoted attention to the young ladies. He knew Rachel when she was a child. Of course he honors her for the sake of her father, with whom he was associated so closely in those dark and trying times. It is said that he is quite wealthy. I think he is a stock-broker in the city. Mrs. Trent has a woman's keen scent in such matters, and thinks it quite likely he will propose to one of the ladies."

I did not say which. My reason in telling Ross of this bit of gossip was as I said ; only I had another in addition. But his bronzed face told no tales. He said nothing.

" It was noble in him, was n't it ? to refuse the bribe, especially as the war had stripped him of everything. I admire such a man," I remarked with warmth.

" Do you ? He is rich, is he ? Guernsey," Ross said dryly, " I chance to know that the scene you describe did take place. Alas, my trusting friend, it was but a bit of melodrama arranged beforehand. It succeeded. The spotless virtue of McAllister was placed thereby so entirely beyond suspicion that from that day he grew rich fast, very fast."

"Here is the house," I said by this time. "You will find the ladies in at this hour, I hope. I will not go in. You will have much to talk about." And I left him upon the step waiting for admittance.

CHAPTER XXI.

NOT YET.

IT may be supposed that I was eager to see my friend when he came that night to our room at the hotel. What had taken place was not written in his face, at least, and he fell, almost as soon as he had lighted his cigar and settled himself in his seat, into talking, to my surprise, of Rachel, always of Rachel.

"I had," he said gravely, "to tell her the details of her father's troubles since she saw him last." As he smoked, Ross told me the whole story of the last days of Governor Beauchamp.

On leaving Ocklawahaw before the war began, as has been described, the old politician entered upon another of the many intermittent stages of his career. The astute wire-workers knew well enough what they were about when they returned in triumph from the Reservation bringing the exiled statesman with them. He was made Governor in a whirlwind of enthusiasm. But it was the old story over again with him of alternate popularity and yet greater unpopularity following swiftly thereupon. In this case there was good reason for it. Hardly had he been inaugurated before the secession of the South came. During the cam-

paign Governor Beauchamp had dealt in generalities.
No man could have been more eloquent than he as to
the usurping purposes in general of the North, that is,
if this, he said, and that, and the other were so. But
when Governor, and called on to take an active part
for secession, he first hesitated, then halted, then engaged in vigorous resistance. To the utmost of his
ability he threw his ponderous person against the
whole movement. Not a drop of liquor did he touch.
There was no indolence now; never had he shown
the energy he now put forth. Wherever he was,
whether in his parlor, at the Governor's mansion,
talking at the door of the post-office with a group of
trembling adherents about him and plenty of scowling
foes hovering around, perched upon the counter of a
friendly store with every straggler along the streets
dropping in to listen to what he had to say on the
supreme topic of the time, whittling, as he sat in the
Executive Department, at whatever white pine or bit
of red cedar he could lay hands upon, — from the
beginning to the end did he pour out, in his slow
and drawling fashion, one unceasing tide of anecdote,
argument, ridicule, denunciation against secession,
with prophecy exceedingly definite as to its certain
and disastrous ending. But he was only one man
against many thousand. Deposed from office, he retired to his plantation, and lived there for a year or
two in deepest obscurity and ignominy. His intense
hatred to secession may have furnished alcohol in
itself more than sufficient, for he never drank again.
There was something unspeakably affecting in the

devotion of the old hero to the Union he had always loved so well. Cast out by those who had once flattered and fawned upon him, his white hairs streaming as it were upon the midnight tempest of the war raging about him, absolutely alone in his unshaken faithfulness to what he regarded, against every personal advantage, as true and right, he was as King Lear bearing in his arms the dead Cordelia. Not a man in his region as large of stature, as vigorous, seemingly, and notwithstanding his years, as he, yet the pure agony of the thing was too much for him. He hoped against hope; with every breath he predicted the destruction of the Confederacy; but, when the cause he so detested seemed sure of success, he could endure it no longer. In his devotion to the Union he seemed to have forgotten the existence even of his daughter, and died at last of a broken heart.

It was after his death that Ross contrived to wring enough money out of the neglected plantation to remit to the daughter; for she was the only heir. Let it be added that, with the downfall of secession, the Governor entered, all the more that he was dead, upon a greater popularity than ever, and one which promises, in the pages of history, to endure forever.

Ross rehearsed the story to me as he had to Rachel. "That man, McAllister," he went on, "will use his old-time companionship with the Governor to advance himself with her. It is natural that she should forget everything now, except the really grand and noble traits of her father, and McAllister, the rascal, will profit by it."

My friend should not have evaded me in my desire to know how he was pleased with the changes in Rachel and Persis, if I had known then, as I did afterward, the depth of his interest in one of them. It may have been intended to throw me off from learning this; for he went on to speak of the condition of things in the State in which he now lived, and of which the old Governor had been the alternate idol and abhorrence. That led me to urge upon him to use his popularity, as one who had fought as he had done, for the best interests of the State, now sorely in need of wise leaders; although I would much rather have talked of Persis instead.

From the moment of his coming I could not but see how shy he was in speaking to me of her, nor could I bring him to do so while he was with me. He told me instead, of his plans, so far as he had any, for, like everybody else in his region, all business for some time to come was broken up. The fact is, for the present, my friend was, although he said nothing to me about it, an almost penniless man. There was reason enough in that for holding himself aloof for the time from even Persis. He was in no condition to talk to any one of marriage, nor could he tell when he would be. Since I have come to know things, I am very sure it must have drained him for the time of his last cent to have made the long journey to see her. But it was little he said to me about her or himself, and in a day or two he had gone. But I could not understand why he seemed to be so reluctant to allude to Persis; it was as if there was something in *me* which prevented!

I was unusually busy those days. In such intervals of my hurried life as I could get, I wrote — some of it on the cars, most of it in hospitals — such a book as the times prompted. When Ross arrived it was passing through the press. Now, a thing looks in print very different from what it does in manuscript. You may be very comfortable in your chosen apartment while the blinds are shut and the curtains are down; but putting your scrawls into print is like tearing open shutter and curtain, and letting in the pitiless sunshine; the revelation of litter and flying dust is remorseless. It was this prevented me from seeing my friends for some time after Ross departed. As soon as I could get away from my work, I called upon Mrs. Trent.

"I have understood," she said soberly, "why you did not call before." Her general aspect was as if I had lost a father or a mother since she saw me last, except that she could not condole with me as openly. There was a tender sympathy in her silence, an avoidance as of something which must be painful to me. More than once, when I spoke of Ross or of the young ladies, she lifted pitying eyes at me, and proceeded to tell me how Jean had hurt her hand, or some recent and surprising smartness of little Guernsey.

"I happened to be with them," she remarked at last, and when she could escape the topic no longer, — "with Persis, I mean, and Rachel, when Colonel Urwoldt called." Mrs. Trent would not have been a woman had she not been more eager to speak about

that than anything; but she did so hesitatingly, as
if she feared to pain me. "Knowing how busy Persis
always is," she said by piecemeal, "I never go up to
their room. That day I was with them in the parlor,
about to leave after a short visit, — they are generally
so busy, — when the door-bell rang. Rachel was looking out of the window, Persis was unusually bright
and well. She was telling me what she intended to
do. A fine situation as teacher is soon to be vacant,
and she was making every effort to secure it. She is
a remarkable girl, Mr. Guernsey, but already too
tensely strung by temperament, and our atmosphere
exhilarates her like wine. Dr. Trent says that, considering the excitements of the city, the air is too
stimulating for enduring health. I have never seen
her looking as well. Rachel is the picture of health,
in her way, you know. Persis was positively brilliant. She seems to develop substance, too. I hope
so; she is always so excited, enthusiastic. Rachel
must have seen to it, for Persis was dressed that day
plainly, but in admirable taste. Her cheeks were all
in a glow of hope of securing the situation; her lips
were like scarlet, her eyes were very bright. She has
fine eyes, Mr. Guernsey."

"Very fine," I assented, not altoget'..r understanding why my friend mentioned it as if it were a
calamity.

"I think she has improved more than she would
have done had she been born here." My companion
did not lift her eyes from the fancy work she was doing as she said it.

"Yes," I assented; "it is as when one has to run before taking a leap, it gives that much more impulse. It is better for her that she was born and had lived so long in Ocklawahaw. The newness of everything here, the contrast with all that went before, is itself an influence upon her. It develops a rosebush to transplant it, you know."

"Yes; she has an energy, a fire, beyond what I hoped for when she first came. You *do* think her a really remarkable woman?" Mrs. Trent looked at me as a mother might at an ailing child.

"I have not met a lady whom I admire more, nor," I added, "of whose future I am more confident. A new order of your sex is coming upon the stage, my dear madam, a race of more highly educated women than has yet been seen, and she is growing to be as fine an instance of it as I know."

Mrs. Trent gave a little shiver, or was it a shudder? "She has always seemed to be so interested in you and in your books, Mr. Guernsey!" And my friend worked steadily on, her eyes upon her work.

"Much more than I or they deserve. It is her kindness, her enthusiasm for books in general. I have enjoyed her society very much. But you were there," I asked, "when Colonel Urwoldt called?"

"I told you long ago how much the Rev. Mr. Adair admires her. It must," said Mrs. Trent, stopping to think, "have been five, no, eight months ago, that I told you about that." It was as if she were defending herself. "You *do* remember that I told you, Mr. Guernsey?"

"I do. Everybody knows that. But," I demanded, "you have not told me about — "

"The visit of Colonel Urwoldt?" Mrs. Trent interrupted me. Evidently she was in haste now to tell me and be done with it. "As I said, Rachel was standing looking out of the window. She is a fine girl, Mr. Guernsey. In her way, you must consent to it, she is also a very excellent girl. She is more matronly in her ways than Persis. I am afraid she does not care for literature in general, not as much so as Persis. You find her interesting company, do you not ? "

"Certainly I do," I replied, and my friend added, —

"So far as physical development goes, I think she is very beautiful, more beautiful than Persis. And, then, she has such excellent sense. It is a pity she does not take to books, but then—" There was almost a pathos in Mrs. Trent's manner as she pleaded with me for Rachel. "Mr. McAllister," she continued, "almost worships her. He is an old friend of her father's. They say he is very rich. I am told he takes her driving very often. He is getting up a superb monument to the memory of Governor Beauchamp. Rachel showed me some of the designs. Persis is full of enthusiasm over the Governor's last days. Yes," Mrs. Trent weighed the matter slowly, and settled it with a conclusive nod forever, " Rachel is much more beautiful than Persis! It may not be a purely intellectual beauty, but she is the most evenly balanced girl I know. You are not going, Mr. Guernsey ? Wait a moment and Steven will be in. But I was telling you," and Mrs. Trent also arose, "of the day Colonel Urwoldt called. As I told you, Persis was in full career, laughing, talking of her plans, her face turned from the door toward me, when the bell rang and the stupid servant showed the visitor into the parlor without a word. I saw a dark-visaged, handsome, stern-faced military man standing there, and touched the arm of Persis. I wish," Mrs. Trent said it very sadly, "you could have seen her face as she turned and saw who it was. I am sorry to tell you, but I feel that I ought."

"What do you mean?" My face must have expressed something more than I intended, for I fancied that the eyelids of my friend grew moist.

"How could I help seeing it?" she said. "How can I help telling it now? As soon as Persis saw him her eyes fairly glittered, her hands went out toward him, she made a joyous movement forward, checked herself, flushed, turned pale, was terribly confused. It looked as if all her years of education were gone in an instant, as if she was only a poor little country school-girl again! And the moment before she seemed," Mrs. Trent said indignantly, "to be so erect and strong."

Dr. Trent came in at the moment, and his wife made no attempt to detain me, when I left soon after.

But even good Mrs. Trent did not know everything. It was Persis she was most concerned for when I saw her next. "I cannot understand you men!" she said to me as sharply as if I had been doing something wrong. She was mortified, angry. "There is no understanding you," she said, "no comprehending one of you!"

"Is that so?" I sadly assented. Little Guernsey was standing beside me with his wonted grasp upon my trousers, and I lifted him between us as a shield, kissed him and set him down. "Why will you cut his curls off?" I complained. "Is it to keep him sheared of all mystery! Poor little fellow, your head is as round as a billiard ball."

"Why did you not bring Colonel Urwoldt to see us?" Mrs. Trent eyed me with suspicion. "I gave him a special invitation to do so that day before I left him to the girls. And Steven was his classmate. I had arranged to have Persis and Rachel meet you at tea. Why was it?"

"He would not come, ma'am," I said, humbly enough for the two; "events have soured him a little. He does not feel at home among us yet. But we shall see him again. Unless I am mistaken, he will take a high position. In his own region he is considered the ablest, the most energetic of men."

"Mr. Guernsey," Mrs. Trent spoke in an injured manner, "I had hoped you had known me long enough to make a friend of me. Do you suppose I am blind? I know you, sir, better than you know yourself. No man has a more loving heart. You have worked hard, have been tossed from post to pillar, are cut off from your own home. I know no gentleman who is more domestic than yourself, more keenly sensitive to the joys of a home life. Nothing is more natural! I would have been astonished, under the circumstances, if you had not!"

"Had not?" I had the aspect of an idiot; inwardly I knew only too well what she meant.

"Had not fallen in love with her. It was natural you should come to love her." Mrs. Trent grew rosy red, with temper too, as if defying somebody. "What could *be* more natural? Persis is of an ardent nature. She worships genius. And then you have been more than a brother to her since she came. Do I not know how highly she esteems you? Rachel is as good, as beautiful, as excellent a girl as lives, but Persis can sympathize with you!"

"My dear madam," I gasped, my cheeks uncomfortably warm, "you forget. Colonel Urwoldt — "

"Colonel Urwoldt!" The name became an epithet as she spoke it. "That is your weakness, Mr. Guernsey. You can no more appreciate yourself than if you were a child of three years old. Colonel Urwoldt! Is he, ignorant, uncultured, a mere soldier as he is, — is *he* fitted to make Persis happy? Mr. Guernsey," the eyes of the good lady lighted up with the sudden intuition, "*that* is the reason he dared not bring affairs to a point. He saw how superior she was; he dared not, dared not!"

"You are prejudiced, madam." I hastened to say that at least before I made my escape. "Colonel Urwoldt is nearer my idea of the original man, the native gentleman, than" — I saw in Mrs. Trent's eyes that she demanded exception to be made for her husband, but I wouldn't do it — "than any man I know! He has been disappointed in people. Unless I mistake, he has set his whole life upon Miss Persis!" It was said at a venture, for I did not dream then how much this was so. "If he is dark and stern," I went on, "he is also the sincerest, most self-sacrificing of men. At heart he abhorred slavery more, because he knew it better, because it was his own region it cursed, than any one even in this city dreamed of doing. If he could have done so, he would infinitely rather have fought against it and for the Union; that I do know! As it is, he is like a man in a swamp who has struggled, is struggling desperately to plant his foot upon solid ground. If you but knew how hungrily he yearns toward what he has not!" Mrs. Trent looked at me in amazement I spoke so warmly, but how little either of us imagined the tragic facts of the case! "The day is coming," I added, "when he will be one of the best-known men in the land. Persis will be proud of him!"

There was no use of saying anything. Mrs. Trent had fallen back into the arctic intrenchments of a woman's sense of infallibility, in comparison to which that of the Pope is a trifle, and she smiled pityingly upon me as I tried to break away. But she added, —

"I will not detain you a moment. And I know that Persis does have, as I said, a certain girlish feeling for your friend. But that is not her true self. She has really outgrown all that. Consider, Mr. Guernsey, that she is one of the most accomplished of women, and she is developing into something higher

every day. It is to you she is suited; she will be a
living and powerful impulse to you as long as you
live. From the first, Steven and myself have set our
heart upon it. You owe it to yourself, you owe it to
her."

Never had I seen Mrs. Trent so much in earnest.
I was half out of the door when she laid her hand
upon my shoulder. "So much is involved," she said.
"I have always been to you as your own sister. If
you will tell me one thing, I will never trouble you
again. Mr. Guernsey, solemnly now, have you not
fallen in love?"

Only a woman like Mrs. Trent would have asked
it. Years before I had been tempted to a wild passion for a Mrs. Thirlmore, a married woman, but that
was a fever from which I recovered. I suppose I *am*
a child, for now I *had* fallen in love, for really the
first time in my life, as desperately in love as a man
can! I do not know what Mrs. Trent saw in my face,
but in the act of my leaving she kissed me impul-
sively upon the forehead. It was the woman in her,
not the sister, but that which is most purely and intensely the woman of a woman, — the mother in
her, — which made her do it.

"I knew it!" she said in triumph, and let me go.

CHAPTER XXII.

PICNIC.

NOT another syllable passed between Mrs. Trent and myself upon the subject which had interested us so much. I think she was sorry she had gone as far as she had, for she tutored her eyes, too, that nothing might remind me afterward of how she had forced my secret from me. I think she had a more tender interest in me, as in Persis, thereafter; but she was doubly careful, was comparatively cold toward us, the more effectually to make us feel at ease.

Persis and Rachel seemed to be about the same. Speaking of the last, it is due her to say that she was, as Mrs. Trent said, improved in every sense since coming among us; she was more refined, if not more placid. The contour and color of her cheeks, the deepening interest and attention in her serene eyes, the very poise of her rounded person, was reaching a repose, too, of manner which was to her sterling sense as the motionless transparency of the water of a little loch, such as one sees among the hills of Scotland, is to its granite bottom.

Persis was developing, also, along the lines of her nature. When it first occurred to me that she was not unlike a racer of the best blood, I cast out the suggestion with scorn. And yet no better illustration has come to me since. I have a fondness for a horse of the purest breed and training such as I have for the sea, because both are in unceasing motion. It is not the sleek sides, the arched neck, the delicate pasterns, the clear eyes, the fine ears, the thin nostrils, of this animal, the next of all to man, which I care for, except as these indicate and answer so easily to its excess of life. There are times when you see the speed of a spirited horse ; you can always feel it struggling against your rein. Now, with deepest respect for Miss Paige, I could no more refrain from recognizing this resemblance in her than I could from noting the likeness of a fox to one man, a jackal to another, a leopard to — Ross Urwoldt, we will say. She possessed a sinewy, even intense intellect, to begin with. Her hard life with her grandfather had developed it, and from too early a period. The long waiting in Ocklawahaw had deepened her purpose while it quickened her impatience. Now that she had opportunity, she had given herself to that opportunity with what would have been called excess had it been an affair of dress, fashion, going into society, instead of education. Moreover, she grew by what she fed upon, until she was coming to feel that a certain repression, almost suppression of herself, was at once her hardest and most essential duty. It was this that I noticed in her, toward me especially, after the visit of Colonel Urwoldt.

"I think that even Rachel has studied too hard,"

Mrs. Trent said to me one July morning, a month or two afterward. "You, too, are worn out, Mr. Guernsey. . Dr. Trent cannot take the time, but your book is out now; we need a vacation, all of us. If you will take us to the Island, we will go. You know that you can imagine yourself at your own island home again when you are there, and this island is not two hours away."

Of course I assented, and it was thus that we came to go together upon the picnic of which I am now to speak. Good Mrs. Trent took along a large hamper, and her colored coachman to carry it; but I knew that she took with her, also, some leading motive in having the girls and myself with her, which I refrained from looking into; like the closed hamper to my incipient appetite, it satisfied me, for the present, merely to know that it was a good and sufficient motive, and that it was there.

The island to which Mrs. Trent referred was a dozen or so of acres of rock and sand and straggling grass and huckleberry-trees, down the harbor. As yet it had escaped the eye of enterprise; not a hotel was erected there, not a steamer touched at it. A lighthouse stood upon its highest point, but I doubt if a kid slipper had ever pressed its lonely sands. Dr. Trent and I discovered it long before when upon a fishing excursion, but we had sworn the skipper of the sailing-boat which took us there to tell no man of its advantages; and it was he, his boat scrubbed for the purpose, who carried us there on the occasion of which I am now speaking.

By agreement we met on the appointed hour at the boat after a very early breakfast and before the sun was up, — Mrs. Trent and her children, Miss Rachel, Miss Persis, and myself. Already it gave promise of being a perfect day.

"I knew it," Mrs. Trent said, as we settled ourselves, hamper, coachman, and all, in the boat, and pushed off from the wharf, — "knew it as soon as I woke. One feels what sort of day it is before the shutters are thrown open."

She was right. There are some mornings when one does not like to be too closely looked at before ten o'clock by one's most intimate friend, when you refrain from bestowing upon the one next you at the breakfast-table more than a glance and a curt good-morning. The weather is to be reckoned by what it does within rather than without you, and the measure of your inner sunshine is that you love to see and speak to everybody, that you see clearly, and do not shrink from being seen. Nobody said so, but I think we all felt this as we took a look at each other and then at the sea opening out before us. For some time we were almost entirely silent in our contentment with the hour. There was breeze enough to fill our sails, but the water was smooth, the sky clear. Overcoats and shawls were in use, but the coolness was not more than enough to give edge to our pleasure.

"I dare say," Persis remarked at last, "that the novelty of being up and out at such an hour has something to do with it."

"Yes," Rachel said slowly; "it reminds me of how

it is with me when I am asleep. I always sleep sweetly, but I love to wake about midnight, and change my position, and go to sleep again."

The eyes of Jean grew rounder as she listened to the words. "O Miss Rachel!" she said, in accents of reproof, and the laugh which followed helped to wake us up.

"What I meant," Rachel explained with rising color, "was that one likes a change. In little things, I mean. You love to walk after sitting, to sit after walking, to rest after studying. I enjoy it."

"And to study after resting. Vacation is only begun," Persis went on, "and I am already looking forward with pleasure to books again. See how crisp the water is!" Little Guernsey, holding firmly to me as he knelt upon the seat, was looking where she pointed, at the foam made by the boat as our speed increased.

"Is it soda-water?" he asked of me in confidence; but Jean, on the other side of me, heard it, and her laugh had in it the same freshness as of sea and air. For what is the peculiar charm of the dawn of a beautiful day but its likeness to childhood? There was a tender veil upon the coming clearness, a creamy hue on sky and water. It may be because one rises refreshed by sleep, because every sense is hungrier and more sensitive at that hour; but nature meets you then as if it also had awakened from darkness and slumber to a new life. There is a tremor in earth and air as of eagerness to enjoy and be enjoyed. The colors of nature, lavender, ashes of roses, dewy

pink, were delicate and variable like those of infancy.
Toward noon our sunburned skipper would have
something to say, but even he was as silent now as
the coachman beside his hamper in the prow. The
silence and the colors seemed to go together; it was
an enjoyment as delicate as the changing hues about
us. We tacked this way and that, as we went down
the harbor, passing now a fisherman's scrap of an
island upon the one hand, and then a fort with cannon threatening and sentinels pacing the ramparts on
the other, and upon all rested the same silence as of
sleep slowly passing into wakening. Fishing-boats
sailed by us coming in from the sea, now singly, now
in little fleets; but these too were as silent as if in a
picture. Then the glow in the east grew rapidly
from gray to gold, giving us the royal reason thereof
in the sun rising out of the sea. As if some pro-
hibition was lifted therewith, we laughed and talked
freely enough until we reached, and landed upon, our
island.

On the instant we were Robinson Crusoes, every
soul of us, with the peculiarity of pleasure which
belongs to nothing else, and we climbed the rocks
with the old, old· enthusiasm which is ever new.
After that we visited the keeper of the light, climbed
his tower, and inspected his lanterns.

"He is so lonely," said Persis as we went, "that he
will be delighted to see us. We will be a joy to him,
a glad surprise."

She at least should have been such to him, so overflowing was she with an almost feverish enjoyment:

but she was mistaken; we were nothing of the kind; indeed, I fear we were little more to him than the sea-gulls. To us the island was a temporary Eden. To him it was so many rocks, such and such strips of sand covered and uncovered by the tide, a few stunted trees, so much work tending his lamps, so many dollars' salary. He had been there for many years; had grown tall and lank and silent as his tower. We were conscious of being frivolous in comparison, as we moved about him asking questions. Evidently he despised our laughter; what was there to laugh at? We could arouse no enthusiasm in him by our questions as to the terrible storms he had experienced, he had grown so used to everything. The only smile which broke like a ray of sunshine upon the wintry coast of his aspect was when, before we left, we shared our dinner with him.

"It would kill me to live here, but," Persis said, "it would suit Rachel admirably."

"Except that it would break Major McAllister's heart, we might," Mrs. Trent laughed, "marry Rachel to the lighthouse-keeper. He is so useful a man. Rachel might love him for that."

"He would do as well as Mr. Adair." Rachel said it with all simplicity, but it was something new to me, the way in which Persis colored, while Mrs. Trent laughed so heartily that I asked who Mr. Adair was. As if I did not know!

"He is keeper of another lighthouse," she explained; "but *his* lantern is of a newer fashion, and revolves more rapidly!"

I fear there was a spice of spite in Mrs. Trent, for I knew very well — everybody knew *him* — that Mr. Adair was a clergyman of a more liberal school than hers, and who, as I had long heard, was paying Persis much attention, being himself unmarried.

"I am hungry," Persis suggested; "suppose we eat our dinner."

We made the entire round of the island, first, that we had resolved upon, peering into every nook and cranny as we went. Then we dined upon the highest point of rock. Our skipper must have made a satisfactory disposition of the share of dinner we sent him, for we could see how sound asleep he was afterward on the deck of his boat anchored out from the shore. Jean and little Guernsey were off fishing in the landlocked pools under the care of the coachman, after he had himself eaten his dinner, and taken to the man in the lighthouse, with our compliments, what was left of Mrs. Trent's superabundant supply of ham and tongue, corned beef and jelly, pies and cakes. "I think he will despise our sardines," Persis said. "They are an insult, they are such little fish, to him and to his ocean. But why is it," she added, when we had settled ourselves, after eating, upon the rocks, — "why is it that one enjoys a rock so when the sea is dashing against it? Is it a sense of security as against danger?"

"Yes," I replied; "but we enjoy it most because it is the contrast of stillness and solidity with eternal motion and variety."

As I said it I glanced from Persis to Rachel, from

Rachel to Persis. The latter was all the more energetic
in that she was taller, but weighed little more than
when she came to the city. Her eyes seemed larger,
if her cheeks were a trifle thinner. By a strange
blending of the two, she was paler and yet more
brilliant of color than I had observed before. Although she was evidently tired, she could not be at
rest. She had on a neatly fitting dress of some drab
material, but she threw aside her hat at the earliest
moment, and was reckless as to her dress in clamber-
ing among the rocks, her hair breaking from its confinement as she went. Nor was she without plenty
to say.

" You know I had not seen the ocean until I came
East," she explained ; " to see ? every day is the best
part of my life here. Rachel says that she could live
in Ocklawahaw again ; I could not. It is so small
there, so close, so shut in and dull and dead ! I feel
as if I began to live when I came here ; everything
going before is like a blank."

I saw Mrs. Trent looking at me from behind where
Persis stood, for she could not sit still — Persis, I
mean — for an instant. What Mrs. Trent said with
her eyes was, " She is growing very pretty, is n't
she ? " What I meant by my nod was, " Yes, she
is indeed. But she will be much more so some
day." I was aware next that the question had gone
out of Mrs. Trent's eyes, and the pitying look at me,
the hovering look, had entered instead. I turned to
glance at Rachel.

" I prefer to walk around these big boulders instead of climbing over them," she had said from the outset, and now she remained where she was when she first sat down to dinner. I do not think her dress was of a finer material than that of Persis, but there was greater care displayed, I should say, in the ruffs about her throat, the cuffs about her quiet hands, the nameless pleatings and arrangements of ribbons. There is a perpetual change about such things, a diversity of cut and color, but I class it with the bewildering variety one sees among flowers, leaf and petal, stamen and pistils. I enjoy it, but I would break down if I were a dry-goods clerk and had to name and put a price upon it inch by inch. Whatever her dress was, Rachel had composed it carefully around her; it had an almost liquid flow about her person as she sat, her hands in her lap, looking out upon the sea with calm eyes. Yes, she was becoming, as Mrs. Trent remarked, so far as face and form went, more beautiful than Persis, and she merely sat and smiled and listened, when Persis, incited by Mrs. Trent, began badgering me about my books. No one would have thought or spoken about them anywhere else; it was part of the picnic freedom, and a going back to our childhood on the part of us every one, to allude to them at all. We had simply nothing else just then to do.

"You have a bad habit of changing the subject when any one speaks about your books," Mrs. Trent said. "It is not polite, is it, Persis? Besides, we are off among the rocks, far away from people."

"If you will count," I said, "it is every seventh

wave which comes against this rock with the greatest force. There is rhythm in nature, and seven is the number of perfection. Count! One, two, three, four, five, six waves — look out for the next — whish! boom! Did you ever notice it before? Keep off the edge of the rock, Miss Persis; it is slippery."

"Which is not the question," the young lady observed. "Tell us about what you have written."

There may have been some small conspiracy, but there was such persistence in the matter that I said at last, "Once for all I will tell you everything. I don't want to talk about my productions for this reason. When I begin at a book it is because I have a mustard-seed of an idea of something I want to say. It is a very small seed, microscopic, but it grows. You wouldn't believe it, knowing the result as you do, but, as I write, I fall into the absurdest infatuation. Day after day I tear away at it until it is ended. One becomes merely the secretary and slave of the men and women in the book, a hard-worked amanuensis whose very existence they ignore. They do what they please, say what they like; one has nothing to do with it except to write it out. Friends blame me for making my characters, as they call them, act in this way or the other. How can I help it! I have for them the yearning of a feeble and helpless parent. It pains me, shocks me, for them to do this and that. I know it is not artistic for them to act as they do. Moreover, I love them dearly, the worst of them the most, although they care nothing for me. As to controlling them, I never attempt to do so. There is the pleasure, as of a faithful slave, in toiling after them; that is all. I say as I work, Surely these people are living people, will live forever. Alas, as soon as I stop writing they are dead. So is my hope."

" I do not understand," Persis said. She had seated herself near me with an eagerness which had to do with something quite beyond what I was saying. " Your hope? What do you mean?" she asked.

" It is hard," I said, " for a mother when her baby boy turns out to be an idiot, and I suppose it was the wildness of my hope; but no man, not an author, can tell how bitterly I, at least, am disappointed in the baby of my brain when I come to get a square look at it! The disgust you have for your completed manuscript was deep enough. To compare small things to great, you remember how Sheridan wrote under the last line of his 'School for Scandal,' 'Thank God, I'm done with this detestable thing at last!' So with me in my poor way, my bitterest critics could not dislike my book as sincerely as I do, except that I have more pity than they, knowing, as I do, the ideal, and the effort toward it."

I talked very freely with my friends; but then I have very few intimate friends, exceeding few, and it is only with such that I can be said to talk at all. This was the first time I had spoken even to these of my books, and I determined it should be the last. So I added, —

" A writer must have enough of what is called the dramatic instinct to put himself in the place of his characters. But it is into the shoes of my unfriendliest critic I put my feet most easily. 'Dear enemy, if you only knew!' I say to him." And then I lifted an honest hand against the kind things the ladies were trying to say. "Being personal friends, you take an interest where," I said, "others care, of course, nothing at all. Do you remember what your ugliest rag doll was to you when you were children? To you it was alive, and, homely as it was, it was your own. So with me. Ah, if you did but know how real to me are my people — until they leave me. And then to see, as they go out into a hostile because clear-seeing world, how little they resemble what I intended them to be. They wander out, hand in hand, like noodles, when to me they were so real, so noble, so true! 'It is not your fault,' I cry after them; 'it is because I could not put you into the decent clothing of such language as would help people of the world to see you as you are. But I did my best. Good-by. I will hear of you no more.'" My friends only laughed at me, and asked me for "more."

"Do you see that cloud on the edge of the Atlantic?" I said. "It is smoke; the steamer which makes it is under the horizon."

"Is it? But what," Rachel said in her matter-of-fact way, "has the boat to do with your books?"

"We assert that only man has sinned. If so," I demanded, "why are those little crabs fighting as they are?" and I called the attention of all to the pool left by the tide in a fissure of the rocks at our feet; "are

I am sure that the others would have let me alone had Persis allowed it. Then, as always, she was so eager to know, to understand! During the time of her regular studies she worked as in a groove; but this was vacation; we were on an excursion for pleasure. She was out of the groove, but the excess of effort under which she had toiled so long and so hard remained. She was reacting already from rest; she was restless beyond her wont, nervous, excitable. "*I* would like to write books," she said.

"It must be such an easy thing to do," Rachel added.

"To men of great powers I dare say it is," I assented. "Not to lesser men. You can judge somewhat of a statue by the heaps of marble chippings and dust out of which it arises. So of a book. It is a little thing, but you have no idea out of what a mass of blotted manuscript and corrected proof it emerges. Only last week one of our best authors told me how he was annoyed by certain words which, in writing, he strove in vain to be rid of. They insisted upon coming to the tip of his pen in almost every line. Each writer has the parasitical words peculiar to himself." .

"As a rose has its own *aphidæ*," Persis suggested.

I made no reply; but what the distinguished author really said was: "Those accursed tautological phrases are to me what lice are to a beggar. I comb my manuscripts of them as well as I can, I comb what I have written over again in proof, and yet the first thing I see, when the volume comes to me from the press, is

that every page swarms with the infernal vermin
still!" I did not put it in that way to my friends,
but I drew comfort at the time from what he said.

"But the reward," ejaculated Persis, "think of the
reward!"

If Mrs. Trent or Rachel had said it, I would have
allowed the talk to end there. It was Persis, however, and there was that in her manner which made
me add: "Reward? Of course my knowledge as to
that is very limited. One thing every writer soon
comes to understand. He may have friends, may
make friends. These will like his productions, possibly, for the sake of the productions themselves. But
these like an author because they are like the author;
because he is a man of their own school of thought,
opinion, feeling, — above all, peculiar taste. What
he tries to say is merely what they, too, think and
feel, even if they do not say it. Alas, Miss Persis,
the world is painfully wide and diversified. There
are other schools of thought, too! These are truer,
possibly, to what all men will think and feel in twenty
years, and these may be as hostile as the friends are
favorable. In fact, it is these who put most energy —
gall is more vigorous than honey — into what they
have to say of a book and its maker. A man is an
idiot if he does not see that he is a prejudiced person
concerning himself, that, in all likelihood, what his
enemies say of him is the truest of all that is said."

"But they, too, are partisan," Persis remarked.

"Yes; there is," I said, "some comfort in that. But,
at last, what can any man do but simply perform

whatever is put in his hands to do, and as well as he can? Whatever I do *must* show the botch of my clumsy fingers. If we could do better work, God knows how gladly we would do it."

"And now," I said, getting up, "I at least have had far more of Guernsey for dinner than I bargained for when I sat down. Let me add only this; no one can be quite as conscious of his failures as the man himself. The critic cares not a penny, but, oh, how much *he* does! Unless the desire is beyond control, Miss Persis, don't — don't!"

"Don't what?" Persis asked, a trouble in her eager eyes.

"I do not know. Be a — a — woman." I knew it was a meaningless thing to say, but I could not say anything else at the instant. "Miss Rachel?" I turned as I said it to her. She was seated as when she made herself comfortable from the first at the table-cloth spread beside her upon the volcanic rocks. Her hands still slumbered in each other upon her lap. She had listened with her invariable kindness and evident good sense, her eyes as steady in their softness as were those of Ross Urwoldt in their sternness. "Miss Rachel," I said, "I want to ask a favor of you."

"What is it?" she said, with freshening interest as I stood nearer to her.

"Please," I said, — "please, please do not become a Madame Genlis, Récamier, De Staël!"

"I won't," she assented smilingly.

"They were noble women, grand women, powerful

women, but," I persisted, " do not allow your coming
to our city to make a Madame Dudevant, a George
Eliot, a Mrs. Somerville, least of all a Miss Martineau,
of you. You will promise me, Miss Rachel?"

"I promise you." She said it with a sincere laugh,
her eyes lifted to mine in a questioning way, doubtful
as to how far I was in joke. Persis was looking
fixedly at me as I turned away and began gathering
up our scattered things toward going home. As I
came to know, she made a point to hunt up and read
to Rachel all she could lay her hands on afterward of
the lives and books of the women I mentioned, of
other women, also, whose names were suggested as she
read. She began to read them to Rachel, I should
say, but she could not wait to do so at last, so eager
was she and so rapid, so much time did she give to
such things.

Our skipper had been shouting to us to come for
some time; the coachman and the children were already on board the boat. The lighthouse-keeper might
have strolled — Mrs. Trent suggested that he probably
would — down from his rock for a moment to bid us
good-by, but he did not. That was his loss, as well
as ours. We talked about fifty things as we adjusted
ourselves on the boat to thwarts and boom and centre-
board.

"We have neglected the children shamefully, and
for things of less interest," I said, as we went bowling
before a good breeze up the harbor homeward. Jean
and little Guernsey had their strings of fish, their
demoralized clothing, their renewed appetite to be

attended to. It had been a charming day to us all,
but we endured also the mild disappointment which
comes like a quieting hand upon the close of every
excursion. There was a conflagration in the west
over the setting sun, perishing like an Indian Rajah
upon his funeral pyre. The water darkened through
all shades of gold and umber, as we went, into a deep
bronze. Steamers were coming in from excursions,
'with swarming decks, brass bands, flying flags, and
surely an extravagant use of their whistles. Pleasure-
boats of all sizes, sail-boats and skiffs, flitted to and
fro upon the water as we neared the wharves, with
here and there a company who yielded to the disposition to sing which, somehow, comes upon every man
even as soon as he is afloat. As we sped along, and
the darkness began to fall, I saw that Rachel was
seated in the stern, her hands clasped in each other,
gazing peacefully upon the scene. But Persis was
standing in the bow of the boat, holding firmly by the
mast, looking into the crowded way we were going,
her garments on the wind.

" I wish the young lady would sit down," the skipper grumbled at his helm. " I can't see how to clear
the craft hereabout." It was a little odd, but I was
thinking something of the same kind myself.

CHAPTER XXIII.

A LITTLE VISIT.

IN calling upon Persis and Rachel I often saw lying about their parlor not only the paper which Ross Urwoldt edited in the State where he now lived, but other journals of the same region. Mrs. Trent explained it to me. "Colonel Urwoldt is an old friend," she said, "and the young ladies take, naturally, a deep interest, also, in the condition of that part of the country. From what they tell me I should say that he has his hands full in trying to bring order out of confusion down there."

"I keep myself as well informed as I can," I replied, "and no name is mentioned in connection with affairs in that section as often as his. He writes with an almost savage energy, judging by the editorials of his which I have seen. He seems to be a leading speaker at the conventions held there; if he speaks with as trenchant a force as he writes, he must be a power for good among his people. I dare say, in his public speaking as in his editorials, he is the more powerful in that he indulges in personal abuse of no man. For this is," I added, "an odd thing about Urwoldt, — he rarely alludes to persons, to persons for or against him; it is of lines of policy he speaks.

More than any one I know he disdains, despises men; so much so that he does not express his contempt, it is assumed as silent matter of course. To him great Nature is everything, — Nature and what he regards as its unswerving laws in states as in stars. Men and women are less to him than insects; they are that species of them which, unlike all other creatures, are untrue to the laws of nature in them, and are therefore as foolish as they are miserable. But he does not say so. He is Indian in his silence also, Indian, too, in his unswerving endurance and persistence toward his end. In all the South I know of no man who has clearer views of what is essential to its welfare, or who toils toward it with such clear-headed energy. If he lives he will be among the first men there of the coming times; he may climb into recognition by the North also, — who can tell?"

"I am glad to know it, glad for *her* sake!" My excellent friend looked at me, as she said it, as one does at a wounded man; but I did not ask whether it was of Rachel she spoke, or of Persis. "I fear," she added, "that, unconscious as she may be of it, Colonel Urwoldt is the chief motive to her in her studies. What a girl she is!"

"So she is," I said as I rose to go. "But it must be an extraordinary woman who can capture and hold in bonds such a man as my friend. I am glad to know that she is improving, developing. She has need to do so if she is to outrun the degree in which he is every day becoming more intensely — Ross Urwoldt."

Now Mrs. Trent is one of the happiest of women in her married life. Indeed, it is impossible to think of such a woman as unmarried. Wherever you saw her comely face, you would say, "I not only know that she married young, but I can tell what kind of husband and children she has." You would be right if you were to add, "That lady, whatever her name may be, takes the pleasure in matching people — no one more ladylike in her way of doing so — that another style of woman does in matching silks. Pleasure! there is nothing on earth which she enjoys quite so much as drawing together and marrying the right man to the right woman, if they be of the very few whom she cares most for. Any one can see that in one glance at her charming, matronly face." Which is all very true, so true that I knew what she meant when she now met my remark about Colonel Urwoldt and Miss Persis with the defiant demand, "What do you mean, Mr. Guernsey?" I understood her. She was defending not Ross and Persis so much as she was her plans concerning them.

"My dear madam," I explained, "I have known Colonel Urwoldt for many years. No man knows him so well. I have said that he thinks little of men. Alas, my dear lady, he thinks even less of women! To him they are, I fear, little more than so many squaws. It is worse than that. In his eyes, so far as women are whiter than their red sisters of the West, by that much are they the weaker of the two. As your husband has told you, as you see every day along the streets for yourself, nine women out of ten have at least the appearance of invalids. I have observed it for myself at the suggestion of Dr. Trent. When Colonel Urwoldt was here I could not help mentioning it to him as we walked the city. All that he replied was, ' Who does not know that ?' with hardly a glance at them."

"Yes, but," Mrs. Trent broke in, "ours are educated women, — educated, sir ! Squaws, indeed ! " She was almost angry.

"Yes, dear madam," I replied, — I was in her parlor at the time, — "but my unfortunate friend thinks that as increase of ease to women is but increase of indolence, as more money is to them merely more dress and jewelry, so of their education even, the more they know, only by that much the more are they — shall I call it artful ? no, artificial is the word."

"He is worse than Mr. Adair, and *he* is bad enough ! " Mrs. Trent said ; but I will not repeat what she added in that connection. It was not safe to accept her version of that clergyman. She was one of the best of women, but a born partisan, and the very warmth of her nature gave her a mortal aversion to one whose preaching, she averred, was as cold as it was brilliant. "It is as uncertain," she explained, "as many-colored, as variable as the Aurora Borealis." I led the talk back to Ross ; but Mrs. Trent was so full of what she feared might prove the seductive power on Persis greater than any other, that I had difficulty in drawing my friend from Mr. Adair to Ross Urwoldt.

"He is a savage!" she exclaimed when I was through.

"He is — Ross Urwoldt," I said. "As to that, pardon me, madam, but his mother was carefully educated. Do you know, Mrs. Trent, education is not always a thing which lasts. A woman can put it on and off like a muff, or a pair of six-button gloves, — they *have* six buttons sometimes, don't they? I know men who took a thorough course in college, and yet, ten years after, you would not be aware of it. Sometimes it is drink which burns up the brain and everything in it. In others, gluttony, greed of money, pure laziness, uncultivated companionship, de-educated them."

I might have told her, but I did not, that I knew at least one man, a fine scholar at college, out of whom licentiousness had rotted his Latin, Greek, mathematics, as utterly as it had his purity. What I added was only this: "Few women are better educated than was the mother of Ross Urwoldt; few women have more native intellect, not one in a thousand has such health, and yet she slid back, as she grew older, into very nearly what she was before she went to school. Persis knows it, knows what Ross thinks of women in general; and it is this, too, which exasperates her into the effort she is making."

Thereupon I fell to asking myself how far Ross had yielded to his almost Mohammedan estimate of woman during the demoralization of the war. God knows; I did not. I came nigh asking myself, also, how far Persis could have thought of such things. She was the one woman who, knowing the life of his disreputable father, knowing Ross himself so long and so well, was capable of leaving nothing out of consideration. It made all the difference in the world that her home had once been in such a place as Ocklawahaw, and not in the city where she now was; that the strands of her peculiar strength had been, if I may so speak, spun and woven by her own hard hands there, while other girls were growing up under soft showers and loving dews, — mere flowers which toiled not neither did they spin. But I said nothing of this to Mrs. Trent.

"Don't go," she said, as I kissed Jean good-by and put his hat on the head of little Guernsey to take him with me. And then she resorted to a subterfuge to accomplish things she thought more important.

"How well your new book is succeeding!" she said, and added many kind words. To me any topic was better, for the present, than the one we had been upon.

"Thank you," I said. "Come here, please;" and as I said it I opened the front door to go out. It was winter again. There were six inches of snow on the ground, and the flakes were filling the air as they fell.

"Do you know," I said, as she looked out beside me, "that each flake is a wonder of beauty in its angles and curves?"

"So Steven showed me once with his microscope," she said, drawing her shawl closer about her bosom. "What of that?"

"Try to pick out with your eyes and follow to the earth any one of those flakes. Now, my dear madam," I said, "any one of the mass of ordinary authors is a ninny if he does not know that his little book is, at best, but as one flake among those myriads. He does not come, do the utmost he can, within rifle-shot, as Ross would say, of even his idea of excellency. However he may toil at the making of his own particular flake of snow, striving at least toward perfection of curve and angle, what is his handiwork, at last, but one of a storm, so to speak, of books? These have their seasons as brief as that of these fluttering flakes. After that what befalls? Look at the snow on the ground. Can you pick your favorite flake out of that? In a week the whole mass of separate flakes, lost into the rest, will have been ground under wheels, sleighs, hoofs of horses, feet of men, into a dirty slush which will disappear before the first rain. What is one book? How long does it live? What definite end does it serve?"

"Our talking about Colonel Urwoldt has made you resemble him," Mrs. Trent laughed. "Suppose your flake *is* lost in the mass, it does its part, does n't it? to make grass greener next spring. It is Rachel who said that."

"Rachel? Persis, you mean."

"No, Rachel. Not that she has read your book as yet. She does n't care very much for books. When Persis reads them to her, she listens. Persis reads to her a great deal while she sews. She reads so well it would be hard not to listen. Yesterday," Mrs. Trent went on, "I was with them, and Persis was saying what a pity it was there were so many books. 'So there are,' Rachel said, 'but I suppose each book does its share.' And then she said that about the snow and the grass. She is not as ambitious a girl as Persis, but," Mrs. Trent insisted, as so often before and after, "a more sensible and a more lovely girl I never knew. If Mr. McAllister succeeds in winning her, he will have an admirable wife. Sometimes I think he is only making good friends with Rachel in order to have her help him secure Persis. For Persis is becoming a really brilliant girl. I never saw any one improve so fast."

I tried to bid my friend good-by. "You may catch cold standing in the air, and," I remonstrated, "what will the Doctor say but that I made you do it? Come, Guernsey. What you need is a new sled, and one as red as money can buy; let us go."

But Mrs. Trent would not release us yet.

"You would have laughed, as I did," she said, clasping her hands together under Guernsey's chin as he stood with his back to her, and impatient to leave. "I happened to drop in on Persis and Rachel last week, and " — here she kissed her boy to quiet him — "I chanced to open the door of their parlor softly. Persis was seated, her face from me, reading one of Robert Browning's poems which I am sure nobody can understand. For that reason, I dare say, she had selected it, and she was reading it aloud. Rachel was — "

"For that reason? What reason?" I asked.

"Persis thinks," Mrs. Trent explained, "that what is hardest to do is, for that reason, the thing of all others which she must do. She took up German during her last vacation to keep herself awake, for she

said, she was very sleepy almost all the time. But I
was speaking of the day I called. While Persis was
reading Robert Browning, Rachel was seated opposite,
ripping up, if you care to be told, an old dress, for she
is very economical. There are hymns one never tires
of, and so," Mrs. Trent was so kind as to inform me,
" there are old dresses which women like Rachel and
myself never tire of making up again and again.
Never mind about that. Persis was reading in her
animated way, and Rachel, her eyes on her work, was
listening faithfully. Yes, faithful is the word. It
does not matter whether she likes a thing or not.
Except that books are not such to Rachel until Persis
imposes them on her ; whatever is a duty, that Rachel
is faithful to. She reminds me almost of a — yes,"
Mrs. Trent hesitated, " of a dog in that. When she
saw me standing in the door she said like a child,
' Oh, I am so glad!' and it was the way her face
brightened that made me laugh ! ' It is very good in
Persis to read to me,' she told me when her friend
left us for her music-lesson. ' Persis likes it. I can't
say I like poetry. I do not like it simply because
it *is* poetry. At least, not very much of it at a
time. If poets would only put what they have to
say in fewer words ! Why can't they tell right out
what they mean, and be done with it ! I know it is
wrong in me to say so, but I cannot help it.' The
poor, dear, good girl had," Mrs. Trent laughed, " such
a penitent look as she said it that I kissed her and
told her she felt exactly as I did. And I, too, Mr.
Guernsey," Mrs. Trent said defiantly, " would rather

any hour hear what my Jean has to say, what little Guernsey will chatter about when he comes back to-day from walking with you, than any poet dead or living." And with that, she let us go.

As has been said before, all the property I possessed consisted of my island cotton-fields off the Carolina coast, which I leased at the close of the war to an East Tennessee man, a Mr. Adkins. For a time I was alarmed lest I should have beggared that gentleman thereby, for, instead of sending me my rent at the times appointed, he wrote me so cogent a set of reasons why he could make nothing out of my fields and former slaves, that my chief regret was for him. I was afterward to learn that he so applied himself to his new venture as to wring from my property a return which must have paid him far better than years of peddling before the war, and extortionate sutlership during it. This I knew nothing of at the time. I could have done nothing then if I had known it. What did it matter? Not a bit of a fatalist am I, and yet, as I might have known then, the corn and tobacco, the bacon and the beans, upon which he was to feed were in a process of growth for him not more inevitable than that of the switches — if I may so phrase it — which were to whip his nakedness in due time. No certainties more certain than that! Poverty was in the end to be a greater blessing to me than his ill-gotten gains were to Mr. Adkins, a blessing to more than myself. If the roar of cannon stimulated Southern men to desperate bravery during the war, I thank God that, as

19

in my own case, the dire necessities of their case
when the fight ended were such as to keep them
aroused, to impel them to yet stouter struggles in the
way of hard work for bread.   Shocking as it may
sound, I am glad that Southern women, also, were
awakened thereby to an exertion which lifted them
to and left them on a higher level of beauty and of
force of character than before.   .

Like many a better man from among them, I was
obliged to work very hard.   Possibly my being of
New England blood and birth enabled me to accept
and adjust myself more readily to matters.   I lectured
far and near, wrote for the daily press, was secretary
of a benevolent society, put out a book or two when
I could, — was very busy from January to December;
with the blessed luxury, as the result, of having a
few dollars to give away to those who were worse
crippled than myself by the war.   Mrs. Trent had set
her heart upon marrying me to Persis Paige.   I often
wondered that it did not come into her mind that I
might be too poor to marry, — it would have been
miserable folly for me to speak as yet of marriage
to any one.

When I returned to my hotel after seeing little
Guernsey home at the time of which I have just
spoken, I found a letter lying on my table from Ross
Urwoldt.   He wrote very rarely, and it must have
been his letter which, in connection with my visit to
Mrs. Trent, produced the absurd dream I had that
very night.   I thought I was among the throngs
which crowded the benches, tier on tier, of the

amphitheatre at Rome. And yet it could not have been at Rome, for we were come together to see a foot-race, and it ought to have been out in the fields at Scyros instead, for it was Atalanta who was to run, against Hippomenes, I suppose. As is always the case in dreams, it was all over in an instant. It is not impossible but that I had eaten too much supper, for the Romans crowded me dreadfully as I sat, and there was a haze as of dust and I know not what difficulty and painful effort upon the scene. Hippomenes flashed past me as I looked. And yet it could not have been he, for I could see no golden apples in his hands as he ran. His face was too cold and dark for that of a lover, and he seemed to be borne on like an image in the hands of an invisible force, without effort or eagerness on his part. As he passed out of sight in the difficult distance, Atalanta sped before me, upon his track. She was kilted for the course, her hair knotted upon the back of her head, her arms bare to the shoulders, a dart in her right hand. Her eyes were sparkling, she bent forward, her fair forehead was beaded with her effort. It was but an instant, and she disappeared. Then came another moment of hushed suspense. Then something took place along the way they went. I could not see what it was; the dust, the difficulty, the pressure upon me of the crowd, was such. It was something that filled the amphitheatre with — was it a shout or a shudder? — and I awoke. The only things clear to me were the set faces of the runners; one was Ross Urwoldt, the other Persis Paige.

CHAPTER XXIV.

A RIDE INTO THE COUNTRY.

I WAS absent from the city for some time after Ross Urwoldt left us. Months fled by without my seeing, hardly hearing from or of my friends. At last I happened to have a day or two to spare during one of my swallow-like returns to the city, and my heart, too, came back to those for whom I cared most. The habit, however, of motion was still upon me, and I went one day with an open carriage and driver to see if the young ladies would not like a ride. It was an afternoon in the early spring, cool but summer-like. I could not content myself in-doors even with them, and I knew that they, too, ought to be as eager to be out as any bird or bud.

I found the Rev. Augustus Marston Adair waiting to see Miss Persis. Like everybody else, I had seen perpetual mention of him in the papers, had heard people speak of him very often. I had not met him before, and was glad of the opportunity, so much the more as he was generally believed to be a devoted admirer of the lady upon whom he was calling, — a fact which made Persis somewhat of a city celebrity. Mr. Adair was an undersized but admirably proportioned gentleman. His clothing fitted him like a glove, as did his peculiarities of tone and manner. He had small quick eyes, sharp and black; his hair was cut short about an oval forehead; mustaches of a raven hue, and waxed to a point upon either side, adorned his upper lip. He had a breadth of chin out of proportion, and the aid lent to his tongue in conversation by his eyes and hands gave fourfold force to what he said.

I record it of Rachel with gratitude that she never kept me waiting.

"Persis is very sorry," she told Mr. Adair and myself after our greetings were over, "but she cannot come down to-day. She is not well."

"I hope she is not seriously sick?" Mr. Adair asked.

Rachel hesitated a moment. "As a rule," she said, "Persis was never so well as she is now. I did not think she could endure so much hard work. It seems to do her good. You would be surprised to see how strong she is, what color she has; but to-day she is suffering from one of her terrible headaches. Last night, as is often the case, she could not sleep. She has to go to a Teachers' Institute at five, and has bandaged her eyes and lain down till then, so as to be able to go. She will be very sorry to miss seeing you."

Immediately upon her coming in, Mr. Adair, in a very gentlemanly manner, turned from me to her. We had introduced ourselves, and he was talking rapidly to me; but his interest in Persis was evident from the many questions he now asked Rachel concerning her.

Interested as I was for Persis myself, it gave me, all the more, an opportunity of understanding her lover. In his anxiety for her he was at his best, for he was his genuine self. Inquiry upon inquiry, he poured them upon Rachel in regard to her friend in measure so fluent and copious that I could see it was but his nature to do so when, instead of Persis, it was a religion he was questioning into. So interested was he to hear and accept what Rachel had to say of Persis that he allowed her time to answer, listened to her with his eyes also. When she left the room to bear a message from him to Persis, his change of bearing, as he took me in hand from where he had dropped me, was great. The trouble with him seemed to be that he had been everywhere and very often, that he knew everybody and everything already and to the utmost. Although his unceasing talk consisted largely in asking questions, he did not care for any reply. Even when he courteously paused, and, for courtesy's sake, to let me say a word, it was so plain I could tell him nothing he did not know already, and perfectly, that I soon subsided into silence, glad to have him say all there was to be said. He was well informed, spoke admirably, putting his sentences into epigrams, which were axioms also. His talk was like champagne, his eyes and hands adding so much of sparkle and movement to what he said; it was not until afterward the doubt came that possibly it was at best but the effervescence of soda-water.

In a little while Rachel came back, and, after some words of unfeigned regret at not seeing Persis, Mr.

Adair withdrew, and we were free to take our ride. This much I can conscientiously say for my companion that, so far as toilet was concerned, she was, apparently, always as ready for company as, let us say, a dove. My impression was that she dressed as much for her own comfort as she did according to her own taste. It was her nature, and one could detect as little to criticise in her simplicity of raiment as in her sober way of saying and doing things. That was the feeling I had when I shook hands with her, that there was nothing in or about her which could distract my attention from her best self. I was glad of it, for I had but a little while to be with her, and I wanted it to be as much a time of quiet, of restful enjoyment, as possible ; which may be pardoned in me when it is considered that I am too restless myself, that I had been all winter on the strain of travel, lecturing, writing, mingling with unceasing people.

"I wish — " I began, but controlled myself until Rachél and I were seated in the carriage and it was rolling away. But she asked me directly, —

" What do you wish ? " That was another peculiarity of my companion. When Persis or Mrs. Trent — when almost any one else was present, she devolved the conversation upon some one else and listened. What she did say was the word, if it was but a word, which needed to be said, and then she stopped. I think she paid the close attention of her eyes as of her lips to any one who happened to be speaking, on the same principle ; she counted upon it that every word would be worth hearing. Her attention always had the effect upon me of causing me to say less than I otherwise would, and to make what I did say better worth the expectant eyes which so waited upon them. "You said you wished —" she repeated.

"If it were not that it would make it *too* blue," I replied, "I wish the Teachers' Institute were sunk in the sea." Her eyes demanded explanation, but also smiled assent. I only added, as we wound our way through the crowded streets, "Please notice one or two things, peculiar, I think, to this city, as we go. Look at the drivers of trucks, carriages, express-wagons, — that long, low vehicle, for instance, coming this way laden with machinery, every horse pulling with a grave, determined step, as of a dignified gentleman, — each of these, every driver of a street-car also, acts upon the rule of going ahead himself, and leaving the other man, who is about to cross his track, to do the reining in. The dirtiest-faced driver of them all shows an unhesitating assertion of self which you would not see in, say, Brazil."

"And yet," Rachel said, "when the other man does halt the instant before the wheels would otherwise strike against each other, did you ever notice with what firmness he does that too?"

"That is another thing; that," I said, "is the habit of obedience, too, to the inevitable. Look at this police-officer at the crossing, how he arrests the current of carriages and wagons until the crowd accumulated at the corners can go over! The blue-coated Moses has but to hold out his silent switch, and the Red Sea of hurry and confusion parts before it as

by miracle. Nowhere do I find self-assertion so determined, and yet so obedient to law, as here."

"Yes," Rachel said, for we had to stop awhile, the
throng was so great; "and I often wonder at the manner in which people give way to each other along
the crowded sidewalks. Men and women are all in
such haste, mixed up, going in opposite directions,
yet they curve in and out, and just miss striking
against each other beautifully. It is like — "

"A kind of music," I said for her; for when one
has to talk to an audience so much, one's facility
of wording things becomes too prompt for politeness.
"Another thing, please notice," I went on, "and that is
that the women outnumber the men thirty to one."

"That," Rachel explained, "is because the women
are shopping, or out for exercise; the men are in
offices, shops, factories, ships. Many of these are
countrywomen who have come in to buy things; their
sons, brothers, husbands, are at work in the barns and
fields. Then there are more women than men in this
part of the world; at least, so they say. You don't
object to that, do you, Mr. Guernsey?"

"Not at all. But that brings up a question we
won't spoil our ride by talking about. Look at those
people," and I motioned with my head toward a man
and woman who were going by; "you never saw
rougher folk than those even in Ocklawahaw."

"No," she said; "but then we did not have as nice
people there as you see here. Men and women grow
old here more beautifully than they do there. Persis
and I were talking only yesterday of how many

noble-looking old gentlemen we see every time we are on the streets, they are so erect and fresh-colored. Not a day but we see some dear old grandmother with a complexion like that of a girl of sixteen."

"Her hair," I added, "upon either side of her forehead in puffs of drifted snow. I fall in love with such every time I take a walk. They belong, I fear, to a generation which is going out."

By this time we were beyond the more crowded streets, and were rolling along rapidly toward the country. I changed my seat so as to sit opposite my companion. It was delightful to me to find myself with an audience of but one; but I remained didactic. "If you were to put," I said, "what this city used to be into flesh and blood, it would stand before you in the old lady, the stately old gentleman, we have been speaking of. Even now it is, in many respects, the best town I know of."

"Is it?" Rachel asked it with interest, yet composure. When in Ocklawahaw she was entirely contented, could have lived and died there without a wish to get away. She felt in the same way about her present abode. Hers was a nature which adjusted itself as silently and perfectly to its situation as water to a cup, and, from the first, she took her new life so much as matter of course that, except for the use of a peculiarly Western word now and then, you would have said she had been born here. "Yes, I like it," she now added, sinking back upon her seat with an air of comfortable possession; "its streets may be crooked, but they are clean. There are so many school-houses. What fine large horses they have even in the street-cars. I like sleek horses. And there are such nice policemen. And the conductors on the cars, too; you see some of them who are genuine gentlemen, who seem as if they were taking fares for a week or two until they could get back into the higher positions to which they belong."

"Out West," I added, "you can tell whether a region is malarious or not by a glance at the first child you meet. In the same way you can judge of this city by its boys; they appear to the merest stranger who passes them along the street to be unusually intelligent and yet under wholesome control. Every ragged, barefooted little Irish Mickey even seems to be in the grasp of an unseen hand, — is it the police or the public school? perhaps both. But why is it," I demanded, for my mind was running too much upon that subject at the time, — "why is it that so many of these women seem to be invalids? Notice, as we go, how many girls wear eye-glasses. There is a child of ten in spectacles. Yonder is a lady who is the picture of health; but she is in a carriage, her coachman in livery. Must a woman be rich to be well?"

My companion did not know it, but in that case there was no lady who seemed to be richer than herself. Her Scriptural name helped toward it, I suppose; but if she had worn a coal-scuttle bonnet and a drab silk you would have sworn that she was the only child, so healthful and serene was she, of a wealthy

Quaker. Her eyes were gone from me with an attention which clung about each woman in passing.

"Why are there so many sick women?"

It was of myself I asked it, but Rachel answered thoughtfully, "I suppose it must be the climate. Perhaps it is hard work, anxious care. Often it is hereditary. Sometimes they study too hard."

She was thinking of Persis. So was I. For the present, however, my interest was, by contrast with the overtasked women of whom we had been speaking, with Rachel herself. As it always did, her dress became her, especially her hat or bonnet. To me a badly arrayed woman attains to the climax and summit, in every sense, of wretched taste, when she crowns the Himalaya of her heaped-up hair with one of the barbarous hats common then and now. But Rachel wore a head-dress of which I only knew that it answered its ends and completed her attire. "I should n't wonder if Mrs. Trent told her how much I would like just that style of hat," I said to myself in my self-conceit. "But how could anybody have known that I would call upon Miss Rachel to-day?"

"Rachel is ruled by Persis in her studies, but she is," Mrs. Trent had told me one day, "more determined than you would think in everything else. In her toilet, for instance, she will not listen to a soul. In everything except their studies it is she who rules Persis."

There was a smile upon the lips of Rachel as I was thinking of this, and her eyes were full of fun.

After a while it broke into a laugh. "Mr. McAllister was telling us last night," she said, "of something he saw in the city yesterday. A drove of cattle was landed at the wharves. One of them escaped. Mr. McAllister's office is in an upper-story front, and he saw it all. The ox came up the street in a fury. Mr. McAllister never before saw such horns, he said; they were so long, so wide apart. The animal tore along, emptying the street before it. The police-officers fled, men in wagons put the whip to their horses and galloped them, the wagons bumping over the cobble-stones. Women ran out to pick up their children. Men, women, boys, shrieked, dodged into doorways and down alleys, and fled every way for dear life. The great brute was master of the situation. With its tail in the air, dashing right and left with its frightful horns at dogs and men, it disappeared up the street, clearing out the city before it. Mr. McAllister said it was infamous!"

Rachel told about it demurely enough; but there was a mirth in her lips, an almost triumph in her eyes, which gave me a new idea of her. "It was a shame for me to do so, Mr. McAllister was shocked; but I only laughed," she went on, "when he told me. The ox was direct from the Southwest. I could not help taking sides with the ox. I would not have it hurt anybody; but," she laughed, "it was not accustomed to anything but prairies, it did not understand cities. Was it very wrong in me?"

"But what has that," I assented, "to do with —"

"With the advantages of the city." She came back

to sobriety in an instant. "Only this. Persis never wearies of saying what an admirable place it is. Such schools, lectures, concerts, art institutions, public libraries, intellectual people. She says that the atmosphere is electric. So it is. No city is more fortunate. I am glad we came. But, Mr. Guernsey," she pleaded like a child, "do you not sometimes think — I am not a student like Persis, as you know. I try very hard, but I cannot like philosophies as much as she does. It may be my lack of intellect; but, Mr. Guernsey, do you not think —"

I was curious to understand her more than to comprehend merely what she was objecting to, and left her unassisted. "What I mean," she said, "is this: do you not think that in this city education, the estimate of intellect is carried too far?"

"In one city," I suggested, "money is everything; in another, the denomination of Christians you belong to; in another, good birth. What you mean is that here the extreme to which people go is the excessive appreciation of talent, literary ability, schooling in all its degrees. Miss Rachel," I exclaimed, and her face brightened at my energy, "you are right! I am glad you agree with me." And I launched into denunciation of excessive study, especially for women, in a way which would have ruined me for life had I been upon the platform instead. "Don't you think so, Miss Rachel?" I asked in the end. "Provided no one was more than badly scared, you would not care if something fresh, like your big ox, from nature were to dash in upon things and scatter them for a while. Isn't that so?"

My companion laughed, agreeing with me with her eyes, but shaking her head. " Is not that a delightful home ?" she asked, pointing to a house we were passing, and reverting, as she always did, from people, unless they were being praised, to things. Our road, hard, white, swept, and watered, was perfection itself, and the hoofs of our horses rang merrily upon it as we went. On either hand were residences, each in its own environment of spruces or elms, horse-chestnuts or apple-trees, which told, some of them, of ancestors extending back through four generations.

" When the house," I said to Rachel, "like this next one, for instance, destitute of trees, is particularly large and fine and new, it tells us of an owner who blends in himself the grim industry of a century ago with the taste and expenditure of to-day. The suburbs are the best half of the city. They are to the city, what his charming wife is to her husband, the red-faced, quick-mannered, energetic business man. You see that the wife is beginning to put on her spring attire. See the tender gray green of the leaves about to unfold on the tips of wayside shrubs. And what a peculiar hue the grass has ! In comparison to what it will have as the summer comes, it is like the colorless water at the edge of the sea along the sands, in contrast to the darkening blue as it deepens into the depths. There is the same uncertain tremor, as between winter and summer, in the air also. You feel as if you wanted to throw yourself summerward, and help it in the struggle."

" I like it," Rachel said, "without — " I had to

wait for her to end the sentence. She was unlike Persis in that. Persis completed in her own mind what you had yet to say before you got through. Her reply waited almost impatiently for you to be done. Not so with Rachel. She went with you to the very end of your remark. If it was in answer to the simplest question, she did not reply on the instant, there was a moment's hesitation before she spoke. I could see her answer coming in her eyes, on her lips, before it framed itself into words, and I enjoyed her slowness as one does a lisp. It had weight in it as of value; it rested me to tarry for it.

"I like the season," Rachel said, "without imagining things about it, without putting what I think into — thoughts. Persis reads poetry. When she sees anything which interests her very much, it always reminds her of what some author has said about it. I know I ought to take more pleasure than I do in what gifted people have written. As it is, I like things," she colored a little in trying to phrase it, "like things," she said, "as they are. Yes."

It was all she added by way of assent, as the driver reined in on the top of a hill, and I waved my hand as I stood up toward the landscape. To our left were villages by the dozen, homes peeping by the hundreds through the trees and from behind the hills. I wanted to tell my companions that the church spires here, there, everywhere, were like marks of interjection, exclamation amid the unheard life going on so abundantly below us; but I was held silent by her silence as she feasted upon the scene. Off, and from our very

feet, toward the right, was the ocean, entering into and
receding from the land, to come again in bays, inlets,
harbors; while, farther to the right, the watery expanse was diversified with little islands, and a mos-
quito swarm of sailing craft, large and small, through
which a black-hulled steamship from Europe was
intent upon its way, leaving behind it a long wake
of smoke above and billows beneath. Here and there
a flag fluttered from masthead or fort, mere vibrant
dots of color, the sky of fleecy blue over all, until
ocean and air blended into one in the dim horizon.

Had it been Mrs. Trent, more so, had it been
Persis, we would have talked to each other without
ceasing, pointing out this and that, demanding admiration for one thing or another. Persis would have
been in a fever of enjoyment, new color in her talk
as in her cheeks, but Rachel sat and looked upon the
scene in silence. Keenly as Persis enjoyed music, I
had observed, when we were at the opera together,
or in the concert hall, that the very best music merely
stimulated her the more to speech, as it did me.
Then, as now, Rachel could not do two things at a
time. She had such a fashion of giving herself
utterly up, now as always to what was in hand, that
I left her to herself. Her face, I noticed yet again,
was broader, the brows particularly, than that of
Persis; her large eyes rested upon what she looked at,
not glancing hither and thither, as those of her friend
would have done. The hands of Persis would have
been as active as her eyes, but I never knew Rachel
to gesticulate. If I did not know how much more

efficient she was in nursing the sick, in housekeeping, in everything except books, than Persis, I would have said she was but a Circassian beauty, fair and round and lazy.

"Upon the whole," I remarked, "I like this city beyond any I have visited in Europe or America. It is inhabited by people each one of whom is a distinct individual, and yet the blending of all into one is so perfect that the city, as a city, is, beyond any other, itself a definite and very distinct person. People have their faults here as everywhere. You cannot help seeing that a little success in literature, for instance, has the effect upon some which wealth has on others; they hold themselves as aloof as possible, touching you with but the tips of dainty fingers. Courtesy is cultivated as sugar is in Cuba. Yet the preoccupation is so intense at times that it will show through. It may be because it contains treasure, but how often it is a man's house and heart here are as a fortress! It reminds one of the rich Jews in Oriental countries. When it is a question of buying and selling, the Jew lives in the open doorway of his shop, is upon the sidewalk, eager to greet whoever comes. So far as business goes, a man is as accessible in his counting-house here as men are anywhere. As to his home, that is another affair. The Hebrew makes the exterior of his house as unpromising as he can, from dread of tax-gatherer and thief. Once within it, you are dazzled by the display of wealth and enjoyment. So of these people. Apart from business, the aspect of the man in this region is cold and almost repellent; but if you are welcomed within, to his home, to his heart, you are delighted at the wealth you will find there, — the wealth of friendship and love. Except in externals, it is absurd to say that they are a cold people. They are so intense at first in regard to any matter which interests them that, in a little while, they are as intensely tired, disgusted even, with the whole thing. Woe to the sensation, whatever it is, man or thing, which imagines it can have and lose and then have again the popularity it once enjoyed! The city is like a boy who so gorges himself at first with a new kind of candy that he sickens forever after at the very sight or smell thereof."

"Not where principle is concerned," Rachel insisted.

"Certainly not! And it is very curious; I know nothing like it elsewhere. Here principle means person. In political matters, for instance, at the first blast of the trumpet it is not merely that every man of them falls into line, eager for the fray; if you look at the warriors, lo, it was the resurrection trump instead, for here, as if in cocked hats and knee-breeches, are their revolutionary sires once more! The youngest man reverts instantly to his great-grandfather, is himself that ancestor to the tips of his fingers!"

"Is that true in religion also?" Rachel demanded; but slowly added, "I think that in regard to books these people are almost — would it be too strong to say it? — almost fanatical. Persis and I are thrown,

in our classes at the conservatories of music, in the
art-rooms, libraries, and the like, with girls who are
destroying their eyes by night study. They know it;
they know everything!" Rachel sighed. "But they
say they cannot help it. They will no more stop,
they *can* no more stop, than if they were opium-
eaters. Many of them are ruining their health! I
am so afraid for Persis. I used to have influence
over her; in this I have none."

"Yes," I said; "we agree that greed of money is
sordid. As if greed for knowledge, except as a
means to some noble end, is anything but another
kind of gluttony! It is vulgar for a man to get
drunk on whiskey, yet I know men and women who
intoxicate themselves more utterly on the champagne
of excessive literature, excessive science, excessive
intellectual stimulus, — it does not matter of what
kind. Do you know what has become of their old-
time fanaticism in religion?"

My companion put so much of deepening interest
in her eyes that, as our vehicle toiled slowly up a long
hill, I could not refrain from becoming a bit of a ped-
ant. "The great discovery of our times," I said, " is,
as you have had lectures enough since you came
here to know very well, the conservation and cor-
relation of force. That is, there is the same amount
of force in these people, for instance, as always, only
it takes different forms, goes in different directions.
A century or two ago, they rushed with excessive
energy toward things divine. To-day, there is the
same measure of desperate effort to know. The only

difference is of direction, of object. What they vehemently attempt now is to know anything, everything, except what was accepted by their grandfathers. The intensity, the fanaticism, of effort is the same."

"You think then," Rachel asked it almost timidly, "that a person can try too hard to know things, to be highly educated?"

"Miss Rachel," I said, "you ought to use, ought to develop all you can, the vigor of your arm and hand. Now, your intellect is but another sort of arm and hand, by which you can reach after, can grasp and hold, certain things. It is your duty and mine to develop our intellect so far as we can do so without neglect of any other part of us. If I attend to my body to the neglect of my mind, I am a fool. If I care for my intellect in such a way as to neglect and injure my body, I am but another species of fool. Besides, the highest objects of desire are as much beyond the reach of the intellect as they are of the hand. Surely I am the greatest fool of all if I become so absorbed in the care of either body or intellect as to neglect that noblest part of me, for which body and intellect exist, by which I alike feel and know in a way and to a degree beyond everything body and mere mind are capable of."

I could see that Rachel was not thinking of herself nor of me. She did not look at the houses or fields on either side of our road as we rolled smoothly along.

"You were speaking," she said, "of the fanaticism of excessive education. People used to be fanatics for faith; is it not possible that they may grow to be fanatical against faith? Mr. McAllister was saying so last week. He has no interest in matters outside of his office. He does not believe, I am afraid, in anything; but we have all sorts of people at our boarding-house, and they *will* get to discussing things at the table until the lady of the house has to beg them to go up-stairs and let the servants clear the cloth. Last week, after listening awhile, they became so violent that he said to them, 'You know I do not go with any of you, but I've made the rounds of your halls and circles, and you radicals are the most dogmatic of all the people I know. It is a blessed thing that no two of you agree, or you would burn us believers in a twinkling!' He meant himself and me," explained Rachel; and I fear that the Major said it largely to conciliate her. "But I am so sorry, Mr. Guernsey — "

She said no more, but Mrs. Trent had told me about it, and I exclaimed, "So am I, Miss Rachel! very sorry!"

"When we first came," she went on after a little, "Persis could not go to church often enough. She must hear this wonderful man and that until she had heard everybody. For a long time she took great interest in it. She would come back full of enthusiasm; whatever she heard was something so new, so deep, so beautiful, so brilliant. And no two of the speakers were, she said, in the least alike. 'It is part of my education to hear them,' she said. Now she is through with it all."

" And does not go anywhere on Sundays ? "

" But she is so very tired," Rachel said.   " If you
knew how hard she works all the week!   She has a
high position as a teacher now, is paid a good salary ;
but the text-books change almost every term, she
must keep far ahead of her pupils.   On Sundays she
always has a headache.   Dr. Trent has given her
medicine.   And you cannot think how he talked to
her !" Rachel said to me with large eyes.   " He
scolded her until she cried.   But she *must* work !   She
is the most conscientious girl I ever knew."

" I 'm afraid," I said gravely, " that hers is something like the diseased conscience of a devotee, Catho-
lic or Buddhist."

" Oh no, how can you say so !"   And my companion
went into the warmest praise of her friend.   I had
never seen her so earnest.   She did not hint such a
thing, but I had gathered from Mrs. Trent that the
terror of Rachel was lest Persis should lose her
Christian belief.   " If there ever was a Martha," Mrs.
Trent had told me, " it is Persis, — a Martha who toils
with her brain, I mean.   She is not consciously selfish," Mrs. Trent explained, " she is so eager, so ignorant she thinks, there are so very many things to
learn, so very, very many things to do, that, beyond
any housekeeping Martha I know," laughed Mrs.
Trent, " she is careful and cumbered about much —
not serving exactly, but work, harder work than the
Syrian Martha ever dreamed of.   Rachel," Mrs. Trent
mused aloud at the time, " is Mary instead.   But it is
in Persis you are chiefly interested.   Mr. Guernsey,"

she said with new energy, "if God ever made a woman for a man, he made Persis Paige for you! Your tastes, your interests, are the same. I am sure she will do anything *you* say. Dr. Trent can do nothing with her. There is no man she admires as she does you. Use the authority of — of the affection you must feel for her, Mr. Guernsey, and insist upon her having more mercy upon herself. I want her to be a true wife to you for many a long year!" But it was nothing less than her motherly care for me which allowed Mrs. Trent to say as much.

But I was suddenly brought back from thinking of what she had said.

The one serpent in the Eden of the suburbs through which we were returning is the Railway; its trail is over it all. Our driver must have been new either to that fact or to his horses. As we made a sudden turn, a locomotive thundered by on one side, the driver fell off the box in the swerving of the vehicle, and our horses ran away with us! I am not strong, but I used at least to be something of a squirrel in alertness. With a word of caution to Rachel, I clambered into the vacated seat, and gathered up the reins, which, fortunately, had not quite slipped off the dashboard. I dare say it was more oats than alarm which inspired the horses, for they were making, although at full speed, for the city. The instant problem with me was how to hold them in, yet keep my seat; but in that instant it was solved. My companion had climbed into the front seat below, had snatched off a shawl she wore as protection against the coolness of approaching evening, had passed it about me as I sat, and, kneeling upon the seat, was pinioning me by the shawl to my post with a grasp as of iron, and all without an exclamation. If it had not been for that, I must have been rocked off my perch by the swing of the carriage, or pulled under the heels of the horses by the reins to which I clung. As it was I was enabled, planting my feet more firmly, to put such a steady strain upon the reins as at last to draw the animals down into a trot, a walk, a halt.

The whole affair was like a landscape seen by a flash of lightning; there was a good deal of it, but it was soon over. I did not look into the carriage until our driver came limping up, all the broader of brogue for the accident. As he mounted upon his box he was, to conciliate me, I suppose, as loud in his praises of my dexterity as in anathemas upon the locomotive, the horses, and especially himself.

I was almost as curious to see Rachel as if, since I last saw her, she had been in Europe. Yet, on looking at her as we sped along, there was nothing to see beyond her former self. She was seated as comfortably as before. Her shawl was thrown back from about her shoulders, since she was warm enough now without it. There was less color in her cheeks, but her eyes were the same. I had all the disposition a somewhat excitable man would naturally have, to say a good deal by way of commendation, explanation, congratulation, joke even, but I know that I said most of it to myself, and not aloud. She, I think, had less to say than I.

CHAPTER XXV.

RIVALS.

I HAD my own reasons for urging Ross Urwoldt to visit me. There came an adjournment of Congress, I believe, an arrest of some sort upon his business in Washington, where he happened then to be, and, at last, he came. A few days after his arrival we called upon the young ladies, but found that they were not in the city. Persis had been compelled to lay aside her work and they had gone into the country with friends for a little rest, but I took Ross with me to see Dr. Trent and his wife.

The instant we entered the house I saw that Mrs. Trent was almost as much upon the alert as if my friend were a savage intent on slaughter. It was not because he was of Indian lineage. There was really so little of any other than the blood of the white man in his veins that it was only the higher qualities of character and few of the mere bodily traits of the Indian which Ross retained. No gentleman in her knowledge was more thoroughly such, few had his intellect, none the experiences of men and of war which made him what he was. His silent and fixed attention to Mrs. Trent when she spoke took the place in him of that deference to her sex which, I fear, he did not possess to the degree he should have done. Had I known it then, I might have seen that he was so attentive to her because, for the moment, she was to him his nearest approach to Persis. But, now as always, it was never of Persis he spoke, it was always of Rachel.

I think it was this which alarmed Mrs. Trent most. It was not for him she intended Persis. Her whole heart, dear lady, was up in arms for me instead. She was alarmed at his coming. Persis was away, but she must be on her guard to defeat his nefarious schemes.

"Persis and Rachel have made many friends during their stay here, many warm friends," she said with some emphasis. "I am glad that some of these have taken them, it was almost by force, to their farm. Rachel does not need it; she looks well, is well always; but she will enjoy herself there as she does everywhere. Persis was in great need of a change. What with teaching and being taught, she is like a factory girl tending her loom; she has to be on her feet all day, and must be on the alert always, lest any of her many threads should tangle or break. You will be delighted to see Rachel," Mrs. Trent added with sudden interest; "she is looking so well, Colonel Urwoldt, and she will be delighted to see you. Persis has time from her studies for hardly anything; but I have heard Rachel speak of you very often. As to Persis, it is a pity —"

"Yes, it *is* a pity," Dr. Trent began; but his wife frowned at him, laughed, shook her head. The mild-mannered physician was a tyrant among his female patients, gentle as he seemed to be in tone and touch; but Mrs. Trent avenged her sex, for I doubt if his most submissive patient yielded to him as he did to her.

I turned Ross over to Mrs. Trent for the rest of our visit. She was such a warm-hearted, frank-spoken, bright-humored matron that, with little Guernsey on one side of her, and golden-haired Jean on the other, she could not fail to interest my friend, she was so much interested in him and in Rachel. It was little he cared for any woman but one, yet Mrs. Trent, with her happy face and ready laugh, was, in comparison to city ladies in general, as an open wood fire is to an iron-latticed register highly polished and set in marble. If any one could make him feel at home, she could.

"Yes, it is a pity." Dr. Trent finished what he was intending to say when he and I were by ourselves in his study that night. "I am called in occasionally to minister to nuns in convents. Their sickness, poor things, is because, neglecting body and mind, they abandon themselves too much to the care, as they call it, of their souls. More frequently too than you think, a foolish girl so gives herself up to loving some perhaps worthless fellow that her excess of affection in and by itself disturbs the balance, and, while over-developing her heart, as it is styled, she endangers herself in every other way. Look at Persis. Almost from the hour of her coming I have had her under treatment. This mania for self-culture is often as much an epidemic as measles or whooping-cough. The vessels of the brain can be over-distended, over-stimulated, by excess of study as by whiskey. If the stomach is not equally inflamed, it is greatly weakened; but the injured organ is, chiefly, the brain. The veins are so habitually distended by the excess of blood during application too great, too long con-tinued, that when the stimulus of study or liquor ceases they cannot contract. That in either case is the cause of reaction, of craving for excitement. If we had time," and the Doctor unlocked the rosewood case thereof as he spoke, " I could show you under my microscope a section, my dear fellow, of a drunkard's brain which proves what I say. What do you sup-pose *that* is ? " And he took from a shelf and held up before me a small jar of liquid with something suspended in it.

"A pickled clam, I should think," was my con-jecture.

"A clam! That, sir," the Doctor said in triumph, "is a section of the brain of the inventor of" — and he named a patented discovery too well known to allow of its being mentioned in this connection. "He had a large brain, the veins were beautifully distended; but there were a good many of us students, and it had," he added regretfully, "to be divided among us. He devoted years of severe study to his contrivance, succeeded in it, was swindled out of it. In a burst of rage he slew the man whom he supposed did it, was imprisoned, killed himself, and his body came into our hands. Had he been an intemperate

man, the alcohol would have consumed the stomach
and hardened the brain.   As it was, the blood abandoned the stomach to dyspepsia, and so habitually
enlarged the vessels in the brain that they could
not recover themselves.   You have *felt* ennui from
somewhat the same cause; if," suggested my friend,
his finger and thumb upon the stopper, "you would
like to *see* ennui under the microscope — "   But
I declined.

"Guernsey," the Doctor complained, replacing the
jar and putting the key of the case in his vest pocket,
" I at least ought to know something about women."

"If any man does ! "   I was right in exclaiming it.
The truth is, it was sympathy for suffering which had
led this friend of mine into medicine.   Once in it, he
had given himself to the study of feminine maladies,
because he found that it was women who suffered
most.   With his study and practice, his sympathy
had grown into a science so clear that a female patient could no more resist him than a school-girl can
resist, distasteful as it may be, the Rule of Three.   I
dare say, had he not been rich, and therefore independent of his practice, he would not, with all his
sympathetic certainty, have dared to be as peremptory
with women as he was.   People knew that he was a
physician largely from love of and success in his profession, and none of his brethren had a reputation, in
that region, and in his own line, to compare with his.
Had female practitioners been as common then and
as well qualified as they are now, they could not have
been as successful as was Dr. Steven Trent; for under

no conceivable circumstance can a woman fear and obey a woman as she does a man.

"I do not understand the sex," he now proceeded, "but I know as much of it as most people. Now, a woman has within her two citadels, into either of which she can retreat and defy the world. The one is her heart, and, back of that, her will. If you can enlist her heart against her will, or her will against her heart, you may persuade her, — induce her, I mean, to persuade herself. Let a woman, keeping her health, and consequently her beauty, up to the highest point, carry on, also, and carry out the equal development of her heart and her mind, and she will become that of which Aspasia was, I presume, but a feeble prophecy, — a human being worthier of love, respect, adoration almost, than any other object on the planet. But — but," argued the Doctor, "if her heart be held, by herself or by circumstances, in abeyance while her life runs almost entirely into the expanding and informing of her intellect, then her will, already strong enough in virtue of her sex, gets to be so strong that she is beyond argument. A theory, it matters not a straw what it is, takes to her the place of a babe; she exaggerates it, idolizes it, spoils it, will fight to the death for it, as she would for an only child.

"No man," said the Doctor, "has a higher estimate of woman than myself. My wife, for instance, is " — for Mrs. Trent was his one weakness; I did n't blame him — "as superior to myself in sense as she is in personal beauty. But truth is more to me than even my own wife; and I do know that there is no loveliness in a woman, any more than in a circle, unless she has symmetrical development. We call them angels. Whatever we do not know about angels, we do know that they are not lop-sided. Crop one of the wings of a dove or eagle, and you will see, when it tries to fly, what I mean."

"But what about Miss Persis?" I asked.

"Persis is a favorite case of mine. On some accounts," the Doctor remarked with the coolness of the dissecting-room, "I hope she will continue to disregard what I say. I want to study the inevitable result. No, I don't mean that! She is a noble girl, a gifted girl. Her improvement delights me, as it does us all; but I wish she would hold up a little. If she were less of a student, and more like my wife, like Miss Rachel, it would be better for her."

"I do not know about that. Listen. Last Wednesday afternoon I was riding," I rejoined, "in the street-cars. It was sufficiently pleasant, and we rode in an open car. As usual, we were all of us, the men at least, in a hurry, — some to get home, some to keep business appointments, some to catch the train. There sat a little terrier-faced man beside me, — you can count their sharp noses by the thousand all over the city, — and once, when the bell struck and the car stopped, he said, 'Confound her!' with so much vigor that I looked up and saw who he meant. It was Miss Rachel. She was standing upon the curbstone. If she had been in a drawing-room instead, she could not have been more cool, composed. She was not going to risk her clean skirts, to say nothing of her person, among the rush of wheels. Not until the car stopped and the way was clear, did she leave the curbstone. I helped her on, seating her purposely beside the growling terrier."

"Yes; that is it!" my friend broke in. "We agree that Americans are thin and haggard because they run themselves down, eat too fast, talk too fast, go too fast in everything. Everybody acknowledges that dyspepsia and defalcation, heart-disease and softening of the brain, speculations, panics, and suicide are the result. Why, sir," exclaimed the Doctor, "it is for that women are made! When they go as fast as the men, God help us! Now that religion seems to be loosening its grasp upon men, rather now that men are-breaking from its hold, if woman cannot restrain them, if she swaps her sex for theirs, like the miserable girls who used to drag coal-trucks on all fours in English mines, and plunges into the pell-mell with men, then are we gone indeed to the devil!

"But no, sir!" cried the Doctor; "antidote always accompanies poison. Cinchona grows in the centres of chill and fever! Because Americans are the most excitable and headlong of people,' therefore is it that — and it is becoming our sole safeguard — in America women are most had in reverence. I like Miss Rachel. She represents the staying power, the — "

"She stopped our street-car, at least. And," I said, "as she stepped deliberately on board and seated herself, not a man of our perspiring crowd but was the better for it. It restored every soul of us to civilization simply to see her." And so the doctor and I turned the conversation into a discussion of the chances in reference to Miss Rachel of her persistent admirer, Major McAllister. It was easy to see that Dr. Trent took as gospel whatever his wife had imparted to him concerning that, and it was a good deal.

"How does Mr. Adair succeed with Miss Persis?" I demanded, after a little; for, through his wife, Dr. Trent could not help knowing about that also.

"I would think," the Doctor said in the end, very innocently, "that, of all men, Mr. Adair would be most to her taste. Like herself, he grew up far from cities and under the most old-fashioned of influences. He also has educated himself through poverty and struggle. You can see how determined he is by a glance at his chin. It is a queer combination; look here!" And the doctor made a rapid sketch with pencil, upon the blotter of his table, of the head of the gentleman. "See," he said, "what a towering cranium he has, egg-shaped like Shakespeare, like Hawthorne. Phrenology is a humbug; none the less, that oval head signifies imagination, ideality. But look at the jaw going with it; it is that of a bull-dog."

"Some one told me his history, the other day," I said. "When he began he was an ardent, even bigoted preacher of the old-fashioned faith. He was a handsome fellow, unmarried, fond of society; he had read everything, was an able man and unusually eloquent. Slowly came a change. He was praised, thronged about, quoted. I suppose you would say, Doctor, that it was a struggle between brain and jaw;

your wife would tell you that the strife was between
head and heart. According to your craniology, while
the massive base held him down, the top of his head
lifted him like an inflating balloon. But the applause increased until it prevailed, and lifted him out
of and clean over his ecclesiastical fence. He has
landed a dozen times since. Each time he is sure he
is finally right, for, wherever he goes, he takes those
vigorous jaws, you would say, with him. Now you
mention it, he is, although of small frame, like a
mastiff, an unsleeping mastiff in vigilant charge of
the premises. It has come to be the law of his life
that affirmation arouses denial. Assertion, almost
any positive assertion, is to him a burglarious tramp
which he assaults on sight. His incessant 'Not so!
not so! not so!' is more monotonous than the bow-
wow-wow of Towser. Alas! bark as fiercely as he
may, he backs and backs, as he barks, toward the end
and edge of everything, — is forced backward as by
the incessant violence of his denials. The first thing
he knows, over he goes, falls whirling round and
round through the empty air, and is forgotten from
among men. Meanwhile he reads everything, goes
everywhere, meets everybody, knows to its last anal-
ysis positively every opinion men have ever held.
Old-fashioned folk slumber upon their assumptions,
and there is an energy in his pugnacity which people
like. He is said to be very good to the poor."

"It amuses me," Dr. Trent laughed, — "the horror
my wife and Miss Rachel have of him. And yet," and
his face sobered, "I hardly blame them. Once only

did I meet Mr. Adair. It was by the bed of a dying lady, one of his parishioners. When I came in she had hold of Mr. Adair's hand with both of hers, and, her hollow and eager eyes fastened upon his face, was listening to what he was saying to fit her for death. While combating something said by the dying woman, Mr. Adair assumed that her fears were purely physical, that the old-fashioned religion was so utterly obsolete these days that nobody believed in it. I thought of the hundreds of millions the world over to whom that religion is the chief motive in life, the sole consolation in sorrow, and wondered at the cool assumption of the man. Because *he* did not believe no man did. Having shut his own eyes, there was nothing seen by anybody!

"Mr. Adair," added the Doctor, "shows excellent taste in admiring Miss Persis as he does. He would marry her if he could. His latest and strongest convictions are in reference to her. It is no laughing matter that she is breaking away from all persuasion. Guernsey," he continued, "Miss Persis has been seriously affected. Her nervous condition has alarmed me more than once. What good does it do to cut off her tea and coffee, to limit her to raw beef and stale bread, to warn her against drinking too much water at her meals and taking too little exercise? She merely tries to make up for obeying me by more intense application. She will not be controlled."

"If a lover were eloping with her," I said, "we might stop her, you think; when it is an Idea which is running away with her, we can't, especially if her

Idea takes the shape of eloquent Mr. Adair. But no, sir, I have a plot to prevent it which I will not confide to you; you could not keep it from your wife to save your life. For we cannot afford to have her marry Mr. Adair. If she were to marry a Methodist preacher, her life would be one of perpetual change, but change of that sort would be a trifle compared to the breaking up and change she would have to undergo as Mrs. Adair. Did you ever see a picture, Doctor, of Francisca di Rimini and her lover, Dante's Francisca?"

"Of course I have," he replied.

"The pathos of it is not," I explained, "that the erring couple are linked forever together, but that, as Dante puts it, the two are afloat forever upon scorching winds. Imagine a hell of that sort, the unrest of ardent and eternal guessing, each one sufficiently aflame already with consuming intellectual effort, and yet mutually exciting each other to more desperate conjecturing still!"

At this moment a messenger came in haste for Dr. Trent; a lady was taken ill somewhere. He bade me good-by and went out merely to come back again.

"I am the most forgetful of men! Mrs. Trent has told me of it a dozen times, but I have so many things on hand I forgot it! Guernsey," the Doctor said, taking my hand in his, "you must excuse and pardon me!"

"Pardon you?" But I felt that the blood was in my cheeks as he stood there.

"Yes, yes. I forgot completely," apologized the

Doctor, " for I am *so* busy, what my wife told me about you and Miss Persis. Forgive me. I ought not to have spoken of her case so freely. Aha," he laughed, " that is why you are so hard upon poor Adair. And you have a plot to defeat him, have you? Good, I congratulate you, my dear fellow!" He shook me cordially by the hand. " What a fool I was to forget such a thing! It is so natural, too. She is a splendid woman. She is intellectual, almost a genius herself. No woman is better fitted to stimulate and sympathize with you. It is the wisest thing you could do!" And he shook me again by the hand, but his smiling face clouded as he did so. " I have made a bungle of it, talking of her to you as I did. Since I have done so, let me add this. Neither Rachel, Mrs. Trent, nor I can influence her. You can! Use your authority over her, — I mean, her love for you. Don't allow her to study so hard, my dear. Tell her to spare herself for your sake, if not for her own. I am glad I *did* tell you. Good-by!" And the Doctor was gone.

CHAPTER XXVI.

THE WINDY WAYS OF MEN.

UPON the first Sunday of his coming, Ross insisted upon going to hear the Rev. Mr. Adair. I did not know then, as I did afterward, of the depth of his devotion to Persis Paige. Really it was to see her, to place himself at last in her hands, and to rest there, that he came at all. From Mrs. Trent, most likely, he had heard of Mr. Adair's admiration for Persis, that when she went to church at all it was to hear him, and he wanted to see the sort of man Mr. Adair was. In the absence of Persis he might judge of her by that; for although I was not aware of it then, Ross was eager to know, even while he almost trembled to do so, wherein the changes in Persis lay.

One rarely hears a more pleasing speaker than Mr. Adair proved to be. He appeared larger in the pulpit than out of it; there he had free and uninterrupted opportunity of letting himself out, and he did so. Ross was a person of such striking appearance that the preacher may have noticed him in the congregation, perhaps knew who he was, for Mr. Adair knew everything. This may have stimulated him to greater effort. As usual he was engaged in denying, disproving, vigorously resenting something, I forget what it was, for I was myself interested only in the clear diction, the terse and clean-carved sentences. Unless I greatly mistake, his congregation cared no more than I did for the subject-matter of what he said. He was to them, as to me, but an extremely skilful musician: it was wholly in his brilliant execution they were concerned; for the sentiment of the piece they did not care a pin. And Mr. Adair was very much of an expert in what he did. Nor was it merely in his effective anecdote, sarcasm, ridicule, superb contempt, that his skill consisted. Purely as a quality, I may say that he had great dramatic force of scorn; it was a more corrosive scorn than I ever saw in the best actor; he took such pleasure in it, so evidently from the very heart of the man did it come. His rhetoric, too, was as the scarlet of a cardinal, he was so dogmatic, so infallible. Against, not for, anything in particular. His highest power was in hatred for and assault of something; what it was he opposed, what it was he held to instead, nobody thought of that a second time.

"As sword-play it was splendid," Ross said, as we came away. "The curious thing about it is, that the adroitness of the man is by reason of a sincere detestation of, an almost desperate determination to slay, the person upon whom his sword is drawn."

"The person?" I asked.

"Guernsey," my friend said in what seemed to me to be a species of contemptuous despair, "you people who profess to believe most really believe as little,

almost, as the rest of us. Look at it. So far as this
Mr. Adair is certain of anything, it is that Christ
was, if he ever existed at all, a good man who said
and did some admirable things there in Judæa, was
killed for it, and has been dead and dust for near
twenty centuries. On the other hand, you, and
Christendom with you, profess to regard Christ as
more than man, as alive to-day as much as ever, as
present on earth now, and more actively engaged with
men than before. You say so; really you believe it
almost as little as he! Mr. Adair don't believe in a
living Jesus: but the amazing thing is, that he acts
as if he did; that is, he strikes, when you get at the
core of his fury and his assault, not at the rabble of
disciples about their Lord, but at the Christ himself.
He does n't care for the mere men, them he despises
as I do; it is the Christ he attacks, the living present
Christ of Christendom. He persists, whatever he may
deny, in considering Jesus a living, a powerful, an
exceedingly active foe, and fighting him furiously.
That is the reason he never tires, is so vigorous in
his cut and thrust. No man could fight as he does
unless with a feeling, under all, that it is with a liv- -
ing, yes, and a very dangerous enemy. I wonder you
do not understand! The Roman soldier was content
to thrust his spear into the side of the crucified Naza-
rene but once; this warrior can never, for all his
efforts, be quite sure he has at last killed the
Christ."

But Persis was absent for some Sundays longer,
and Ross went with me the round of the churches.

As I came to know afterward, he did so with a despairing desire to see, as a last resort, if there was anything among us upon which he could rest as with final assurance : to win Persis and to learn that were the objects of his coming, and he was almost as intensely desirous of the one as of the other.

One of the speakers Ross liked, in his way, very much. He was a broad-browed, earnest, apparently sincere and philanthropic man.

"He is a noble soul," my friend told me as we walked home from his church. "I enjoyed what he said. His church is what a church has to be, I suppose, these days, — nothing more than a lecture-hall. The preacher is a clear-headed demonstrator in science. He makes experiments. I could almost smell the chemicals upon the air. With a dead doctrine upon the table before him, he is very good at dissection, explanation. He made some striking suggestions, some daring guesses. He and his people are intelligently interested in conjecturing, experimenting. Who knows, they think, but something may come of it some day ? I will go again next Sunday and see."

We did so, but could scarcely believe it was the same speaker. He must have had some severe sorrow during the week before in his household or among his people. Perhaps he had read something, heard something. For some reason he was not in the mood for speculating that day among the uncertainties. To our surprise he stood as upon rock, was almost impassioned in assertion of those things upon which men must rest if they are to rest at all. I was so delighted that I told Mrs. Trent of it. After Rachel's return from the ·country she and Mrs. Trent hurried there to hear him and to rejoice that his experiments had arrived at last at some result. They came away indignant, not so much at him as at me. He had reacted to something more radical than before. "He was worse than Mr. Adair! You ought to be ashamed," Mrs. Trent scolded me, "of playing us such a trick! People should not make practical jokes, Mr. Guernsey, of serious matters. I am grieved that *you* should do such a thing!"

During his short stay Ross and I gave every Sunday to hearing some minister. Our review could not but be as limited as it was superficial. "In no city," I told him, "is there a larger number to the population of able, eloquent, devout, successful pastors. Nowhere are there, perhaps, more thriving churches, or members who work harder or give more to all benevolent objects." There was much during our rounds that I heartily liked. So, although in a wholly different sense, did my friend. He listened closely, gave to each speaker his due award of praise for logic, illustration, pathos, rhetoric, personal appearance, but to Ross it was so much enjoyment of a varied eloquence, that was all.

"Whatever thorough training, vigorous talent, fierce competition, can do," he said to me, "for men, your speakers of every kind have long possessed. All that men anywhere can do as the result thereof, they do. They do it most admirably. I have heard things I knew before strongly put. It is when they try to tell me of the things I do not know, of the underlying forces which must make a man do what he already approves but does not want to do, it is when they try to get at the things which I would die to be assured of, that they break down. Do you think," Ross said almost violently, "that I care a snap for the opinions of Tom, Dick, and Harry in regard to things unseen? Here are men straining themselves to stand on tip-toe and look over the wall. For thousands of years men have made nothing at that. I am as tall as any of them, can see as far into the invisible. Poor fellows, they do not see anything, and yet they want to lift me to look! I am sick of everlasting conjecture."

"In regard to much of it, somebody," I remarked, "has said that, at last, it is but the swing to and fro of a pendulum which can tick only an unceasing *Ego, Nego! Nego, Ego!* You may take, if you will, the spluttering electricity of Voltaire and his race, I prefer the steady fires of St. Paul, the glow of heart and intellect fed by the unchanging certainties."

"Do you? One hears," Ross groaned, "so much speechifying! I might have known it was so before I came. I must fall back on the tree lizards and cat-birds!

"While *I* am talking let me tell you one thing. I admire," Ross added, "your famous city more than I have confessed. It is magnificent. Your business blocks, philanthropies, city management, libraries, public schools, free baths, ships, factories, inventions, are wonderful. More amazing still is the persistent, highly skilled, I may say overflow of, intelligent

force. Nowhere on earth is it more concentrated
than here. Your success in regard to things material strikes me, as a stranger, very much, but not so
much as the pitiful failure of the vast effort in regard to everything else. As soon, I mean, as you
bend yourself to things unseen, I am your equal. I
can speculate about God and the soul as successfully
as the best of you!

"Guernsey," Ross went on, for he had cherished
small expectations, but they had ended in a large despair, "your people bring to their guessing in regard
to the unseen an energy more desperate than to their
daily business. In the last they accomplish everything; in the other nothing, nothing, absolutely nothing! The results in the one case and in the other
come too close together for the contrast not to amaze,
if it did not amuse. That is all!"

On account of the connection too in which it took
place I shrink from speaking of myself. My excuse
is that, really, it is *not* of myself I speak. The facts
were these. Before the coming of Ross I had produced a lecture which aroused more interest than any
as yet, because I was myself more interested in it
than in anything, so far, of my handiwork. What it
was about does not matter. It was timely, but whatever force it had lay in its undeniable truth. Everybody had been saying the same thing to himself for
some time; my sole merit was in speaking out what
many felt even more clearly than myself. It so
happened that I delivered the lecture in one of the
city halls during the sojourn with us of my friend.

When the audience heard what I said, tried to say, in my lecture, it was listening, in fact, merely to its own deepest intuitions. My words were less than their own conceptions.

I was glad, the night of my lecture, to find myself at last off the platform and with Ross in his room at the hotel. He was kind enough in what he said, but we were sufficiently stimulated to get away for the time from ourselves. "It is odd," I said to Ross, "how matters happen. Listen. Once on a time I was in a barren region out West where a man was boring for oil. My interest was not in the work, but in the man. Day after day for months had his drill forced its slow way down and down through what seemed to be the unending variations of gravel, clay, sand, rock. One day, at last, a strong torrent of oil spouted up from below, driving like straws the tools and the man himself before it. So it is with all of us. We toil on, for years it may be, but some day we strike the deepest and richest fountains within ourselves. You knew as little as any man what was in you, but you are beginning to see, at last, what you may arrive at. But, listen! A man says and does and is his best not until he drills his way through the accursed crusts of things, and gets at the central certainties. That will do; tell me something about yourself," for a man is never so apt to say foolish things as immediately after a successful address.

But the character and enthusiasm of my audience that night had excited Ross beyond his wont.

"That explains!" he said. "For your success lay

not so much in what you said as in your joyful confidence. You assumed that every one agreed with you in his inmost heart, and — "

"The clapping of their hands was," I said, "but an outer pulsation of their hearts assenting to undeniable facts. That is so, because I tried to travel only on solid certainties. When there are such fragments of rock all along for my feet, why should I flounder in the mud, or flutter upon feeble wings? 'The Devil is an Ass' is the name Ben Jonson gave to his play; for the Devil is the supreme fool of the universe, always thwarted in the end, because he prefers lies to certainties. Ross, dear old chap," I said, my hand on his shoulder as he sat, "why will you plunge forever on, as through a cypress swamp? Plant your feet, man, on the everlasting certainties!"

"Certainties?" he asked.

"I am not speaking of the notions of Tom, Dick, Harry, Aryan or American; as you say, we can guess as well as the best of them. The unseen certainties only God knows, only God can make known. He has done so! We have had them for eighteen centuries, and no more are to be told us. They suffice; look at them, — God; the soul; life, a gymnasium for the development of eternal character; every worst event overruled for our highest good!"

"How can there be a good God," Ross demanded, "when there is so much rascality and wretchedness among men?"

"I don't know. It hurts me as much as it can any man. All I know," I said, "is that God come to us in Christ accepts sin and suffering as tremendous facts; endures them for a lifetime; suffers all any man can suffer under them; undergoes the utmost that mob law, civil law, church law, God himself can do; dies crushed to death under them. When God comes in flesh, and takes, endures, survives that, I try to take the Christ, to cling to the Christ, without knowing anything else, as the supreme and sufficient certainty. In him I rest, and am contented to wait and see!"

"I can understand," Ross said, after a long silence, "that when a man *does* stand upon your absolute certainties, as you call them, he stands very firmly. The forefathers of the people living about here had such hold upon your certainties that they have sent them down with amazing force. Their personal notions everybody laughs at; these certainties of theirs and yours are in the blood and bone of their children. Can a man grasp a thing so vigorously," Ross asked of himself, "unless it *is* a fact? You can hang on to a bit of gold; if you grasp a bubble, it breaks. Anything but a fact is crushed the harder you grasp it. Certainties? Those old-fashioned believers have made America what it is,—that's a fact. This city is flooded with foreigners, yet these certainties, as you call them, are strong enough in their minority of descendants to overmaster and to leaven the new and hostile majorities, here and over America so far. Did it ever strike you," Ross added, "in regard to those who have departed from their hold upon your certainties, that in so short a time they are already a spent force? The certainties hold out, in the past as in the present, here and over Chris.endom, better and longer than that. Guernsey," Ross added with one of his steady looks, "I will say this: I know men who are worn out by debauchery, idleness, the owning of too much money. A *blasé* man is as weak as water. Mr. Adair is intellectually a *roué.* Alert as he seems to be, he is, except in violently opposing everything, as weak as a man can be, as to the definite doing of anything, as to the going in any definite direction, because he is the victim of ennui. You see, a man must exhaust his brains sooner or later; there is but a saucer full of them at best; why should the brain not give out as much as the nerve or the stomach?"

"Yes," I 'd, "Mr. Adair is, at heart, as profoundly disgusted with his present position as you or I or any man could possibly be. His resolve to escape from it is desp. No man has a clearer head, yet when he asks of himself, Where shall I go? he falters like an idiot. He must get out of his Moscow crumbling about him to ashes, but, like Napoleon, whither shall he go through the trackless snows? If he could but come to see that, in this matter, it would not help him were he a Socrates and a Plato, a Bacon, Newton, Shakespeare, all in one! The divine certainties are apart from men, are as clearly revealed as they are eternal, inexhaustible."

"Oh, well," Ross added, "this I will say: the *power* is with you who believe in them, — the power, because with you is the heart. I fear some of even your churches, as churches, are dying; the *heart* in them

seems to be ceasing to beat. But I am not interested
in such things; let us talk of something else."

Of course I knew that I might do more harm to
Ross than good, but I had a hope in a promise my
friend had made Mrs. Trent, that he would go and
hear her pastor, good Mr. Brown. He was a plain
man, sincere in his faith, excellent, hard-working,
humble, seeming never to think of himself. His creed
was that in which I was born and reared, and I was
anxious as to the result when one Sunday I went
with Ross to hear what he had to say. Mrs. Trent
was lingering for us in the vestibule of their modest
church, and I saw her eagerness in her eyes as she
gave Ross her hand, forgetting me entirely. I imagined I saw her lips move in prayer as she seated
herself next to Ross in her pew, my seat being on the
other side of him.

While the people were singing I was thinking of
the cañons in the Sierras, how they run a thousand
feet deep this way and that through the solid rock.
"Ross is, in comparison to other men," I said to myself, "as a cañon is among the glens and valleys. He
tends, as it were, due north; is deep, is rock, is
seemingly unchangeable. And yet there are fires and
internal forces which can and do alter the trend of
the deepest valleys. If Ross is changed into a happier direction, he will be Ross Urwoldt in that too,
and to the end." I glanced at him as Mr. Brown
took his text. His eyes were fastened upon the
speaker, and he remained motionless to the end in
his fixed attention. It had been my fortune imme-

diately upon the close of the war to help feed the
starving men taken from Andersonville prison, and it
reminded me of them, — the gaze which Ross riveted
upon the speaker. His face was gaunt as with want;
the features were sharp, pinched. He was a very
strong man, had vigorous appetites; he had nothing
to satisfy his soul so far, he was hungrier than he
would let me know. Everything else had failed. So
far as churches went this was his last chance.

I try to hold on to the Christ, but it is scant faith
I have in any Peter or John whatsoever, however
near Christ they seem to stand. My experience now
but established me in this. Had Mr. Brown known
the result, he would have died rather than have
done it. Alas, all he said was about something, I
forget what, in connection with Christ, not about the
Master himself. It was as if he held up for our admiration the holy coat of Treves, the seamless vest-
ure of Christ; but it was not the Son of God himself
whom he showed us. As the sermon advanced, Ross
still listened, but took — how could I blame him? —
as little interest in it as he would have done in any
other bundle of rags. After service Mrs. Trent had
not a word to say. Ross had already forgotten Mr.
Brown and what he had talked about. As I came to
know afterward he was saying to himself, as we
walked away, —

"I am done now with everything else but Persis."

CHAPTER XXVII.

EXTEMPORE.

PERSIS and Rachel were still absent, and I was walking along the street one afternoon, when Dr. Trent, who was driving rapidly by in his carriage, reined in his horse and beckoned to me. "I have seen to it," he said, "that the young ladies in the country know nothing of the visit of Colonel Urwoldt. It is essential that Persis should have a good rest from all kinds of excitement, and for that it is necessary Rachel should be with her. Mrs. Trent tells me that Urwoldt is here, chiefly, she believes, with reference to Persis, and it is partly her suggestion that Persis had better remain away, for the present at least. I think it is due to you," the Doctor gravely added, "that I should speak. There are times when a physician must be frank. Miss Persis is, I fear, very inconsiderate. Confound education!" he broke out; "they distil knowledge, these days, into strong drink, and the use of it, where women are concerned, has grown into an intemperance!"

I knew that Dr. Trent was becoming almost rabid on the subject, and answered him lightly. "People, you mean, are abandoning the flowers of garden and field for perfumes in bottles of cut glass. It is an age of telegrams, you mean, and the distillation and condensation of everything. The essences of men and women, as of nature in general, are so sublimated into novels and poems that we prefer the books to everything else."

"It is no joke," Dr. Trent said, almost roughly. "Persis always was, I learn, of a high-strung, excitable temperament, liable to intense excitement; of late she often sinks into deep depression. She has worked herself too hard ever since she came. A few weeks ago a much better position as teacher was offered her, — a large salary attached. It is such an opportunity as few women have even in this city; it is a great compliment to her, and I was so alarmed for the result that it was by my arranging, unknown to her, that she is to-day among kind friends. Before she enters upon the new position she must rest. She has allowed herself to be drawn off, as if she had not distraction enough already, by Mr. Adair and others, into doubt and everlasting discussion as to the very foundations of what had been her faith. Poor child! she is completely at sea. Tell Urwoldt she is sick. He can visit her some other time."

I fancied I saw Mrs. Trent's hand in that suggestion, but the Doctor said to me, as he gathered up his reins, "We regard you as her next friend, and, I assure you, she is in a critical situation, and — I cannot answer for the result." Thereupon he insisted upon telling me of a number of young lady patients of his who had graduated with high honors at this institu-

tion and that merely to sink into melancholy wrecks
and die.

Before he was done, Ross crossed the street toward
us, and Dr. Trent waited only to shake hands with
him, and drove on. I could not define to myself why
I shrank, as I did, from repeating to Ross what the
Doctor told me. As we sauntered along the street, my
friend stopped before the entrance to a public hall
at which there was displayed a staring placard. "I
saw a notice of this affair in my paper at breakfast,"
he remarked, "but had forgotten it. Let us drop in
a moment. We don't have this style of thing everywhere, and I may never be in this city again. We
need not stop more than a minute or so."

Knowing as I did what was going on within, I was
sorry that Ross should, in his present mood, be even
a momentary spectator thereof, but there was nothing
to do but to go in with him and take what came.

It was a long hall, narrow and poorly lighted from
without. At the farther end was a platform, upon
which, to my surprise, several ladies, old and young,
were seated, with here and there a man or two. The
audience was small, straggling, no individual man or
woman seeming to have relation to any other. One
or two were reading the papers. It is more than
possible that I was prejudiced, but I was struck as by
a malarious chill, there was something so dreary in
the aspect of everything. At least so it seemed until
I looked up at the presiding officer, who, as we entered, was addressing the meeting. Evidently he
was, or had been, a clergyman, and might be a bishop,

so patriarchal was he. There was more than clerical dignity in his towering height, his iron-gray hair, his paternal gestures, his benignant and persuasive accents. You would have taken oath that, whatever his abilities might be, he was an eminently good man, one who had endured with patience much persecution for righteousness' sake.

"The sole article of our creed, dear friends," he was saying, "is the most perfect freedom, — freedom for everybody, freedom for everything. It has been exemplified upon this platform since our Convocation met. We have had the pleasure of hearing every variety of views from almost every variety of individual. A distinguished rabbi has addressed us, — a rabbi of a large and wealthy synagogue, and of the liberal school. With great pleasure we have heard from his lips the assurance that the Jews are rapidly abandoning their belief in Moses as any other than an able lawgiver. The pretended inspiration of the Old Testament, the ridiculous stories of miracles attending the history of the Jews, the superstitious rites and ceremonies, — all, he tells us, will soon be, to the Israelites also, among the refuse of the past, with Buddhism and the miserable fetichism of the poor African. The expectation of a Messiah is definitely given up, and we have been charmed with the story of Jewish love for America as the only Christ or Canaan desired by them. We have had, also, the pleasure of listening to the eloquent lady who spoke so well for female suffrage ; to a medical friend, also, who assures us that, with due observance of the laws of health, all disease and death itself will be unknown. I could not assent wholly to our female friend, following after, who has depicted before us the horrors of marriage and the blessedness of perfect freedom of divorce, but there is much truth in what she advanced. We have been amused by the earnestness of the Christian enthusiast who addressed us so vehemently; nor have we failed to learn much from the lady who spoke to us, as she believed, under possession of the spirit of Thomas Paine. The living *and* the dead," the speaker said in a fatherly manner, " Calvin and Voltaire, sceptic, atheist, Spiritualist, Mohammed, Jesus, Joe Smith, Methodist, Swedenborgian, — we are glad to hear whoever comes. If there were a Satan," and the benevolent bishop smiled upon his laughing hearers, " he should be as welcome to say his say as God, if there be a God. That is the peculiar glory of our platform, that it is free, — free as the air, as the light!" Great applause followed this statement.

He proceeded for some time in this strain. More people dropped in, some went out. Here and there little knots conversed together. I was tired of it, but Ross would not go out with me. He seemed singularly interested. When the speaker sat down after a hearty invitation to any one to speak who liked, quite a number complied with the request. I cannot remember them all. One woman with close-cropped hair and spectacles was so very plain in her language as to the tyranny of man as a husband that the benignant presiding officer was obliged, although in a very fatherly way, to warn her that the police were present. When she had flung herself from the platform in a rage, a mild-eyed Quakeress had her say; after that, a long-haired, pallid-faced individual freed himself of the bitterest of assaults upon religion, any and every religion.

Then followed a lull. No one seemed inclined to advance anything further. People arose here and there and yawned. A small and active man passed along the seats, soliciting subscriptions to a radical periodical; conversation rose into a universal hum; men and women began to go out. The officer looked at his watch. "I see, dear friends," he said, "that we have some time left us. Is there *no* one who will favor us? Feel entirely free, whoever of you, dear friends, may wish to attack anything, to defend anything!"

There was no response. The worthy bishop fastened, to my dismay, his persuasive eyes upon my companion. "I have observed among us," he said, coming to the edge of the platform and rubbing his episcopal hands slowly and softly together, "a friend who has listened with great attention, and whom I take to be a stranger. Perhaps, sir, *you* will give us the pleasure—"

Without a moment's hesitation Ross arose, went down the narrow aisle, took his place beside the president, and looked deliberately around him. From our coming in I had observed that, whoever spoke, there was applause. Whenever any point was made, it mattered not what it was, for or against, if it was amusing everybody laughed, if it was striking every hand lent its cordial tribute of clapping. When my friend faced the audience there was a pause. He was so tall, erect, vigorous, there was so much of meaning in his aspect, his sad face was so dark and determined, that during the hush people asked of each other in a whisper who he was; evidently he was a man of distinction. Then came a round of applause. The reporters looked up from their desks below, while the patriarch whispered to Ross.

"Our friend declines to give his name or abode," the presiding officer remarked, still rubbing his genial hands together. "What does it matter? It is not himself, but what he may say, which should interest us." And the applause ratified the words.

I had read much in the papers of the power of Ross over his hearers, but had never heard him speak since we were together in college. What wholly indescribable quality is it in mere aspect and tone which compels us to yield to such a speaker, as one does not so much to music as to weight? Before he had opened his lips every one present felt that there must be value, yes, weight, in what this stranger had to say. His first accents strengthened the conviction.

I report merely such points as I can recall of the remarks made by my friend.

"Stranger as I am," he began, "I know that there are multitudes, large majorities I dare say, of the people of this city and region whom you do not represent. What I say is to you, and to those whom, organized into associations or not, you do represent. Please accept what I say in a few definite statements of the way in which you as a class, an increasing class, impress me.

"First, it is plain, from what I have seen here and elsewhere in your city, that you are consumed by a great desire to learn something you do not already know. It is natural. All men feel it. I do, perhaps, as deeply as any. An unspeakable desire!" And the depth thereof was, as he spoke further, in his eyes, his whole aspect. Thereupon the hearers applauded; they agreed with him in that.

"Another thing I have observed," Ross continued. "You are, I suppose, as intelligent a people, as resolute and persistent a people, as any alive. When you go at making money, you make it. If any needed improvement is pressed upon you, it is invented, invented out of the apparently impossible. Above all things you crave, must have, as you think, a new religion. For how long and earnestly have you striven to invent a religion which shall supersede the old! Thus far have you hit upon anything which will serve as even a temporary substitute for it?"

Ross waited for a reply. There were several moments of silence, and then applause, always applause.

"So far as I can see," he went on, "the only clear conclusion you have reached is that any final certainty to rest upon is impossible. You have lost your last hope of such a thing as truth, ultimate truth, final fact. It is purely from the force of habit, because you have nothing else to do, because you like to talk, to hear other people talk, that you keep up

even the show of trying to get at something upon
which to rest. You are like divers who, having
abandoned all hope of securing any pearl from the
depths, having given up the last lingering belief that
there are or ever were any pearls, are plunging about
in the brine hither and thither from love of the
sport, grappling with and eluding each other, laughing, chattering. But in all the wide ocean there is
not a pearl; the diving is all!" The pathos of the
words had for an instant a stilling effect; but then
followed the invariable clapping : they did not care!

"Then what is there of practical use," Ross was
only less scornful than Mr. Adair, "in your efforts?
Except to unsettle yourselves the more, what do you
accomplish? Do you constrain men to do what is
right, to hate what is wrong? Say that you help
men in every other sense, do you soothe the suffering where it becomes agony, the suffering of the
soul? In every business beside you are the most
practically successful of people. As to religion, what,
unless it is the destroying in men the very sentiment of religion, — what do you *do?*" And from
out of the sadness of the speaker the demand flashed
like lightning across a dark cloud, it was said so
fiercely. The applause was none the less, rather the
more vigorous.

"To what rest have you attained? You are," he
proceeded, " the hardest-worked people on earth.
With your hands, with your brains, you toil as was
never required of slaves. It is consistent in you to
war upon the Sabbath; to all rest, *rest,* you are the

deadliest of foes. This mill of yours runs more
st⟶   ⟶ louder clatter than any other, but the
            nd therein is — yourselves ! There is
        ⟶.ainty upon which you even profess to
⟶ow your head or heart for a passing instant.
Eternal thirst for repose, eternal and desperate effort
for repose; and so far what have you obtained but
t   ⟶rofound assurance that for you such a thing as
        is forever impossible ? You stand upon ice;
    ⟶u think," Ross said with sudden ferocity, " that
⟶ ho also feel my feet slip from under me, will
⟶ld on to *you* for support ? " No one was offended.
There was general laughter, with applause coming
after. Nobody cared one way or the other.

"Let me tell you one last thing." And my friend
drew nearer to his audience. "As a city you inherit
more from your forefathers than any people that ever
existed, — schools, wealth, free institutions, health,
unusual vigor of mind, renown. You have inherited
as men never did before, — reputation, influence
reaching across the land, over the world. And yet
the most precious part of your heritage has slipped
utterly through your hands. You have lost it so
entirely that you refuse to believe it ever existed.
You think your ancestors were hypocrites for pretending to possess it. Do you know what I mean ?
Greece no longer enjoys the artistic skill which made
it the wonder of the world. The Roman of to-day
scarce knows that his nation was once the mistress
of all lands. ·What remains of its former supremacy
to the Spain of this century ? The one thing you

have lost, which did most to make your fathers what they were, that one supreme thing is — the fear of God. Do you fear him?" Ross waited as if for a reply.

"Yes," he added at last, "as much as you do Thor or Jupiter. How many of you have the smallest fear — *fear?* of — anything? To you, when you regard him at all, God, before whom your grand old ancestors trembled, the only object they did fear, — God is as an aged grandfather, a good old soul in his dotage! You may cherish a lingering, compassionate affection for him. But fear, — the *fear* of God! — it has perished from your nature!" And then Ross paused. "Because I am with you in that," — a thrill ran through the audience, the stranger stood erect, his hands extended, there was such unspeakable sadness and sincerity in his face, — "because I am side by side in your hell in that, I say it! Of all that you inherit from men who possessed it as men rarely do in this world, you have let slip, have cast away, your chiefest birthright, — you have lost your God! In place of God what have you found? — what? *what?*"

It is out of my power to tell the manner in which it was uttered; it was like the wail of a lost soul. As Ross said it he descended the platform. After a moment the applause broke forth louder than ever. The people were delighted. One or two women with smiles on their faces arose as my friend came down the aisle, and extended their hands to thank him.

"You did it very well," one said, and another.

"It was the best speech we have had."

"I was quite interested!"

Ross looked at them in a dazed way. He could not understand. Yes; even the capability of believing anything was gone, — gone from the very women! Without a glance at me he picked up his hat from where he had been seated beside me, and kept on down the passage and out at the door.

He was no believer, but as he walked away he had but one thought: "Is Persis become like this? — Persis?"

"I see," he said at last and in an absent way as we neared our hotel, "that these foolish folk do not make you miserable."

"Me? miserable? My dear fellow," I remarked, "the people who are most ignorant of, who most oppose, the blessed result toward which all things and every soul of us tend, these work as effectively to bring it about as any. The sun itself has not a surer orbit than the silliest comet, a mere flying fleece, as it is, of gas. No, sir, I hate no man, have a kindly feeling even for the shortest-haired of those poor women, knowing that, all unconsciously, they are helping toward the august end!" I waxed jubilant as I went on, but I fear Ross did not listen.

CHAPTER XXVIII.

CHRISTMAS.

CHRISTMAS came, and Persis was still absent, and Rachel. It is hardly necessary to say that Ross would have gone to them if, from day to day, he had not hoped they would return any hour, Dr. Trent and I holding him back from going after them meanwhile. They were to return with the new year, and there was nothing for Ross to do but wait. "I *must* see her!" he one day said, rather to himself than to me, and abruptly; at the time I thought he meant Rachel, for of Persis he never spoke.

"I am glad you will be with us at Christmas," I told him. "You can nowhere find it so set forth, as it were, by contrast. These barren fields, these lines of stone fences, these severe winds and snow-hidden plains at which you shiver with a deeper than bodily chill, — it is these things which produce these people. This State, for instance, is the steel die out of which comes the coin of gold with its bold and sharp-cut bas-relief thereupon of Liberty. What an intense, anxious-faced people it is, you have often remarked. Remember that, for centuries now, the very quietness of the Sundays has been because of their deeper intensity then of thought and feeling, a thought and feeling of which all word and act are but the noisy overflow. Two holidays only they have had, Fourth of July and Thanksgiving ; and the sermon is perishing out of the last as the oration has out of the first, leaving little beside the smell of pop-crackers in the one and the fragrance of turkey in the other. Even Sunday is passing away."

"And Christmas is becoming the only holiday," said Ross.

"You see how it is." I threw my hands apart toward the proofs of that in the streets along which we were passing as we talked. "Look at those dry-goods palaces," I said. "From the days of Eve and the apple, we men have always been flanked at our austerest through the women. Tougher, more vigilant men never lived than those who settled and built up this city, as they did, in fact, our whole civilization ; but they, too, have had to surrender. Do you see those windows of plate glass, the rich and varied millinery heaped within them in easy reach, apparently, of every hand, as well as hungering eye ? Year by year those windows are widening, the brilliant display becoming more luxurious. In view of Christmas see how they outdo all they have attempted so far ! You said that our liquor-shops are innumerable ; did you ever think that the confectionery establishments are to the women and children what the dram-shops are to the men ? The theatres are larger, finer, more crowded here than elsewhere. Now I know that the harder men work, so much the more eagerly do they rush, in the reaction therefrom, into amusement, if not into drink. So it is with us. Look at that window! The creams, cakes, candies, — these show, here as elsewhere, the reaction of children from their incessant books, of the women from their hard housekeeping, if not from their excesses in hearing lectures and dabbling in the sciences and the metaphysics. It is by the swing of the pendulum between, between — "

"The intellect and the stomach," Ross rather coarsely interrupted, "that the clock-work of your civilization is kept going, is it?" But I knew that he enjoyed the brilliant display as much as myself. The air was clear and very cold. Before we were up that morning the deep snow had been cleared, under stress of the police, by every householder from before his own door, and the snow-ploughs had done the same for the tracks at least of the horse-cars. Every now and then, as we went, some man, hurrying along a little too fast, slipped and fell, and spectators laughed louder than they would have done had not Christmas been so near. More than once groups of ladies and children were startled into shrieks which ended in laughter, as small avalanches of powdery snow fell upon them from the house-tops high overhead. The toy-shops were in their glory, Saint Nicholas himself parading up and down in front of each, with hoary beard and profuse liberality of advertising chromos.

It was the only season of the year in which Ross would have done so, but he went with me into the warehouses of toys, consenting meekly to the crowd-

ing of the throngs about the laden counters, — for he
insisted on adding to the purchases I was making
for Jean, little Guernsey, and the rest. Except for
the universal good-humor which prevailed, we might
have been in a baker's shop during a famine, in
a dispensary during a pestilence, so multitudinous
and eager were we in the making of our purchases.
There was something delightfully absurd in such
eagerness after dolls, tin wagons, trumpery gimcracks
of all sorts, which could not last a week, and had no
practical use while they did. But it was in Ross I
was most interested. He was more of a boy than
I had supposed possible, — more, I dare say, and by
reason of Persis, than he ever was before.

There was something in him for which the brilliant
day, the happy crowds hustling us hither and thither,
the infection of good-humor, could not fully account.
I wondered at first if he had heard from her, his
eye was so bright, his smile so ready, his participation
in the mood of the hour so hearty. Why it was so
I did not then know, but Persis might have explained.
He had centred his one hope in life upon her, and
upon her alone. Very slowly, but now for a very
long time she had come to take, to and in him, the
place of everything for which men care. Home he
had none. Not as yet had he come to see in the re-
united Republic something unspeakably greater than
his lost Confederacy. Even the love and trust men
give to God, Ross reserved for Persis. What she had
come to be he did not know; how she would receive
him he could not say. Nearer to nature than other

' men, his instincts were deeper and truer in that too; and there was something in Christmas itself which strengthened his intuitions concerning Persis into certainties. As I afterward learned, he had been out that very day, in behalf of Rachel, but especially of Persis. Now he insisted on helping me bear to our rooms the purchases we had made; he would not wait to have them sent.

We were not the only ones bearing brown-paper parcels. Our way lay past one of the railroad depots, and, at his own suggestion, we lingered within it to watch the crowds of people swarming in and out.

"They live," I explained to him, "ten, twenty, fifty, a hundred and fifty miles out of town, in villages or on farms. Men and women, young men and girls, they come in every day except Sunday to business, most of them, and go back at night. The tides are not as regular. From five until ten of mornings they are at their flow; from five till ten at night they are at their ebb. To-day they are reinforced by those who have come in to buy presents. They will pay as much, if not more, than if they bought nearer home; but this city gives, beyond any other, a peculiar glory to what is bought in it. Look at the people!"

It was late in the afternoon as we halted in the wide doorways of the depot, and the movement was homeward. Fat and lean, tall and short, old and young, male, but chiefly female, — it was a procession of bundles, big and little, with all sorts of people attached thereto. The current ran into the depot at that hour as steadily as a swollen brook; and now it was a brook in autumn, laden with brown-paper packages in place of the sere leaves of the forest.

Sharp-visaged women, thin and spare, whom we knew at a glance to have given over their last hopes of marriage; sandy-bearded men, recognized by their weather-beaten faces to be farmers; women stout or scant of flesh, mothers evidently of children; fragile girls, pallid from work at sewing-machines or weary standing at looms or counters, at four dollars a week; old men whose intense shrewdness had puckered their lips and eyelids into microscopic consideration of the veriest trifles, — every soul of them had, thank Heaven! a parcel.

"Yonder," I pointed out to Ross, "is a lad with a cigar, which he will be very careful to be through with before he gets home. He is a clerk at a hundred dollars a year; but he takes a glass of lager already, as he does his cigar and oath, in order to be as tall a man as his companions. They do not know at his house all he is up to; but see! he has saved out of his daily twenty cents for lunch enough to buy a velocipede for his little brother. Do you observe that poor fellow with a crutch? He has that box under his arm because he did not have money enough left to send it home by express; and he enjoys carrying it. Look at that hollow-cheeked woman in black, — the one stopping out of the rush to get through with her attack of coughing. You can count her children by the bundles under her arm, — one, two, four, six; not one of them old enough yet to help her. That red-faced scamp on the left has no bundle;

everything has gone for liquor; but he is n't drunk to-day; he is carrying himself home sober for once, as the only present he can give. He will make fifty promises to-night, and his wife, poor fool, will try to believe he will keep them this time; but he won't."

"Where are the children? I see very few," said my companion.

"If you want to see children you must go into the Irish quarters. Your section has its sins. Here a dastardly crime is one answer to your question. But there are children, children waiting at home in a fever of impatience. These people will steal in through the back door with their bundles when they get home, will hide them under beds and behind chests until to-morrow, rebuking the children meantime for foolish expectations. What children are here have been in town at work. Yonder is a little girl with a bundle bigger than herself. You might know that she is the oldest, and has to support the other orphans."

"Your people," my friend said, "are, as I have often remarked, the thriftiest, saddest people alive, but they don't seem so to-day." He had heaped his packages at his feet, and was considering the crowd which poured in past us, stroking down his black mustache with the palm of his left hand, the scar across the back of it.

"The old force is in them," he said. "The war showed that. Just now the force has taken to frolicking. How hard they go at it! It is like the flourishes a man makes after he has signed his name,

— the foolish curlycues, you know. It makes me figurative to be among you."

"There *is* something in Christmas!" I said.

"It is largely the doing of Dickens. He has popularized it by his sentimentalities."

"He is but one of a myriad influences converging to one end. I belong, as you know, to no church, but," I urged, "as matter of fact, is Victoria a queen as really as Christ is a king? No, sir; kingship is not waning more evidently from czar and emperor than it is increasing in the man whose birthday is becoming the chief holiday, and the gladdest, of all nations. This universal glow of joy and generosity which is melting the midwinter into more than tropical happiness and plenty, what is it but the flush upon the sky, the mildness on the air, which heralds the sun soon to arise? That, my dear fellow, is the most radiant of my certainties."

"If I get my wish this Christmas season, I," Ross suddenly said, "will try to believe as you do."

I did not understand, but made no reply, and we went on our way to our hotel through streets thronged by the burden-bearing crowds, and brilliant by this time with lighted windows, joyous with the unaccustomed good-humor of people plodding cheerily along through the snow and the crush of the multitude.

Next day we were to have met Rachel and Persis to dinner at the house of Dr. Trent. I did not know why, but I was almost afraid to look at Ross when, on our arrival, we were told that they could not be with us. Neither did Mrs. Trent look at him, as she

said to us at table and over our turkey, " Persis is
still quite unwell, and Rachel, dear girl, is unwilling
to leave her. Don't be cross, Doctor," she added, in
the same breath.

"I am not cross, my dear," her husband replied.
"I ought to be used to it by this time." He certainly did full justice to our excellent dinner. But
a cloud rested upon us : any stranger could have
seen that by the effort we made to talk about too
many things. Jean was a tall girl now, and a very
pretty one. Ross sat by my side, and I did not care,
as I said, to look at him. He had come with me to
the house in such almost boyish gladness of heart,
and now he was so silent. His face was reflected,
however, in the clear eyes of Jean sitting opposite
him. There was that in it which darkened her happiness ; even little Guernsey glanced at him with apprehension, and both of them were glad to get away
from the table sooner than they would otherwise have
done. We could hear them rejoicing in the parlor
over what Mrs. Trent declared to be the shameful extravagance of the gifts to them of Ross and myself.

My friend was too much master of himself to show
his disappointment, not at least beyond the first half-
hour. In some way Rachel and Persis had learned
at last of his presence in the city, and had written to
him through Mrs. Trent. It may be that the one or
the other of them said something to her, too, in a
letter, for I could not help seeing that some new
mood had fallen upon Mrs. Trent. It was plain she
took a deeper interest in Ross, — in me, too, for that

matter. There was more than anxious uncertainty in her manner toward him and toward me. She seemed to suffer under some apprehension. This helped Ross and myself, I think, to do what we could to make the time pass pleasantly. We would have succeeded better if it had not been for her husband. When a patient was concerned, he would have his own way against even his wife. Moreover, he was too much absorbed in the case in hand as a "case" to remember other persons and things as he should have done.

"I used to be dreadfully concerned," he now remarked, "about people. When I undertook a difficult case I would rush from it to my books, from my books to it incessantly. All night long I lay awake worrying. If I had kept it up it would have killed me. More than that, it would, before I died, have killed my patients. Now I am bravely over all such nonsense. When I know all that the books say, when I know my patient almost as well as a Yankee clock-maker does his clock, I simply do what is to be done and then stop. If men and women will not do what I want, since I cannot call in the police and force them into doing as I wish, I let them alone. Many a time, I know the woman will get well if she will do so and so, or not do this and that; if she don't, she will die. She may be as good, as lovable, as necessary to her family, as Mrs. Trent there, if you please, but when she won't obey me, I sit down and eat my dinner, and *let* her die! Sixty thousand persons kill themselves with their own hands every year in Europe. As yet," Dr. Trent said sententiously, "only ten thousand suicides a year are recorded for America. But, think of it! Every year, in Europe, two thousand boys and girls take their own lives!"

A man accustomed to the dissecting-table can say anything; but, with Ross to hear it, I would have been glad if Trent had held his tongue.

"There is but one thing in the world — By the by," the Doctor interrupted himself, "it is Christmas, and I give it as a conundrum. Colonel Urwoldt, what is the only thing on earth stronger than a woman's will?"

"Don't answer him, Colonel," Mrs. Trent broke in; "it's an old riddle of his; he says it is a woman's 'won't.' You cannot think how dreadfully he slanders my sex." And, with a warning glance at her husband, she hastened to change the subject.

But her husband was either as forgetful as a babe of the situation, or, more likely, he was surgically determined and obstinate, now that the theme was in hand. "The time was," he persisted, not heeding what we were talking about, and at the first opportunity, "when I was terribly exercised about matters which do not disturb me now. You read of some horrible affair in every paper you open, some outrage, abominable cruelty, murder. Once I used to groan, 'Why was I not on the spot to stop it? If I could but have been on hand at the instant with club or revolver!' I don't worry myself that way these days; why should I?"

"Let us talk of something more pleasant," interposed his wife, for we all felt that the Doctor was about to say unpleasant things.

But, no, there is a fatality in it; he persisted, although he knew he ought not. "There is death, for instance," he remarked. "To us death is the most appalling of events. What folly! Looking back from another life, it may seem the best thing which could befall a man. Read of the ravages of plague and war, of famine and disaster! A baby dies as easily as a flower. Put a particle of prussic acid on the tongue of Hercules and —"

"Steven!" Mrs. Trent exclaimed.

"No, sir. Our Maker does not attach," the Doctor went on, "the value to life we do. All of us do die sooner or —"

"We won't listen to you!" His wife got up from the table, and we all arose, not until I remarked that Ross was listening, looking in his old way so steadily at the speaker. Evidently he was struck with the idea, and he went with the Doctor to his study, while I gladly remained with Mrs. Trent and the children. As I supposed, Dr. Trent was as angry as it was possible for him to be with Miss Persis for her imprudent course in regard to her health.

"He thinks it would have been better for her," Mrs. Trent told me in the end, "if she had never come to the city. The Doctor is dreadfully old-school in his notions. He says that women may come at last to take the highest positions. Extraordinary women have done so in the past, it may come to be a common thing for them to do so, but it will require

generations going before. During many a long year
they must slowly toughen themselves, he thinks,
before, as a sex, they can stand it. Many a poor
thing," Mrs. Trent mourned, "must fall as a martyr
before that."

And then we talked about Colonel Urwoldt, and
again the flutter of uncertainty, of apprehension, came
into her eyes — for me? for my friend? I could not
tell which.

Dr. Steven Trent gave himself so much to his practice among women that he made a hobby of it. It is
a pity a man cannot become a specialist without being
afflicted, more or less, as by mania. To escape becoming brutal the Doctor cultivated the poetic view of
things, especially as his sympathetic nature found, I
suppose, its only relief therein. More than once,
woman, he told me, being to man what music is to
the words, it follows that, unlike man, she must be
rhythmic, varying, alternative in her moods. I listened, amazed at the analogies he drew from nature.
Man was the rocky coast, woman as the ocean coming and going in its tides; and much more to that
effect.

"The charming difference between herself and us,"
he said at last, "the essential loveliness of woman,
consists largely in the variableness of her health and
consequent states of soul as of body. At one time,
and herself as powerless in regard to it as a floating
feather, she rises to the highest crest, so to speak, of
her nature. Then she reaches a height, Guernsey, far
beyond us; she does things, says things, feels things,

yes, and writes things, quite above us, nearer the stars. But then, and because, alas, of that, she has her ebbs of being also. Then she is less than herself. We do not get as high, Guernsey, as she does; but then we cannot get quite as low, — low, physically, mark that, — and therefore mentally, I dare not add morally. We cannot equal her at her highest; we should keep away from her at her lowest!"

The Doctor had much more to say to the same effect before and after the day of our dining with him, and I remembered it, ah, how well! afterward.

CHAPTER XXIX.

A SOCRATIC SOIRÉE.

RACHEL and Persis were to return to the city as soon as the health of the latter allowed, before long, it was hoped. Ross spoke about them less than before, but I fancied he was growing restless, although, as I knew better afterward, if ever a man hid himself in .,unself from others, and because he was feeling so deeply, he did. A few days after Christmas the meeting of one of our Socratic Soirées, as they were called half in joke, took place, and I was glad to secure an invitation for my friend. The assemblages comprised, at times, some of the best people, in certain lines at least, in the city, and was held from house to house of its members, a card thereto being considered quite a prize.

When the evening arrived I took Ross with me. Ensconcing ourselves in a corner of one of the large and handsome parlors, I explained things to him as the company dropped in.

"Here," I told him, "are men and women holding all conceivable views upon every possible topic. Now and then a merchant or inventor attends to hear us talk, and to see any distinguished person who may be here ; but such people consider themselves, I fear, as having already climbed about the only practicable Olympus in reach, and care little for our discussions. That substantial citizen by the mantel is one of them. Yonder is a celebrated Professor; that white-headed gentleman is an eloquent divine; the person beyond him is a sculptor; the lady at the window is a fine musician; that gentleman is a painter; the lady conversing with him is an authoress;" and, naming each, I went through the list, as far as I knew those present, of the diversified gathering. "I do not suppose," I said in the end, "that there are two individuals here who hold precisely the same opinion upon politics, art, religion, education, philanthrc'" 'al endeavor; but the fact that a person is here at àn is itself proof that each one is as willing — not quite, almost so — to hear as to speak, either in defence of or opposition to anything, everything, which can be held by such as are essentially gentlemen and ladies. Few cities in the land," I added with some pride, "can show a room full of persons more variedly yet distinctively influential, so far as ideas have influence. I am glad you can be with us to-night. There is Mr. Adair."

For that gentleman came in as I spoke, ushering, to the astonishment of Ross and myself, Persis into the room. But I did not call her Persis even to myself; beyond all doubt she was now Miss Persis Paige. Her dress was a well-fitting yet flowing fabric of some shade of green, which became her so wonderfully well that I murmured to myself, "I know it is Rachel's selection," and I knew also that Rachel had come back to town by the way in which the hair of Miss Persis

was arranged. I was right. At the moment Rachel
herself entered with Major McAllister. The Major
was arrayed in the glossiest of linen, the finest of
broadcloth. His whiskers were fresh from the hand
of his barber, for he was one of those gentlemen who
remind you of that artist as inevitably as a freshly
mown lawn does of the gardener. He wore a yellow
vest and heavy chain of gold. His cravat was as irreproachable as his manner, each having in it starch
sufficient to enable it to retain to the end its correct
set. He was broad, bald, eminently commodious, and
you wondered that he was not married, as in passing
upon the street a desirable but vacant lot, you wonder
why it has not been built upon. Rachel was looking
well, with that peculiar charm which does not mark
city life. One never thinks of Mary, or Martha
Washington, except as living in the country. The
broad low brow, the full cheeks, the old-fashioned
freshness of complexion, speak of Mt. Vernon, of
its substantial sideboards, ample porches, grassy
yards, fat kine, wide fields, the Potomac flowing near.
So was it with Rachel. You knew at a glance she
too was from and of the country in distinction from
the city; that she would rather live there than in
Paris itself. As I looked at her I saw that I could
no longer speak of her without adding the Miss to
her name, as in the case of her more intellectual
friend. Throughout the evening she listened to what
was said with the pleased attention of one who has
only to listen. No one asked her to say anything;
her repose of manner forbade it.

As I said, neither Ross nor I was aware that our friends had got back from the country. The fact, as I afterward learned from Rachel, was that Persis could no longer be prevented from coming. "It was hard enough to keep her there before she knew of the arrival of Ross; after that," Rachel said with a meaning more than her words conveyed, "it was impossible! She was far from well enough, the nearness to her of Ross excited her almost dangerously; but she would come." They reached the city barely in time to dress for the soirée. Persis was sure I would have Ross there with me, and persisted in coming.

It was now that I began fully to understand matters. Ross did not seem to know that Rachel was present. From the moment Persis came in his eyes were upon her; and, considering how strong a man he was, what experiences he had known, they were such wistful, such hungry eyes! He had not seen her for so long, she was so greatly changed, who can say what he thought as he watched her? It was little he listened to me, but I went on with my duty to him as to a stranger.

"Did you ever notice," I whispered to Ross, "how the habit of public speaking stamps itself upon the face of a man, upon his whole person? I could show you trees along this coast which tell of the wintry winds. Now, look at that man!" And I indicated with my eyes an advocate of reform in the room who had been all his life in a forlorn hope of one kind or another. "Do you not see the same blown-backward, yet persistent aspect one observes in the struggling trees? More or less it is true of every public speaker. There is hardly a gentleman here who is not such. They have faced audiences until, look at them! they have the aspect of cliffs washed by the seas."

Ross, looking at Persis, had nothing to say. On coming into the room she had looked almost wildly around; had seen him; her cheeks flushed, then paled; her eyes glittered. After that she guarded herself from looking our way any more.

As I came slowly to understand things, I also looked keenly at Persis as she stood talking to Mr. Adair, and then to one friend and another. Her face was thin, but so full of color that I was ready to pronounce Dr. Trent a quack; there was no sign in her of ill-health. She held herself erect, was outwardly as composed as any woman present. To my eyes no lady there — Rachel excepted, and she in a totally different way — was to be compared with her. Her beauty suggested so much more than mere beauty that I heard the question buzzed around Ross and myself, "Who is she?" "Who *can* she be?" "What books did she write?" Then something was said about Mr. Adair. Unless I mistake, envious glances were mingled with those of admiration. I winced lest Ross should heed a criticism or two upon her which fell upon my ears. I need not have feared. Oblivious to everything beside, he was asking himself if she could indeed be the sunburned Ocklawahaw girl whom he used to see in her calico frock, her feet bare and very brown. She was to him as if he saw a striking portrait of her instead, idealized, in a costly frame, and by the hand of a master. He had forgotten that I was with him. Drawing myself back, I glanced again at his face. His eyes were settled upon her with such steadiness as is not allowable in good society. There was an unpleasant suggestion in them of the eyes of a panther crouched in ambush and watching a doe grazing nearer and nearer. If he had said anything to me about her, I should have liked it better; he was too entirely natural for the place we were in. She must have felt his gaze. One feels it when a lens brings the sun to a focus upon one's hand, and it was impossible for her not to know it, when love so deep, so single, love which had waited for so long, love like that of this man of the earlier ages, was centred upon her. By the paling of her cheeks as by the flushing I saw that she did feel it; what I did not know was, that it took all the strength she had to hold herself in hand. Even then, while she loved him, she defied him as she defied herself! Not for nothing had she been training herself all these years; she would be such a woman as he did not imagine a woman could come to be. She would be stronger than he, than herself, and he should see that she was!

There was a movement in the room. The host of the evening arose, manuscript in hand, to read an essay. With the rest of the company, Persis settled herself in her chair to listen, and Ross, seated beside me in the rear of the assembly, was fain to transfer his gaze to the face of the reader. I came, as has been said, to know it afterward, as I did not even then, that my friend had an almost wolfish hunger while with us to learn whatever we could tell him. This Pilate did not ask, What is Truth? and turn away not waiting for an answer. His mind was in at least as vigorous a measure of health and appetite as his body, and it pains me now to the heart as I think how intensely he wished to know, wished to know while then and there, at the very table, so to speak, of the very men and women of all the land who professed to be best able to impart the food for which he was dying.

It so chanced that the essay was upon "Truth." No man in all that region had more reputation for wisdom than our host. He was a pallid, slight man, who gave in the reading whatever was lacking to the writing. We accompanied him with breathless attention. From the first sentence we had the feeling that he knew and was on the point of announcing something new, valuable, of the utmost importance. He was a miner who was being followed by eager friends to the spot among the Sierras where he had found and left, hastening back to tell us of it, the largest nugget of gold eyes ever saw. And now, striking, so to speak, straight across the rocky ridges, our leader hurried on with steps so rapid and confident that even Ross himself almost shared his confidence of finding treasure; the luck of my friend having been, alas! so bad hitherto. Arrived at last upon the edge of the inmost ravine where lay the priceless prize, in the very act, as it were, of pointing it out to our ardent gaze, the distinguished pioneer suddenly ceased reading and sat down, leaving us staring into vacancy. With lips still parted by reason of the hope and haste with which we had hurried after him, each of us looked with blank inquiry in the face of his neighbor, and, while all smiled, it was so ludicrous, Ross forgot himself for the moment and laughed aloud.

"What struck me," he said when I remonstrated with him for it afterward and in private, "was the politeness of your people. It reminds me of what happens when I am hunting wild turkeys. As you may know, they are the shyest of game; and the company last night were like people lying low, alert but quiet, in the brush, with a drove of fat turkeys nearly but not quite in range of their rifles. The one thing the hunters do is to keep silent; there must not be, however excited they are, a whisper, a motion. What that indispensable silence is to these, politeness is to your philosophers. Whatever you think, feel, have to say, and however strongly, the essential thing is to be polite. That is all right, of course; half civilized as I am, I admired it; your friends have reached the self-control of heroes."

That was afterward. When the essayist ceased to read, the company, after a decorous silence, were called upon in turn for their opinions upon the essay and its topic. It was impossible for language to express more tersely, lucidly, even strikingly, the ideas which the reader had advanced. Hardly a sentence but was an epigram, and each person was full of deserved eulogy upon what was presented, adding thereto some suggestion of his or her own, in dissent or assent. " It was remarkable," Ross told me when we talked it over afterward, " what bright things people said under the impulse of the essay; the dullest man there caught from it the trick of smartness. For the moment the reader actually inspired the intellects of all, — only their intellects, mind, — as the Christ is said to inspire also the heart and the soul."

Ross was right; the essay had the effect of champagne. Many beautiful and suggestive things were said until, nearly the last of all who were called upon, Miss Persis Paige was asked for her opinion. It was the first time she had had such an opportunity. I knew that she could not but be much interested. We have all heard the music which a cunning performer can draw out of the rim of a glass goblet, and there was a certain subdued intensity in the little she said, which thrilled the others almost as much as Ross and myself, it told us so well the depth of her—shall I name it excitement? After expressing her thanks to the essayist, she strove to gather up the criticisms and suggestions of those who had spoken. Yes, Truth was the harmony of things, the symphony of all conceivable sounds, the choral melody of all movement, the blending of all contradiction in the end into an absolute unit, the passing of paradox into proverb, the evolution of doubt into assurance. I cannot repeat all she said, for I was sympathizing with her in her evident alarm at her own earnestness, her haste to say as little as she could and stop. She ended, I remember, in saying that Truth was like the statue of the veiled Isis, upon which was inscribed, "I am all that hath been, is, or shall be, and my veil no man can lift;" but my chief impression was of perhaps exaggerated pride in the lady. herself, of admiration exceeding surprise.

There was a murmur of applause when she was silent, and I did not need to see the face of Mr. Adair to know what he thought of the eloquent woman.

Even before Ross Urwoldt was called upon, I shrank a little from him with apprehension, it was so much like a personal encounter, too, between Persis and himself; then I recalled to myself that he was as essentially a gentleman as any man alive, and rested on that. All along, people had glanced at him with respectful curiosity. When he began to speak, there was that in his tone and coolness of manner which confirmed the impression that he was, in a deeper sense than of birth and abode, a foreigner. After a brief tribute to those who had spoken before him, he apologized for differing from them. Because of what followed afterward I remember almost his very words, so few were they and deliberate.

"It is very beautiful and interesting," he remarked, "the much which has been said in regard to Truth. For one, owing to defect, possibly, of education, association, temperament, I have no idea even of what is meant by Truth in the abstract. To me the truth means nothing whatever but simply that which is so. That so much oxygen and so much nitrogen go to make up the atmosphere is one truth; another truth is, that so much sulphur, so much charcoal, so much saltpetre will make gunpowder. That the rings of Saturn are so many, that the sun is so many miles away, having just such dimensions and force of heat, light, attraction, is another truth. It is a truth in mathematics that twice two are four. The same of everything. On investigation, the intellect seems to possess such and such faculties, and these only, — that is truth. Men have found that, in the long run, virtue is best and vice is worst for a man. That is truth in moral science. Why say anything further? Truth is Fact. That which is *so* is Truth! Beyond that, I, for one, have no belief in any phantom, ghost, spectral something named Truth."

As Miss Persis had spoken with small reference except to her lover seated behind her, so Ross said what he did with her only in mind. As to the rest of us, his feeling, I fear, was scorn, where it was not disappointment amounting to disgust, despair. In his perishing hunger we had given him for food the most vaporous, if beautiful, of abstractions. From beginning to end no one there was more courteous than he; but there was a bitterness, too, an almost fierce impatience, under and through it all, which conveyed what he meant beyond the words he employed. He was a gentleman, but of the type of Ishmael and Esau, that was evident. Nowhere in the world do men and women detect and appreciate character more surely and swiftly than those among whom my friend then was, and I was not ashamed to introduce him to more than one of them as we broke up our assembly and parted.

I did not see, in the throng, what took place between Persis and himself. As both Rachel and herself had escorts, there was nothing for Ross and myself but to walk home together.

"You tell me," he said, as I took his arm, "that ministers of every denomination and shade of opinion were there, to say nothing of the others present, as able, decided, diversified, and intelligent in their views and beliefs. Now would you like to know the thing which impressed me most of all? What were the subjects which came up for discussion? According to the avowed belief of many present, they related to exactly *the* matters of fact which are the most tremendous of realities known to men. And yet," asked .Ross, "were they handled as such by any man there, believer or unbeliever? I admire the courtesy, — it is the condition, I know, of any coming together at all of people of views so radically opposite, — and yet, and yet!" He rubbed an impatient palm over his forehead. "It is because I am so up and down in my way," he said, "so used to dealing with facts *as* facts, but may I be damned if I understand it!"

"What do you mean?" I demanded, for he had not sworn in my presence before.

"Mean? Look at me, Guernsey! Do you suppose," he said, his black eyes holding mine as in a vice, "that .if I believed as you say you do, I could discuss my surest, most essential belief as one does a matter of dress or art, a point in politics or science, the newest poem, the latest novel? I'll tell you what, Guernsey, as sure as you live, man, it is not because you must be so polite with each other, it is because that, really and truly, not a man or even woman of you believes any more than I do! It was worth my coming here to find that out. It pays you for the bore of having me here for you to be told it."

"I hardly think," I remarked, "that faith is perishing from the earth. Since the year 1800 the population of this country, for instance, has increased nine times, the membership of the churches twenty-seven times."

"It was not the number of Christians I was speaking of," Ross said, "but the measure of personal belief."

It had no effect upon my friend; why, then, should I record a word of what I said in reply? While I spoke he was rather looking at, than listening to me. "One thing," I remarked in the end, "even you cannot deny. When a cannon goes off you know that the explosion and the ball come from within the cannon. No one denies that light and heat are from the sun. Now a man is a fool who does not agree that the source of the largest manifestation of sheer force known to men is in the Christ. Say he never existed, none the less out of the *idea* — delusion, if you please — of the Christ issues the sublimest measure of energetic force the world knows of. Yes, force, influence, power, — power to make men write, sing, paint, carve, give money, do hard work, endure, fight, hope, believe, die! Here is a force in direct opposition to the wish of men, the habit and custom of men, which is more effective, statistically, than when it began to operate twenty centuries ago. You can no more ignore it than you can a locomotive at full speed, a thunder-storm, a —"

"None the less, I don't believe in it! Guernsey," Ross said coolly, "I 'll tell you one thing. You think Christ made deaf people hear, blind people see, dead people live. Very well. Let me tell you that his greatest miracle is to make a man believe. You are yourself a stronger proof than anything you can say. Belief *is* perishing from men."

"I agree with you," I said, "and it will go on perishing until men see it is so, and dash through everything to Christ to be miraculously made to believe by the one who alone can do it. Yes, belief will, at last, so nearly perish from the earth that, in their desperation at what follows on that, — and who knows what terrible calamities may attend it? — men will break their way through the official disciples to their Master for this, as they did when he was visibly on earth."

But, as I said before, Ross did not listen to me. "Rachel," he now remarked, more to himself than to me, "is what she is in virtue, I suppose, of being a woman, in virtue of her perfect balance of body and mind, which is another name for her excellent sense. You are what you are because you have had so much suffering. Is n't that so, Guernsey?"

"What I am? I do not understand you." And I suppose my color must have risen, his steady eyes were considering me so.

"It is you, not what you say, which has any weight with me," he said; and I cannot repeat what he added except that he closed with the remark, " You are the happiest man I know of, Guernsey, and it is because of your faith, I suppose. I don't care for your faith, but I do care for you, — as a sort of phenomenon," he added; but, of course, in that he was satirical. So far as Ross preferred me to others, it was because even he could not remain indifferent to my interest, as has been before mentioned, in him.

"If I am the happiest of men," I said, " it is because I am so rich in my certainties. I can ring them down to you, one by one, on this table," for by this time we had reached my room, "as a man rings down upon his counter his twenty-dollar gold pieces! Take one of them. I do know that the Supreme Force is seeing to it that out of what now seems to be the worst thing in my lot shall come to me my greatest good, that — " But Ross was not listening.

" 'It is charged upon us,' " he quoted, " 'that our only creed is that in Judæa eighteen hundred years ago nothing particular took place.' When the liberal clergyman said that in his jocular way, every soul of you agreed with him that it was a good joke. It bewilders me! Supposing," Ross said, "that there was, *is*, a Christ, would Peter, John, even Herod, have considered it funny? And yet, Rachel excepted, everybody laughed! The fact is," he added, " you believers have really no more faith than the unbelievers. Your belief, Guernsey, is less than you imagine. Curse your shams!"

There was the sudden anger in it of a man bitterly disappointed. It does not matter what I replied. He seemed to dismiss the subject with contempt. I had much to say, but Ross was not listening to me; it was of another Messiah he was thinking.

CHAPTER XXX.

ROSS AND PERSIS.

ROSS may have been unfortunate in timing, as he did, his call upon Persis next day. Men have moods enough, but mood means more where a woman is in question. Marc Antony spoke from personal experience when he alluded to the infinite variety of Cleopatra. What woman more lovely than Melusina, yet how could she help becoming a mermaid during Saturday night? Considering the temperament of the barefooted Ocklawahaw girl, and to what a pitch she had kept that intensity strained during the years since, the wonder was that the intellectual over-stress of school and parlor did not, as with women of her kind always, react into something worse than dishabille and deep sleep.

But Ross had already remained a longer time than he intended when he came. His business elsewhere was pressing upon him. Moreover, love, like every lesser hunger and thirst, comes at last to a point where it must have its supply or perish; and when a man like Ross has waited so long, the moment arrives when he cannot be put off, and I tell his story at all because to me he was Marc Antony come again,—in love as in everything else.

Once, twice, he called to see Persis. Rachel knew the strong, stern man as if he were a child, — knew and pitied him with all her heart, so haggard he had come to be, so silent under his anxiety. When she excused Persis to him, she encouraged him so far as she could. " Persis was not very sick, she was overtaxed; she would soon be well." When the lover came the third time even Rachel's prudence gave way, and she consented that Persis, too weak to do so, should go down to see him.

Like every other lover, Ross had arranged what he would say and do. It would be very simple. He would tell her that he had always loved her, that was all. Persis knew his direct manner of doing things, and she was ready to yield to herself at last as to him. She had come East with great expectations. What was there at last to compare with Ross ? Rachel was alarmed for her when she saw her pallid cheeks becoming crimson, as she felt her thin hand tremble; but Ross was astonished to see how strong she seemed to be when she came into the parlor.

"Why, Persis," he said, "they told me you were sick. You never looked as well in your life."

" Do I ? " she laughed, and was glad of it, he seemed so pleased; she was proud of it, he so evidently admired her. It deranged his plans, she was so erect, so beautiful, her eyes were so bright. "I am a rude fellow from the West," he said to himself. "There is not a woman to compare with her in the world. I must be careful." And so they fell to talking of indifferent things for a while. The trouble with both of them was that they were so certain of each other they could afford to wait; there was pleasure in dallying with rapture. They spoke of Dr. Trent and his wife. Then Ross told her of his plans for the future; he was going into politics; he had schemes about schools to be established over his State; he was organizing a society to encourage emigration thither.

"I see you have learned much since you came here," she said; and she went off into praise of the city, its people, its institutions. Here was, to Ross, the fruition at last of the hopes of a lifetime. She was thinking only of Ross; it was Ross she was rejoicing in, and the city, for which she cared not a straw in comparison, was but the nearest topic; her heart overflowed, she must praise something. As they talked she became more exhilarated under the admiration, adoration almost, of his eyes so dark and steady. She knew that she was saying brilliant things, and she felt so strong, too, and well. "How can you endure to go back," she said at last, in sheer wantonness; "it is so dull there, so slow and behind the times! I know that you like everything here best. You do, don't you?"

Her lover was burning to get at that which was nearest the heart of each, but he said something in denial. What did he care for anything but her? He would come to that in a moment. But she was full at the instant of her admiration for this author and that, several of whom she knew personally. He loved to hear her talk, noticing that she was so much more improved than he had thought possible, then forgetting even that in her vivacity. "And you do like everything here?" she repeated.

If he could have been a little cooler! The day when, as a boy, he had crept upon and brought down his first deer had seen him more composed than now; but then Persis had become more to him than life itself. If he could have reflected, he might have known that her great liking for these writers was but the irrepressible expression of her love for him! But her excitement was contagious. "No; I do not rate them as you do," he said. "What author of them all compares with those of other lands and ages? People hereabout have deft fingers; they take English or German bullion, and draw it out into fine wire and weave it into all sorts of fancy work," and much more to that effect.

Ross did not care a penny about it; he only wanted to aggravate her to further speech; he loved to see the play of light in her wonderful eyes, the motion of her restless hands. His was the curiosity of a big boy come into possession of a new and wonderful toy; he examined it carefully, tried it this way and that, wanted to see how it would work, — was it not his own? He was more of his father's son than he knew. There was in his manner of playing, so to speak, with her an appearance of ingrained contempt for a woman as a woman beyond what he knew. It may be because Persis was too tensely strung at the moment, but she felt it so. His face, the familiar tones of his voice, brought Ocklawahaw back again, and she remembered vividly what women were there.

She had rebelled against it when she was a child; these last years had been spent in another place than Ocklawahaw! Moreover, she was weak, nervous; she had drawn upon her health as a spendthrift does upon money which he considers immeasurable. She had engaged in her studies with such energy, such velocity, so to speak, that she had not strength left wherewith to check herself. Now, as she talked with her lover, her cheeks grew hotter, her lips became dry.

There was no excuse for Ross! He had fallen into his hereditary trick of continuance, as after game; as if, drawn aside by a squirrel when pursuing deer, he had persisted in pursuit of the unworthy object from mere habit of persistence. Neither of them cared anything except for each other. Had he told his love when he first came, she would have given herself to him without a thought of anything but him. From that hour their mutual affection would have melted and moulded them into one by a flame more than the double of that which glowed in their hearts while apart. But Ross had fallen now, only for the moment, he said to himself, into another mood. Could it be that, born and raised as he was, he felt a secret jealousy of this Persis whom he so admired and loved,—jealousy, that is, of her as a woman? Was it only her imagination that this strong man was provoking her to say things, as he would have done a precocious child? "She ought to know," Ross was saying to himself, "that, whatever I think of her sex in general, she is to me the one exception to all women that ever lived."

What he said aloud was: "It is natural that these people should seem to you as they do. The change from Ocklawahaw was very great; you were quite young, and merely an impressionable girl. To a man, accustomed to a rougher, stronger life, things seem different. These people spend their days in furbishing up and grinding down the broadswords of their stout old grandfathers into razors, razors wherewith to split hairs. The way it strikes one from ruder regions is, that excessive over-culture is the law of your life."

"What Vandals and Goths might think — " Persis began; but Ross had already listened long to what she had to say, he would not be put down.

"Thank you for the suggestion. You know," he said, "the condition of Rome when the Goths and Vandals broke in. The masters of the world were sunk into a luxurious effeminacy, — womanishness, that means. The difference with this Rome is that its womanishness is not sensual, but intellectual. It resembles paralysis; that is, even in matters of thought and the deepest thought, the hand shakes, is uncertain, as with perpetual palsy. Your leading minds are undecided. Therein lies the reason they effect so little. Nobody can accomplish anything by indefiniteness. There never yet was a man who conquered except in virtue of strong personal conviction, — conviction positive, sharp, final. It is worse than nonsense, it is feebleness!"

Colonel Urwoldt had been used too long to the handling of soldiers. His accents were too much

like words of command. He may have known Persis
up to the hour when she left the Reservation; he
did not know her as she was now. He loved her a
thousand fold more for what she had become without
at all understanding what that was. Moreover, he
had a deeper aversion than men in general have to
seeing the women they love under the influence of a
priest. This lover had no faith in any religion; yet,
strange to say, he shuddered to see that Persis had
none, yet the influence over her of such an unbeliever
as the Rev. Mr. Adair was more offensive to him
than if that gentleman were a Jesuit instead. He
had no faith himself, but he unconsciously clung to
his faith in woman's faith. Ross was in a state of
transition, little as he knew it, and what should have
been in Persis a woman's faith was to him the sole tie
to life, as of a babe through its mother. Mr. Adair
he hated; and it was the outcry, although Persis did
not know it, of his soul as of his heart, when he said,
"Biddy yields to her priest; don't yield to yours,
Persis, don't do it!"

Persis felt her lips grow parched as he said it.
She was very weak; and that much the more she
was excited, exasperated. I will not detail what
followed. Must manliness become brutal, and as
by its very completeness? And Persis? Alas, the
sweetest music breaks into a scream if it soars too
high! yet it was merely the excess of womanliness
in her which made her the more bitter as she replied
to her lover. For Ross seemed to be possessed of a
very devil of teasing; he intended no more than that.

She had become attached to the persons and things about her, knowing what they had done for her; but of that he did not think. He might have seen in her dilated eyes, in her hot cheeks, how feeble she was. Had he taken her hand its trembling would have taught him. All that he saw, as he talked, was her brilliant beauty. He had no feeling but of ardent affection, affection on the edge of possession at last, as he gave vent to his gladness in ridicule of authors, lectures, literary clubs.

"The emptiest nonsense of all," he said at last, " is the everlasting disquisition going on here in regard to matters which are hopelessly beyond the reach of even the ablest. Persis, it is the sheer frivolity of this which makes it so acceptable to your sex."

In view of what came after, let it be remembered how her grandfather, yearning after a regenerated world, and despairing of existing instrumentalities toward it, had taught Persis that it might come by means of a race of women better qualified for the work than any going before. From a child she had studied her Bible to that end. Christianity had slowly wrought the world up to its present estate by the unsuspected force of the meanest things. Yes, woman was the undreamed-of force which was to revolutionize and complete the salvation of the race. She had, then, found many a scripture for it. If this Joan of Arc had left all that behind her of late, it was because she had come out into the open field where flags were more avowedly unfurled to the same result. How keenly she felt the contempt implied even in jest, for her sex, and by Ross of all men, she alone could know. He had told her long ago that the intense determination of the North at the outset of its war upon the South was itself an assurance of its success, and she believed that the very earnestness of feeling by woman for woman, these days, was itself a prophecy of what, purely as women, they were to be and do.

" You think that at last we are only squaws, " she said, and he began to see in her eyes fastened upon his something he did not understand. Was it the dawn of a morning he had not anticipated in her, in any woman ? Was it the first flash of a coming storm ? He shrank before it. If Persis could have known !

Strange as it may seem, the chief hunger of the man since he could remember had been for a home of his own. It was in his nature from the first; he had been deprived of it by his father's brutality and then by the marriage of his mother. To this he had looked forward through his years in camp and the uncertainties following upon the close of the war. He hungered for peace, for rest, for time to think, for a period during which he could come to some final decision in regard to matters which, often as he denied it, made worse strife within him than Federals and Confederates had ever made without. Even as he spoke his one desire on earth was for a home, — a home, and for Persis as the wife who alone could make that home.

Perhaps Persis could have endured any measure of joy. Rachel had allowed her to come into the room, hoping in that as in the best medicine in reach, in that and in the rest of soul which could not but come to Persis when her years of hope had found assurance at last. "Her future will seem to her," Rachel thought, "a heaven of repose. After that, after she and Ross have come to an understanding, the long strain will be over. What does she care for except for him?" Persis had gone down to see her lover with the craving, under show of strength, of weakness, utter weakness. She loved him with her whole heart, she knew that he had never loved any but her. He was so strong; none but she herself understood how strong he was, how tender he would be, how true! She already saw, and before she entered the room, his eyes fastened upon hers with the steadiness of a love which would never change. Already she felt his arms about her. "I am so tired," she had almost sobbed. "I can trust to nothing else in earth or heaven. Everything else is emptiness. He will take me to his heart. It will rest me so! rest me, rest me!"

And then befell what has been but imperfectly described.

"You think we are only squaws!"

She lifted herself by grasping the marble of the mantel, and, holding herself apart, she stood before him there, the one object, stern, pale, which was to come between him and everything else for many a day to follow. Even then he could not help seeing how her dress fell away from her as she stood, how much she had lost of flesh. Her cheeks were hollow, even if they were brilliant, and her eyes were too bright. She could not remember afterward what she said to him. It was an irrepressible torrent upon which she was but as a floating leaf. Nor could he remember what she said. He saw in a stupid way the mischief he had done. Not regarding what she was saying, he studied how to remedy it. Once or twice he was on the point of taking her in his arms, of soothing her upon his bosom, of begging all manner of pardon, of stifling her angry words with kisses. He dared not attempt it. He was afraid to risk it. He loved her the more for the terrible things she was saying, even while they angered him and drove him off. Then she stopped and began to laugh; she could not help it! As he looked at her in amazement she broke into a violent weeping like a little child, and, before he could stop her, she had gone out of the room.

Left alone, he stood in the centre of the apartment, staring at nothing, like a fool. Then he began, as he stood, to curse the city to which she had come; but when he entered upon the profanity due himself for his brutality the subject was too vast. He could do that more justice afterward. Then he rang the bell and sent up a line by the servant. He had hardly supposed the note could be delivered when the answer came back.

"*Persis is seriously ill. Neither she nor I can see you now, nor for a very long time. You need not wait.*   RACHEL."

Even then it struck him that the writer had not written before, so far as he had seen, in a hand so

full and bold and clear. But he held it in his grasp
as he walked down the street, and entered again upon
the task of cursing himself.

My knocking at his door that night brought no
response, although the hotel clerk became irritated
at the number of assurances he had to make me
that my friend was undoubtedly in. As I learned
afterward, he called again and again upon Persis and
Rachel; but neither of them would see him. They
could not. He was not the kind of man who resorts
to writing; nothing less than a personal interview
would suffice for him. All this time letters on
pressing affairs of business had been pouring in upon
him. He was needed at Washington, then in the
South. Large amounts of money depended upon his
immediate return thither. Indignant telegrams began
to follow each other in rapid succession. So sure was
I that he avoided seeing me that I was as careful at
last not to be seen of him, and in a day or two he
was gone. The only memento he left was his card,
with the words scrawled in pencil upon the back : —

" Called off by business."

CHAPTER XXXI.

OCKLAWAHAW AGAIN.

WHEN Ross Urwoldt returned from the East to his plantation, it was to enter upon his affairs with a species of cold energy such as he had never before shown. If such a metaphor is allowable, his arrival was as sudden as that of an aerolite, and he struck, so to speak, with such force as to bury himself in the soil. For a time he saw no one but his overseer and the freedmen, and, rising with the dawn, he gave himself, and exclusively, to the making of corn and cotton. Apparently, but not for more than a few weeks. When the change of season enforced a relaxation in his planting interests, he turned from it to other things with such vigor as to dismay his rivals, — for this one law seemed laid upon him, he must work without cessation; why it was so he did not define to himself, but he dared not stop. The paper he edited had sunk during his absence into that most mole-like of things, a "local paper," and he took it in hand and lifted it out of its narrow circle, breathing such breadth into it as alarmed its patrons for his "soundness" on State affairs. His success at Washington in things legal brought him new clients, and he took every case that came with the avidity of a man who had his bread and his reputation yet to make.

With it all he went into politics as a candidate for the State Senate. Everybody knew him as one who had fought with desperation during the war, and the comment ran the round of friends and foes, "The Colonel always was as ambitious as Lucifer. He has been in Washington and knows the ropes. When he gets in the Legislature, won't he make Rome howl!" For weeks he toiled, in his paper and upon his round of speech-making at every cross-roads. There was a fierceness in what he wrote and said which slow-going people could not understand. "He has fought so long," they said, "that he cannot stop fighting. You can't get the hang of what he is after. He is harder on us than he was on the Federals. The hotter he gets the harder it is to make out what the Colonel is after. But he is all right, you bet! They say he is to marry the daughter of the old Governor, who is at school up North somewhere. Smart move!"

How could others comprehend him, seeing that he did not stop long enough to comprehend himself! For this friend of mine did not have an atom of sentiment; you are imagining a different Ross Urwoldt from the man of whom I am speaking, if you think he had. He stripped himself of his last dollar during the war that Rachel and Persis might not, so far as he could help it, be inconvenienced, and no man ever loved woman more than he did Persis; but the passion Persis had for him was because he by no means did his wooing upon his knees. He sought or did not seek her, as opportu-

nity served. He had taken his time about it. In mid-
torrent of his greatest ardor he had held himself in
check, and her. But, and so much the more, would
he make — and none knew it as well as Persis —
a husband who, till he died, would be even truer to
her, as he came to know her, than he was to himself.

No man, meanwhile, so sick of strife as he. During
his political canvass he spent night after night under
the hospitable roofs of planters, the whole household
coming about him after supper to hear what the candidate had to say. While husband, wife, and children listened to his talk about Washington City, about
the schools the South must have, how best to deal
with the negroes, and the like, the wiry, stern-featured
man was envying the dog, even the cat sleeping upon
the hearth, — these had at least a home. A home with
Persis! in the universe there was nothing he cared
for except that!

He was elected to the State Senate, but he was not
popular there even while he was acknowledged to be
the ablest man in the Legislature. His was a nature
which could not sour; but how could he be patient
while the war was fought over again in his hearing,
day after day, with impassioned but futile oratory?
It was in vain that he introduced and urged what he
regarded as measures of the utmost importance; in
almost every instance they were voted down, and he
found himself upon his plantation again at the end,
a very tired and badly beaten man. While this was
going on, his practice as a lawyer ran down; his
paper lost its circulation and stopped. The day of

his return to his home he learned that his overseer had been swindling him and had fled. State enterprises in which he had invested money failed; the titles to much of his land in the Reservation had fallen into dispute, owing to Spanish grants which had been found or forged. Even the husband of his mother, indolent Amasa Clarke, became in some way a contestant, in behalf of his wife, for large possessions which Ross's father did bequeath, or should have bequeathed her, and long letters began to come to him, first from Mr. Clarke and then from the lawyers.

Except for the sickness of his early childhood, he did not know what illness meant; but now he lay prostrate in body as in mind. The indomitable will remained, but mind and body both were to the will as broken arms. If Persis had been his wife he would have arisen from his troubles, and have been, by virtue of having her to fight for, a stronger man than before. As it was, he was as much alone in the world as if wrecked on a rock in mid-ocean. There was something worse still. Along the Atlantic seashore there are trees which strive to lift aloft vigorous branches. But they draw their existence from a soil of only a few inches in depth; beneath that is a bed of clay, white and barren as marble, into which the roots strive to thrust themselves in vain. Having no grip, as upon the globe itself, how can the tree resist the storm? And that was the curse of Ross Urwoldt, that he could not lay hold upon the world with the grasp of any living interest.

For weeks he lay as in a stupor. Beyond a neighbor or two, almost the only person he saw was the freedman whom he had made overseer; and he came in every night with the same old story that not a freed-woman could be got into the fields, and that the men were little better; "de hebbiest crop of cottin you ebber saw a perishin' for de pickin'!" Who can say what passed through the mind of this man as he lay? Everything had failed him. Persis? When he was upon his feet and strong, he had been confident of what she would have said if he had asked her to marry him. In his weakness he was not so sure. She knew everything, was very beautiful; but now that he was sick himself, he doubted whether, with all her education, she was at last anything more than a nervous, capricious, hysterical woman. His mother had been highly educated in her day, and why should not Persis, too, slide downward again into the same limp womanishness? He remembered, as he lay, what Dr. Trent had said of the sex; their weaknesses, perversities. Dr. Trent? Yes, and he had said, too, that life does not have the value, by any means, which men attach to it.

"Let me look at it as one does at the raising of cotton, — what does it pay me to live?" Weak from fever, his whole life passed languidly but distinctly before him. Ocklawahaw — and here was his black-eyed mother, loving him so; no, it was Mrs. Amasa Clarke, Mrs. Pooga-Dooga, dirty, stupid, ignorant; the other woman was his childish delusion. The Big Meetings — what good had they done? Parson

Williams — so poor all his life, and dust for so long now! Then his bloated, red-faced father stood over him as he lay. Ross could smell the whiskey-breath of flesh consuming in alcohol, as he did that day he rode with him after the thief. Yes, and there he lay dead among the gravel. What good did his land operations and browbeatings of people do him?

"And there is Governor Beauchamp, orator, buffoon, Congressman, lying drunk under the sycamore! Governor again, with a yell and a whoop, dragged out of office by the shoulders, making a pitiful stand for the Union, dead, and this time for good and forever! And here comes the war! what ardor, and beating of drums! what speech-making, and glorious prophecies! how the boys were hurrahing! Then the fighting! Victory. Defeat. Victory again. Defeat once more. The fields covered thick with the dead! And they were so brave, too! Prison, hospital, camp, nearly four years of it! What was it for, anyhow?

"I went to the city to see Persis. And if they had anything to tell I wanted to know it. What did I hear? Guesses, clatter, contradiction. Persis lived there, she knew all they had to say; what did *she* believe? Nothing. Persis? Poor thing, what does your fine education make of you?" A fragile woman stood before the sick man, talking, arguing, getting excited like a peevish child, her hands tremulous, her face white and drawn. Her eyes glittering, she talks, she laughs, she storms, she cries, she can't be silent, she can't be still. "She can't wait to see when a man is only teasing. Know? She does n't know *me*, and after all these many years! Know? She knows so much that she has lost the power of knowing the simplest thing. Know? Yes, but she does not know how to love!"

When the end came, I, Guernsey, was selfish enough to be almost hurt at the little influence I had exerted upon him. I had wanted to do him good. I had tried not to say too much to him. All that he said in his last letter before his sickness was, "I like you, Guernsey, more than any man I know. If I could be as certain as you, I would be a happier man than even you can ever get to be. But I do not *know*. What is more, I *cannot* know! You would not be me, I cannot be you."

The one person in the world who could influence Ross Urwoldt was Persis Paige; but Persis? She had learned a vast deal, — had learned, if you please, everything else. But in learning it she had broken herself down from doing the one thing she was created to do.

It was because he became as weak as a child that, like a child, he was seized, as he lay, with a desire to get back to Ocklawahaw, — not back to his mother, not back to the mere woods and prairies of his childhood, but to his childhood itself. Leaving his affairs to take what course down-hill they pleased, he got out of bed, and journeyed back, as he could bear it, to the Reservation.

The keeper of the old log tavern in Ocklawahaw did not at first recognize him when he dismounted at his door. "Had chills an' fever, hain't you?" Mr. Golson demanded.

Emigration had brought in men and money, but these, too, had so yielded to the inertia of things as to make matters worse in the town. Everywhere appeared dilapidation and decay. The keeper of the tavern, the men loafing about the store, the old Indians and half-breeds prowling through the neglected streets, the half-naked children rolling in the dust, the small farmers driving in with unpainted wagons and rawbone horses to sell their produce, — all were in keeping with each other. What Ross had grown accustomed to in the East, and even in his own State, made Ocklawahaw seem doubly down by contrast.

All the way, as he walked through its well-known streets that day, he tried to make things look as they used to do when he was a boy. Hardest to do of all, he tried to bring to mind his mother as she used to be. Not an ounce of paint had been applied to the house in which she lived since he had left it; that and the broken pickets were the things most noticeable as he drew near. But who could that fat old woman be upon the front porch, rocking herself in a hide-bottomed chair, her hair about her shoulders, her dress an old calico, a baby in her arms, a pipe in her mouth? It was impossible for Ross to believe that she could be his mother. She had fallen below what he had feared when he saw her last; but now? Weak and tired out, he sank into a chair and looked at her with eyes sad and steady. Yes, although she was the master so far as her husband was concerned, his shiftless indolence had degraded by infecting her beyond all that Gerald Urwoldt had done. It is sad for a man or a woman to possess health and lose it, to possess a million in money and lose it, a throne and lose it. Men and women have had character and pre-eminent reputation and have lost it. "This mother of mine," he thought, as he looked at her, "has lost her education as completely as I have lost my faith in everything. The worst of it is that she does not know it." The squaw-like cringe of manner at first sight of her son, that was there still. Almost with her first words she began to ask him about her brand of cattle. The baby in her arms began to cry; other of her children, fat and dirty, came in and clustered about him with their beady black eyes. Amasa Clarke might return at any moment. Ross made his stay as short as possible.

"Did you know," she called after him, "that they have got back again?" But he did not hear, or hearing did not heed her.

Before breakfast next morning he got up, went over the street to the old store, managed to find his way up into the loft. As when he left it, the low walls were covered with the paintings of his father. Ross forced open a little window and looked at them. They were coated with dust, the rats had gnawed them here and there, the rain had got at and washed out much of the color. The largest of the pictures was at the gable end of the loft, and reached from the floor to the slanting roof. It represented a hunter

in the midst of a herd of buffalo. Notwithstanding
the dust, the damp, the general decay, Ross could not
but observe how true to nature, although but in spots
here and there, was the transparency of the sky, the
rolling of the prairie slopes. Even then he saw that
the tangle yet elasticity of the grass was that which
he had so often observed. And the buffalo too, the
confusion of the stupid yet infuriated brutes, with
their small eyes gleaming through their matted hair,
their distended nostrils, their gaunt flanks, — Ross
had himself often been in the midst of such. "Never
have I," he thought, "been other than in the surging
brutality of some such beasts since I was born!"

But it was the hunter upon the frightened horse
amid their throng which fastened his eyes. Ross
recognized in the man in his buckskin suit and
broad-brimmed hat, his rifle in poise, cool, athletic,
exultant, what his father must have been before he
himself had any existence, recognized himself!. The
horse the hunter rode was a spectral smear, but the
head of the rider projected from the discolored canvas, its eyes glittering like the last lingering sparks
in a heap of ashes.

"You had your day!" It was the sole tribute the
son could offer as, turning away, he rummaged under
the joist beneath the roof and drew out of the dirt a
short gun. He almost smiled as he remembered the
day he had hidden it there so long ago. Lying beside
it in the dark, was the old shot-pouch and powder-horn
which Ross had forgotten. He examined them eagerly. Yes, it was his mother who made the pouch out

of the skin of his first deer; every stitch was familiar
to him. And the powder-horn? There were his
initials, "R. U." He could not have been more than
eight years old when he scratched them upon it. He
had fitted the bottom in and the stopper; the charger
he had made with his own hands out of a boar's tusk.
He was too weak to be ashamed of his emotion as he
handled them now. As he took the weapon in his
grasp and looked it carefully over, the first thrill of
pleasure he had known for many a day passed through
him. It was a double-barrelled shot-gun, yäger pat-
tern, the first fire-arm he had owned. It was rusty
with years of hiding where he had put it under the
drip of the eaves, but he took it over to the tavern,
rubbed it up and cleaned it with an almost personal
affection, remembering that day in the snow when he
had brought down with it his first squirrel. Not a
dog or horse he once owned remained to him. "This
is the last friend left to me," he said, "and it may
prove to be the best to me of all."

An hour after, Ross was seated on the stone beneath the sycamore outside the town. He had slept
like a babe, so tired out was he, the night before;
but there was that in the familiar scenes around him
now which crowded upon and dazed him, like the
darkness and stillness of another night.

"Governor Beauchamp used to sit on this stone,"
he tried to state it to himself, "and talk. How often
have I seen him lying just there!" For the moment
the purple-faced patriarch lay at the feet of Ross, so
vivid was the remembrance. "He was but a bigger

grain of dust," the wearied man tried to think, "an atom of dirt whirled by the winds this way and that, dropped when the wind stopped blowing, picked up again, hurried by the gust here and there. Now he is dead, is dust and nothing else."

But what did he care for the old Governor? And he fell, as he sat upon the stone, his head against the sycamore, into a dreamy dulness, to awake out of it with a start. "Persis? Yes, it was here Persis used to sit, poor little thing, in your calico and trying to hide your little brown toes! '*Penna, pennae, pennae,*' was it? What did you get out of it at last? Persis? Did I love you? Did I ever love anybody? It is all too long ago. Let me see — see —" To keep awake he forced himself to get up, and walked slowly on to the river, and then up its ragged bluffs into the belt of dense forest separating the town from the prairies beyond.

"Yes, here you are again, old river." He sat down on a rotting log to look at the muddy stream, while he tried to think how he used to swim in it, to paddle up and down in his canoe, to fish, and shoot alligators caught sleeping along the shore. "Halloo, old pecan-trees, how are you? Have they gathered all your nuts yet? Let's see." He had forgotten for the moment the season of the year; but, yes, the earth was thick with dead leaves, it was late in the autumn, the ground was covered too with the brown hulls, what nuts he could find were rotten. "Any mustang grapes left?" He went peering about through the tangle of vines. "There used to be so many," he complained. Finding a cluster or two, he sat down on the dead leaves, laid his gun aside, and ate the grapes very slowly, picking them off one by one. The pulp was at its sweetest, but the skins were at their bitterest, and he ate these, too, as when a boy. Then he sat, his hands fallen between his knees, and thought, — tried to think, for the woods were closing in upon him as in a dream.

"It used to be so much to me," he murmured to himself, "used to be everything. Is it because I have got behind this stage-scenery, too ? I am so dull, so stupid." It was a cloudy day ; there was no wind, and the trees, except where the poison oak-vine clambered up their trunks, were almost leafless and silent. Now and then a lingering leaf detached itself and fluttered slowly to the earth, a squirrel ran from tree to tree, the stealthy tread of opossum or raccoon was heard, a chipmunk darted across the openings, in the distance a rotten bough fell to the ground, a blue-jay chattered, a catbird called, an owl whooped ; but all sounds so neutralized each other that they made themselves into a murmuring silence which pressed upon the brain, a hush that was also a force.

He had counted upon relief among the scenes of his childhood, and found only depression. For a long time now he had thought and felt until it was impossible to think or feel as he had done. Beyond mere earth and wood and water; beyond mere light and air, and such animals as he chanced upon, there was to him — nothing. A hand gloved, so to speak, in these things, was laid, could he but have

known it, tenderly upon his eyes, soothing him
thereby into that solitude, silence, repose, out of
which comes recovery. As he sat he fell asleep. Re-
laxing in his exhaustion from his upright position,
he lay at last upon the thick mattress of dead leaves.
Often when a boy he had slept all night beneath
those very trees, and now he had been pressed back
by a living hand out of his manhood into his boy-
hood, pressed back of that into his infancy, back
of that into an unconsciousness such as goes before
birth. To his utmost he had asserted himself and
failed. His was the submission which comes at last
to every man at death. For hours he lay, his dark
hair tangled with leaves, his hands cast out helplessly
on either side of him, almost as utterly done with
himself as if he were dead. Almost, not altogether!
A mother need not fear she will awake her child
when she creeps at midnight to its crib and bends
over it; not so when the child has grown to be a
man, at least not so if the man is of strong person-
ality. Stand over such a man when his sleep is at
its soundest, and suddenly you will see his eyelids
unclose; he is back again, and in a moment will have
you under his knee and throttled if not recognized
as a friend. So in the case of Ross Urwoldt, lying
dead asleep. What is the inmost self of the man?
What was that which was within Ross as a man is
within his clothing? It was a Ross Urwoldt so
much apart from his sleeping body that suddenly
he awoke as if aware of, and resenting and resisting
the presence with him of another, even of that

invisible presence bent over him only in tenderest care.

Angry with he knew not what, he arose to his feet, and, picking up his gun, he struck through the woods and out into the prairie beyond. "I can remember," he said to himself, "when, as a boy, I counted over a hundred varieties of flowers which I found among the grass here. They must long ago have ceased to struggle against the hoofs of the cattle!"

When he reached the first eminence he stopped, threw his hat upon the ground, and looked around. It was a hill too high and too conical not to be, as he well knew, one of those mounds in which slumber a buried race. He had been present at excavations made in others like it, and knew what it contained, — rude implements, bits of pottery, and bones, heaps of the ashes of what were once multitudes of living men whose name and history had perished with them. "But that much more dust," he thought. "It was dust from eternity. In the whirl of things it became men; ate, drank, slept, fought, slew, suffered, died, and so was dust again. Is there among it a smaller atom of dust than myself? And this — what is this?"

The clouds were broken, and the sky was blue, the sun shining brightly. His eye slowly swept the entire expanse of earth and heaven, trying to recall the amplitude and glory of what it had been to him in days gone by. "Is my brain sodden," he said, "that I can make nothing of it but a vast prison? What good is there in mere size? It is, at last, walls

Who can tell by what instinct he followed, as he walked slowly on, the road along which he had driven that day with his enraged father? He was very tired when he sat down at last upon the spot beside the creek where his father had fallen and died. The road ran abruptly down to the water and through it, and so up a steep incline, and out again toward the farms beyond. It was the way most travelled by those going in and out of Ocklawahaw, and the gum-trees and willows grew thick on either side, making a shade deep and dark over the current, gurgling as it went.

"You need not sing it so steadily," he murmured, his voice sounding far off to him as he said it. "Do I not know, know, know it? Yes, —

> ' Men may come and men may go,
> But I go on forever, — '

go on forever, ever!" His head sank upon his bosom. It was late in the day, and he had walked many miles forgetting the food in his deerskin pouch.

There was a sound at last of wheels coming from the town, and, looking up a moment with a blank stare, he hastened to his feet, and, barely in time to do it, he stumbled rather than sprang into the thick undergrowth until it should pass, whoever and what-ever it was. He might have known, had he cared to do so, who were in the vehicle as it drove by. It was impossible that he should not have recognized their voices, for, halting mid-stream to allow their horses to drink, they conversed together, talking of the death, near by, of Gerald Urwoldt, and all that had followed. But Ross heard the sound as he did that of the babbling water, and when they were gone on he came out of his concealment and sat down again upon a stone, his gun between his knees.

"Do they?" He looked up in surprise. Who was it was saying so loudly, "Accidents do happen, you know?"

"Do they? So they do? I wonder who said it? Yes," and he repeated it over and over to himself. "That is a fact. On that very spot —" He looked dreamily at it, putting forth his foot to touch it.

Even now it was not that the Niagara swept him downward beyond his strength; it was because he deliberately refused to put forth his strength and swim ashore. Wilfully and deliberately he gave himself up to the effects of loss, defeat, sickness; took luxurious pleasure in letting go and drifting with the torrent.

"I am glad I wrote the letters. She will understand!"

He sprang to his feet wide awake, resentful. "Coward? Who said I was a coward? You are a liar!" A moment after, "I must be crazy." He laughed as he said it. "No; I never was more sane. I know that all is but dust, a whirl for a moment of dust. How angry she is, how beautiful, and how weak! Dust, only dust."

CHAPTER XXXII.

SOLUTION.

" PERSIS is not well enough to see any one." That was all the satisfaction Rachel afforded me when, as soon as I could after the departure of Ross, I called at their house.

"I hope she is not seriously ill?" I asked, there was so much of what I may call determination in Rachel's face.

"Dr. Trent does not allow her to see even Mrs. Trent," Rachel said; and the resolve in her face took so much rising color, almost as of anger, but not at me, that I began to talk of Ross instead. She listened to me, as she always did, with eyes serene and attentive, and to the end; but she would not converse concerning him either, and under disguise of chatting upon indifferent topics, I gave myself up, as I always did, to a fresh study of Rachel herself. When I say that she had improved as much if not more than Persis, it is not in my power to explain what I mean. You must know such a woman for yourself to understand her. Both of them had developed in intellect, as in personal beauty. Whatsoever charm comes to their sex from frequent hearing of the best music, from daily association with the best society, was theirs alike. Will it help us if I say that, beyond this, Persis was a specialist and Rachel was not? That Persis was an enthusiast in reference to certain branches, while Rachel accepted whatever she learned in equal measure. In conversing with Persis I noticed that her entire education manifested itself in her strong preference for this and that, with dislikes equally decided, while Rachel was interested but impartial. In Persis culture was an electric fire quivering in her eyes, tongue, finger-tips, as in brilliant points; in Rachel it was the glow of a higher health which suffused her entire person.

The day, for instance, of which I am speaking, her silence in reference to Ross and Persis, her control, after the first salutations, of her color too, had deeper effect upon me than words could have had. But it is of Persis I wish now to speak, of Persis only. "Persis has as much regard for me," Dr. Trent told me when I next saw him, "as Elizabeth had for Burleigh, and is about as obedient to me as the Queen was to her counsellor. When Urwoldt saw her last, she had reached a climax of some sort, Heaven knows what. Things went wrong. If she had succumbed at once and cried herself out, she would have been over it by this time. But she would not. She is a woman of that kind, and, setting her teeth, she made a desperate effort to hide matters, to go on as before. Her strength was already exhausted and — down she came."

"Surely there is some remedy," I said.

Dr. Trent sympathized with my anxiety. "Opiates

react," he explained. "What she needs is natural rest." He paused, but I knew as well what was coming as the traveller does who waits beside the empty basin of a geyser. "Do I not believe as much," he said at last and with vehemence, "as a man can in education, in the highest education for women as for men? But when," and he was lifted from his chair to his feet, "a woman takes to knowing as a toper takes to whiskey — !"

"But men, — do not men — ?" I began.

"Not as often; not with such womanish intensity. Besides, they cannot stand it as men can. Let them learn everything if they will," and the Doctor threw his hands wildly apart, "but there is one thing a woman must do. She may know much or little, but, being a woman, she must love, — must!"

"Her parents died," I began, "when she was a child; she has no brother, has no sister —" But the Doctor broke in upon me.

"I never could comprehend how matters stand between her and Urwoldt, between her and yourself! Mrs. Trent does not, never could! For what I know, Miss Persis has no lover unless it is Mr. Adair. Like many of our noblest women, she has not married because," with sarcastic emphasis, "she has as yet found no man worthy of her. You have disappointed us, Guernsey," he added, "cruelly disappointed us! Never was there a woman so admirably suited in every way to you."

"Perhaps there are reasons," I stammered, "circumstances which I cannot expl—"

"Oh! ah! Pardon me. I am beginning to under-stand! She would n't have you? Mrs. Trent did not know that. Then," and the warm-hearted physician seized my reluctant hand, "it is in *her* I am cruelly disappointed. Yes, yes, I will say no more! Except this, that, being a woman, she must love — some-body. A woman cares nothing for science, for any system of truth whatever, but solely for detached facts; nor for a separate fact, except so far as her feeling is enlisted for it in some way. For the race she cares nothing; only for her mother, child, lover, husband. You cannot feed the ears with splendid sights any more than you can satisfy the eyes with music. Persis could not stop the craving of her brain, if she should try to do so, with loving. How, then, can she satisfy her heart with knowing, and when her heart is really the largest part of her! If there is no man she thinks worthy her love, she can love God, can't she? When a woman has no God, it is ten times worse with them than it is with men." And he illustrated it from his experience to a degree I do not care to repeat.

"That is the reason," he added at last, "why Persis perplexes Rachel so. Rachel does not talk about her, but Rachel cannot even imagine any one without a faith and a love, at least for her Maker, which comes first and before everything else. To her Persis is a painful puzzle. If she were a sceptical brother in-stead, Rachel would say, 'Oh, it is because he is a man, and a wicked man, for what I know,' but for a woman to doubt! To Rachel it is an unfeminine peculiarity, an absurd crotchet; worse, really, than if her friend should adopt boots and trousers. She never reasons about it with Persis; it is something too eccentric to be reasoned about. Rachel cares less for learning on that account, but she has on that account a more pitying love and care for her friend. I admire Persis, but Rachel I admire and love," said Dr. Trent.

That was all he would say about his patient; he would go into no details. When wrought up he used frightful language concerning the follies in general of women; as to particulars he was as silent as if it was of his own wife he was speaking.

I was very busy in the days which followed. Whenever I was in the city, and had time to do so, I preferred to get my information in regard to Persis from Rachel, especially as Dr. Trent and his wife grew shy of speaking freely to me of her. There was a sudden pity, too, in Mrs. Trent's eyes the instant we met. She would check herself from her usual high spirits when with me; would say, by way of comforting me, more things about my lectures and books than facts warranted. She was so careful in her allusions to Persis, was so consolatory that I almost liked it in the end, as one does a new species of confectionery. For I had, from ignorance, maybe, no fear that Persis would die, even that she would be ill for any long time. She possessed, whenever I saw her, an elastic energy which reassured me. One afternoon Jean came into the office where I was seated waiting for her father, and putting his microscope out of order while I did so. Jean is not fourteen as yet, and, by reason of her golden hair, we are great friends. After standing for some time in silence beside me, she remarked soberly, —

"Miss Persis is very sick, is n't she, Mr. Guernsey?"

"Yes, no, — oh, no, not very sick," I said.

"Mr. Guernsey," Jean planted herself full in front of me to ask it, "do you love Miss Persis very much?"

"Certainly. Don't you love her too?" But I felt my face growing hot under the compassionate eyes of the immature woman, who kissed me by way of silent consolation, and walked sadly away, as if she knew things which I was not prepared to hear as yet. There had been many weeks, even months, during which Persis was out of the city with Rachel somewhere. I also was forced to go away again, and I had a general idea that Persis was so ill that, however anxious I might be, it would be best I should not inquire into it too often or too closely. But Jean must have been mistaken, for when, on my and their return, I arranged with Rachel to have Persis take a ride one lovely October afternoon, Rachel was sure it would do her good. Obtaining the most comfortable carriage, and the safest horses and driver to be had, I rode to the door merely to see the ladies off; but when Persis was comfortably nestled beside Rachel on the back seat, they begged me to go with them. I thanked them, declined, replaced my hat on my head, and was walking off, when Rachel remarked, "Mr. Guernsey, please get in," but in such a way — some women have it — that without a word I took the seat opposite them, and we drove off.

Not until we were out of the city did I take a good look at Persis. She had on a dress of what is called, I think, myrtle-green, with a fleecy wrap of some cream-colored material about her head and shoulders. Except that she was thinner, I could not see that she was sick. Her cheeks were bright, as were her eyes. She had larger, finer eyes than I had supposed, more intelligent, they seemed to me. For I tried, very quietly though, to interest her as we rolled at last through the woods ablaze, by this time, with the glories of autumn.

"I had no idea it was so beautiful," Persis said, and I felt as if winter itself had touched me when I saw a subtle likeness between her and the foliage on either hand. The manifold gradations of gold, from black which is becoming bronze up to brilliant yellow, with reminiscences of a more ardent red in the pink which streaked and tinged the leaves, — these told of a ripeness which was hastening toward decay.

Why is it that one is sure to say, and from one's very eagerness not to do so, precisely the thing which should not be said ? It was so now. "To think," I remarked, "that last June all these woods were of a tender green! The year is a babe stricken with these colors of age and death before it is five months old !" And I saw my blunder in the tears which gathered in the lashes of Rachel, but I was glad that she was too much occupied with her friend to look at me as I deserved.

"It is so beautiful," Persis said, loving the foliage with lingering eyes as we passed slowly along. Her

accents were in unison with the waning life of the
woods. It clothed her like the crape of a nun, her evident abandonment of things. She was so exhausted
as to have lost the desire to strive. Something
stronger than herself had come upon her, and so
tamed her that she loved the subjection.

"It is merely a passing weakness," I thought; "she
will get well." But I dared not look again when I
noticed how the tears of her utter surrender were
moistening her eyelashes. Her silence seemed to
subdue even Rachel into a quieter affection, but she
looked at me at last in such a way that I began again
to talk lightly of this, of that. And I did succeed in
bringing the smiles to the face of Persis at last. For
not even then did I know how long and how well
she had loved Ross, how her hard work was but a
means toward that, how she was sceptical because
" she believed that," as Rachel told me afterward,
" even if books failed her she had Ross. When he
failed her, too, and was gone," Rachel added, " she
broke down utterly. Then she rallied herself, and
made so frantic an effort to go on with her teaching
— for she had a noble position — that when she fell
in the effort it seemed impossible she would ever recover. I will never speak of those dreadful days!"
Rachel vowed, and she has kept her vow.

There were many things taking place at that time
which I cannot mention as yet, but out of our ride
that day came one result.

"I intend to go to Ocklawahaw," Persis announced
as we returned homeward.

"Will Dr. Trent consent?" I asked in amazement.

"I am going in any case," she said.

It was not that she was not submissive, but it was to another man than to Dr. Trent. Ross had always had firm hold upon her since she could remember; now he was drawing her to himself through all that lay between. I dare not say that Rachel and myself could feel, through Persis, the irresistible grasp which was laid upon her, but we knew that we must go with her if she persisted.

In this remarkable world things fit with accuracy, and the fit — there is no other word for it — of its burr to the chestnut, of its air to the lungs, of the light to the eyes, is but an instance of the universal adjustment. For there was a sort of parenthesis in my affairs during which I had nothing else to do, exactly then, but to go with the two friends. It is not necessary to detail all that.

"Go? Yes, by all means!" Dr. Trent assented. "It is the best thing that can be done for Persis. I do not want," he added, "to distress you, Guernsey, but if I were to tell you what might befall her, it would break your heart. Be sure and start soon."

We took our time at it after we were started. By rail, by steamer, by rail again, by steamer once more, by private conveyance, we reached Ocklawahaw at last. We had arranged beforehand for rooms with the family which lived in the house once owned by Rachel. Mrs. Amasa Clarke was there to greet us. She astonished me. It was hard to think that so coarse a woman could be the mother of Ross, the

mother he used to boast of to me when we were in
college. He had told me how she had changed, but
I was not prepared for change as great. The poor
woman was glad to see Rachel and Persis again, and
yet she saw the change in them too, and shrank from
it, I could see that. There was an old negro woman,
Seelye, who was beside herself with joy at our coming.
I do not imagine that she could have changed in anything, Persis and Rachel were so glad to see her.

I confess that I was not quite prepared for Ocklawahaw. It is true that I had seen many of the
roughest regions during the war. Our journeying
had, of late, been through a cypress swamp which
ought to have made the town an Eden in comparison.
Moreover, Ross and the young ladies had never described their old home to me in any other light.
Most of all, my introduction to the Mitchabuna of
other years should have qualified me for what followed. And yet, when I sallied out the morning
after our arrival, I was long in accepting the fact that
this was indeed the place in which Ross, in which
Persis and Rachel, had lived so long!

Let me acknowledge it frankly, I was borne up
and over even Ocklawahaw, as I had been during our
coming thither, by Persis. She grew stronger with
every mile since leaving the East. The morning after
we came to Ocklawahaw she was radiant, not with
joy but with excitement. But her eagerness looked
beyond Ocklawahaw to that which drew her, and
more vigorously now than ever, to something beyond.

Rachel had put on a new beauty the moment we

went down the steps of the porch and out into the
November coolness. "Here is the same dear old
silkweed," she said. It was nothing but a low brown
shrub, with queer bowls full of flossy silk, but she
took the silvery streamers in her hand as lovingly as
if they were the locks of a child, herself a child
again. "And this is our Indian-weed once more,"
she cried, seizing upon one of the myriad stalks of
an ugly growth with which the country was disfig-
ured. "Listen, Persis!" And she shook it till the
pods rattled again, and both of them laughed with
glee at the sound. "Yonder are the same old, old
Indians wrapped in their blankets and sitting in the
sun," she said, as we walked on. "If you were an
artist, Mr. Guernsey —" And she pointed out the
children who had grouped themselves to stare at us,
as we went, half naked most of them, chilly as it was.
Nor did my companions seem at all afraid of the
men loitering about, with beards as portentous as
their flapping hats. That these companions of mine
should have originated in such scenes, it was that
which bewildered me. Until, at last, like a man
swept downward by a muddy torrent, I laid hold
upon the low-hanging limbs of the live-oaks everywhere about me, with their leaves still green among
the swinging masses of gray moss, nothing could be
more magnificent, and by their help I regained my
feet, so to speak, and entered into the nature of
things, understood it all, and was myself again.

Rachel and I yielded, as we had done all along, to
Persis, when she halted in front of a disreputable log

tavern, and begged me to go in with a question for the keeper. Was it pure intuition on her part? Perhaps Ross had written to her. She may have heard in some other way, I never asked. But the tavern-keeper told me yes; that Colonel Urwoldt had come to town. He was not in the house; he was out "a hunting," and my informant threw his hand in a general way up street. Could he let us have a light wagon and a pair of horses? That he did not know; and he came out upon the front porch to think more clearly, scratching behind his ear, looking suspiciously at me as he did so.

Some people are fond of ferns; others have a passion for dogs, for horses. As I have already remarked too often, my chief interest is in people, and I watched my newly made friend as he stood, shirt-sleeved, upon the steps, and stared at Rachel and Persis waiting on what ought to have been the sidewalk. It was not often that he saw ladies. Never had he seen such ladies, never!

"Mr. Golson," said Rachel, "don't you know us? This is Persis Paige. I am Governor Beauchamp's daughter, Rachel. Have you forgotten us so soon?"

The man was the roughest of the rough, pitted with small-pox, a scar across his left temple, and now, his hand still in his shock of red hair, he stood and stared. Both Persis and Rachel laughed and blushed, and Persis, strange to say, the most, so excited was she, the flattery of the man's astonishment was so sincere. It was some time before he could adjust himself to the circumstances. But he knew from the instant of his recovery that he *did* have horses and wagon, and it was not long before I had helped the ladies into it, had gathered up the reins and was driving off. The last I saw of him he was standing on the ground gazing after us, his hand in his hair, endeavoring to realize things.

I knew, without looking back, as I whipped the hard-worked plough-horses along, that Persis was greatly elated; that Rachel had firm hold upon her hand, and was whispering to her as we went. I turned here and there at a word from Rachel; there was a half-suppressed exclamation as we passed near an immense sycamore, under which was a large stone. Soon after we emerged from the village, and the woods which belted it in, upon a highway leading between fields, and then on and on, up and down, over a rolling prairie. None of us felt disposed to talk. As I checked the horses for a descent toward what seemed to be a creek winding its way through willows, I glanced back. The remark I was about to make died on my lips! Persis must have had a letter, must have had information of some kind, for she was seated, her face now dark and cold, drawn tense and silent by I know not what. As we stopped in the stream to allow the horses to drink, I said something. Rachel replied to me, but Persis, held firmly by Rachel, was looking to the right and left, like a deer in search of its fawn. There was nothing to be seen or heard, and we drove up the ascent on the other side. By what I caught as I drove, I judged that Persis had given way and was weeping. Rachel was whispering in a soothing tone, and said to me, after we had gone two or three miles, "That will do, Mr. Guernsey; please turn and let us go back."

I think we could not have been two hundred yards from the creek on our return, when, looking back, I saw that Persis had ceased to weep, was rigid again as with intense expectation. Even Rachel sat pale, and almost terrified. At the instant there was the report of a gun, and with it Persis had risen to her feet, was struggling with Rachel, who had thrown her arms about her.

"It is all right," Rachel said, clear and calm; "drive on, Mr. Guernsey!"

What came after was swift beyond measure, yet exceeding slow as in a dream. Before I could cross the stream Persis had broken furiously from her friend, had leaped into the water, had dragged herself through it, had thrown herself moaning upon the earth, her head upon the bosom, her arms about the head of Ross Urwoldt, lying where his father had died, a shattered little gun beside him, wounded apparently to death.

I think, looking back at it, that when a woman is most a woman she enters upon the possession of qualities which are those of men, but of men never except rarely, and then only when at their best. It was Rachel, not I, who took command. Weeping, but not interrupted thereby an instant, she had cut open the coat and underclothing of my poor classmate, had torn something into strips, was stanching his wounds before I realized what had happened. Under her directions I untied the bucket hanging between the hind wheels of our vehicle, and brought water. Then I spread the old buffalo-skin in the bottom of the wagon, helped make Persis get in and sit down on it, throwing out for the purpose the movable seat upon which she and Rachel had ridden. After that Rachel and I lifted Ross in, laid his head in the lap of Persis, Rachel seated beside her. Then I drove toward the village as rapidly as I dared.

I had placed the bucket in the wagon before starting, and Rachel continued to bathe the unconscious face, to stanch the ugly wounds. Not a word was said by us, and I am sure that Persis was aware only that Ross was lying there. She did not know where she was, who we were. With a hand on either side of his head, smoothing out his matted hair, untangling his heavy beard, she was kissing his lips, and crooning inarticulately over him, like a child over its dead bird. It was Rachel who wept as she worked. The eyes of Persis were dry and glittering.

I had not observed things as we went, but now it seemed to me as if sudden winter had smitten the world. The prairie stretched brown and barren on every side. The fields, as we passed among them, the corn in stacks, here and there, looked desolate enough among the stubble. So tense was every nerve that I could hear their leaves, brown and dry, rustling in the breeze which was rapidly rising. When we drove beneath the live-oaks the breeze had become a strong wind which was swaying the hanging moss like banners on the blast. It was raining, and I saw a bit of hail lying upon the exposed forehead of my friend as I glanced around, before driving on more swiftly. Then there was a rush, a roar, as if all at once a cataract had fallen from heaven upon us. The air was full of flying leaves, of shreds of moss, and then it was as if the clouds themselves had descended upon our heads! I had entered upon my first experience of a norther, and so blinded were we by the sudden tempest that it was all I could do to guide the affrighted horses to the house at which we were staying.

CHAPTER XXXIII.

CERTAINTY ITSELF.

I AM obliged again to go back to events which took place before our coming to Ocklawahaw. If I seem indefinite as to the precise date to which I wish to return, the uncertainty has reference to that alone; in everything else I am as thoroughly assured, as vigorously confident, as the dryest mathematician could desire.

Not the smallest intention have I of telling at this late hour the story of how, and all along, I had wooed Rachel; it is with the blessed result thereof alone that I have now to do. This I must add, though I am sure to say it over again before I am through, — that both of us, and from the outset, were confident how it would end. An oak is an oak from the acorn, and our mutual affection in its germ, growth, flower, fruit, was and could be none other than of the order of the certainties.

Dr. Steven Trent knew nothing of it! His knowledge of the sex was the result of long, thoroughgoing, sympathetic study, but round-headed little Guernsey knew as much of the matter to which I allude as he. When it broke upon him at last, it so staggered him that I do not think he will ever again be quite

as dogmatic concerning women as he was before.   As
to Jean, she had always considered me as merely the
larger of the two Guernseys, in some respects younger
than her brother, the one over whom she could tyran-
nize most. *She* had no idea of it. During the minute
of her coming, at last, to know, I grew many hundred
years older in her estimation, and have been to her as
a beloved but venerated grandfather ever since.   Persis had acquired the art of knowing everything under
and beyond the sun, as a gifted musician gains, and
by never-ending practice, the command of the piano,
yet Persis did not know, for a long time at least,
there was anything in that direction *to* know !

What gratified me most was that the knowledge
came upon Mrs. Trent, when it did come, like a something — shall we say a shower-bath ? — which took
her breath away.   This was the stranger since Rachel
and herself are of the same type, not so intellectual,
it may be, as Minerva, not as intense in pursuit of
an object as Diana, but of the gracious, beneficent,
altogether lovable womanliness, I will not say of
Venus, but of Ceres.   Yet I know why Mrs. Trent
was, when she did learn the amazing fact, most
amazed of all.   If they do belong to the same type,
the highest to me of all, none the less does Rachel
surpass her in the peculiar and divine excellences
of the same, in virtue of being so much the younger
and therefore the more advanced of the two.   For, as
has been said, while men are stationary as a sex,
women in all their types are ascending.   You can
measure their ascent during the past; how much

nearer they are to climb toward himself in the future, God alone knows!

I do not blame Ross so much for not knowing how Rachel and I stood toward each other. It was of Persis I said most, when I had written to or talked with him, because she it was who, by her incessant activity, by her striking success in certain things, gave me most to say. Now I recall it, I must have shown that enthusiasm which enthusiasts always have for enthusiastic people provided their tastes and occupations run, as in this case, in the same channels. Yes, I must have produced in him, as in everybody else, the impression that I was in love with Persis.

And so I was. But Ross would not have fallen into his mistake about me if he had known! One word to Persis would have relieved him. Rachel understood it! From the day I first saw them after their coming to the city she knew that it must be Persis, not herself, with whom, in certain respects, I would be most occupied. It was Persis who took the lead in asking me as to what studies she should undertake, what books she should read. Afterward it was natural my conversation should be most with Persis, and not as regards her education only. So of our conversations concerning what I had written, was about to write, while Rachel sat by and listened, came into the room and went out as she pleased, many and long and animated were the conversations I had with Persis. Of course, as her intellect developed, as her improvement advanced, my interest in so gifted and determined a woman increased. Driven here and there as I was, how could I fail to find particular pleasure, during my hasty sojourns in the city, in talking with such a woman and upon such topics? The keen variety of it to my ordinary life gave special zest to this; Rachel understood that perfectly.

"And, then, Persis is coming to be a strikingly handsome woman." It was to Rachel I made the remark when we were alone together one day. "That is," I explained, "when she is excited."

"And conversing," Rachel added while I was stopping to say to myself, —

"But you are beautiful instead, and *you* are always the same." What I uttered was, "When Persis comes into the parlor she is pale and worn. Her face has almost the alabaster whiteness of the globe of an unlighted lamp. But it is an electric lamp, and conversation is the machinery which lights it. When it is about things of interest to her, almost from the first word her fires begin to burn. She cannot keep her hands still, she becomes more and more interested, radiant, to the end. When the revolving magnets of conversation are stopped, then comes reaction, I fear."

"She is so *much* interested, and in so many things! Yes, she kindles at a word. If it were not for the having to come down again, I almost wish," Rachel laughed, "that I could go into raptures. But I love to see Persis in them, she becomes so beautiful."

"And is this what the Rev. Mr. Adair thinks when she talks speculative theology with him?"

"Yes," Rachel assented slowly, "except that all his ideas were new at first to her. She thought there was something wonderful in them. But Mr. Adair had entertained them long before. He was nearly through with them," Rachel said simply, "when Persis began. What he was interested in was in her interest. There was something positive in *her*, you see. *She* is not a — a — " Rachel was in pain for a simile thin enough.

"A vapor," I ventured.

"It is thinner than that," and Rachel shook her head without a smile. "I am so sorry for him! Mr. Adair got through all his speculations, got at last out of them; yes, clear through the last of them into — into — I do not know what to call it — into — nothing. He told her so. Persis cried about it. He told her that beside her he had nothing left him to love, to believe in. 'Neither have I,' Persis told him. You see, she, also, was through with all the theories by that time. 'Neither of us has one solitary belief left,' she said to him; 'it was your beautiful reasoning I loved so,' she said. 'Now that neither of us has anything left us, Mr. Adair, we are too poor to marry.' Persis laughed when she said that to him, but she cried over it afterward in our room.

"Oh, yes, Mr. Guernsey," Rachel came back to where we began, "when I hear you and Persis talk, — talk so long, so eagerly, — it is something like that. I understand!" She had quite a motherly air as she said it. We could not disquiet her!

For not only had I fallen in love with Rachel from

an early period of her coming to the city, but I told her so as soon as I did. She was gentle and yet firm, intelligent yet silent, good yet perfectly sensible, Christian without a particle of cant, sympathetic yet not effusive, beautiful yet unconscious of it — If it will help any one to understand my feelings, I will say that, while I can enjoy a good sonnet as much as any one, I greatly preferred to the best of them a peculiar way she had of arranging her fair and abundant hair. No man I know of has, or possibly can have, a greater pleasure than myself in a well-ordered and flowing poem, but I had, and from the first, yet more satisfaction by far in the color and flow of her drapery. Persis said strong things, brilliant things; but there was a uniform sense and sweetness in the conversation of Rachel, to which I turned as one does from confectionery to — breakfast? to breakfast, dinner, supper. As I told Ross, Persis was one of the most original women in what she thought and said; what I did not tell him was that, to me, Rachel was herself such an original as Eve was. There was a virginal freshness in Rachel herself, — in her beauty, her voice, her way of not saying and doing things — Our affection for each other was as natural as food and sleep and drink. I did not have to come down again after talking with her. We walked as in the summer meadows of daily life, side by side, but each at his or her own gait. There was not the least exertion on either side. We were simply ourselves —

I would not be so broken and abrupt in what I am trying to say, could I have begun at the beginning, and told of all this as it took place. But I assure you I did not hesitate in telling Rachel about it. I seemed to myself to be not more than ten years old at the time, Rachel vastly wiser, yet only a year or so younger than I. Living, therefore, as we did, in an old-fashioned period, apart from more modern people and fashions, I fell desperately in love with her from the start, and just like a boy. Not that I had not known the gust of a feverish passion before, but, in all sincerity, she was my first sweetheart. It was part of our childish pleasure to tell nobody about it, having excellent reason for not doing so, and having many a childish laugh about it all along. Nobody imagined such a thing of people so unlike. We contrived to see more of each other, Persis was so busy, than you would think. Whenever we were separated, as was often the case, we corresponded closely. I wrote to her wherever I happened to be, almost every day, and it was the chief pleasure to me of the day to do so. Rachel did not write as often, yet the first thing I did in arriving at the town or distant city in which lay my business, was to go to the post-office, and I rarely failed to find that she was awaiting me there in the form of a letter in her clear, round hand, — a letter so sensible and precisely what I was craving for that it was only less to me than herself.

For Rachel has a singularly clear mind, and she saw her duty almost from the first. She had always been in the habit of having somebody in charge. I made it plain to her that I needed her more than Persis did. Moreover, I must have assumed things in a

28

way too ardent for a kind-hearted girl like her to resist.

"You are the first woman I ever loved, the one
woman I ever can love," I told her.

She knew me, and knew it was the simple fact,
knew that I needed her more even than her poor old
father had done; and what else could she do but
begin to love one who would be so dependent upon
her? Yes, dependent! Not for what we call knowledge, but there are things I need infinitely more than
I do knowledge! Even in my own life-long line of
things she was of great help to me.

"Persis likes my writings," I told her one day, not
long before going with them to Ocklawahaw; "but
there is vast difference between me and my books,
and it is *me* you love! Persis praises me, and sincerely too; but you detect and tell me of my faults, —
faults of matter, faults of manner, accursed faults in
the very bone and blood. You are as quick to see
them as you are to notice places in a table-cloth
which need mending."

"Yes, I know how to mend," she laughed.

"I wouldn't have loved you," I said, "if I had
not known how much I needed you. Never fear, I
intend to be a good boy and mind you," for which
she rewarded me — we had got that far along — with
a kiss; adding, before the sweetness was departed, —

"Yes, I intend to see that you do!"

"It would never do for people to know," I began,
"how very much you are to me."

"There is no fear of that. They will not know it

from *me*," she smiled. "And you do not need me except to correct, now and then, the little things. I appreciate you more than you think." And her eyes, fixed tenderly yet proudly in mine, praised me so that I felt happier than if an opera-house crowded to the dome were applauding me. The breeze, strong and steady, which bears a ship along, is not a more practical force than to me is Rachel. Whatever I am attempting to do by the press or on the platform, although I may not get an idea from her, yet am I upheld and borne along by my unceasing sense of her loving approval.

"There is the matter of money," I said to Rachel from almost the beginning of our affection. I mentioned it ruefully, and she understood and commenced to laugh.

"I know." She nodded a mother's head at what she was too well aware of.

"But I always feel as if —"

"You had millions. I understand."

"Because we were originally created," I argued, "to have everything as abundantly as we do the light, the air. After death we shall, and eternally, have everything heart can wish in infinite measure. Meanwhile I can't adjust myself to anything else."

It was remarkable how wonderfully Rachel improved under the influence of our mutual affection. It was to her what to Persis was her love for Ross and her passion for study. Moreover, I am sure that Rachel, for my sake, was more of a student than she would otherwise have been.

But we kept our secret. As I told her from the beginning, I was too poor to marry as yet. Nor did we have, as the time rolled by, the remotest idea when we would be able. All along I felt like a hypocrite of the blackest dye, when with good Mrs. Trent especially. It was sorely against my nature not to let her into our secret, but it was small proof of my strength to hold my tongue, seeing that I had passed under the influence of a woman who influenced me yet more. Neither Mary nor Martha Washington would have revealed a state secret, and Rachel, for her sake as for mine, held ours as something sacred.

"There is plenty of time in which to let them know. And it is *our* matter," she remarked, and controlled me in this as in everything else. Which confession I would be ashamed to make if I did not know how greatly I need to be controlled.

"There are things," she was pleased to say to me one day, "which you can do at all only by doing them alone. I cannot make a suggestion as to them. For me to intrude then would be worse than if you were to come — when we go to housekeeping — into the kitchen and pry into oven and stewpan. I am proud of you, dear, and I hope I know when to be silent and to leave you to yourself."

From almost the hour of falling in love with Rachel every lesser good began to come to me as naturally as could be. I had more occupation than ever in my profession; better paid because, I dare say, I worked better. I was able to save more money, having now something to save it for. For years I had tried in vain to dispose of my plantation, and the day came when, and without any effort on my part, I sold it, and for much more than I had hoped. "It is your doing," I told Rachel, although how she did it I could not have explained.

With all our care it did leak out at last, soon after Ross left us,—through me, it is scarce necessary I should say,—how things were. What followed I dare not describe, save that it was so entirely natural that Rachel and I should love each other that every one, even Mr. Adair, was amazed that he or she had not thought of it before.

CHAPTER XXXIV.

ASSURANCE.

IT was this which made it easier for me to accompany Persis and Rachel to Ocklawahaw. What befell after we arrived there I have already related, — our drive, our finding Ross by the wayside wounded, our bringing him to the house. As soon as possible a surgeon was summoned from the nearest military Post. The mother of Ross prohibited her husband and children from showing themselves, and assisted — her hair about her shoulders — in the nursing, Rachel taking the general control, and Persis remaining in tearless misery.

The breast of the wounded man was dreadfully torn, so much so that the surgeon could not understand it until I rode out, within an hour of his coming, and brought in the gun which had done the mischief. It was a short double-barrelled shot-gun, such as I had not seen since my childhood, — a cheap toy at best, and rusty from long disuse. Both barrels seemed to have gone off at once, and the discharge had burst them both, making wounds not deep but wide-spread. From the first the surgeon had slight hope of saving my friend, and he took me aside and told me so. As soon as I could, I told Rachel, and was surprised at the calmness with which she took the news. "For it will be the death of Persis," I went on to say to Rachel, who was scraping lint upon a table in the kitchen as we talked.

"I do not think so," she said. "If Ross dies she may sink for a time into a stupor, but she has too much strength to die. You have no idea, dear," Rachel whispered, "what hidden vigor she has, what will. Yet I would almost rather she should if Ross is to die. I dare not think what, in that case, if she survives, she may come to be."

"I do not understand," I said.

"Because you have never known her as I do. If," Rachel said, "she regains her strength, unless Heaven takes that way to break her down, she will become a bitter, heartless woman. I dread to see her go back to the city, go back to her studies, go back to be the woman she may become. I love Persis," and the tears of Rachel began again to fall, "but, knowing her as I do, I would rather she should die! You think you know people; you have no idea," and she ceased from her work to look up at me, "how bitter, how miserable, how desperate for evil, Persis may become.

"But I do not think," Rachel whispered to me, "that doctors know everything. Not even Dr. Trent. Ross is very strong. He has been terribly shaken, he is dreadfully wounded, but — Guernsey, dear," Rachel said, her eyes in mine again, "Persis and Ross are other people than either you or I. They are like iron, — like iron," Rachel said, "which God can do great things with if he wants to."

"And passes them through fierce suffering to fit them for it," I thought, for Rachel had stolen back to the wounded man.

After a while Mrs. Clarke went home to see to her baby. The surgeon had ridden all night, and, having done what he could for the present, was trying to get a nap in a back room. Rachel rested for the moment in a chair by the window. Her hands were lying in each other upon her lap, and, dressed in some brown material, having on a white apron, she looked in such perfect health, was so fair and yet so rosy, was so fresh and strong and sweet, that, not having anything I could do for Ross at the instant, I could not help saying to her with my eyes, "If you had upon your head the fly-away cap of a Sister of Charity, a child would know that you were the Superior of the order throughout the world; that is, until somebody put a crown upon your head instead, and then they would see that you were born a queen."

But she shook her head at me, and I too looked at Persis. The poor thing was seated on the floor by the side of the low lounge upon which Ross lay. Surgeons care little for the proprieties at such times, and he had allowed her to remain there through his examination and dressing of his lacerated breast. The more so as she seemed to be as quiet and as immovable as if carved from stone. She had lost a shoe in her leap from the wagon, and her stocking, stained with the red mire of the creek, showed from under the skirts of her dress still damp from the water.

Her lap and bosom were spotted with blood where

the head of her lover had lain; for, unless we had torn
her away by force, it was impossible to remove her,—
not even Rachel had that influence over her. I think
she was conscious of nothing but Ross. She had driven
him off from her by her weakness when she last saw
him; nothing should part them now! Her face was
set and haggard, her eyes dry; there was something
almost of the wolf in the watch she kept over him.
"No, no, it does not do," I thought, "for a young girl
to stretch herself upon the rack of intense effort as
she has done. It is a devilish fanaticism. Whether
it be from love for any man, or from love for knowledge, it is murder. Whatever makes a Catherine de
Medici, a Brinvilliers, a Messalina, a Madame Kru-
dener, is equally wrong. Accursed be excess whether
it be in drink, in dress, in study, or religion! From
Bacchantes of every sort, from Mænads of all kinds,
good Lord, deliver us!" And I let my eyes rest
with fresh satisfaction upon the peaceful aspect of
Rachel.

None the less I saw some excuse for Persis in
Ross lying upon his back, his breast swathed in clean
bandages. He had been fully conscious while the
surgeon was at work upon him; his eyes were closed
now, and we knew by the involuntary twitches about
the lids and beneath the bearded lips that he was
enduring mortal anguish. Not a groan, not a murmur, escaped him. Persis had not kissed him since
he came to himself; but she had held his hand in
hers, and waited the will of this her lord as to whether
he would take her or not, as to whether he lived or

chose to die. Ah me! how have I failed in trying
to tell in what sense this friend of mine was unlike
ordinary men! Men may be but duplicates of each
other, as much so as silver dollars; but Ross was
fresh, at least, from the mint. Not an edge or a line
was dulled, in face as in accents, in bearing as in
manner, in silence as in speech, in anger as in love;
he was simple, sincere, frank. Never opening his lips
about it to any but me, he lied to himself in trying
to assume that he was, at last, but of the best breed
of animals; but, having got into the swamp of such a
notion, he had persisted in it to the end. For Persis
was the one appointed to lead him up and out of that
bog; and Persis, Heaven help her! had tried to fit
herself for him by perfecting herself in mathematics
and metaphysics; in the languages, music, and the
study of the Aryan religions!

Ross opened his eyes at this moment. Rachel came
and stood beside me. As he looked at us, a sudden
surprise dawned in his steady eyes like a sunrise, a
sullen film rolled away from them, he understood
so well that he almost laughed. Persis glanced up
at us, then her eyes returned to his bronzed and
steadfast face, which had already yielded to her as it
had not done to disappointment and deadly wounds.
His hand closed on hers, — closed so hard that there
was the wincing in her lips of pain, while her eyes
grew brighter. The surgeon had forbidden him to
speak, but I answered what I saw in his eyes.

"Did n't you know *that*? Why, man, I have been
in love with Rachel"— here I kissed her — "ever

since "— and I was defeated in trying to kiss her again —" I first knew her." Purely for the purpose of having him understand beyond doubt, I would have illustrated my meaning still further if Rachel had not put me away from her, but very gently, laughing and blushing. I was rejoiced at the new gladness in the face of Ross and Persis. But he was asking me something more, his lips were helping his eyes to frame it. I did not understand. Rachel did, and whispered to me.

" Married ? " I replied. " Of course we are married ! We were married before we left the city, a month ago." Whereupon Rachel was so intent upon helping me make Ross understand, that she put her arm about her husband's neck, and her head upon my shoulder, looking down upon the wounded man with eyes serene and satisfied, adding a little kiss thereafter by way of postscript.

How could it fail to be infectious ! Ross turned his face toward Persis ; his eyes half entreated, wholly commanded her. As she lifted herself to kiss him, Rachel and I drew away ; but when we saw that the arms of Persis were about Ross, that she was weeping with the sudden letting loose of her long-suppressed tears, Rachel, crying as heartily as she, had to interpose, very firmly too. Ross was not to falsify her hopes of recovery by being agitated in that way.

There was such a look in his eyes when, at last, I stood over him again, Persis weeping quietly, humbly, by his side, that I could not but say, " Yes, old fellow, there *are* certainties in this whirlwind of

dust we call a world.   There are certainties of evil,
absolute and most terrible certainties, if we go or
allow ourselves to drift downward.   And there are
certainties, divine certainties, if we will but climb by
them upward.   I can put them all in one word,
Ross," for I felt, as well as saw, that he was listening
to me ; " the supreme certainty is — "   And with a
happy face I threw my hand upward.   " Of all the
many certainties I know, that is the nearest to us,
the easiest for us to accept and rest upon !

" And there are lesser certainties," I added, after a
while, " all along.   The old order of things is passing
away.   Many things outside the South, things you
and I detest, are as dead as negro slavery.   They
are already struck through and through by the arrows
of Heaven, by the sharp certainties of the almighty
Christ, which always hit and kill.   We are both
young as yet.   Both of us have served a severe ap-
prenticeship.   Each in his own way, we will have
as much to do as we know how ; yes, and we will
pocket the rewards of it, too ! "

I spoke as I felt, soberly, gravely.   Never before
had I been as conscious of strength.   It was the
entire weight, serene force, priceless value of my wife,
added to me.   " Persis, Rachel," I laughed, " are certainties to us, ab-so-lute certainties.   They will help
us through life.   Beyond it are the higher certainties
into which they and we and all things shall come to
be, — blessed and eternal certainties !   Why should you
and I spend our life in whirling like bats, half the
time in, half the time out of, the caves of darkness

and all uncertainty ? " People are very quiet when speaking of or hearing about that which, at last, no one can deny. " Why," I urged, " should we not settle down upon the primeval rock of what, in our deepest self, we know to be true, — settle down upon it both to rest and to be firm-footed for hard work ? " And a peace fell upon us as when head and heart, as when lover and the one beloved, are at one.

There was peace even after the surgeon had made another examination. His trade lay in wounds as that of a florist does in flowers, and he assured me as coolly as could be that my friend could not get up from his hurts. I am sure *I* know nothing about it, but Rachel says that Ross will recover. How can I tell which knows best ? Possibly I have too much faith in my wife, love and faith so cling together. We will see.

THE END.

Cambridge : Electrotyped and Printed by John Wilson & Son.

THREE NEW NOVELS

BY THREE OF THE MOST POPULAR "NO NAME" AUTHORS

I.

THE HEAD OF MEDUSA. By GEORGE FLEMING, autho
of "Kismet" and "Mirage."

II.

BY THE TIBER. By the author of "Signor Monaldin.'
Niece."

III.

BLESSED SAINT CERTAINTY. By the author of "Hi
Majesty, Myself."

ROBERTS BROTHERS, PUBLISHERS,

Boston.